The Baker's Boy

T·H·E
Baker's Boy

A Novel

BARRY KITTERMAN

SOUTHERN METHODIST
UNIVERSITY PRESS
Dallas

This novel is a work of fiction. Names, characters, places, and incidents are either the product of the author's imagination or are used fictitiously.

Requests for permission to reproduce material from this work should be sent to:
  Rights and Permissions
  Southern Methodist University Press
  PO Box 750415
  Dallas, Texas 75275-0415

Jacket and text design by Tom Dawson

Library of Congress Cataloging-in-Publication Data
Kitterman, Barry.
  The baker's boy : a novel / Barry Kitterman. — 1st ed.
      p. cm.
  ISBN 978-0-87074-520-1 (alk. paper)
  I. Title.

PS3611.I89B35 2008
813'.6—dc22

                                                          2007042696

Printed in the United States of America on acid-free paper
10   9   8   7   6   5   4   3   2   1

*For my children Ted and Hannah, whose lives
are beautiful stories, and for Jill, loving and
patient and wise these many years.*

Acknowledgments

I owe a debt of gratitude to those who walked the streets and roads of Belize with me years ago, and to old friends at the Uptown Café. I am grateful also to the late Thom Gunn, who told me to keep writing, and to Bill Kittredge and Earl Ganz, who offered to teach me how; to Robert McBrearty and others at the Fine Arts Workshop in Provincetown; to my colleagues at Austin Peay who weather the storms of academia with me; to Stephen Bauer, who read earlier versions of this novel and had faith in it and in me; to Harrison Taylor and Rick Long; and to the Sunday night I group. Finally, a gratitude that cannot be measured goes to Kathryn Lang of SMU Press.

1

There is a café on Franklin Street run by a woman I know, a young mother with two small girls who love her fiercely. They would come down to the café with her every day if their mother allowed it. The woman's name is Stacen, and she puts in long hours selling bakery goods and coffee to a town that isn't geared to what's popular everywhere else nowadays: cappuccino and latté, the espresso drinks. Last August, Stacen hired me to work the morning hours in her café so she wouldn't have to get up so early, so her children, who share the bed with her, could sleep until dawn. She wanted to give her husband Tony a chance to sleep in, too. He's a student up at the college.

The café is a lot like the other jobs I've had. I've had a lifetime of jobs already. I've done construction. I've sold half the products you can imagine, and a few items you can't imagine. True-crime magazines. Christmas trees. Salmon eggs. I grew up in Tennessee, but I went to sea twice before I came back to Tennessee for good. I worked in a sporting goods shop for five years where I became knowledgeable about fishing tackle. People who come into the café sometimes remember me from the sporting goods place. To me, a job's a job. I've been paid by the month, by the week, by the hour. I've worked for tips. I've drawn unemployment. I went to college, but college didn't change me. I've never done anything illegal on purpose, although for six months I moved rental cars around the state for Equity, and some of the time the trunks of those cars were full of marijuana. A guy told me about it later. I wish he hadn't.

I'm known as a good worker, so it puzzles some people when I move from one job to the next. People get used to having me around. I told Stacen I'd be good help, but I wasn't counting on some of the confusion. Four months on the job, and I can't remember the difference between a mocha and a latté without looking up at the little sign above the machine. I can grind the beans from Kenya or Madagascar, and I know how to steam milk, even if I don't always get it right. Or so the customers tell me. I'm not an espresso drinker. I don't do that to myself. It doesn't matter, though. Stacen didn't hire me to make coffee.

I am the baker. By the time the café opens, I've already been in the kitchen for three hours, mixing the day's bread, getting the frozen bagels and croissants into the oven. A lot of what Stacen sells comes to the back door in big trucks from New Jersey. We're in the middle part of Tennessee here, a long way from New Jersey. The customers don't ask which baked goods are frozen and which are fresh, and Stacen doesn't tell them, but I can't take pride in anything that's frozen. It's different with bread. We make it the way we're supposed to, from flour and oil and yeast and salt. And water, of course. Bread is like a story I can tell again and again. Each time, I change the details a little, and sometimes I forget a detail or add one on a whim, and the story goes somewhere I didn't intend for it to go. Still, the new version of the story is as good as the old one, and I may decide to tell it that way the next time.

When I put in my time as a deckhand, and this was a lot of jobs ago, a lot of years ago, I knew an old salt who used to drink gin in his bunk in the afternoon, and by dinnertime he would tell us how he survived Pearl Harbor and went on to defeat the whole of Japan. He said it was all true. He told me once, "You know what the difference is between a fairy tale and a sea story?" I didn't know. "A fairy tale begins, *Once upon a time*," he said, his eyes a little moist, as if he was remembering his childhood. "On the other hand," he told me, "here's how a sea story begins: *This is no shit . . .*"

I'll tell you a story. It's no sea story. You wouldn't get me out on the ocean again. But, like the man was trying to say, every word I'm telling you is true. This is how I came to be in Stacen's café the night of the ice storm. This is how we all came to be there. My life is changed now and everything in it looks different to me. The first will be last and the last will be first, and the rest is often forgotten. But this is a good place to start.

• • •

One night last fall, I slept poorly and I knew, no matter how late it was or how early, if I didn't get out of my bed I was going to find it hard to get up an hour later, when I needed to get up and go to work for Stacen. So I left the apartment I'd just moved into, and I rode my bicycle across town to The Unreformed Temple of Caffeine. It's what Stacen has named her place, though everyone else in this town still calls it Toddy's Café. Toddy was the first owner, a little bald man with white eyebrows. These days, Toddy hides out from the IRS in Florida. Stacen gets the occasional postcard from him, but we're not supposed to tell anyone. Toddy's failure was Stacen's business opportunity. She talked the bank into letting her reopen the café, and it's a nicer place now than it was during Toddy's time. She's had it two years, but so far she hasn't been able to shake the old name. People are funny about names.

That night, it was a Thursday, I let myself into the café a little before three. Across the street, Mr. Liu, who owns the Chinese restaurant, had set his garbage cans on the curb. Stacen won't have anything to do with Liu. She says he makes the street smell like fried pork, and it keeps her customers away. I've eaten at his place but only if I'm sure Stacen won't see me over there. I'm not hard to get along with. People say the Chinese revolution drove Liu and his wife from Shanghai, and they showed up in this town looking for a professor at the college, a Chinese woman who had been dead for years. They found Toddy instead, and Toddy gave Liu a job and he bought Liu's wife a warm coat. I hear a story like that, I don't know how much of it is true. It may be a little lacking in the no-shit department. But I usually go along with it.

Something I know for a fact: it's odd going to work before dawn. It's like going to a foreign country and finding out you get to eat all the old familiar food, but at the wrong time of day. Soup for breakfast. Those first weeks at the café, I didn't know if I was heading off for work in the dark of night, or if it was the earliest moments of the morning. Either way I felt on edge. I unlocked the door and let myself in that night, that morning, whatever, and I looked out the window at the street. I got spooked by some little movement, a stray cat drifting from one alley to the next, a shadow passing behind Liu's garbage cans. When I stopped to watch, the shadow turned into a man. He looked like he might be twenty-five or thirty. I don't know what made me think I could guess his age, a man at night in the shadows poking through Liu's garbage as if he'd lost something. I saw him take a small brown object out of the garbage and eat it. It was the size and shape of a potato. God knows. I've never done that. The man didn't look too shabby in the dark, though he was thin. If he had looked a little more desperate, I might have called him over. It seemed awful to be that hungry. I stood at the window and watched him, thinking he could have a mental illness, one of the dangerous ones. I've met a lot of crazy people, and not all of them taught at the college. I was also thinking he'd have had better luck earlier in the evening, before everything in the garbage cans got cold.

I turned on the fluorescents in the front of the café. Light slowly flooded the sidewalk and carried halfway into the street, and the man looked up, the way a raccoon or a possum will look up from the same job. When he walked away from the garbage cans, he looked grumpy. It bothered him to be interrupted that way. He stopped at the corner to look back at the café, then crossed to our side of the street and came down the sidewalk, stepping up close to Stacen's front window. I knew he was going to put his hands on the window, maybe breathe on it. I'd have to go outside and clean the glass before we opened. I should have gone straight back to the kitchen to my morning work. Already, I'd lost most of the extra time my coming in early should have bought me. But I didn't move from the window, and when the man stepped closer, out of the shadows, I could see he wasn't fully a man. He was still in some sense a boy. He wore several layers of clothes, three or four at least. He wasn't Chinese, either. I thought he might be Chinese, the way he showed up like that in front of a Chinese restaurant.

"You wish you didn't know me," he said. His voice, not yet a man's voice, came distant through the pane of glass, a soft accent, from the Caribbean. It was an accent I'd heard before. Of course I knew him. I didn't want to, but I'd known who it was the moment I saw him step away from the garbage. The walk, the way he tilted his head. Only the clothes threw me off, and the years. I should have waved him away. I knew better than to be helpful to people. Still, that morning I opened the door partway to talk to him. I wasn't hardened enough yet.

"How did you find me?"

This black man, this boy, this youth, he was of indeterminate age. If I counted up the years, I still wouldn't be able to say how old. I can't explain it. He stared silently at the doorpost, the places under his eyes darker than the rest of his skin, his hair kinky, the color of smoke. He didn't want to look directly at me. He must have sensed my life had slipped a few rungs down the ladder. I thought about how fifteen years ago, Mr. Liu, the refugee Chinaman, stood at that door one morning and asked Toddy for a start, for a leg up the ladder. Toddy was a good man before the business with the IRS. In those days Toddy would have opened his door right away whether it was Liu outside or this boy or some runaway New Orleans harlot. He would have taken this boy back to the kitchen and fixed him something to eat. Toddy would have slipped him some cash. I had five dollars in my pocket, but I didn't want to give it to anybody. I gave a boy money once before, a long time ago, and it was a mistake. Money wouldn't help. This one at the door didn't ask for it and he didn't try to come inside, which was good. Stacen would not have been happy to find this shabby boy sitting at a table when she came in at six. She would have blamed him for the lack of business, and she would have blamed me, too.

"I can't do anything for you," I said.

"Of course not," he said. "You never could."

"For any of you," I said.

He smiled at me, a smile that was part pain and part anger. I knew the threat in it. I was taller than he was, but older. He might not have aged properly, but I had. Even in the sad shape he was in, if he wanted to hurt me, what could I do? Call the police? What would I tell the police about a man, a boy, who sprang up whole out of my memory?

"Still telling *stories?*" he said. I didn't know how to answer him. It was as if he had accused me of a crime, one for which there wasn't an excuse. It was my turn to look at the doorpost. It wasn't an interesting doorpost. It didn't deserve that much of our attention.

"Put me in one of your stories," he said. I closed my eyes. It felt as if he had struck me. When I opened them again, I looked at the tables, at the chairs, anywhere but straight in front of me. I looked at the floor. Sometime the afternoon before, some kid had sat at the table in the corner and shredded a muffin into crumbs and I needed to sweep it up. When I looked out the window again, the sidewalk was empty.

"For true," I said.

I don't know why I said those words. Those were words that just came to me. I've said them for years. I say them every time the boy shows up, and he shows up again and again, like a song on the radio, like an ad on the television. And every time he shows up, my life changes. For true it does. For true.

At first light, Stacen appeared at that window, keys in hand. She let herself into the place, her café, Toddy's Café, The Unreformed Temple of Caffeine, before I could get to the door. I had the croissants in their baskets under the counter and the first loaves of bread in their pans. I'd mixed up the honey-oat recipe, a bread Stacen found in one of the cookbooks she keeps in a pile on top of the refrigerator. The air was heavy with the smell of yeast and flour and honey. I'd have liked to make that recipe less sweet, substitute molasses for part of the honey maybe, but I didn't know if I could get away with it. Stacen is not an understanding woman in the morning, though she is beautiful always. She is tall and dark-haired, and on her left shoulder there's a tattoo she's proud of, a little cup of coffee with a wisp of steam rising off it. She has a smile for the public, but once she's back in the kitchen at the stove or the sink, her worries wash over her. I've seen it on her face. She has those two bright-eyed girls and she can't find a reliable sitter, and she overextended herself when she bought this café. Her husband Tony is tall and strong and good-looking. He's starting his seventh year of work toward a bachelor's degree in history up at the college. It's good to stay out of Stacen's way until the café fills with customers and she has the chance to restock the shelves at least once. Most days, that's when Tony brings the girls down. They play at waiting on tables, bringing him coffee and muffins until he goes to class or takes them to the park.

I closed the door to the glass case so Stacen could see what I had accomplished.

"I was hoping you wouldn't be here this morning," she said.

That sounded worse than she meant it to. What she meant to tell me was this: she was hoping she would find, one morning, that I'd gone back to my wife, and maybe my old job with the fishing tackle, that I'd remembered how to be of use to somebody besides her. My weeks were numbered at Toddy's Café. The number pretty much corresponded to how many weeks were left before my wife gave birth. If I was still living in my room downtown when Katherine's time came, Stacen was going to throw me out of her café. She was going to toss me onto the sidewalk and throw my jacket out after me. She was going to do it the moment Katherine called her with the news. She meant to do it in front of the customers. She told me so.

"Tanner is seriously screwing up his life story," Stacen said. "Tanner needs to get his story straight."

2

That is a sad story. Let me tell you another, one that begins a few months earlier, on the eve of my forty-seventh birthday when my wife Katherine discovered she was pregnant. We'd been married three years. We had just celebrated our third anniversary the weekend before in the house I used to share with her and two cats and two rooms full of books. We ate a nice dinner, had a bottle of wine. I thought I liked being married. Katherine is eleven years younger than I am, and it was the third pregnancy for her, the only time by me. She ended those other two pregnancies quietly, the first when she was still a teenager. From the way she felt this time—she felt ready—she must have known about this baby even before she peed on that little strip of paper in the bathroom. She wasn't worried about her state of health in the coming months, or the baby's state of health. If she had anything to worry about, it was me. She waited until we were in bed that night to tell me. She was excited, and sure somehow that she was going to have a son. Not that it matters, she said. I'd love to have a little girl. But I know this baby is a boy. I can't say how I know it, she said. I just do.

I told her I was happy for her, for us. I told her this wouldn't change anything, only make everything better. I told her I saw a bright future ahead of us. I lay awake long after she fell asleep, staring at the clock on the dresser until the hours changed from night to morning. I don't know if I fooled Katherine with anything I told her that night. Our bedroom window was

open, but there was no breeze, only the sound of the first cicadas of the summer from the woods behind our house, then the quiet of the night, and finally
the early sounds, the birds and their pointless cheerfulness. I listened until I
heard a car out in the street, the old man who brought our newspaper in the
mornings. When it grew light, I got up quietly. I put on the coffee, plain old
Folgers. I hadn't learned about the good stuff yet. I was still working at the
tackle shop then. The air hadn't cooled in the night, and as I walked down
the drive to get the paper, the closeness of that early-summer morning in
Tennessee brought back a lot of other mornings to me, when the damp scent
of flowers came with other smells. Warm smells. Kerosene and coconut oil,
the human odor of an outdoor latrine, all those smells that had once mixed
together and made my life too rich. Too full of boys and want and violence
and the threat of violence.

A bank of trees stood at the end of the street. With the trees in leaf, I
couldn't see through them to the cornfield I knew was on the other side. That
still morning, thinking what it would mean to be the father of a son, I stood
before the wall of trees in the cul-de-sac and I lost twenty years of my life. I
imagined I was back on the edge of the bush in Belize. I imagined myself standing over a boy with a length of rope in my hand, watching the thing I called
my life slipping through my fingers, the way that rope could slip through
my fingers. I listened carefully, half believing at any moment a small black
schoolboy would ring the big iron bell to begin another day at the New Hope
School, the place where I once tried to be a teacher. I was filled with the fear
and dread that come from remembering, and I don't know how long I stood in
the street or what it was that let me move my feet again, back to the house and
my sleeping wife. I knew it was time to do something different with my life.

That's when I got interested for about the thirty-seventh time in taking some
classes over at the college. I had all summer to get up my nerve. Those classes

were just going to be review at first. I finished a degree once, though it was years ago, and it wasn't in one of the useful subjects. It was one of those subjects where they always want you to do a little more, get another piece of paper with your name on it. It was English, and I don't have to say anything more about that. But if I was going to use the education I got and abandoned years ago, if I was going to resurrect my old degree and maybe even get another one, I needed to brush up before I went any further. I needed to sit in a classroom and read books with freshmen, get used to the feeling of being a student again. It had been a while. I was trying to do good is what I was trying to do. That's what my life has been all about, trying to do good, trying to understand what *good* is. If I could stick with school long enough this time, prove to myself my brain still functioned after the recent years of selling fishing tackle, if I could plug away until I got certified in math maybe, or one of the sciences, then I could try teaching again, could even teach part-time at the college as long as I didn't make anybody up there mad at me. They need teachers. It was in the newspaper. It would please Katherine if I went that route. It was a plan I'd contemplated for some time. Admit it, for years. From a lifetime of making plans, this was the plan whose time had come.

The summer passed so quickly I have almost no memory of it: two trips to the pool, a first visit with the midwife. And then before I knew it, we were in the third week of August and I was sitting in a narrow smelly college classroom, up near the front because I couldn't see the board anymore from too far back, and over near the window because I needed the fresh air. It was the beginning of a new semester, and I had a new plan for my life. Sort of a new plan. I'd dusted off an old plan. I watched the other students filter into the room. They studied the pictures on the walls of Venice and Rome and the Italian Alps. There was a definite Italian theme in that room. I looked around at the young women, beautiful on the first day of class, dressed in sleeveless blouses and shorts. The men looked less comfortable in their new shirts and blue jeans. They all wanted to sit in the back row. The professor came in and wrote his name on the board and the title of the course, English 202. The students looked at him suspiciously. He wasn't what they had hoped to find. He had trouble with clothes. He looked like a biker with a court date.

The students kept coming until all of the chairs were taken. I could tell which of them were new to college, eighteen, nineteen years old. Their high school teachers had told them they were on the edge of a great new adventure. They could be anybody they wanted to be. The world was a party and they had invitations. I didn't like those younger students. I looked around at the Italian mountains and the fancy projector hanging from the ceiling and the shiny white board at the front behind the teacher's podium, and it made me wonder a little. You go through school, it takes a long time. You have, what, one or two years of kindergarten and then eight years of elementary school, and after that four years of high school and four years of college, if you don't screw it up too badly. That's seventeen years or more. Then if you aren't paying attention right after college, if you fall asleep at the wheel, they can make you a teacher. That's the way it happens for most people. For the first seventeen years, I didn't ask myself enough hard questions. For those years I was a student. But I have been on the other side of that podium, too. The first morning I ever spent as a teacher, I stood in front of a very different kind of classroom, a different kind of school. *New Hope.* That long-ago morning, a question sprang up unexpectedly, as if someone had whispered it in my ear: *Is this really your life, or has there been some mistake?*

Over twenty years had gone by since I first heard that question, and nine o'clock on a hot Tennessee morning, I was forty-seven years old and I still didn't have an answer. The younger students watched each other, planning their alliances. The older students had slipped into the room earlier: a woman in a wheelchair, a heavy-set man who looked like he was on medication. They knew each other and sat together. When the woman spoke, her voice filled the room. I didn't like those older students either.

"They told me I couldn't take this class," she said. "Not this semester. Not after what happened with Dr. Myers." She looked at me, as if I should know about Dr. Myers. No, no, I thought. Don't talk to me. But it was the same as always. She had to talk. I felt dizzy. I felt closed in.

The heavy-set man smiled at her and waited. He was polite.

"I had to set them straight on a few things," she said. She divided her attention evenly between the two of us. She wasn't going to play favorites. "It's my taxes that pays these damn professors," she said. "I tell you what."

The woman put her hand over her mouth, which I thought was a good sign. It might help. I tried to center myself the way the books say to. Deep breaths. Think about a rod that goes from the center of the earth right up to your very soul. But not like it's up your butt. Not like that. The man nodded to the woman in the wheelchair to go on. He meant to encourage her. He wanted her to tell me what.

"I was in the military," she said. "I know how these people are."

"You're right about that," he said.

"No different," she said.

I will say I felt bad for her. I can still do that. Compassion comes from sorrow, and even on my good days, I have enough sorrow left to patch up the ozone layer. Compassion was once my chosen profession. I felt bad, but I looked at her and I knew she felt worse. Then somehow I didn't care so much. We both wanted this first day of class to be over so we could go home and hide. At the stroke of nine, a single last student eased into the room and stood arms folded at the back near the door. There was nothing unusual about that. Some students like to wait outside the building until the last minute so they won't have to talk to anyone else. But it wasn't just any student. It was him, and he was the person I didn't want to see. I felt him actually, his presence back there. I could say I smelled him, though that's misleading. It's not a bad smell when he shows up. It's never been a bad smell, or the same smell. I thought the others should feel him, too, but nobody else noticed him, his worn clothing, the leaves in his hair as though he had slept on the grass the night before. He wore a thin shirt without sleeves. Sweat glistened on his black arms. He wasn't wearing shoes, and he didn't have any books with him. He looked like the guy who mowed the school lawn. I wasn't feeling well. I closed my eyes, thinking he might not be there when I opened them again, hoping he wouldn't be. When I opened my eyes, I refused to look to the back of the classroom. I looked at the desk in front of me instead.

The professor read over the course outline, stumbling over words he probably wrote down the night before. He held up the textbooks so everyone could see what they looked like, as if maybe we would head to the bookstore later and order the books that way. *I don't know what the title is,* we could tell the woman at the cash register, *but it's a big fat book. A blue one.*

The woman in the wheelchair complained about the reading list.

"Who are these guys?" she said, looking at the names on the list. "Are these guys Greek or something? I'll read the Bible," she said. "God is my king."

"Tell you what," said her friend.

"We'll start with Homer," said the professor. That professor was kind of fat, and he had a white beard that poofed out on one side as if he'd been sitting with his head in his hands all morning. It didn't seem to me anyone was likely to listen to him. I wanted to speak up, let him know I was listening, but the smell was getting to me. That room smelled like a gym, like dirty clothes, and there was an electric smell, too, like lightning had just struck a power line. It smelled like the boy in the back.

"Does anyone know who Homer was?" said the professor.

"Does anyone know what this is?" said the woman in the wheelchair, and

I looked up to the clock on the wall, right beneath the poster of Venice, and I saw it was exactly 9:23, before I looked at her again, at her hands in her lap, and saw she was holding a gun. Below my window a car tried its brakes in the parking lot, and some woman with a throaty laugh found life funny as hell out in the hall. I didn't find life funny. That gun was pointed in my direction. It was small and it was black. It was so small I found myself thinking it probably shot little bullets. I hoped little bullets wouldn't hurt as much.

"Not that it matters," said the woman in the wheelchair. "You don't need to know what this is and it can still kill you." And then she laughed, too, the way the woman out in the hall had laughed, only this time it was an idiot giggle, and the students in the first row turned around to look at her. A pretty girl with a ring in her eyebrow turned a shade of gray. She didn't say anything, but her lip trembled a little. She wanted to cry.

"I guess you got their attention," said the loud man. "Praise Jesus." He took one of those little notebooks out of his pocket, and a pencil. He opened the notebook.

"Praise Jesus," said the woman in the wheelchair. Then she shot the younger woman, the one with the ring in her eyebrow. The bullet entered just below the girl's breast pocket. It may have come out the other side, I don't know. The gun made a loud noise for such a small gun. It was an unmistakable noise.

"Get you another one," whispered the man. But he wasn't looking at her. He was writing as fast as he could in his notebook. "For the newspaper," he said.

"Praise Jesus," said the woman, and she turned and shot a boy two rows back who was trying to get out of his desk. He settled again into his chair, doubled over as though he had been slugged in the stomach. His sack lunch fell out on the floor beside his desk. An orange rolled away toward the classroom door.

"You don't look like much," said the woman. She was talking to the professor now. The old guy, it was as if he was welded to the podium at the front of the room, if you could weld a person to anything like a podium. If you pushed on that podium, he would have fallen right over.

"But you are the teacher," she said. She pointed her gun at him.

"Don't," he said.

"What are you going to do about it?" she said. Something about the way he looked disgusted her, made her hesitate. She wanted to shoot someone better than him, someone in a tie and a tweed jacket, someone who looked like an Englishman.

There were students in the back who weren't sure what had happened. The ones closest to the woman in the wheelchair sat quite still at their desks, all of them, except for a very large black woman who stood up slowly, holding her big cloth purse in front of her. She glowered down at that woman with the gun.

"Motherfucker," she said. "You ain't no good woman."

The crazy woman shot her, too, but the one with the purse fell forward and pulled the other gal out of her wheelchair onto the floor. A small bottle of oxygen fell out from beneath the wheelchair. I wondered what that would be like, I longed for it, a measure of extra air just like that when a person needed it.

In time there were policemen in the room and the sound of ambulances and stretchers to carry students out to those ambulances.

"Praise Jesus," said the wheelchair woman from where she lay, pinned to the floor.

Someone got the gun away from her. I don't know who. It wasn't me. That's when I saw that her friend, the loud student, had a tape recorder in his pocket. He'd given up taking notes and he was talking into the tape recorder. I heard him say the word *abortion* several times and other words like it. *Holy Spirit* and *Thorazine* and *financial aid.* I heard a soft moaning sound that wasn't any recognizable word, and I realized I was making it. I stayed at my desk the whole time. Even when the police asked me to leave the room, I couldn't stand up without help. I knew whenever I got to my feet, I would not sit in that desk again or any other desk like it. Still, I was aware of what was going on around me. I was more observant than the police officers, who are paid to be observant. I was the only one who saw the door open a little bit, maybe halfway, although I couldn't see who opened it. I saw the barefoot boy with the leaves in his hair slip out of the room. It's always like that. He shows up. Something bad happens. And he goes away.

I don't know what I did the rest of that afternoon. I walked around, I guess. I got myself tired out. I didn't eat anything and I didn't drink, though I walked past every bar on Franklin Street at least twice. I got home that night and Katherine was already in bed asleep. She never watches TV. She didn't know what happened at the college. I took my time moving through the house. The furniture, the magazines on the coffee table, the dirty dishes in the kitchen, all of it looked different to me now. Before she'd turned in that night, she'd made out a list of the tasks she wanted us to complete before the baby came. There was a small room in the back where we could put a crib. I needed to get the boy next door to help me move some boxes of books, a file cabinet. I didn't want to do any of it. I was afraid.

To anyone who has children, or anyone who desperately wants them, my fear of becoming a father could seem foolish. You could say, it was just the bad day. You might say if I gave myself some time, I could get centered again. The rod from the core of the earth could connect to my soul the way it's supposed to. But it was more than one bad day. It was a bad life. It was a bad world. The fear grew stronger as I stood in the kitchen. The fear walked through the living room with me. It walked through the house like a companion, like a lover, until it washed over me and I went out to the backyard to be sick. I couldn't tell Katherine how frightened I was. I was sick for a long time, and I thought it wouldn't be so bad if I died in the backyard so I wouldn't have to tell her. I knew I was going to break her heart. She is a kind, good woman who has forgiven me for much already. This time would be too difficult. She wouldn't be able to understand it. I seldom spoke to her or to anyone else about my fears, about Belize, or my life before I came back to Tennessee. About the boy who has followed me for twenty-five years.

I should have told her. I don't know why I didn't. I never got around to it.

3

The night I saw the boy go through the garbage in front of Liu's like some sort of ghost, only I didn't think it was a ghost, I'd been on my own for a couple of weeks. I was talking to Katherine every day, but I didn't tell her about the boy. There were things I told her and things I didn't tell her. The next night, I made myself get up and go to work early again. I kept a pickup parked in the alley behind my apartment, a truck I bought years ago when I first moved back to Tennessee, and maybe the truck wasn't reliable anymore, and maybe I didn't want to put gas in it, and maybe I didn't actually drive it anywhere, but it made me feel good to know it was there. I rode to work every night on a bicycle I found leaning against the back wall of my building. It was there for the taking, or at least for the borrowing, a girl's bike actually, a three-speed somebody once tried to fix up with a little blue paint when he should have been working on the mechanical parts. The only time I ever tried to shift gears, the chain came off. I coasted as much as possible, and I returned the bike to the same place in the alley every morning, a practice Stacen's husband Tony called *a piety for common things.* That sounds like a quote from some ancient-of-days history book, but I'm pretty sure Tony made it up.

When I walked in the door of the café, three o'clock and the moon in the sky just a little sliver at the end of the street, the first thing I did, even before I turned on all the lights, I went to the back and measured yeast as gently as I could into a bowl of warm water. If I set the yeast quietly in the water, in no time at all a certain magic would take place at the bottom of the bowl. The yeast would come to life. It's like the beginning of the universe as far as bread is concerned, even more dramatic if I remember to put a little sugar in the water. I looked around for my apron, listening to the night sounds in that old building and keeping an eye on the bowl. I wanted to be there when the yeast started to blossom. Not everybody feels the same way about yeast. When Stacen bakes, she proofs the yeast like I do, but she doesn't share my feelings about it. Sometimes she has to swear off bread completely for a week or two and drink dark cups of tea made from the bark of trees. Those trees grow only in the Amazon. She has to beat the yeast in her body down to an acceptable level, and that tea is death to yeast. I stay away from her tea.

I heard familiar noises through the ceiling that morning, the young couple who lived above the café. It sounded like one of them was moving the bed across the room a couple of inches at a time, an odd thing to do at four in the morning, but I didn't stop to think about it. If I thought about the noises they made, it wasn't going to do me any good. They weren't what you expected to see in a couple. He was well over six feet tall, and she was short, her hair the color of glowing embers. They fought a lot, sometimes with each other, sometimes with Stacen. Fighting was one of the noises they made in their bed.

It was Friday, and I wanted to bake rye bread from a new recipe—cracked wheat and rye flour and caraway—and I thought about how when a customer came into the shop, she would pick up one of those loaves of dark whole grains, and her eyes would grow wide at the weight of it. I have always loved to make a woman's eyes grow wide, but I'm not talking about that exactly. I stood in the middle of the kitchen where the light was good. I read the list of ingredients, and I got a knot in the string of my apron, and I swore and pulled the knot tighter and swore again but not as loud as before because the couple upstairs had quieted down, and in the quiet of the night in Stacen's kitchen, nothing to break the silence but the radio turned down low and the hum of the refrigerator, I couldn't swear with conviction. It's like swearing in church. I picked up the bag of yeast in one hand, wondering at how light that bag was and what work I was going to ask it to do. I looked at the grains of yeast I had dropped into the bowl of warm water. And nothing was happening.

So there it was, out of nowhere, a small gray doubt. My old friend.

Doubt, I have found, is the enemy of yeast. Doubt is even harder on yeast than Stacen's tea from South America. If you're a baker, you have to believe in yeast like a swimmer believes in water. What happened that morning, I had nobody to blame but myself. Although I know better, I am a doubtful person.

This is everything I know about doubt. It's also everything I know about swimming.

When I was a boy, I was a great swimmer, amazing, a prodigy. The summer I was eight, I joined a local swim team after I finished all the lessons the Red Cross people could come up with. My coaches were high-school girls with broad hips and peeling noses who walked the pool deck with whistles around their necks. I won races, I came in second, sometimes I came in last. But no doubt about it, I could swim. My mother was timid around water, which is why she took so much pleasure in seeing her children swim, myself even more than my two brothers. My brothers were so much older than I was, it was as if I was an only child. A menopause baby. As much as my mother loved to see me swim in a meet, or just to see me work out, hundreds of passes up and down the pool until she knew I'd sleep that night like an old man at the rest home, she was afraid of water that wasn't tame. She didn't like lakes or the ocean or the river that ran through our county.

I had a friend in those days, Henry Bowman, a boy who lived outside of town on a farm and whose mother wasn't afraid of a river. There were other things his mother wasn't afraid of that my mother would have thought the woman should be afraid of, if my mother had known about them and about the other woman's general lack of motherly fear. There were pocketknives and Bowie knives and box-opening knives and knives to cut your thumb off. A twenty-two rifle. A John Deere tractor that would almost start if you rolled it as fast as you could down the hill behind the Bowmans' barn. One morning it was hot and it was going to get a lot hotter, and Henry's mother let us go with some older kids down to the river. I was happy to go, because I had been absolutely forbidden ever to go near that river. My mother had nothing to worry about. The river was slow and the other kids were Mormons. I didn't know anything about the Mormon religion, but to me, Mormons sounded steadfast and cautious. You were safe with them around. There was a boy Mormon who seemed like an adult to me, so he was probably fifteen. He was old. His sister was a year or two younger.

These were poor Mormons, which is why we were all swimming down at the river and not at the pool in town. The girl wore the suit she had owned for two or three summers. It was too small, and it showed me more than I ever thought I would see of a Mormon girl. I watched her without knowing why. I'd never enjoyed the company of girls and here was this one in her funny swimming suit with her funny laugh. I played in the river the whole morning and on into the afternoon, wading close to the bank. I watched Henry Bowman and the girl and the older brother, too, as they drifted into the deep water and swam against the current without going anywhere. I was a better swimmer than they were, but I couldn't see the bottom, and I didn't know what the river looked like when it disappeared around the bend. And I had a mother who was even then watching the street from her front window, wondering if I would come home alive from the Bowman farm. I was my mother's son, a good son. I didn't go out in the deep.

We stayed in the water until the sun dropped out of the sky, and the girl climbed the bank to lie down on a flat rock, hugging the warmth of it. I wanted to lie down next to her. I couldn't say why. I wasn't tired or sick. I just felt like lying down all of a sudden. I'd noticed it once or twice before, how being around pretty girls could make you want to go lie down. A tennis ball drifted our way from some mysterious, upriver location. She was the first to see it. She pointed it out to me, never moving from where she lay on the bank, knowing all she had to do was point and I would run after the ball like her favorite dog. I tried to imagine people playing tennis on a farm like the one where Henry Bowman lived. It was a funny thought, as if you had found a picture of Henry's father in a tuxedo or his mother having tea with Jackie Kennedy. That tennis ball was a magical tennis ball floating just beyond my reach, the kind of tennis ball Mormons discovered, not the tennis ball a person of little faith like me was meant to find. I presented it to the girl the way I would have given her a treasure or a beautiful fish, but she wasn't interested, which is why Henry and I found it necessary to throw that ball back and forth across the river, Henry to me and me back to him while the girl watched us. It took a while but we made her laugh. Her brother smoked a cigarette on the bank. He knew none of us would tell on him.

I couldn't stop looking at that girl and she couldn't stop looking at me. She was studying the front of my swimsuit when she laughed, and I didn't get the joke at first, and when I did get the joke I didn't know what I was supposed to do about it. Henry threw the ball to me again, and this time I stepped out to it, stepped away from the bank of the river and found myself floating, first through the air and then down into the water, the deep water. I held the ball in one hand and let myself sink down to where the river was colder, wanting that cold water to fill my swimsuit. When I finally remembered to strike out for the shore with my free hand, in the blink of an eye I forgot everything I had learned from those Red Cross girls with their furious whistles. I had to struggle just to get my head above water. I looked at the girl on the bank, who frowned at me in a curious way. I couldn't hear her, but I watched her lips form words, and I tried to imagine what the words were. I thought she might have said, *you little fool.* I thought she might have said, *you go ahead and drown.* I looked down into the muddy water, and I couldn't see my feet beneath me, and I believed in my heart I was going to die.

Upstairs, in the room above Toddy's Café, the noises stopped altogether once they were done moving the furniture around for one night, which was good because when they really got into it up there they made the plaster fall from the ceiling, and I had to run around and cover the bread and the bagels with dish towels. It would make Stacen crazy to know about the plaster. I never told her that part. The afternoon crew, which is what Stacen likes to call herself (as in, *I've given the afternoon crew a raise, too bad about you*), had left dishes for me to wash. I turned to them, looking over my shoulder far too often to see if the yeast had bloomed. I tried not to think about the bowl on the counter, but after twenty minutes I had to check it again. The water I poured over the yeast must have been too hot. I threw out the whole mixture and started over, this time adding a truckload of sugar to give the yeast a crazy boost. I went out front and wiped tables that were already clean, glanced at the clock, tried to figure out how much time I had before Stacen showed up. When I came back to the yeast this time, it lay there very doubtful, like silt at the bottom of the bowl. I wasn't sure. Maybe I'd smothered it with all that sugar. I poured it down the sink and tried again.

I didn't know the names of the young people who lived upstairs. I thought they were down for the count, but then I heard a door slam over my head and the two of them were shouting at each other up there, something about a girl called Naomi. I was pretty sure the redheaded girl wasn't called Naomi. I threw a damp towel over my bowl of yeast and water, and I tried to tune them out. If Stacen had been in the kitchen she would have run to the back landing and yelled up at them or maybe just shouted up through the ceiling, *don't tell us about Naomi, we don't care about someone called Naomi.* Stacen expected me to have bread rising on the table when she came in. She didn't expect me to know anything about a Naomi.

I didn't look in the bowl this time. I looked out into the dark street and I thought about people I'd known, boys like Henry Bowman and other boys, too, like the one who had been following me around, a boy named Albert. And I wanted to blame all my problems with doubt on them and on others like them. I could imagine those boys out there, as if they might have gotten to know each other and compared notes. They might be waiting to get hold of me. I could forget Henry Bowman for years at a time. He grew hazy to me, the way he looked, the sound of his voice. It was Albert who still conjured himself up clearly, like a bad dream. I was watching out for Albert, especially on my way to work, the same way I watched out for drunk drivers when I rode the blue bike in the dark. The bars closed an hour before I got up, but the younger barflies, students of the bottle, were apt to head from their last drink in the bar to someone's apartment where they played the evening out a little longer. When the young couple in the apartment upstairs invited people over, they kept their music loud, full blast, until their last friend saw reason and went home. They liked the music loud when they rolled out of bed in the morning, too, just before eight. They thought their music covered the other noises they made. They used to stop in for coffee on their way to work, but Stacen gave them the cold shoulder. I wondered if I sometimes passed them on the road at night when they were coming home from the bars. You can never know which car coming your way is going to be the dangerous one.

I heard some sort of glass break upstairs, and I went to the door that opens to the alley. The young woman who wasn't Naomi came down from the landing. She wasn't dressed to go outside, and she stopped at the foot of the stairs as though she'd just realized how little she had on. Her red hair billowed out around her small and lovely face. The boy followed her downstairs to the sidewalk. He wasn't rough with her. I don't know what I would have done if they had taken to fighting right there outside the door to Toddy's. He was asking her to go back in, all bent over because he's taller than she is, saying he was sorry, saying he didn't feel anything toward Naomi anymore. That's when they both realized I could see them through the window. They looked at me in that way people will look, as if I might have been able to say some words to them that would make sense of their quarrel, or of their lives.

I tried not to stare at the girl. She wore a flannel shirt and little else, and the shirt was misbuttoned. The boy had only his underwear on, but he didn't look as cold as she did. She looked so cold I opened the door that stood between us.

"What?" she said. "What do you want?"

"I don't know," I said. "It's just, it's so dark out tonight."

She hugged her shoulders. Neither one of them had shoes on.

"Please go back inside," I told her. "This is a bad time of night. You could get hurt. It happens all the time. You could drown."

The way she looked at me, she couldn't believe I said that. She thought she'd misunderstood me. Her boyfriend heard me clear enough. Maybe if he hadn't laughed it wouldn't have been so bad, or maybe nothing could have helped. She gave me the finger—I didn't hold it against her—and she started off down the sidewalk with him trying his best to follow. He wasn't used to going barefoot. He looked back at me as if I was to blame, but there wasn't much time for blaming people, not if he meant to catch up with her.

Sometimes you don't know what to do, so you don't do anything at all. Like that afternoon with Henry Bowman when I was suddenly filled with doubt in the middle of his river. It was as if I had never learned to tread water. I couldn't remember how to float. I didn't put my head down and strike out for shore. I did a pathetic one-handed dog paddle, and I didn't even call for help. I could only make a sound like a deaf boy would make if he wanted to get someone's attention. In my fear, I drank brown water and got mud in my eyes, and I went under and came up and went down again. The Mormon boy, that girl's older brother, watched me from where he sat on the far bank, trying to understand what kind of trouble I was in. He slipped into the water, though I think he finished his cigarette first, and he crossed the current in four long strokes to push me back to the shore. I wasn't sure he'd gotten to me in time. I lay on the bank with my eyes scrunched up, a lifeless body, until I heard him laugh, and Henry laugh, and finally I heard the girl laughing, too.

"You're not drownded," the boy said. "You're not dead. You're just a dope."

Henry laughed all over again at that, and the girl smiled kindly at me, which was worse than when she laughed. The brother shook his wet hair out of his eyes and threw a rock into the water, and Henry threw a few rocks. Henry kept laughing and repeating what the other boy had said, *you're not dead, you're a dope, you're not dead, you're a dope,* until I knew I couldn't be friends with Henry Bowman anymore. I wouldn't go over to his house for anything after that, even when his mother called and talked to my mother. I didn't like the Mormons either, not for a long time, not until I got older and understood the world better.

I wish I hadn't turned my back on Henry. The next summer, he slipped out his back door one night when the moon was full, and went down to the river by himself, and without me and the Mormons to keep him out of trouble, he fell on the rocks and didn't come home when he was supposed to.

He didn't come home at all. His father found him the next afternoon, his face still in the water where a branch had caught him by the shirt.

Maybe Henry lost faith in himself. I don't know. You ought never to stop believing in your own story. Stop believing and you drown. When Stacen showed up at the café, I had nothing to show her that morning, no bread rising, ready for the pans. I didn't tell her about the couple upstairs, and I didn't tell her about Henry Bowman. I told her about the problem with the yeast, and she called up her supplier and yelled at him over the phone. She closed her account. It was a new bag of yeast I was working from, a pound of the stuff, and she had me toss the whole bag in the trash. That yeast had died from some mysterious miscue at the yeast-making factory. She wanted it out of her café. I didn't argue with her. There were dogs outside at the garbage can. I had to shout them away before I dumped the yeast and got the lid back on the can again, tight. We put a sign in the window next to the coffee cakes: *No Bread This Morning We're So Sorry.* Stacen threw flour and sugar and soda together and cursed the entire yeast-producing industry of America while she prepared muffins to feed the town. I felt bad for her. I knew the town wouldn't show up to buy her muffins. I felt bad about the couple upstairs. I felt bad about Henry Bowman. I decided not to think about them, any of them.

I thought about that bread, the loaves I didn't get to bake. I could imagine the coarse round shapes that would have come out of the oven, brown and solid. They would have weighed a pound and a half apiece. I would have loved that bread. I loved bread a long time before I learned how to bake it. It's like that with most things I have loved. I learned to read before I learned to write. I wanted to swim, so I stood on the side of the pool and watched others move through the water, a yearning in my heart, before I let someone talk me down the ladder. I ate someone else's bread before I learned to bake my own. It's the normal flow of humanity. It starts out fine, but it hardly ever ends up fine.

This was what I liked about working for Stacen: I went against the normal flow of humanity. When I went to work in the middle of the night, there were people who hadn't made it home yet. People were in the middle of their problems at that hour—sex or drink or some other addiction—and I was going to work, thinking about bread. I was setting the yeast to proof or checking on the sourdough I'd mixed up the day before, while most everyone else who was awake had lost his purpose. I got the coffee going, and the first customer stumbled in saying *goddamn this hangover,* or *goddamn my kid,* because it was a woman who stayed up too late waiting for her teenager to come home, and I was awake, a little tired from three or four hours of work, looking forward to my first break. If Tony had come in early, or if he'd stayed up all night reading his history books, I bummed a smoke from him. If the place wasn't too busy, I liked to sit out front at a table with a cup of tea.

Later, midmorning, I'd put my sweater on and grab a small loaf of the bread I'd baked and I'd go out to my bicycle. People would be waiting in line to buy their coffee, or they'd be rushing out to their car to return to work in time for the office break, taking a sack of bagels with them, and they watched me get on my bike, a middle-aged man with a stoop and a reasonable belly, the same guy they watched restock the shelves a few minutes earlier. They thought I was a person of leisure. When I got to my room, I could lie down on my bed with the newspaper and read it as slowly as I wanted to, read it until my eyes grew so heavy I couldn't fight sleep anymore, knowing all the time that the professors were in their offices and the preachers were in their churches and the drug dealers were on their street corners slogging through their day while I was about to take a long nap. And I was as good as any of them.

That Friday around eleven, just before I left the café, I took the sourdough starter out of the crock and mixed up flour and water and put it in a large pot to sit all day and overnight. I had a perfect record with sourdough. I could count on it. I wanted to go home and get some sleep and later take in a movie or go to the library to read the newspapers. I would get myself straightened out. When I came in the next day, I would see the lovely sourdough mixture, I would add the rest of the flour, the oil and the salt, and I would bake up wonderful loaves with a crust that once you cracked it open, the aroma would come out with the steam, like life itself. I would overcome doubt.

I left by the alley door. The dogs were at the garbage again, and I told them to scram. One of them had a gray froth at his mouth. I stopped. I backed away, but it wasn't any kind of sickness. It was the yeast that dog had discovered in the garbage can, the same yeast that had refused all morning to come alive. Now it was bubbling in the can, and on the dog's face, too. I had a feeling like somebody was watching me at the far end of the alley. When I looked, nobody was there. But I had the feeling, watching that dog, and it was a bad feeling. I felt like I was drowning.

4

A woman in a wheelchair, a woman with Jesus too much on her mind, goes into a college classroom with a gun in her lap, and everyone's life is changed. I don't know how else to say it. Four months ago, I still had my job at the sporting goods store on the morning that woman went to class early and shot three people: a girl with a small silver ring in her eyebrow, a boy who sat back down in his desk like he'd been punched in the stomach. And a brave woman who stood up armed with nothing more than a big black purse. Their lives would never be the same. Everything changed for me, too. After it happened, I couldn't sell fishing reels anymore, even the expensive kind. I became a baker. On the morning of the shooting, I was living with Katherine, but I couldn't live with Katherine afterward or with anyone else. I needed to live alone. I was soon to become a father, trying to get used to the idea, but all that changed, too, and after that morning I wasn't going to be any kind of a father except a deadbeat fly-by-night voluntary-sperm father. I worked at the café and slept during the days, and I watched out for a Belizean boy named Albert who I shouldn't have seen around there in the first place, and surely not after all the years that had passed.

Sometimes I didn't get my sleep in the afternoon because I had to go to the courthouse and talk to the police or talk to some lawyer about what happened in the classroom. I didn't know we had that many lawyers in this town. They all asked the same questions, and I didn't have anything new to say. Yes, I was there. Yes, I saw the gun. No, I didn't remember what it looked like. Well, it was a small gun. No, I didn't own a good suit. No, I'd never been arrested for anything, even drugs. I don't know much about drugs, which ones will make you talkative and which will make you stare at the floor for an hour or two. Maybe drugs would have helped.

One afternoon, when I thought I'd talked to every lawyer in town and most of them twice, I got called to the office of an attorney named T. John Croker. (I don't know what the T. stands for and Croker has never told me. I'm sure it's something awful.) It wasn't the first time I talked to Croker. He owned the building I was living in, and before I could move in, I had to meet him at the apartment to sign a lease. That first time I met him, when he found out I was one of the people in the classroom where the shooting took place, he took a special interest in me. He told me he could give me a break on the security deposit if I would come see him in his office once I settled in.

I would have avoided him if it hadn't been for the security deposit. But he called me and asked me to come by, and he said it was important, which is how I ended up in the lobby of his building, looking for Croker's name above a little row of buttons, some sort of doorbells that were supposed to ring upstairs. Croker's button was broken, so I found the stairs and walked up the two flights to his office without ringing the bell. Croker had a thing for old buildings. The place smelled musty, like small wet animals. At the top of the stairs, his door was open part of the way. I stood outside the door and tried to clear my head, and he knew I was out there, but he waited for me to knock. He waited a long time.

"You can come in, too," he said. "Whenever you're ready."

I followed his voice into the room. I couldn't see where he was sitting at first. In most of those lawyers' offices, it was just me and the lawyer and a woman in the room to take notes, although one time the lawyer was a woman and she had a man taking notes. I wondered how you got a job like that, taking notes for a lawyer. T. John Croker was not like those other lawyers. He was not like any lawyer anywhere in the world's history of lawyers. For one thing, he took his own notes. He worked for the city, and he worked for the county, and sometimes he worked for himself. He didn't have a receptionist, and instead of a desk he had a big table in the middle of the room, and he had papers and manila folders piled on top of the table, all the folders the same color so don't ask me how he knew what was in any of them. He's a short little guy, and some of the stacks of paper came up to his chin. If you went to his office today and you sat down behind one of his stacks, he might not be able to see you on the other side of the table. Underneath the table where his knees should have been, he had cardboard boxes with the word *Budweiser* printed on them in red letters. Those boxes didn't contain beer. They were full of more papers. It was all information to Croker.

I stepped into the room, but I didn't know if I was expected to sit down. A girl was there ahead of me and she wasn't sitting down. I felt like I wasn't supposed to be in the room while she was still there, so I stared at the things on the wall. Croker had a framed certificate that said where he went to law school, and next to that another one said he was a licensed notary. Off to the side, two smaller certificates said he could drive a riverboat in Kentucky, and he could do weddings, too. If you thought you wanted someone like Croker to do your wedding. I recognized the girl standing in the middle of Croker's office, surrounded by all that information. She still wore the little ring in her eyebrow. She wasn't there to take notes.

"Here," said Croker. He grabbed up a handful of books and envelopes from a chair. "Let me move some of this stuff."

"Never mind," she said. "It's okay." She leaned up against the windowsill, dreamy. I tried not to think of her the way I'd last seen her, lying on the floor in the classroom, the medical people working to save her life. I tried not to look at the place just beneath her shirt pocket where I remembered the bullet going in. It was too soon, but I wanted to imagine that place all healed up now, maybe a little pink scar left to mark the spot. Croker introduced us like she was someone I'd never met before, which was true in a way.

"Sara," he said. "Do you remember Mr. Johnson?"

"Please," I said. "Call me Tanner."

"Why?" said the girl. I think she was wondering if it was okay to smile.

"It's my name," I told her.

"Tanner was at the college that day, Sara. He was with you in the class-room. He knows what you've been through."

"You were there?" said Sara. "You know about it?"

"She's the girl who got shot," said Croker, this time to me. "She looks pretty good, doesn't she?"

I agreed with him. She looked fine. Healthy, even.

"It's a miracle she's alive," said Croker, and I'm sure he was right. I sat down in the chair he'd cleared off, and I tried to think about the idea of miracles, but I couldn't stay concentrated on it. What I kept thinking about was the girl, how someone tried to kill her but she was still alive, and how great that part was, but there was something else, too. How she reminded me of someone. I couldn't make the connection at first. If you sell anything long enough, like burial plots or kennels for little dogs or fishing tackle, it's only a few years before the majority of people remind you of someone else, someone you liked, another someone who disappointed you. This girl at the window, her name was Sara and she was there to see Croker because he was her lawyer, and what's more, her uncle. He was her lawyer uncle. She was small and dark with long pretty hair she wore up off her neck. There was so much of it, black hair pinned in random loose folds, it must have fallen to her waist at night when she brushed it. She had a sweet smile. She only halfway bothered to pay attention to Croker, happy enough reading the titles of the books on her uncle's shelves and watching the street out the window. I tried not to stare at her.

"Do you ever go fishing?" I asked her finally.

Croker looked at me from over the top of his stacks of paper. His eyes grew narrow. He wasn't alarmed yet, but he was watching me. The girl was a little spooky after what she had been through, and he was probably wondering if I was spooky, too.

"You ever shop at The Bobber?" I asked. The Bobber was the name of the store where I used to work. In addition to fishing tackle, they sold sleeping bags and backpacks and swimming goggles, and jewelry. I didn't get involved with the other products. Sometimes it's good to specialize in just one thing. The girl was reshelving one of Croker's books. She showed me the title: *The History of the School Bus in Tennessee, Vol. II. By T. John Croker.* The title surprised me. I wouldn't have expected two volumes.

"I quit school," she said. I didn't ask her about school. She just wanted to tell me about it. "I want to be a stewardess," she said. "I'm taking some classes on my own." She mentioned a technical college in Nashville where they teach bartending and massage therapy. She was all over the place. "I'm going to learn how to throw pots," she said.

"Throw pots." I said. "Where? They have classes for that?"

"You know what she means," said Croker. Give him credit, the way he tried to cover for me. He might have his eyes buried in a manila folder, but he didn't miss anything. "Throw pots," said Croker, "make pots. Ceramics."

I felt foolish, but Croker kept a straight face. It made me think he might be a good guy. The girl let it pass, too. She wasn't a mean girl, even after what had happened to her. A little confused maybe, wanting to do everything and nothing. I couldn't stop looking at her, but it wasn't in the way you might think. Everybody looks at girls, even blind guys do, but this was different. I knew that girl, and I had to find out how I knew her. I was going to ask her if she worked around town or if she went to the same grocery store I went to, something. Sitting in Croker's window with her bottle of water, she looked as foreign to me as a gypsy, and she looked like someone I'd known all my life.

Croker left the room to do some kind of lawyerly thing, or some kind of thing other lawyers would not do. I wasn't sure I wanted him to leave the room. He had those glass doors where the glass was all frosty, and while he was gone somebody came and stood for a moment on the other side of the door with his hand on the doorknob, as if he was thinking about coming in. The girl and I watched the door, she out of curiosity, me out of terror. But the shadow on the other side of the door walked away, and when she raised her hands to tuck a loose strand of hair away from her face, I realized who it was she reminded me of. I had to stop looking at her then. Croker came back and dove into one of his cardboard boxes, and the girl drifted out of the office waving good-bye to me, telling Croker she had to get home to her cats.

"Where'd she go?" Croker said when he looked up at me. "You're sweating. Is it hot in here?"

"I knew a girl like her once before," I said, afraid to look at the corner of the room where the girl had been standing.

"Who?" said Croker. He had this little mustache and he touched it all the time. He was checking to see if it was still there.

"Her," I said to Croker. "Sara. The girl who was just here." I went to the window, hoping to get another look at her, but she didn't appear on the sidewalk below. She must have gone out another way.

"I got that part," he said. "I'm not an idiot. Who does Sara remind you of?"

"Someone I used to know," I said.

Croker put his files down. "Tell me her name. Tell me all about her," he said, just like that. As if he and I were old friends, as if he had a right to know. "I'm the girl's uncle," said Croker. He wanted that to explain everything, and maybe it did. "We're not connecting the dots these days, Sara and me. Not like before. I'm worried to death about her. I'm all the family she has."

"You wouldn't know this other girl," I said. "Someone I was in love with once."

I held my breath then. I mean, I'd just said a personal thing to a lawyer. He'd caught me off guard. You have to watch what you say to the powers that be. I had to wait and see if I was going to get in trouble for it. And if he asked me, I wasn't sure I would be able to explain how this Sara, who had been shot in my class by the wheelchair Jesus woman, resembled a girl I used to love.

"Someone I haven't seen in a long time," I said. Croker nodded at me to go on. "It's not her fault," I said.

"Fault?" said Croker.

"It's not anyone's fault."

I knew I should stop talking, no matter what else Croker asked me. I'd already told him what I remembered about that morning in the classroom. I didn't want to think about it anymore. And I didn't want to remember anything else. I didn't want to remember Belize. I didn't want to think about my life.

I looked up at the plaques on the wall next to the window. One of them said Croker was in the historical society, and according to the others, he was an honorary Cumberland Colonel and a Friend of the Library. A yellowed newspaper clipping had print too small to read, but it showed a picture of Croker visiting a little kid in the hospital. The Croker in the newspaper was a younger version of the one sitting in front of me, and he had a big dog in the picture, one of those dogs they let walk around in a hospital. The dog was the reason some photographer took the picture. But I was looking at the kid.

"It's her, isn't it?"

"It's her," said Croker. "Sara was eleven years old when that picture was taken."

"What happened?" I couldn't say why, but it was important for me to know. "Why was she in the hospital?" I asked Croker. "Where are her parents?"

"Sara's father was never part of her life," said Croker. "He's in jail somewhere. We try not to know where, exactly. Her mother was my sister. She died eight years ago. A house fire."

"That's awful," I said, and Croker frowned, but it wasn't like he didn't agree with me.

"Was she hurt? The girl?"

"No," said Croker, "not physically. Emotionally, she was devastated. And the smoke made her sick. She stayed in the hospital overnight. I took her home the next day."

"You raised her?"

"She lived at my house until this past June. That's when she moved out, got her own place." He mentioned an apartment complex on the other side of town, the sort of place young people like to live.

"She wouldn't rent from me," said Croker. "She said it wouldn't be real independence. She thought I'd forget to cash her rent checks." He felt sad that she wanted to be on her own.

"You ever do that?" I said. "You know, forget? About the checks?" I tried not to sound hopeful.

"No," said Croker.

I took another look at the photo.

"Poor kid," I said.

"Poor kid," said Croker.

"Things are tough all over." I don't know why I said that. It must have been something I heard someone else say, a long time ago.

Croker closed his eyes and took a slow breath. "Who does Sara remind you of?"

"That was a whole different world. Different time, a different place."

"Tell me anyway," said Croker.

"Why do we have to talk about that?"

"Please," said Croker. "Look, I'm grasping at straws here. You can see how it is. The girl's in trouble. She's been knocked off balance, and the thing that connected her to me, to the rest of the world, it's disconnected. I don't know what to do. I can't follow her thinking anymore."

"Talk to her friends."

"You don't understand. Sara's not like that. She doesn't make a lot of friends."

I was starting to get it. Croker didn't want to talk about the shooting any more than I did, about what party was going to sue what other party. It was personal.

"I'm trying to do right by her," said Croker. "I'll try anything. I need all the help I can get." He was gathering information is what he was doing. He was casting his net wide.

He got up from his table and walked to the window to see for himself if the girl was there, or if she had gone back to her apartment in a building he didn't own. The little guy's shoulders were slumped. He rubbed at his mustache until I thought he was going to rub it right off.

I was tired and fighting a cold, and it was that time of the afternoon, late, when everything gets fuzzy, the light outside and the sounds fading away in the street. Croker stood with his back to me. When his shoulders trembled a little, I thought the man might be crying. He was undone by what happened to the girl, what was still happening to her.

"Tell me everything you can," he said. "Let me sort it out."

I couldn't stand to watch it, one more person hurting. It's what made me tell Croker the things he wanted to hear when I knew I should have kept all of it to myself. It's why I said the name *Ellie Embry* for the first time in years.

A lot of years. Croker nodded and he cleaned his glasses. He tilted his head, but he didn't say anything. This is a trick some people have. It's supposed to make you keep talking. I recognized the trick. I don't know why I couldn't shut up.

"I think it's the hair," I said. "Mostly."

I tried biting my lip.

Then I said, "Her hair was so black it could look blue this time of day. Like Sara's just now."

But it wasn't just Sara's hair. And it wasn't the old dress or the boots Sara wore, although sometimes I see young people in the same clothes we wore years ago, as if they invented the styles themselves. As if we did. More than anything, it was Sara's hands that reminded me of Ellie. It was when she brushed the hair out of her face, the shape of her hands, how strong they looked.

"I'm talking about a long time ago," I said. "Sara wasn't born then."

And it was as if I'd opened the door, I'd started the engine, I'd turned on the tap. Words were coming out of my mouth when they shouldn't have been.

"It's nothing," I said. The thought occurred to me that if I were to shut one of my own hands in Croker's door, hard, I might be able to stop talking. His little smile kept me from doing it.

"Go on," he said. "This is better than the nothing you've told me up to now. I'm listening."

Another thought came to me. I'd watched enough television to know it wasn't safe to speak openly to a lawyer, even one who was a riverboat captain, too. A lawyer has all those certificates and degrees. You can learn too much. Whatever words I said might not be the same exact words that passed from his ears on into his mind, so to speak. Words can be dangerous.

"You need to tell somebody," he said. "You're here. I've got nowhere to go."

"I couldn't take advantage of you," I told him.

"I don't mind," he said. "Take advantage."

If I'd had any energy at all, I would have left his office. I would have faded into the dusk, the same way the girl had.

"I'm going to close my eyes," said Croker. "I'm going to close my eyes and just listen. It may look like I'm dozing off, but I'm not. You keep talking," he said. "I might take some notes."

That afternoon, with a look and a nod, some other trick he learned in law school, he won me over, this lawyer named Croker who started out wanting me to remember the events of recent weeks. We ended up talking about things that happened years and years ago. I talked. I didn't tell him all of it the first afternoon or the first handful of afternoons because there wasn't time, and because telling him about it made it seem like a story I was making up, and I didn't want to make any of it up. The weeks went by and Croker became my friend, more or less my only friend. It was a job that didn't pay well. The thing was, Croker was lonely. All those books and all those files, and he didn't have a life. Which was rough for him, but good for me. I had a hunch he might be a bad lawyer. I didn't care.

This is what I told him. This is how I met Ellie.

It was a time in my life when I didn't know I was young, when I didn't know what I was missing. I hadn't developed my enormous potential for doubt. I had never been to Florida, and I've never been back, but I was there that week in Miami, twenty-five years ago, standing in a line with a dozen other people who all claimed they thought the way I did about things like foreign aid and voluntary poverty and temporary insanity. We could have been Buddhist nuns or social workers, but we weren't. We weren't that glamorous. We were ordinary people, filling out paperwork, waiting for another round of vaccinations, headed for positions in the Peace Corps. *El Cuerpo de Paz. Le Corp de la Paix.* We stood outside in a kind of courtyard with the sun shining through the trees, making leaf shadows on the bricks at our feet. I could hear some vague music from inside the hotel, Latin music. Actually, it wasn't the music that was vague. I was the vague one. So much new stuff was happening to me, and it was all happening too fast. I was standing behind a beautiful dark-haired woman much shorter than me, a woman who looked like she could be the great-great-granddaughter of the Mona Lisa with that secret smile, the rosy skin, the lovely easy way she wore her black hair on her shoulders. I had to pretend I wasn't looking at her, so I looked over her head across the courtyard to where the nurses had opened a metal cooler. The vaccine was in the cooler.

"This is the last shot I'll take in my arm," said the woman in front of me in a deep voice I didn't expect from someone her size. Standing close to her, I got the smallest hint of her smell: part soap and part ocean from where she'd been swimming the day before, and part another odor, vanilla or cinnamon, that made me think I might be hungry. We had these ridiculous paper name tags that said *Hello, My Name Is* _____, and most of us had written something misleading there. *Willie Mays. Holden Caulfield. Captain Ahab.* She had written the name *Ellie* in plain graceful letters. She moved her arm in a circle, as if it was tender.

"The next shot has to go right here," she said, patting herself on the back pocket of her jeans. I told her I would do the same, although my arm wasn't that sore. I just wanted to talk to someone. Ellie was so pretty she looked edible and friendly and she was right there in front of me. She smiled a sleepy gentle smile. Her smile gave me permission to keep talking, a way to begin. In three days, we were leaving for Belize. We didn't know how long we would be gone. It was a two-year program, but lots of things could go wrong. We were hoping nothing would go wrong. Ellie was going down to the Teachers College in Belize City. I was headed for the New Hope School for Boys in the western district, the Cayo.

Even when she stood in a line, Ellie carried herself as if she knew what she was all about. I admired that. I admired her before I felt anything else for her. She told me about herself, some of it then, some of it later. She had a degree in education. She was five years older than I was. She had just ended a love affair with a married man, her college professor, and she wanted work that would let her forget the son of a bitch, the weasel, the *pedagogue*. Son of a bitch was what she called him most of the time. She used words I didn't know when she talked about him. I tried to write them down. *Gynophobe* was one. *Poetaster. Shit-for-brains.* I knew what she meant by that. She must have really loved him once. Standing in line I tried to act confident and worldly like her. I hadn't been out of the country before. I hadn't been to graduate school or slept with anybody the whole night through, much less a professor.

We stayed at the Capitan for a week, a sleazy hotel but the ritz in its day. Al Capone stayed there once. I wrote postcards home, told my parents the Capitan had been Capone's favorite hangout in Miami. I didn't mention the astroturf, or the paint peeling in the shower. I was inventing Capone. I was inventing myself. We sat around the conference room and told half-lies. I was surprised the others couldn't make themselves more wonderful. Like this gray-headed woman from Pennsylvania who showed up with a mouthful of cavities and a fugitive expression. Any room she was in, she kept her eye on the door. She hoped nobody would figure her out until we got on the plane. The third day, she was gone. You couldn't join the Peace Corps to get your teeth fixed.

I shared a room with a mild brown-skinned man who had an album full of pictures of Filipino girls in dance costumes. I didn't know what nationality he was exactly. I mean he was American, sure, but what kind of American? What flavor? He was too tall for a Filipino, too dark to be Italian. Some kind of Italian Filipino. I figured he was okay, compared to the lady with the dental problems, though I wanted him to put the photographs away. His name was Dicky Roy, and he was delusional for sure. He told me about backpacking through Europe. *I went alone,* he said, a sad look in his eyes. He spent a lot of time in the shower.

One evening late in the week at Al Capone's, I wandered in a daze from conversation to conversation until I fell in with two other people who were similarly getting themselves volunteered, this thin boy with a neat beard, the kind you grow because you want to look older than you are and you can't smoke cigars, and the beautiful woman from the vaccination line. Ellie. The three of us made excuses to leave the hotel and we walked to the next block, to another hotel that had a bar, where we eyed each other carefully while we waited for someone to take our order.

"Raise your hand if you still want to save the world," said the boy. His name was Price Donelly and according to him, he was from Minnesota. I had no reason to doubt it. Earlier in the conference room, he'd talked a lot, but mostly it seemed like he was telling the truth. He was going to teach biology to high-school girls. I thought it might be safe to get to know him. If he turned out to be delusional, too, he would be in the city, far away from where I was going to live. Ellie raised her hand when he asked about saving the world, and it made Price smile a sad smile. But in fact it wasn't like that at all. She was only signaling for a waitress. That night was the first time I got to sit next to Ellie. I didn't enjoy it as much as I might have. I wanted to ask her if sitting was as painful for her as it was for me, but I wasn't going to come right out and say, "Is your butt sore?" I wouldn't say that to Ellie. I thought of all the other words for a woman's butt, and none of them worked. Ass, bottom, fanny. Derriere. Rear end. I was going to ask, "How's the old keister?" but it sounded like something my father would say, or one of my high-school teachers.

Ellie's keister was small. She was small everywhere, not just her keister, though you didn't realize how small until you sat next to her. When Ellie spoke, she used her hands, and her hands were the part of her that people noticed. They were larger than you expected them to be, and powerful, without a scrape or a scar anywhere, hands that could sail a boat or build a garage. The first time I saw her hands, she was sliding her pants down a few inches so the nurse could put the gamma globulin into her hip. My eyes were drawn to her hands even then, and not to her pale white keister. I wondered what it would be like to touch those hands, to have her perfect fingers touch me.

"I was really looking forward to meeting everyone," she said. She followed the waitress across the room with her eyes. "I guess I'm a little disappointed." She laughed to let us know it wasn't Price or me she was disappointed in, but it was all right. We knew what she meant.

A television was on above the bar. I couldn't see the screen at first for the crowd. I made out a familiar annoying voice: it belonged to a sportscaster who's dead now, who used to announce all the boxing matches. Then a bell. Muhammad Ali was fighting Ken Norton that night, and Ali had already lost the early rounds before we came in. The sportscaster sounded depressed. Price Donelly didn't like the way the fight was going either. I didn't care about boxing. I couldn't watch men pound each other, even on television. I couldn't see the future in that sort of thing.

"Here's an idea," said Price. "Let's have eight or nine beers and cheer up." He brushed his hair into place with his fingers and sent a strange vibration into motion under the table. I looked down there to see what it was. He was jiggling his leg up and down, burning a million calories just sitting in a chair.

"Sorry," he said. He tried to stop. He tried all night to stop, off and on, and for all the nights after that, but he couldn't stop. His knee moved with a life of its own, as if he had a small engine up his pant leg.

"You believe any of this shit about Al Capone?" said Price. "I believe it." He liked to answer his own questions.

"I more or less have to," he said. "Do you believe the Peace Corps really exists, or is it some kind of black hole created by my parents to get rid of the likes of me?"

"The likes of you?" said Ellie in that voice that was too deep for someone so small. She caught on before I did: you had to interrupt Price Donelly. He needed someone to interrupt him.

"Lost souls," said Price. "Adult children of adult children. People who don't remember exactly what it is they're looking for, but they're going to look for it anyway." He tugged on the end of his beard, which was white at the edges from the sun. A razor blade commercial came on the television. Price watched it in horror as if he had never seen anyone shave.

"Good lord," he said. His hand covered his throat.

"What do you guys want?" asked Ellie. There was a little menu on the table, and Price picked it up and looked at it. Ellie took it away from him. She wasn't talking about ordering drinks. She wasn't talking about a sandwich.

"What are you looking so hard for?" she said.

She wasn't making fun of Price or of me. It was not her way to make fun of people. There was nothing ironic about Ellie, and if I had been alone with her, I might have tried to tell her that first night what it was I was looking for. Maybe not. It's a big deal to talk about those things when you've just met someone.

"This is all you need from life," said Price. His leg slowed down for a moment. In time I would learn that when his leg stopped, it was a warning that what came next was going to be outrageous. He told me once, a long time later when we were riding around Belize City in the back of a pickup truck, it was okay to be outrageous as long as we lived in an outrageous world.

"I think I can get what I need almost anywhere," he said, "but I want to try it out someplace new. You need, every day," and he held up three fingers and ticked them off, "to go for a run, to take a shower . . ."

He looked up at the waitress who was setting three schooners of beer on our table. "The third thing I won't mention," said Price, but it wouldn't have mattered. The waitress might have been serving beer to corpses. She had that dead look in her eye.

"You can do all these things alone," said Price, "or with another person. The rest is gravy."

Ellie wanted to laugh, but she couldn't tell if he was serious or not. It was like that with Price. "You wouldn't want to break your leg," she said. "Or your good right arm." But she said it softly, and I don't think Price heard her. He was watching the TV where Muhammad Ali had come to life.

"The rope-a-dope," said Price. Ali was pummeling Ken Norton on TV, and Price pummeled his own Ken Norton. Price knocked his Ken Norton down, but Norton got back up and Price had to push him against the edge of the table, where Price stung him with blows, lefts and rights, until he could deliver a terrific uppercut, and his hand hit the edge of the table. Even the dead waitress looked over at us then. Price grinned at her and stopped. He sat on his hands, but he stayed on the edge of his chair. He ordered another beer, then one for Ellie and one for me, and then he ordered for a table of young women next to us. He tried to resuscitate the waitress, but it didn't work. They couldn't get on the same channel. She didn't perk up. His leg jumped with its own secret life.

It was late in the evening. Ellie shivered and lay her head on her arm.

"Jet lag," she said without looking up. "Gamma gamma something."

I felt beat, too. Maybe it was the vaccinations. Price had brought along a windbreaker, and he draped it over Ellie's shoulders like a mother would tuck her sweater around a child who needed to sleep. Across the room, the bartender smiled at us. He looked Cuban, so many muscles he could have been wearing his little brother's T-shirt by mistake. He made the TV louder than before. They were giving the decision from the fight.

Price allowed himself to look at Ellie, who this time really had fallen asleep.

"You think we'll make it okay?" he said. He kept looking at her, but he was talking to me.

"We'll do fine," I told him. "There's nothing to worry about." I was worried about everything.

"I don't want to mess anyone up," he said. "I'm not sure the world can be saved, not without a lot of work." Late at night, Price had his doubts, too.

"It's not the sort of thing you want to dwell on," I told him. "You'll go insane." I was thinking about the woman with all the cavities, and about Dicky Roy back in my room, lying in the dark, dreaming of brown dancing girls. I was thinking about all the people I knew with delusions. The thing about delusionals is, it's best to leave them alone. If you try to buddy up to them, they get nervous. Give them some room, they'll be your friend, though it's not always easy to recognize that they're your friend.

"You could fall in love with her," said Price. He knew Ellie was asleep. He whispered the words anyway. We watched the referee on the television take Ali's hand in one of his hands and Ken Norton's hand in the other and turn to the camera. The referee raised Ali's arm into the air and a large inebriated man at the bar decided to swear in a loud voice and to pound on the fellow who sat next to him.

"We just met her," I said.

"I can tell about these things," said Price. "Look."

The bartender came around from his side of the bar to break up the fight, not the one on the television, the one there in the bar. The two drinkers had already separated and the larger man was shouting, "It's okay. It's okay. We're *friends*."

Price held his hand out over Ellie's shoulder, not quite touching her, just holding it there as if he could feel something in the air rising from her body. "Who knows how this will all turn out?" he said.

Sitting in Croker's office, I felt self-conscious, guilty even. I had been married for three years, and I was telling a lawyer with a little mustache about stuff I'd barely touched on with my own wife. Or was I telling the notary public? Or the riverboat pilot? He was a born listener, that Croker. He wanted the information. I didn't tell the man everything in one afternoon. I went back to the office again and again, and the girl Sara might be there, or another lawyer might be, and maybe I'd have to wait to get Croker alone. Sometimes he forgot the original reason I was there, and we didn't talk about Sara or the shooting or lawsuits. We just talked. I liked those days in the fall when the light came through his window and made the papers glow where they were stacked up on his desk. I told him what I remembered of Belize. He wrote some of it down and put it in a folder. I surprised myself, the things I remembered, even if I couldn't remember anything he wanted me to remember about that morning at the college, the woman in the wheelchair or the other woman, the heroic lady with the big purse. That was a different story. That was too recent. I'd tell that story to someone twenty years from now. In Croker's office, I talked about Belize and the New Hope School, about Price and Ellie, and how I fell in love with bread at New Hope and with Ellie in Belize City. I told him about the time I drowned among the Mormons. I told him because I had to and because he thought it might help Sara. I told him because he wanted to hear.

5

I rode the blue bicycle home after my shift at the café, keeping to the sidewalk as much as I could. By the middle of September I had a regular route: down the alley behind the café, cut across the back of the Marathon station, three blocks up the hill past the day care, wave to the children in the yard and try not to think about Katherine my wife and the boy-child she is carrying, coast downhill through the Kroger parking lot, watch out for the garbage guys on Thursday, watch out for the fast drivers who would kill me on my bike, stand on the pedals to the top of the street, pray the chain doesn't slip, squeeze past the rusted pickup, ignore the flat tire, don't let the Rottweiler next door scare me when it barks, it's on a chain, it's always on a chain, it's a big chain, and finally ease around the side of the building and park the bike beneath the sign for Martha White Flour, a sign that has been on the brick of that building for fifty years. Nobody followed me home, no housewives hopped up on espresso, no young men with grudges, no dogs driven mad by yeast.

I sat down at my kitchen table next to the radio I brought with me when I moved to the apartment. It wasn't a good radio. There was only one place I could put it and get any kind of reception. Before I moved in, the owner of the building (T. John Croker, local attorney and part-time slumlord) had one wall of the apartment painted a sickly cream color. The radio had to sit in front of that wall. No place else would do. I hadn't been there a week when I noticed a handful of letters, red letters, trying to fight their way through the fresh paint. It was a note or a sign someone had stenciled waist-high on the wall. Each day that passed, the words grew a little more visible. The top word was *PEOPLE*. Below that I could read the words *ARE* and *NO*. I supposed I could count on more words coming through the paint, too, before long. I positioned the radio so I wouldn't see them if they did come through. I didn't care what people *are* or *were* or what they *would be*. But the radio was small, and the letters were large—four inches tall, stenciled with care. At night they gave off a glow.

I was too tired to care what music they were playing on the radio. I just wanted the noise. I fell asleep at the table, dreaming my own dreams instead of the stuff coming over the airwaves. I dreamed about Belize and about the baker's boy. In that dream, the night is still, no moon, and he's in Belize City climbing a tall fence, climbing with just one hand because in his other hand he carries a bundle wrapped up in his shirt. When he gets to the top of the fence, he looks back over his shoulder. I want to call out to him. I want him to come down from the fence, but I can't call to him because I'm not there. I'm never in that dream. The dream ends always the same way: the boy lies on the ground, a bright light sweeps the fence, there are voices in the night. He lies in the shadows as still as he can be so no one will see him.

I didn't tell anyone about my dreams, not even Croker. I didn't tell Katherine. She didn't need to hear about any of that, not while she was growing a baby. Stacen didn't want to hear about my dreams. She said I spent too much time dreaming, I needed to think about what I was doing, not what I was dreaming. She said I acted compulsively, and she was probably right. The big decisions came to me all at once, like how for a short while I became a teacher of boys. It explains a lot, maybe everything.

I was twenty-three, and I had some ideas. I'd finished college in December, a semester late. I won't say I loved going to college, but I didn't hate it. I was ready to put it behind me, get on with life. I needed a change. I needed to move away from my family and my friends, away from all of it, the cars and televisions, the stores filled with books. I hoped if I went far enough away, I could leave *me* behind, and what I would end up with would be a better me, someone capable and fearless. Most of the people I knew from college had the same idea. They went to Alaska to fish, or they went to the army, hoping for a war they could survive, or no war. It was all in the timing.

That winter after I graduated, I kept my apartment near campus. It was funny how hard I tried to finish college, and then I stuck around, seeing a few of my friends, walking across campus for no real reason. It felt like freedom to know I didn't have to go to a class, but I also realized how little purpose I had. I met some people that winter. Two Moonie girls took me to Atlanta for a weekend. What they wanted was to feed me vegetables and play these old creaky folk songs on their guitars, songs I knew from summer camp. One of them was pretty, but the other one played the guitar better. The second night at their house, when I sat next to the pretty one in the kitchen and took her hand, she broke down in tears and told me to leave. She wasn't one of the happy Moonies, she said. She told me there were two kinds. She put a bruised pear in a paper sack for me and showed me the door. I hitchhiked home from Atlanta, but not without getting stuck at a truck stop for half the night.

Another night, I rode up to Indianapolis with three guys I hardly knew. I kept calling the driver *Ed* the whole ride when his real name was *Michael*. I guess he didn't like that. He asked me to find another ride home. I ended up at the house of a girl I knew a little, a house where there was some kind of party. I talked to a boy in the kitchen who was home on leave from Jim Jones's colony in Guyana. This boy was a basketball player, a good one, and he made it sound like a lot of fun living where he lived, traveling around, playing ball against local teams, trying to do some good. Fanatics turned me off, but he didn't say a word about Jim Jones or his people being fanatics.

This was before they all killed themselves in the jungle, the boy, too, I guess. We talked most of the evening. Jonestown was just basketball to him. Me, I was looking for something new. As long as it didn't involve dressing up in odd clothes, I don't know. If he'd had a plane ticket for me, would I have gone?

I gave up my college apartment in the middle of February and went home to stay with the folks. The old man wasn't drinking then, and it wasn't as bad as I remembered. I know it was February because the further it got from the Christmas holidays the more it felt like I was supposed to be doing something, not just hanging around. I kept meeting people who were doing more with their lives than I was. This boy I knew a little from high school had just come home from Africa, from Senegal, where he'd been in the Peace Corps. He was hanging around like me, temporarily out of ideas, shooting baskets on the playground while he tried to figure out what he would do next, but see, he had *done* something. I played a lot of basketball that winter. Where the folks lived then, a part of Tennessee you've never heard of, we could play outdoors year-round if we wanted to. We could play basketball until the cows came home. This Peace Corps guy told me he'd been changed by his time overseas, but I didn't know him before so I couldn't say if it was true. He had a dopey smile as if he was a little bit lost, and he laughed at jokes he didn't share with the rest of us. He wasn't much of a basketball player. He never would have made the team in Jonestown.

But the afternoon I met the Peace Corps boy from Senegal, the planets lined up in some strange and wonderful formation. It all wanted to fall into place for me. I didn't have a girlfriend. I didn't have a prospect of a girlfriend. I was finished with my last semester of college, living in the converted garage of my folks' house. I needed a job, but I didn't want a job. I didn't have a girl-friend with a job. The Peace Corps was calling to me. I had less doubt about that than I'd had about anything in years. I sent away to an address in Washington for certain papers, and when they came in the mail, I filled them out right away. If I was going to find myself, if I was going to do good, I needed to get started. People wrote letters for me. I took a physical and peed in a cup and handed my cup to a man who didn't find anything wrong with it.

One day not long after that, the big letter came, the one I was waiting for, and the truth of what I had started into motion that afternoon on the basketball court washed over me like a warm and unpleasant tide: I was on my way to Central America. For three days, I stayed in bed suffering from a case of the flu that could have turned into a nervous breakdown. I told my parents about my idea. We sat in the backyard over iced tea, though the old man looked like he wanted something stronger. I told them I'd been invited to teach at a school for troubled boys. They didn't believe me at first or they would have asked harder questions. They thought *I* was troubled. They didn't think I would go, not really, not until the day they drove me to the airport to see me off. My father acted like he was happy I'd found a way to do what I wanted to do and no soldiers from the other side would be shooting at me. My mother didn't understand why I had to go so far away, but teaching school was a safe ambition. There were schoolteachers in our family. Most of them lived a long time without slipping into drug abuse or sin. Some schoolteachers went to church.

In Miami, I met Price and Ellie and the deluded Dicky Roy. I got vaccinations in my arm and more vaccinations elsewhere, and I watched Muhammad Ali win his fight against Ken Norton on the television. Early one morning we drove away from the Capitan, eleven of us in all, and caught a flight to Belize City. On the plane, I watched out the window the whole time, as if I might recognize the place as soon as we flew over it. Dicky Roy passed around a reprint on Belize from an old *National Geographic,* and Ellie tried to get me to read a book of flowery poems written by a man from the fisheries department, but I couldn't read anything. I felt like I didn't know enough to be on that plane, as if I hadn't been to college at all. I didn't learn anything about Belize in college. I didn't know about the Carib Indians or the Creole language, or Guatemalan generals who wanted to cross the border and retake the lost province of *Belice.* I'd been given an envelope with some notes about my new job, along with a letter from a man named Hobson who was waiting for me to relieve him. The letter talked about boys who had been abused or neglected. I didn't know much about abuse or neglect, or about boys who couldn't learn to read, or boys with drunken whores for mothers whose brains were addled by syphilis. There was a lot I didn't know.

The morning I stepped off the plane, I was green and well-fed and scared. Price and Ellie and I spent a month together in the crowded city. We tried to get used to the heat and the smell from the open sewers. We watched huge catfish school up near the swing bridge, where the sluggish river emptied into the Caribbean like a leaky old toilet that never quite got the job done. We listened to Creole women laugh in the marketplace. We drank beer in the late afternoons, waiting for the air to cool and the flies and mosquitoes to drift away into the night. It never happened, the cooling off part. And then the month was over. On a Sunday morning, Price and Ellie helped me pack my things and load them into the back of the Peace Corps pickup, and they waved good-bye to me as the pickup carried me away, out the Western Highway toward the Cayo district.

An old man named Herbert, part Creole, part East Indian, drove me to New Hope. He did odd jobs around the Peace Corps office in Belize City, smiling, always smiling. Herbert talked nonstop for the first hour of the trip, as long as we drove on pavement. He talked about his six brothers, two of them in the States, and his four sisters who were all beautiful except for the ones who weren't. He talked about his nine children in detail, even the ones who caused him trouble. He talked about his Uncle Patel who lived in San Ignacio del Cayo, who was rich and smart enough to out-trade the Guatemalans.

Once past the capital, the pavement played out, and he didn't talk so much. It hadn't rained for weeks, and the road was little more than dust and potholes. Every time we hit a rough spot, Herbert gripped the wheel tighter and said, "Uncle Patel, Uncle Patel," as if he was praying.

It wasn't any hotter in the Cayo than it was in the city, but this heat felt different, country heat, no city smells, no city noises. After another hour, when I thought my tailbone had disintegrated, we turned down a lane lined with tall stately trees. I was grateful for the shade of those trees, and more grateful when I could finally get out of the truck. We'd stopped at the end of the lane in front of half a dozen wooden houses set up on stilts, and two or three low concrete buildings. A sign hung from the veranda of one of the houses: *New Hope School for Boys.* Underneath that, someone had written with a black crayon: *no way out.* Whoever tried to wipe those words off the sign only managed to smear them a little. I could smell farm animals. I saw boys everywhere, black boys and brown boys and boys with a touch of red to their skin, and two white boys with long hair and freckles. A tall black man in his early thirties stood in the middle of the boys, Fairbanks, the headmaster. He was obviously inspecting them.

"Mr. Tanner," he said. He seemed surprised to see me, as if he hadn't believed I would come after all. "Welcome to New Hope."

Fairbanks nodded to Herbert, but the driver had grown more and more quiet the last hour, and once we got out of the truck, Herbert had positioned himself so he wouldn't have to shake hands with Fairbanks. The headmaster shrugged and pointed across the way to the small wooden house where I would live, and Herbert helped me get my bags and boxes out of the truck, doing his best not to stare at the lines of boys forming silently outside the school's main office. Four lines, ten boys each. They stood exactly an arm's length apart, waiting for permission to enter the dining hall.

"Mr. Tanner," said Herbert. "Good luck with those ballies there." And like that he was gone, turning back only once to whisper to me so that nobody else would hear, "If you have trouble here, call on Uncle Patel." He drove twice as fast down the lane as he had on the way in.

It's hard to imagine what a fool I must have looked, alone, surrounded by my bags and boxes. I had the letter from Hobson in my duffel bag, telling me all about this place and the boys who had been sent here by the courts. According to Hobson, most of them had only committed small crimes. Some of them had been picked up after dark for sleeping on the streets, some because they were fighting for food in the marketplace. They were thin and barefoot, dressed in ragged cutoffs, and they looked me over without smiling as I walked across the grounds with my bags. Two boys fell in beside me to help carry my things. One complained about having his evening meal delayed. The other one laughed at him. "You've got a sweet life in this place," he said to his friend. Only he said it in Creole, so it sounded something like this to me: *You di got wan sweet life inna dis yah place, bwai.* That's not quite right either. It hardly sounded like words at first, more like a strange song they were singing back and forth.

Hobson was waiting for me on the veranda of his house.

"Leave the bags out here," he said to the two boys who had stopped on his top step. The boys dropped my bags and turned to leave without a word. When I thanked them for their help, it startled them. Maybe they thought I couldn't talk. They looked at each other and laughed, and Hobson said something to them in a low voice that made their faces get serious again.

He had cold beer waiting for us in the kerosene fridge, but first Hobson wanted to show me the farm—the fields of corn and beans, a small garden plot, two pastures where half-wild cattle and sheep grazed. There were forty-five acres in all, a ball field and a feed shed, and chickens in a henhouse behind the dormitories. A gang of pigs roamed wherever they wanted, slipping through the fence when they felt like rooting in the bush. Hobson didn't talk much. He pointed at things. I tried to keep up.

We returned to the veranda of his house, which would soon enough, I realized, be my house. Hobson lit a mosquito coil and set it at our feet, and he handed me a beer. He was taller than I was, thicker around the middle, and that evening he drank with a purpose. Maybe he was saying good-bye to two years of his life, or maybe drinking was a regular thing with him. Before he came to Belize, he'd worked at a prison in Illinois where he watched the inmates trade drugs for sex. There weren't any drugs at New Hope. I thought he sounded disappointed when he told me that. He kept two dogs, and he'd hoped to train them to sniff out drugs, but he never got the chance. Instead, he trained one of them, a large white shepherd, to chase a boy who stepped out of line. The dog didn't bite, but she could knock a boy down and stand over him until Hobson came along to thump the boy on the head.

"You have to let them know right from the start you're not going to put up with a lot of foolishness," he said. Hobson was a great believer in thumping. He made his hand into a fist with one knuckle sticking out to show me how he thumped them.

We stayed up too late and talked too much. At first, the beer helped Hobson find his voice, but sometimes we stopped talking and stared into the dark bush beyond the fence. I lost track of how many drinks we put away. I only knew I was falling behind. The cicadas were loud, and the more Hobson drank, the softer his voice went until I had to ask him pretty regularly to repeat himself. I'd already wandered through the house he was leaving me. It was three rooms and stood on stilts, with a large vat to catch rainwater off the roof. I could walk underneath the house without having to duck. Some of the older boys had painted the inside green for my arrival, the color of a half-ripe banana. They had painted the windows shut while they were at it. Hobson had three fans blowing inside, pushing the damp air from room to room.

"Don't bother to free up the windows," he said. "You leave one open, some little shit will crawl in and steal you blind."

From the veranda, I could see the single classroom and the dormitories, solid and squat, built low to the ground out of concrete block. The nearest dormitory was for the smaller boys, some of them only ten years old. On the other side of the dormitories, a light shone in a window of the office where the headmaster kept the phone and the logbook. The Salvation Army had built New Hope, but it had been years since any men had come across the sea from Liverpool or Cornwall to work with the boys. Now the men who ran the school came from just down the road, from villages called Teakettle and Black Man Eddy. Hobson had introduced me to three of them before dark: the cook, the woodshop instructor, and a tiny Salvadoran who was in charge of the animals. They were walking out to the road together on their way home. Once Fairbanks finished up in the office, he would leave, too, and there wouldn't be an adult on the grounds except for Hobson.

I asked why that was. I asked how long the boys stayed at the school. I asked if they ran away. I wanted to know everything before I was left on my own.

"It's a small country," said Hobson. "It's hard to disappear." He wore glasses, and I couldn't see his eyes in the dark. "Anyway, most of them have no place to go. Their parents are dead, or don't want them. If a boy runs away, he'll be brought back. Then Fairbanks has to deal with him." Hobson said the headmaster reminded him sometimes of the prison guards back in Illinois. I asked if that was good or bad.

"What's good is good," said Hobson. "The bad parts are bad."

"Sure," I said. "Of course. I see what you mean."

"I know one thing," said Hobson. "If I were Fairbanks, I wouldn't use the strap as much as he does. I wouldn't have to. That strap is evil, but it's a necessary evil. I hope you're not a fucking liberal when it comes to children."

I didn't know how to answer that. I thought I probably was a liberal. I thought I was supposed to be one. *Cuerpo de Paz,* and all that.

"Never hit a boy unless you mean it," said Hobson. "Only, once in a while you'll have to show one of them who's in charge. Then knock the hell out of him. Make it hurt."

A boy named Albert had come to sit on the steps below us, a mixed-race boy with dark eyes and long curly hair. A fine trace of flour clung to his black arms. Because of his job in the kitchen, he was called the baker's boy. From time to time, he laughed quietly at the things Hobson said.

"You know what I'm talking about, don't you?" said Hobson.

"I know Mr. Fairbanks put salt on that strap," said the boy. "That could burn."

"Behave yourself, and you won't get the strap," said Hobson.

The boy pushed on the tip of his nose and made his eyes go crossed. I didn't know what it meant when he did that, but Hobson leaned forward quickly in his chair.

"Do it again," he said, "I'll throw you down the stairs."

The boy laughed. When Hobson got to his feet, Albert ran off through the buildings to where the others had already gone to bed. Hobson's dog started after him. She didn't have her heart in it, though. It was too hot. As quickly as she got up from the porch, she came back to lie down.

"Don't take any foolishness from that kid," said Hobson. "I shouldn't let him hang around. He likes to feed the animals." Hobson reached down and stroked the shepherd, who panted bright-eyed at his feet. His other dog, a short-haired retriever, picked her head up suddenly to look around, as if she had just remembered something she had failed to do.

"Albert's been one of the lee boys," said Hobson. "Sorry. You don't know what that means. He's been one of the small boys. He's not one of the small boys anymore. He doesn't know it yet." The shepherd got up and placed her head in Hobson's lap. She knew something was up, with the packing and the empty boxes lying around. Hobson figured dogs were smarter than people that way. They could sense change, but they didn't go looking for it.

"The big boys used to chance Albert a lot," said Hobson.

I'd heard that expression once already. Early in the afternoon, two boys were kicking a ball in the dirt near the office, and when it was the older boy's turn, he kicked the ball as far as he could over a fence and into the pasture. The small one watched his ball roll between the legs of a startled bull, and he turned and called out to the bigger boy: *you chance bastard.* I tried to ask Hobson about it, but he found ways to leave my questions unanswered.

In the morning, Monday, I woke up with a dry mouth, and my eyes burned when they were open and burned a little more when they were shut. There was a large cast-iron bell hanging near the schoolroom. One of the boys came out to ring it with enthusiasm. When he saw me on the veranda, he smiled as though he had been ringing that bell just for me. The clamor of it made my teeth hurt. Once the ringing died down, I heard shouting from the office, and I saw a boy run across the pasture and disappear into the tall grass near the fence. Two boys had been fighting and it wasn't breakfast yet. Three or four of the others went after the one who was trying to get away, and soon they led him back and inside the office to the headmaster. From the sounds alone, I knew what was happening. Fairbanks had taken a length of rope down from the wall behind his desk and he was beating the boy with it on the legs. I'd seen the rope hanging there the day before. A short gray piece of frayed cotton. It would be soft to the touch if you passed it across your hands. I could hear the boy crying and Fairbanks speaking to him in a low insistent voice. I could hear the sound the rope made. At last, it was just the crying of the boy, and then he came out and Fairbanks made him kneel in place while the others filed into the dining hall.

I didn't feel like eating anything, which was good because Hobson didn't have anything to eat. Soon a different boy came to ring the bell. It looked like this bell ringing would take place throughout the day and fervently. On the third ringing of the morning, eight o'clock, I walked across the grass from Hobson's house to the classroom and stood just inside the door. Hobson and I hadn't said three words to each other that morning. When I looked out, I could see him sitting on his veranda in the same chair as the night before. I thought Fairbanks might come by to introduce me to my students, or bring me a list of the boys' names, but the headmaster was content to have Hobson show me how it was done. And Hobson, I was pretty sure, had been waiting for me to leave his house so he could pour himself a drink.

The empty schoolroom was quiet. Even on my first day, I could tell it was eerie to have that much peace and quiet. Then the boys came, some of them running into the room wide-eyed, as though they were chased. Others came slowly, trembling, remembering other schools, other teachers. I stood at the chalkboard and watched a change come over them as they stepped through the door. Outside, it was okay to run and argue and kneel in the dirt and call each other names. Indoors, they were wild birds suddenly in a cage, flying up against each other, fighting, always fighting.

The schoolroom had the essentials: two chalkboards, a small stage on one end. The chairs and desks were ancient but clean enough. I asked the boys to sit down, and three fights broke out over who would sit where. I passed out new pencils I had carefully sharpened, then took them back when one boy went after his neighbor. My tongue was thick in my mouth, and there was a new and strange rhythm to the pounding in my head.

Fifteen boys for morning classes. I wanted to begin by writing down their names. Fairbanks only sent the younger boys to school, the small ones, and most of them went by nicknames: *Broke-hand, Mouse, Snot. Milkboy, Corky. Cowboy, Whiteboy, Redboy, Bigboy, Leeboy, Blackboy.* I tried to get their real names from them, but I hadn't learned how to listen in Creole. A boy who didn't belong to me came and stood outside the schoolroom window. He was tall as a man, and he looked strong, but his eyes were all wrong. They were empty.

"You know da where for me ma?" he asked. I didn't try to answer him. I wasn't sure about the question.

"This boy is called Simple," said Albert. "He wants to know where his mother has went to."

"She mi go way," the boy said. "USA. Someplace like that." The other boys laughed at him, and I could see the confusion on his face.

"Them boys," said Simple. He shook his head sadly.

"Them boys," I repeated, and everyone laughed again.

I don't know how long he would have stood there quietly watching the younger boys at their desks if Fairbanks hadn't collected him and led him to the fields to work. I was happy to see him go.

"Carib," said one of the smaller boys, and he made as if he would throw a book out the window at Simple's back. Most of the boys were Creole, but there were Caribs in the room, too, boys from Dangriga with a red tint to their skin. They were supposed to be descendants of runaway slaves and a race of island Indians, and maybe it was true. One of the Carib boys looked about the room as though he was frightened, and another older boy whispered to him, soothing him in their language.

"Dirty Caribs," said a boy whose forehead was covered by a large scar. "Unu don't talk the filthy language." Then everyone was shouting again, as if it was a football game and somebody had just scored.

"If you don't all sit down," I said, but I didn't know how I was going to finish that sentence. The first day and all, I wanted them to like me. Albert, the baker's boy, smiled at me to let me know how foolish it was to think they would like me.

"Now, people," he shouted. "Everybody. Just pipe down."

He said it more than once, and it had absolutely no effect. I didn't know why he kept shouting the same words over and over, until I realized he was repeating what I'd been saying from the moment they walked into the classroom. It made him so happy to make fun of me I didn't say anything. I wondered if Hobson had as much trouble on his first day.

I moved to the board and picked up a piece of chalk, trying to remember everything Hobson had told me: I had no idea what kind of work each boy could do. Some boys could add and subtract, others could only count, some were working on their ABCs, a few of them—I didn't know which ones— could read, sort of. I didn't know how old anybody was. Albert was neither the largest nor the smallest boy in my classroom. The smallest boy, Darnell, had a head shaped like a melon, long and narrow. He sat in the corner and talked to himself.

I didn't expect so much noise and heat or the way the sunlight poured in through the windows. I wasn't ready for that first day, but I don't blame Hobson. "Show them who's in charge," he'd said. Boys were shouting at each other, shouting to each other, shouting with each other. Hobson had told me not to hit them, and to make it hurt when I did. Several boys began to push their desks across the room like bumper cars at the carnival. Each crash of their desks echoed inside my head the same way it echoed off the walls of the schoolroom. Two boys slipped up to the small stage where they danced together in perfect time, though there wasn't any music. A cold sweat gathered under my arms and ran down my sides. I had a quick and unwanted image of my grandfather, the meanest man I knew growing up, reaching up and breaking off a small branch from a tree and using that branch to sting the back of my legs as I tried to hold still, the tears coming, the words he wanted me to say. And my father walking away toward the house, his head down, muttering the words *he* wanted me to say. I could not find any words of my own.

I did all I could for as long as I could to ignore Hobson's advice. Class had started at 8:30, and I looked at my watch. It was 8:37. I took a deep breath as one small Hispanic boy who had the preposterous name of Feliciano began an obscene new dance to top those other two dancing boys. Feliciano swung his hips and batted his eyes at the others. He smiled coyly at me and said words in Spanish I didn't want to know. When his hand went to his zipper, I reached the end of my patience. I laid into him. I gave him one on the ear, and then I came down hard on his head with my knuckles, the Hobson way.

"Is this what you want?" The words came out in a growl, as if I'd been storing them somewhere in the back of my throat for my whole life. The boy ducked at first, still grinning, but I slapped him again, more than once, until his face shone red and I could tell he wanted to cry. I was trying not to shout, though the words were hoarse and desperate. I turned on the next boy, and the next.

"Is this what you need?"

I watched them, saw one grinning face after another change, if not to fear, at least to anger. Nobody dared laugh. The ones who escaped getting hit tried not to look at the others, as they dropped one by one into the nearest desk. They sat down and they were still, but I didn't fool myself into thinking I had achieved anything lasting. I figured I might have to hit someone again, every day, for as long as I taught there. I thought I was willing to do it.

Hobson stood in the doorway, a look of disgust on his face, disgust for me, for the boys, for all of us.

"Put them in groups," he said, then turned and walked away.

So I separated them into groups. Four of them I put to work on some arithmetic problems I found in my desk, a page torn out of a book. The boys in that group were all roughly the same size, so I hoped they could do the same work. I set another group up with some Canadian reading books that had been donated to the school in an ancient time. I put three boys in that reading group because I only had three books. If I asked four or five of them to share the books, I thought they'd kill each other. The story I told them to read, "Winter Fun," was about sledding in the snow, and the joy of singing "Oh, Canada."

I brought the four smallest boys to the board and gave each of them a piece of chalk so they could write the alphabet. I had to go to the corner and lead the melon-headed boy named Darnell to the board. Everybody called him Leeboy. He could only write the A and the B of his alphabet. When I asked him for more letters, he had trouble keeping them in his head.

"While I help Darnell," I said to the others at the board, unable to keep my voice from dropping into a growl, "you work on writing your names. You write *Earl*," I said to one. He was surprised I'd figured out his name. His nickname was Boomba. "And you write *William*," I said to another. The boys called him Bus'up. He was the one with the scar on his forehead. I glowered at a little boy who looked not like a boy at all, but like a circus midget, an old man in a child's body. He had a bald spot on his head, probably ringworm. I remembered his name, too.

"You," I said, "write *Geoffrey*."

The boys at their desks, the ones with the arithmetic books, moved their pencils over their papers as if those papers were on fire. I was afraid to look over their shoulders. I didn't care if they were getting any of the problems right. I just wanted them to be busy and not to stab each other. I remembered the constant fear of my own teachers back in grade school, how they were always afraid one of us would put out an eye with a pencil or a compass or a tree limb. I wondered what would happen if one of my students put out another boy's eye. I wondered what would happen if I did it myself.

The reading boys slouched in their desks. Maybe they weren't reading, but they were faking it, which was good. At the board, Darnell couldn't get

past the letter *C*. I thought it might be better to stick with something familiar, so I wrote out his name on the board with the other names, and I told him
to copy it ten times, twenty times, a hundred times.

"He doesn't know what one hundred means," said Albert. "One hundred
could be one zillion to him."

"Tell him to do it a lot," I said to Albert. I probably sounded like I was
begging.

"Boy," said Albert. "Write your name till Jesus comes."

The smaller boy stared at Albert, shaking his head slowly from side to
side.

"Boy," said Darnell. "That's one lot of letters."

Lunch was an hour and a half away. I watched William and Earl fill the board
with their names. They were ready to come to blows because the names were
crossing the line I'd drawn in the middle of the board, EarlWilliam and
WilliamEarl, EarlWilliam and WilliamEarl. I erased what they had written
and told them to start again, and this time to have a little respect for their
neighbor.

"Neatness counts," I said, though I didn't give a goddamn about neatness. It was something to say.

I looked to where I had left the last boy, the circus midget with ringworm, the old man. He stood in front of the last available chalkboard,
behind the small raised area that served as a stage. He hadn't written anything yet.

"Write your name," I said. I was tired of fooling around. "Write *Geoffrey*."

The boy scowled, his eyes straight ahead.

"You won't cooperate? Don't you know your letters?"

"I know my letters," said the boy. He spoke clearly when he wanted to, in
the voice a grownup might use. He held a piece of chalk in his hand, staring

at it carefully, as though it was something he'd found by the side of the road, but he didn't make any marks on the board with it. It occurred to me that his name might be spelled *Geoffrey* or *Jeffrey*. At least, I had to ask him.

"Do you start your name with a J or a G?" I said. I made it clear I wasn't going to put up with any nonsense.

"With a G," he said.

"Write it," I said, and he wrote the letter G.

"Next letter," I said, "is E. Write it."

But he wouldn't write any more.

"Bastard," muttered the boy called Bus'up. "Do what the man says. Write your name."

I wrote out the whole name, GEOFFREY, and told the midget to copy it ten times. Then I went back to Darnell, who was studying what he had written with pride:

DARNELL . . . ARNELLD . . . RNELADL.

The letters were huge.

"Mr. Tanner, sir," said Darnell, gone all thoughtful. He stood at the board, a new pained look coming over his face.

"What is it?"

"Me want stool," said the boy.

I had no idea what he wanted from me.

"Me want stool," he said again. He looked at the others for help. "Me, I . . . want go . . . stool."

For once, the other boys didn't laugh.

"He wants to do his ablutions," said Bus'up, who meant to be helpful. Albert, the baker's boy, nodded.

"*La trine,*" said Feliciano, and he started another more perverse version of his little dance. I tried to get my hands on Feliciano again, but before I could grab him, Darnell bolted outside. I followed him to the door and saw him running across the grass for the outhouse, trying to get his pants down before he soiled himself.

"Well, motherass," said Feliciano. "That lee bastard, he could run, boy."

I sent them all to recess. Nobody had said how long or how often I could set them free. I let the recess last forty-five minutes and would have left them out longer, but I had to believe Fairbanks had his eye on me. Hobson, who was loading his belongings into the same cardboard boxes I had just unpacked, was careful all morning not to look my way. I knew he was watching me, too, measuring me to see if I had what it took. When I felt it was time to start again, I didn't know how to get them all back inside.

I called them, surprised at how thin my voice sounded out of doors. The boys, of course, ignored me. I called them louder, but it was the sight of Hobson standing on his veranda and pointing at the door to the classroom that made them hear me. I stood on the threshold and counted them as they came back in, and I tried to put names with faces. Outdoors, they had re-energized, as if they'd taken turns sticking their fingers in a wall socket. At their desks, I knew they'd get after each other again. The stubborn boy named Geoffrey, the old man who wouldn't write his name for me, came to the door last. He still had the piece of chalk in his hand. He'd been holding on to it the whole time he was outside.

"Boy, nobody's going to steal your chalk," I said, hoping what I said was true.

I took a last look toward Hobson's veranda before I turned to go into the room, and I saw, out of the corner of my eye, that Geoffrey had been writing his letters after all, only he'd done it outside on the schoolroom wall. I didn't care about that. It moved me to think he would practice his name during his recess, afraid to make a mistake in front of me. A warm feeling came over me, a Peace Corps feeling. Something good could come out of that rough morning yet. I went outside where I could get a closer look at the letters on the wall. I wanted to make sure he wasn't having any problems. But he had written the letters clear enough, and the letters made words that anyone could read: *Fock You Mr. Tanner Sir.* He had written it again and again in a neat script, though the letters bumped and dodged over the rough surface of the concrete block. All the anger of the morning came back to me, leaving my vision yellow and clouded, as though I had been rubbing my eyes too hard. I left the others to do whatever harm they could to each other and I hauled this one as roughly as I dared across the school grounds. Fairbanks looked up and smiled when he saw us come up the stairs to his office.

"Good morning, Mr. Tanner," he said. It was the first time I heard the silky voice he used when he knew I needed something from him. "What can I help you with this morning?"

"This boy," I said. I struggled to catch my breath in front of Fairbanks. I didn't want to sound out of control. "He refuses to do the work I've given him, which is bad enough. He also feels the need to write ugly words on the schoolroom wall."

"What are these ugly words?" asked Fairbanks. He smiled at me. He had a perfect smile. "You mean, obscenities?" The subject interested him greatly.

"No," said Geoffrey. "That wasn't me."

"Don't deny it," I said to the boy. "You wrote 'Fuck you Mr. Tanner.' You wrote it more than once."

Fairbanks was already reaching for the rope hanging behind him. He doubled it up in his hand as he stood from his desk.

"Couldn't be me," said Geoffrey. "Me no know how for spell that word."

Fairbanks raised an eyebrow at me.

"He got close enough," I said.

I watched Fairbanks force the boy to stand still, his hands on the desk in front of him. Then Fairbanks brought the rope down hard against the boy's bare legs. With the first blow, Geoffrey began to cry. A welt rose across the back of both calves. With the second blow, the boy let go of his bladder, and Fairbanks stopped smiling. I left the office, the boy's cries in my ears. I hoped the others would know from then on that they had to be reasonable and try to do the work I set before them.

When I got back to the classroom, they were gone. I didn't care where they had disappeared to. I only had to spend my mornings as a schoolteacher, not my afternoons, and it was nearly twelve o'clock. I gave it up for the day. After their dinner, the boys would work in the fields or the kitchen. I had other projects, too. The next day, we could make a fresh start. My legs and arms were heavy as I locked the schoolroom door and went to Hobson's house to wash up. Hobson showed me how to pump water from the rain vat into a smaller holding tank up on the roof, where it could provide pressure for a shower. The water was cold, but I stayed in the shower as long as I could, until Hobson pounded on the door.

Hobson had an old Toyota Land Cruiser, one the Peace Corps staff had lent him after they wore it out on the streets of Belize City. It was against regulations to provide a volunteer with a vehicle. I wanted to ask him about that, add it to my list of questions. Before we ate lunch, he showed me how to take the air filter off the Toyota and choke the carburetor with my hand. He frowned when he saw I wasn't half a mechanic.

"This car will come in handy," he said, "but you have to get it started. It'll take you to town for groceries." Hobson wiped his greasy hands on his pant leg. I did the same on mine. "If there's an accident," he said, "you might get to the army doctor before someone bleeds to death."

A group of the older boys filed past. They were coming in from a back pasture where they had been cutting grass. They carried their shirts in one hand, their machetes in the other. Their black bodies were wiry and muscled and shiny with sweat.

"It's safe to give them machetes?"

"You keep an eye on them," said Hobson. "They fight, but I've never seen them do it with machetes."

"What do I do if they start in?"

"I don't know what you'll do. Stay out of the way, most likely." He handed me the air filter. Even to my eye, it looked old and worn.

"You need a gun?" he said, but he had his head under the hood again, and I wasn't sure I'd heard him right.

"You have a gun?" I wished I hadn't said it so quickly. I wished my voice hadn't caught on the last word.

"A gun," said Hobson, pronouncing the word the same way I did. "I have a motorcycle, too, which I'm thinking I might not even ought to show you. I had a pickup for a while. They made me give it up. They were going to send me home."

With a screwdriver, he scraped at the corrosion caked on the battery cables. *El Cuerpo de Paz* had rules about everything, about where we could live, who we could hang out with, what sorts of things we were supposed to live without. Everything Hobson did and half of what he owned was off the charts. He pried up the caps on the battery to see if there was water inside. Two of the cells were dry. He swore and added water to them from a jar.

"I put off selling the truck as long as I could," said Hobson. "They need some kind of transport here. I took a boy to the hospital last Christmas on the back of my motorcycle. I had to put another boy on behind him to hold the first one in place." He stepped away from the Toyota and wiped his hands on his pants again.

"What was wrong?"

Hobson pointed at the air filter.

"With the boy," I said.

"Which one?"

"The one you took to the hospital."

"Him," said Hobson. "Some other boys pushed him into a hornets' nest. He got stung twenty or thirty times. His face swelled up like a soccer ball. A good way to choke to death." Hobson gathered up his tools and headed back up the steps to the house.

"So what happened?" I followed him out of the sun. My throat felt swollen and thirsty. I'd been drinking water all morning, but I couldn't get enough. Drink and drink and drink some more.

"You made it, didn't you? He was all right?"

Hobson went to the tiny refrigerator in his kitchen to see if he had ice yet.

"It was the baker's boy," he said. He kept his back to me. "Albert. He's okay, I guess. How would you ever know?"

I ate part of a sandwich and lay down on Hobson's spare bed. I told myself I'd stop calling it Hobson's bed when I had the place to myself. In the afternoon, I was supposed to start work in the garden with a group of the older boys. I didn't want to work outdoors. The sun was brutal. It was closer to the earth than it was back home. I fell asleep for an hour and woke up with a strange and different kind of headache. I heard Hobson moving slowly down the lane on his motorcycle, his dogs running alongside him as far as the gate.

When I went to Fairbanks's office to find the boys who were supposed to help me in the garden, Geoffrey was there at the foot of the stairs, kneeling in the dirt. I could see the marks on his legs where Fairbanks had struck him, and other marks where he had pissed on himself. The boy's face was stained with tears.

"I told him to stay there until you came back," said Fairbanks. "He wants to apologize."

I didn't want to think about how long the boy had knelt in the sun.

"Apologize to Mr. Tanner," said Fairbanks.

"I sorry," said the boy. I could barely hear the words that came out of his mouth.

"It's okay," I said. I felt dizzy. I felt as if my head was going to explode. "We can try again tomorrow."

The boy got up slowly and rubbed furtively at his knees. He didn't dare leave until Fairbanks told him he could go.

"Get a bucket of water and a brush. You can clean up this floor," said Fairbanks. I thought he was talking to me at first, but he was talking to the boy.

"And, young Mr. *Gordon* . . ."

Fairbanks said the name slowly and clearly.

"Gordon, Gordon, Gordon," he said with a little laugh, as if he was remembering the words to a song he'd heard but couldn't quite get right. It was all for my benefit. The boy's name was Gordon. I had to reach out and touch the wall next to me because I couldn't swallow and I could barely breathe, and I was thinking, this must be what it's like to have a stroke. What do you do when you know you've been that wrong? What do you say? Is there a way out? I thought about finding the brush and the bucket of soapy water and cleaning the floor myself. I thought about offering the boy the rope and asking him to hit me a few times, or maybe he could just wrap it around my throat like a necktie, only real tight. I thought about resigning from the damn *Cuerpo de Paz* and going home, but how can you resign from anything when you're only a volunteer? I thought about taking another long shower or drinking all of Hobson's beer and his rum and whatever else he had, just drinking it and drinking it until I couldn't remember this day at all.

Someone started ringing the bell again. A boy ran past the office with Hobson's clean laundry in his arms, followed by one of Hobson's dogs hot on his trail. One other time in my life I'd said something so wrong, so shameful. Maybe twice. There was the time in college when I asked a girl out on a date, or she asked me, and I said I would go, and we went to dinner and to a play and had a wonderful time, and all the while I was realizing I couldn't remember her name, because it was one of those things where I didn't get her name straight the first time I met her, and I was afraid to call her the wrong name, so all night long I kept calling her "my friend," as in "thank you, my friend, for dinner," and later "thank you, my friend, for the show," and later "my friend, do you want to come up to my apartment," and she said, "If you had only been able to remember my name, just once, Tanner, and you will realize that I've had no problem remembering yours, this would have been your lucky night, asshole," and after that I was watching her car drive off into the evening.

Or maybe it was like when I was seven years old and I said the word *blowjob* at the barbershop, because I didn't know what the word meant—I thought it was something like a cross between a snow job and a blowhard, like when a blowhard tries to give you a snow job. And all the time the word meant something different, something nobody was willing to explain, and when the room got real quiet and the barber stopped cutting my hair and my mother sitting in the corner started to cry, I knew I had said something I would never be excused for. There was no way out.

Fairbanks pronounced the name slowly and clearly one more time. The boy wasn't a Geoffrey or Jeffrey or Joffry or Gadfrey, or any other name like it. Gordon. He was Gordon.

"I don't care what Mr. Tanner calls you," said Fairbanks. "You do the work he tells you to do. I know you hear what I'm saying."

Gordon. I repeated the name to myself, unable to say it out loud.

The boy shuffled toward the bathhouse for his bucket of water, but I couldn't remember where I was going or why. I saw the welts on the back of his legs, and I had a bad taste in my mouth, like when you wake up in the morning after being sick in the night.

"Don't worry about the names," said Fairbanks. There was more laughter in his voice. "Geoffrey, Gordon, Gregory. Ronald. Most any name will work with a boy like that one. You'll get them straight after a while."

I excused myself and went back to the house. I had forgotten my hat, and I couldn't find it for a long time. It turned up in the bathroom. My head was expanding, blowing up from the inside, and when I got my hat from the hook next to the sink, I was afraid to see what I looked like in the mirror.

I got through the days of that week. Hobson drank hard every evening, disappointed when I didn't drink with him, but it was no use. I couldn't keep up with him, so why try? I made a start in the garden. I walked along the road at sunset. I longed for mail, but when I stopped to think about it, I realized there wasn't anyone to write to me. My brothers didn't write letters. I wasn't sure the oldest one could read. There would be something from my mother at Christmas.

Hobson's plan was for us to take the bus to Belize City on Friday, since he didn't think the Toyota would make it to the city. Sixty or seventy miles. It wasn't much of a car. Friday was when Hobson would say his good-byes to the place. By week's end, he had sold his motorcycle to a man from San Ignacio. He had lined up a home for the dogs, too, with an American family who had farmed the Cayo for twenty years.

"At least they're not missionaries," he said. I didn't know what to say to that. When they drove up to the office and across the grass to Hobson's house, there to pick up the dogs, I stayed inside. A bit later, Hobson came up the stairs.

"We can go now," he said to me, quietly.

Hobson had cleared most of his boxes from the house and ferried them one by one to the bus stop. That morning he'd placed Albert out on the highway to guard his boxes against thieves. The house looked bigger now without his belongings in it. The Western Highway led back to the new capital, Belmopan, and from there to Belize City. If a boy ran away, he would walk the road, or if he had money, he would ride the bus east like we were going to do. He would not go to Guatemala.

We carried Hobson's last two bags out the long drive to where Albert waited for us. Hobson gave the boy a quarter for watching over his things. Perhaps Hobson sensed what I wanted to say, that the day was hot and he was cheap and the boy deserved more than a quarter.

"Never give them too much money at one time," said Hobson. We watched Albert walk away from us, back in the direction we had come. The boy knew we were watching. He held himself with dignity as he moved up the dusty road in an old pair of Hobson's shoes and a Chicago Bears sweatshirt.

"I told him to cut the sleeves off that shirt," said Hobson. "He must be burning up. Never give them too much of anything," he said.

Hobson looked at me then, as if he was angry. "Hell," he said, "I don't care what you do." I was still chewing on those words when the bus pulled up. It was nearly full.

We didn't have to stand. Hobson and I got seats but not near each other. The driver stopped every couple of miles to pick up the next passenger who waved the bus down from the side of the road. At one stop, an old woman pulled herself up the steps. She asked the driver how much the fare was. From the way he told her, it was clear he thought she should already know. She counted it out in coins and two folded dollar bills and looked around for a place to sit down. If there had been another empty seat near the front, she would have sat anywhere instead of next to me.

"Wait," she said as the driver tried to put the bus in gear. "I wan' tell Junie I going."

"All right then," said the driver.

The old woman leaned across me and lowered the glass. She smelled richly of cooking oil and burlap as she hung her head out the window.

"Junie," she called. "Junie." I looked toward the house she was yelling at. There was nobody on the porch or in front of the house.

"Junie," she said again, louder this time. "I going."

The driver waited another moment.

"You done then?" he said.

"Done," she said.

"Anyone else want to say something to Junie?" asked the driver. Laughter carried through the bus.

"Make we go," said the old woman, laughing with the rest of them. A sleepy head, a young boy, appeared at the window of the house, and she leaned across me once more, crushing me so she could wave as the bus pulled back onto the road.

"You're a nice fellow," she said. The bus had resumed rocking and pitching down the highway. "What are you doing here? A tourist?"

"I'm with the Peace Corps," I told her. "I work at the New Hope School."

Her face was very black, but somehow at the mention of the school, it got darker.

"That place. Me no like that place for true," she said, slipping away from the classroom English she probably thought I wanted to hear.

"You hush, Miss Penny," said the driver over his shoulder. "He's new there." He looked up into his rearview mirror, but not at Miss Penny or at me. He was looking farther into the bus, somewhere toward the back.

"This one is not the other one," said the driver.

I didn't want her to hush. I wanted to find out what she had to say. But she repositioned herself so that she could prop her head on the seat, and right away she fell asleep. It was an act of will to fall asleep like that. She rode as far as the capital, where half the bus emptied out. She got off with the others to buy fruit from a stall beside the road, then stood near the steps and waited for the new passengers to buy their tickets. When she boarded the bus again, she moved to the very back. She had three large mangoes in a string bag, and when she passed Hobson, dozing in his seat, she let the fruit swing into his face.

"Careful," he said. "Careful." But she walked on to the back of the bus, as if she hadn't heard him.

6

When I woke up from my nap, I dragged myself out to the front room. The woman who delivered the mail had dropped a couple of bills through the slot in the door. I found a note from Croker on the floor. Croker was my confidant. Croker was my new best friend. Then I read the note. The note said I was behind in my rent.

It would be good (and Croker had underlined the word *good* carefully) *to bring me a check by Monday.* Croker was my landlord. That's all he was. Croker was nothing to me.

I made a mental note: pay the rent. Then I made another mental note: ask Stacen for money so I could pay the rent. The rent looked like a problem. I was trying hard not to think about my recent problems, but it was already afternoon, the hard part of the day. I leafed through some magazines I had by the bed. I read the cartoons, hoping one would cheer me up. I made a pot of tea, and I checked the label carefully to be sure about this tea, nothing in it to kill yeast or send yeast into hibernation. While the tea steeped, I looked out the window into the backyards of my neighbors. The man next door came down his steps with a bowl of food for his Rottweiler, the same dog who growled and snapped at me every morning when I came home on my bicycle. I watched the dog wet himself to get at his Purina.

I waited that day as long as I could before I picked up the telephone. I was calling Katherine every afternoon a little after four, when I knew she would be home from work. She's the librarian at her elementary school, and she planned to keep going to work right up until the day the baby was born. Being pregnant doesn't slow a librarian down. I wanted to tell her about my day, about the bread that wouldn't rise and all those muffins Stacen made. I wanted to tell her how Stacen's freezer was going to be full of muffins come five o'clock. I wanted to tell her how disappointed I was in Croker. I would rather talk to Katherine than anyone I know. Katherine is six feet tall with blond hair that is beginning to gray and a face so soft when she smiles, her chin disappears. I have loved her completely since the Saturday evening I first met her. It was at a party for employees of The Bobber. I used to go to parties, reluctantly. I can talk about movies, and taxes, and who's been a jackass at city hall, that sort of thing, but I never know if I'm going to enjoy myself or if I'll stand in the corner for an hour, then duck out for home. Katherine didn't come to that party to talk politics. She was invited by my boss's wife, who we called Mrs. Bobber. Mrs. B. asked Katherine to come over and look after the children so the grownups could relax over a bottle of gin. I gave up drinking long ago—I have my reasons—and I don't know if Mrs. B. counted me as a whole grownup or not, but I always got invited to her parties, me and two or three women with short hair and loud throaty laughs who smoked too much and ended up gasping for air, their eyes watering at their own jokes. Those women were trying to get back into the swing of things. Maybe I was supposed to be the swing of things.

When I let myself in the side door at Mr. and Mrs. Bobber's house, Katherine was standing exactly in the center of the hallway, a lighthouse in a sea of children's boots and jackets and washed-up toys. She was getting the kids ready to go to the park by the river, kneeling in front of the smallest of them, the littlest Bobber, who was in a life-and-death struggle with his shoes.

"We can't go in the water," said the boy. I couldn't get past him in the hallway, not until he got right with his shoes, so I stood there more or less looming over him. I remember the way he looked up at me, as if what he said, "We can't go in the water," was important, a fact I needed to know. His name was Thomas, and his face was round and serious.

"No," said Katherine, humoring him while she made the laces work. "It's too cold for the water."

"For God's sake," he said. It was a phrase the kid had picked up from his father. Everything was *for God's sake* at The Bobber, though nobody was religious. "We can't play in the water ever," said the kid. "We have to be more careful than that, Katherine. We could drown, for God's sake." And I thought, who was this little kid, and how did my mother get inside his head?

"I would never let you drown," said Katherine. "It would spoil your father's party. Now get your coat, mister."

I listened to the way she soothed the boy. I watched as she tugged his coat on over a bulky sweatshirt and struggled with his little snaps and little zippers and his little paranoia. She knew I was watching. She looked up at me and held my gaze, and I slipped down into her brown eyes. I was a goner. If she left, I didn't want to be at that house anymore. I wanted to go with her. "How about me?" I said. I don't know where I got the nerve. I wasn't brave. "Can I come along?"

Katherine smiled up at me, her small chin disappearing as she blushed. She saw the boy in me, or she heard it. She wanted to say yes. She wanted to say no. She had a weakness for boys.

"Okay by me," said Thomas. He was no fool. Where Katherine was, we would both be safe. "You stay out of the water, though."

"Of course," said Katherine. "He will, he will."

I nodded, careful not to look at her again, not to let our eyes meet. We were too old for innocence. We knew what it could mean if I went along.

"Oh for God's sake," said Thomas.

I left the party before it got started. I had to lie to Mrs. Bobber about coming down with a cold, but it wasn't hard to lie to Mrs. Bobber. I drove to the park and waited in my car until Katherine arrived with the children. I bought her a coffee from the gas station on the corner and we sat on a bench while the children played. Every so often, when one fell down, she got up and scraped the kid off. Those kids had good parents, all of them did, but they loved Katherine better than their own mothers, at least on a Friday night in the playground by the river. They weren't so smart, or they would have seen me for the rival I intended to become.

The next night Katherine and I went to a movie, and the night after that I cooked dinner for her at her house, and the phone rang and it was Mrs. B. asking if Katherine could come over to be with the kids, a last-minute thing, and Katherine said no, she couldn't, she had someone over. That night it was candles and music and tangled sheets and clothes on the floor. Two weeks later we were talking about getting married. Katherine is the only woman I have held in my arms since that night in the park three years ago. I hugged her by the pavilion when the children weren't looking. Later, I used to go to her school, to where she worked in the library. I volunteered to read to the kids. It was a way to make points. What I was after was a chance to hold her, to bury my face in her neck and feel safe. I would kiss her between the bookshelves if there weren't any kids in the room. We had to stoop a little to stay hidden because she's taller than any bookshelf. She towers over the children in her library, but she's good with the ones who need help, especially the awkward kind of kid with broken glasses and half his lunch on his shirt. I've seen her calm a kid like that down.

She had just come in from school when I called. I actually preferred the telephone to seeing her in person. It hurt too much to see the changes coming over her. Just hearing her voice, I could picture her, the way she held the phone in place with her shoulder as she moved around the kitchen. She had gained a little weight and her breasts were full, like in this photograph she used to let me look at, a picture of her as a teenager swimming with friends at a lake in the mountains. I used to get sad when I looked at that photo. It made me wish I had met her sooner.

When I called, everything I could think to tell her I told her, everything that had happened since the last time we were together. She was angry at me for moving out. Who wouldn't be? But mostly she was too focused on the pregnancy to act on her anger. Sometimes she yelled and threw things, sure, but you expect that from a pregnant woman. She threw my clothes out in the yard, but she called me first and told me she was going to do it so I had time to get over there and pick them up right away. And she only threw a few shirts. It was the principle of the thing. She was making a point. She brought me out a cup of coffee after I picked everything up. She wouldn't let me come inside to drink it, though. She said when I was ready to come home, I had to ask her first and I had to mean it. She wasn't running a bed and breakfast.

Katherine knew the score and she knew all the players. She and Stacen had been friends since they were kids. She knew Mr. Bobber from before he opened his own place, back when he sold worms and crickets to the big chain stores. She knew Croker well enough to laugh at his cluttered office and his little mustache.

"Why don't you go see a real shrink," she said, "instead of talking to Croker?"

Actually, Croker has a certificate that proves he's taken some courses in counseling. But I wasn't talking to Croker anymore. The man was too mercenary for me.

"Croker's no shrink," I said.

"My point, exactly," said Katherine. "This is bigger than Croker."

I wondered what she was after. Katherine had a way now that she was pregnant of jumping up and saying things before I had a chance to get my defenses in place. I had a familiar panicky feeling, like when a crazy woman points a gun at you on the first day of school. Exactly like that.

"With a real shrink, you could talk about Belize," said Katherine. "Talk about that school where you taught. Tell him about the baker's boy."

"What did I ever tell you about the baker's boy?" I said. I was trying to remember so I would know what it was safe to leave out.

"He's important to you, Tanner."

I thought about it for a minute. "A lot of people are important."

"I guess so," said Katherine. She sounded far away, as if she'd set the phone down and taken a step back.

"Don't hang up," I said.

"I have to, Tanner."

I heard her open the refrigerator door. From the sounds she made, she was fixing herself something to eat. She ate whole grains and dairy products and every kind of green vegetable. And cheeseburgers. Now that she was pregnant, she ate a cheeseburger every day.

"Are you afraid of your own story?" she said.

"Why would I be afraid?"

"Of course you're afraid," said Katherine.

"It's true," I said. "I'm afraid."

"I'm afraid, too," she said. "I'm afraid for us and I'm afraid for you."

I heard the sound of a jar being opened. The microwave went on.

"Can you do that?" I asked.

"Do what?"

"Can you make a cheeseburger in the microwave?"

"Oh, Tanner," she said. She sounded worn out, done in. Like at a party when the fun is over and the only thing left is to clean up.

"Look," said Katherine, "I have a lot to do. I don't mind being a single mother. I really don't. You want to be a numbered account at the sperm bank, you can be a numbered account. Be just like Switzerland. You want to be a friend, be a friend. You want to be something more, you want to be a husband . . ."

I clammed up. We sat with the phones in our hands, neither of us knowing how to say the next thing. Sometimes we did that. It wasn't easy, this talking to another person. I couldn't seem to have a conversation all the way through without getting sidetracked, in the same way I couldn't bake the day's bread for Stacen without changing my mind at least twice about the ingredients. I'd start with a simple whole wheat recipe, and I'd decide to add some seven-grain cereal for a little texture, or if there wasn't any seven-grain cereal, I'd add oats, and then I would see the raisins on the shelf, and they'd look good to me, plump, eager to jump in the bowl, and I'd have to go out front and let in a delivery and when I came back to the bread I wouldn't be able to remember which recipe I was more or less following, so I'd study the ingredients in the bowl, and I'd wing it. The bread came out okay. It almost always did, but Stacen knew if I'd been cheating on the recipe. When she asked me what I'd baked for the day, if I hesitated, not sure what to call it—Honey Whole Wheat Oat And Raisin Seven Grain Bread—she gave me one of those looks, and she rifled through the stack of books and manila envelopes on top of the refrigerator until she found the help-wanted sign. She stopped just short of putting it in the window.

"So listen, Tanner," said Katherine, "because this is the way it is." She spoke carefully, as if she might have rehearsed what she was going to say. "I have loved you, Tanner Johnson, and I can love you some more. I would like you to come home."

She paused to let that sink in. She ran water at the sink. She was putting the clean dishes in the rack to dry.

"But if you stay away too long," she said, "it will be too late for that."

"I know," I told her. "I understand. I do. Completely."

"I don't have the patience to fuck around forever."

The phone tried to jump out of my hand when she said that. This way of talking was new for her. I couldn't get used to a librarian who swears.

"So, tell the story," she said. "Tell someone. Tell Croker your story. The whole story."

"Tell nothing but the story," I said. I had the phone in both hands. I had a good grip.

"Don't fool with me, Tanner," said Katherine.

"All right, all right," I said. "I heard you the first time. Don't shoot."

"What?" she said.

"Just kidding," I said. "I meant, don't shout."

"Tanner?" she said. "Are you okay?"

But I couldn't talk more. I had to get off that phone. The red letters on the wall were speaking to me. *People Are No Damn . . .* said those words. I didn't have time for reading a lot of words on the wall. And I sure as hell wasn't going to go see Croker. That little man with his barely legal mustache, what did he know? All he wanted was his rent. How could he help me? What good would it do to talk to him? If that was what it was going to take for me to please Katherine, then I wasn't going to please her. And if I did go to see him, I might not talk about Albert. And if I did talk about Albert, who said I had to stick to the one subject and not wander around a little on the back roads of life's great conversation? I was so tired of people telling me what to do, who to talk to, how to bake the morning bread. Nothing Katherine said could make me go talk to Croker, absolutely nothing.

I went to see him. He was working late as usual. Croker agreed to sit and talk because he was a listener, a gatherer of information. He didn't know what to do with the information after he gathered it, but that didn't matter to me.

Croker was hoping he would hear something that could help him with Sara. He could write it all down and file it away in his cardboard boxes. I had a lot to tell him.

I never knew why Albert attached himself to me. He wasn't much of a student, and I was a poor teacher, and the boy hated anything I ever fixed him to eat except for the rabbits. Albert loved rabbits, alive or in the frying pan. A soft look came to his face, and he whispered to them in the evenings when it was his turn to bring them food and water. He loved all kinds of animals. Some nights when I went to bed, I left the boy sitting outside in the dark. He knew he could get in trouble if he didn't go to the dormitory, but if nobody was around at night to check on the boys, Albert didn't see any reason to turn in. If he was still sitting on my porch in the morning, I had to wonder if he'd spent the whole night outside my door. He missed Hobson's dogs. Maybe he missed Hobson.

I didn't miss Hobson. I found a routine at New Hope: classes in the morning with a dozen students and the Canadian reading books, followed by a poor lunch I fixed and ate on my veranda. I could have gone to the dining hall, or Albert would have brought me a plate of rice and beans cooked with coconut milk. The coconuts grew next to the football field, tall trees the boys climbed when it was time to knock the green fruit down. Rice and beans with coconut milk tasted better than rice and beans without coconut milk, but as Albert pointed out, it was still a plate of rice and beans. The boys might find a small piece of chicken on their plate or a slice of cucumber. The next day they would be served up the same rice and beans without the cucumber, and the day after that the cucumber would be back, but the chicken would be gone. I didn't bother with the dining hall. My own cooking was bad, but it was bad in a different way at every meal.

When I went to the city, Price took me out to eat. He was teaching biology and something called Science For Life at his girls school. He used to fill out his progress reports with this line: *As a secondary project, I am fighting hunger in the Cayo district.* It sounded grand. In fact, the only person he knew in the Cayo district was me, and all he wanted to do was find me a decent meal. Price couldn't cook water. If Ellie didn't feel like cooking for us, we had to go out to get fed.

He took me to lunch on a Saturday. He'd discovered a place where the menu was written on the wall in beautiful flowing letters, the words large enough so we could read them from the street: steaks, chops, three kinds of fish, all too good to be true. When we sat down, I didn't know what to order, so he told the waitress to bring me a steak and a beer, and nothing for himself because he said he was just going to watch, that it would give him pleasure to see me eat. She brought word from the kitchen that they were out of steak, and the only beer was Belikin. Price called for the barracuda fish, but they were out of the barracuda fish. He asked for pork chops and a ham sandwich, then fried eggs and chicken salad, and macaroni and cheese, and none of it worked. Finally, Price asked the girl (who was young and should have been in school) what it was exactly her father or her mother or her older brother, whoever was cooking in the back, could fix me to eat.

"Rice and beans," said the girl.

"Okay," Price told her. I saw the wind go out of his sails. "Bring him one plate then. With chicken."

"Yes, man," she said. "Only no chicken."

I was hungry most of the time. I lost weight. Price blamed it on the heat, but it wasn't the heat. And it wasn't that little girl in the restaurant either. It was my own fault. If food didn't come out of a jar, I didn't recognize it. In the lean-to kitchen behind my house, I was hopeless. I thought vegetables might help. I worked with Albert and some other boys in the garden. I found out vegetables take their sweet time coming out of the ground. Albert was strong but he was thin, and with each passing week I looked more like a taller bleached-out version of him. My pants wouldn't stay up. I made new holes in my belt. Albert looked at our shadows one day and made a sound with his teeth that I'd heard old women make in the marketplace when they picked up a piece of disappointing fruit.

"We must eat better," he said. "We need meat, no true?"

I knew what he was after. He had his eye on those rabbits.

We kept them behind the henhouse, and all the boys liked to watch them, but they were a project that belonged to Albert more than to any of the rest of the boys, more than they belonged to me. Hobson had brought the first of them to New Hope from the 4-H center one at a time on his motorcycle, six white rabbits with long ears and pink eyes. They were willing breeders. They bred like rabbits. And each afternoon, Albert asked if we could eat one. I put him off the best I could. I told him we wouldn't know how to cook a rabbit.

"What?" he said. "Of course we could know. No must." It was the way the boys spoke to me, in wild layers of English and Creole. "I am that baker's boy," said Albert. "I could fix it right up for we in that lee kitchen. Nobody no need for know."

I knew better. It wasn't that I didn't want to eat the little bunnies. It was Fairbanks I worried about. I knew how closely he watched over everything that grew on the place. He went out to the garden at night and counted the cucumbers. But Albert had a powerful argument: hunger. My hunger. The boy wore me down. One afternoon when nobody was behind the henhouse but the two of us, he happened to bring along a large pan and a sharp knife. I was weak. I let him take one of the rabbits and do her in.

Albert was as good as his word. He had the doe skinned out and into my kitchen in five minutes. He dusted the meat with salt and pepper and half a cup of flour, and he fried it in coconut oil he borrowed from the big kitchen. It smelled better than anything that had come from my stove in a long time, maybe ever, but when it was done, the pieces brown and crispy and piled high on our plates, I felt so guilty I hardly touched mine. I watched Albert eat most of it. Late that night, he buried the bones and the skin in our garden plot.

Only he didn't bury any of it deep enough. I was in the office the next morning filling out some papers for Fairbanks when one of the boys brought in the pelt. The pigs had dug it up and made a mess of the garden, too. Fairbanks shook the dirt from the smooth white fur. He ran his hand along it and placed it on his desk so he could study it. I pretended I didn't know where the rabbit skin came from. I said there might be wild rabbits living in the bush. Fairbanks stared at the white fur harder, embarrassed for me. He sent for Albert, who was working for Brother Constant in the kitchen. The boy came into the office smelling like the fresh loaf of bread Brother Constant sent along for Fairbanks, and smelling a little like coconut oil.

Brother Constant was the cook and the baker. He baked twice a week, fifty loaves at a time, a simple white bread, no frills, no labels. Albert set his loaf on Fairbanks's desk. A tiny shimmer of heat rose off the loaf. There was a crack in the crust, and I could see the delicate white part inside, the most beautiful thing I had seen in an often beautiful country. I had never appreciated a loaf of bread before, the shape, how it overflows the pan in a hot oven, how no two loaves can ever be exactly the same. The aroma that came from that bread and from the boy who baked it was like the aroma of the home I wished I'd had, more wonderful than any memory. Fairbanks saw how I couldn't take my eyes off the bread. He smiled a thin smile and looked at the place on the wall where his rope usually hung, and he sent the baker's boy back to the kitchen to get a loaf of bread for me.

"Bread is the staff of life, Mr. Tanner," said Fairbanks.

I tried to finish filling out the paperwork for him, but when the second loaf arrived, when Albert set it down in front of me, the smell of bread over-whelmed me. It was more than the smell. Even with my eyes closed and my nose pinched shut, I still could have sensed the presence of that bread on the table. It made my hand shake so that I couldn't hold a pen.

"This is a good bread," said Albert, pushing it a little closer to me. "It makes you want to bite your finger."

I breathed in the rich yeasty heat and had to hold myself back. I wanted to break the loaf in half and swallow great bites of it there in Fairbanks's office. Fairbanks sent the baker's boy to the kitchen once more, and this time Albert returned with a basin of water and a cup of salt.

"Thank you," said Fairbanks. "Albert, sit over there a moment." Fair-banks seldom used the boys' nicknames. He smiled at me and waved at the basin. The rope lay across his desk.

"For my ablutions," said Fairbanks.

He waited for me to leave. I gathered up the papers in front of me, and I held that loaf of bread in my arms as though it were a child.

"I hope you enjoy that bread," said Albert.

I walked back to my house while the loaf was still warm. I had a stick of butter from the Mennonites in the refrigerator and half a jar of jam. I knew there was something else I was supposed to be paying attention to, but I was so hungry all I could focus on was the bread. I ate the first piece without but-ter or jam, and I didn't stop until I had eaten all of it. I didn't let myself think about anything else, not Albert, not Fairbanks, not any of it.

I didn't see the baker's boy for a few days. He was lying low. But after I tasted that first loaf of bread, I went out of my way on the next baking day to walk past the kitchen where he worked, so I could breathe in the odor of fifty loaves placed on every available countertop to cool. No one bothered to bag them up. In three days' time all of that bread would be gone, and even before that,

Brother Constant and the baker's boy would start over on a new batch. Baking day gave Albert an excuse to come back to see me. When the last bread pans came out of the oven, he brought me a loaf so hot he had to juggle it from hand to hand as he ran across the grass to my house. The word *loaf* was a new word to Albert, but he heard me say it so he tried to remember the word when he brought me the bread. He ran up the stairs and stood outside the screen door, dancing from one foot to the other.

"For you, Mr. Tanner," he said. "One lunk of bread."

I hoped it was all right. The boy was proud of himself for looking after me that day, and every baking day to come. I never asked, though, if he'd cleared it with Fairbanks. Once I tasted that bread, I didn't know if I could live without it.

"The way you feel about bread, then, goes back to that place," said Croker. "That school in Belize." It was late in the day and we were sitting in his office and his watery eyes were red and tired-looking. "And the boy is part of it," said Croker.

"Yes," I told him.

"The baker's boy," said Croker.

"Yes."

"It's a sad story," said Croker, fingering his mustache. "You're not always the hero."

"I'm not," I said. "Am I on the witness stand here?"

"Slow down," said Croker. "Nobody's on trial."

"I'm on trial. For taking leave of my pregnant wife Katherine. Ask Stacen. It's desertion." All of Katherine's friends used that word. They didn't understand why Katherine let me call her in the afternoon, why she agreed to meet me every other day in the park by the river. Katherine's midwife thought I should be stood up in front of a firing squad. Stacen's feelings ran in that direction, too. Stacen loved Katherine. For a while she loved me just because I was Katherine's husband, but she quit loving me once I started working in her café.

"Is most of this story true?" asked Croker.

"Yes," I told him. "I think a lot of it's true. And the part that isn't true happened as well."

"I'm sure it did," said Croker. "Why don't you tell me the rest?"

"The rest?"

"You're leaving something out. You always leave something out."

"Says who?" I said.

"Oh, come on," said Croker. "Spill it." That's the sort of thing he used to say. "Spill the beans," he would say.

"All right," I said. "Don't rush me." That's the sort of thing I would say.

On the days Albert brought me my bread, I stopped by the kitchen after the boys ate their dinner. I had to thank the baker, Brother Constant, for remembering me. And I needed the company. Brother Constant was someone to talk to. I'd introduced myself to the man who ran the woodshop, Mr. Montrose, but he was so quiet he might as well have been a mute. Mr. Montrose had the amazing ability to fall asleep while sitting upright in a wooden chair or even, more than once, while he stood in the doorway to Fairbanks's office. Another time, I tried talking to the Salvadoran who cared for the cattle and the pigs. He only spoke a little English, and my high-school Spanish failed me. The boys called him Señor Muerte because he kept a short, very sharp blade in a scabbard at his waist. He used his knife to kill the animals he raised on the farm. The meat went to Belize City, to the prison. Sometimes Señor Muerte sent meat to the women's prison, too. He was seldom allowed to feed the boys at New Hope with what he raised. It could make him angry.

"Today, I kill a sheep," Señor Muerte said to me the afternoon I tried to talk to him. "Next week, a young cow. A man one. *Pues,*" and he glanced around to see who was listening, "I kill Fairbanks."

Señor Muerte worried me. And Mr. Montrose was no conversation starter, though he could have told me what it was like to live in a coma. I had to look for Brother Constant if I wanted someone to talk to. The baker was a short man, black-skinned, with streaks of gray in his hair. He'd worked at New Hope for thirty years, back to the days when the school belonged to the Salvation Army. Sunday afternoons, I used to see him preach by the side of the road with a bass drum and two or three stout women, all of them dressed in white.

One night, I was leaning on the railing outside of the office watching the sun go down across the pasture, listening to the sounds the insects made at sunset in the bush. I'd made plans to drive the Toyota into San Ignacio for groceries. I usually took one of the boys with me for company, and Albert was hanging around near the car trying to catch Brother Constant's eye. On those evenings when Fairbanks left Brother Constant in charge, the baker carried the rope everywhere he went. He made it snap in the dirt or he struck the chair next to where a boy sat. The bigger boys teased him. The quick ones stayed out of his reach but someone smaller, some new boy, would likely end up bruised and crying before the night was over.

Brother Constant brought out two chairs and motioned for me to sit down. He wanted to talk. He was a little stir-crazy, too, that evening. He told me his story, how he once was a boy at New Hope just like these boys, how he joined the Salvation Army, how he grew up and fell in love more than once and fathered eleven children. He spoke with one hand over his mouth. The week before, he'd steered his bicycle off a small bridge and knocked out two teeth. It made him shy. Some of the boys loitered in the office or sat on the railing outside. It was too late to give them more chores.

"The boy named Albert?" I said. "He's your son?"

"That baker's boy?" said Brother Constant. "Oh no, no, not that boy. No, man. Different boys. Boys and girls, too. By more than one woman."

He held up four fingers. He forgot about his missing teeth long enough to give me a weary smile, as though the thought of all that fathering made him want to go lie down. Then he noticed the boys were listening.

"All of that," he said, trying to look displeased with himself, "it was a lot of damn foolishness."

In the half-light, the younger boys played on the ball field. Soon enough, they would have to wash up for bed. Fairbanks had gone to his house in San Ignacio, and I suspected that once the boys were asleep, Brother Constant would ride his bike home, too. He would come back at dawn to slice the bread for breakfast and chase the boys out of the dormitory with Fairbanks's rope.

"When did you start?" I asked him. He looked at me like he didn't understand. "When did you have all those children? Before you took up preaching?"

"Oh, for true," he said. "This was before I got saved. A long time before." He examined one of his fingernails thoughtfully. "And after, too. God is good to a sinner like me."

He got up from his chair on the veranda and stretched. The boys moved away from him, warily.

"Enough for now," he said. "You want to go."

He sent Boomba and Feliciano to ring the bell for the evening roll call. Albert stood up next to the Toyota, trying to look official.

"Boy," said the baker. "Get in the car. Mr. Tanner wants to go."

The bell rang out into the night and the others fell into their lines, envious of the baker's boy for being the one chosen. And most evenings, I would have been glad to take Albert along, glad for the company. He could have showed me where to shop. He could have helped me push the car if it came to it. But that evening, I told Brother Constant I needed the time to myself.

I wasn't ready for Albert's disappointment. The baker's boy ran across the compound and climbed a tall tree, and he refused to come down no matter what the baker or the others said to him.

"Boy, get down, boy!" yelled Brother Constant. He struck as high up the tree as he could reach with the rope. Albert cried out and climbed farther up into the branches. Brother Constant sent for a ladder.

"That boy," he said, "he always have to climb some thing." He swung the rope again, jumping a bit so as to reach higher. He wasn't young but he had a little spring left in his legs.

"Children need a father in their lives," he said. He smiled sweetly at me, not minding the gap in his teeth. "I do what I can do," he said.

It would have been simpler if I had just taken Albert along, but I wanted the company of someone older than Albert, someone who knew the same life I used to know. More than anything, I wanted to be with Ellie, the way we had been together every day in the city. We'd taken long walks after lunch and listened to talks about the Creole dialect, the move to independence. The many causes of diarrhea. It had been difficult sometimes to pay attention as long as she was sitting next to me. One afternoon Price taught us the names of snakes and how long we would suffer if we got bit by one. I remember that part, which snakes lived on land, which ones in the river. I missed Price and Ellie more than they missed me. A month after I moved to New Hope, Price met a woman named Candace who was young and pretty and related in a complicated way to the minister of education. She was taller than Price and so dark we never got a decent photograph of the two of them together. Our cameras were drawn to Candace, to her smile and her bearing. Next to her, Price came out looking like a body that had been trapped too long underwater.

"Black *is* beautiful," Albert murmured when he first saw those photos. "White is, well, somewhat cheesy."

Price didn't mind the bad photos or the fact that he had to look up to Candace. He enjoyed being seen in public with her, though the young men on the street made rude comments when they passed. He tried to organize the four of us—me, Price, Ellie, and Candace—into having dinner at the Chinese restaurant.

"Don't you see?" he'd say. "The beauty of it? Nobody will feel left out. Nobody's Chinese."

But Candace had a child at home, and her own friends. She didn't want to spend all of her time with Americans. It ended up the three of us, Price and Ellie and me. We ran into Ellie's friends from the Teachers College, and those big good-natured women teased her about Price and his appetite. They teased Ellie about me, too, but they were different when it came to me. They liked the fact that I was younger than Ellie. In the restaurant, Ellie's Creole friends looked at her, small and beautiful, always smiling, and they looked at me, all angles and needing a haircut, as if I'd been lost in the bush for a month or a year, and they asked her if she was getting enough to fill her up. Even I knew they weren't talking about food.

When I moved out to New Hope, those women thought I should come back to the city every weekend, but I didn't go every weekend. I didn't want Ellie to get tired of me before she got to know me.

Ellie got letters from her professor. He was lonely, too, pining for her, talking about booking a flight to Belize over Christmas vacation.

"You need some help with this," said Price. He wrote a long Dear John letter for her, filled with ornate language and Creole proverbs which Price himself didn't understand. (*The member of the parliament is the member to remember.*) We had Candace with us that night. She gave Price the proverbs. When he read his letter out loud for us at the restaurant (*Every John Crow cannot remember to leave his member home*) Candace laughed, flashing a gold tooth.

"Member me," she sang in a little girl voice, but she smiled like a woman who had memories. It sounded like a song off the radio. The gold at the edge of her smile drove Price crazy.

"I think you're making these up," said Ellie. She loved the proverbs and sent the letter to her professor more or less the way Price and Candace wrote it, along with a photograph. Candace took the picture, and she told Price and me to put our arms around Ellie so the professor would think Ellie was in love with one of us or both of us. Price hammed it up. I came out looking serious. It was the first time I put my arms around Ellie.

The night the baker's boy climbed up a tree, I was trying to slip away from the school by myself. I wanted to get to a phone so I could call Ellie in Belize City and ask her to come to New Hope, and I wanted to do it without anyone on the school's party line listening in. I wasn't sure how Fairbanks would feel about visitors. He had an occasional lady friend over. I'd seen his friends walking out the lane early in the morning. Mr. Montrose, the zombie woodshop man, had three girlfriends he shuffled in and out the rare nights he stayed at the school, large sad women who only came out of his house to sit on the veranda. Brother Constant was more or less faithful now to the woman who played the drum during his sermons. I decided to invite Ellie, and Price, too, and Candace, though I doubted Candace would come away from the city. She was terrified of snakes. Price said she wouldn't make love to him if it was completely dark in the room.

"She wants to know what that is under the covers," he said. "That big snake thing."

"You flatter yourself," said Ellie. She used to let Price carry on, until every so often he said something that embarrassed her and she wouldn't want to see him for a week or two. Price would go back to Candace then. He took Candace dancing and bought her presents. He bought presents for Candace's little boy. It was all adventure to Price. I went with him to a grocery store a couple of times, a long bike ride from his house to the only place in the city where he could buy the powdered orange drink the little boy craved.

"It keeps him quiet at night," said Price. "Besides, it's good for him. It's what the astronauts drink." He opened a jar of the stuff and we tasted a pinch of it there in the store. I had forgotten how sweet it was. I thought I might get some for Albert.

"I wonder what this would taste like," said Price, "with a little rum."

I drove to San Ignacio alone and wandered the town for an hour to build up my nerve. An ancient Creole named Miss Beard ran an ice cream shop near the center of town. She had a phone in the back. Her place was lit up like a police station, the walls a shiny white, no pictures anywhere, just a calendar from the Mennonite feed store, a Bible verse in German for each month. I knew she couldn't read German. Miss Beard smoked cigarettes at a small table behind the counter, and anytime I went in there, she pretended she wasn't listening to every word I said on the phone.

Ellie didn't have a telephone. I had to call her landlady, who lived next door, and wait while the woman sent a small boy across the yard. Ellie was out of breath when she came to the phone. She had run up the stairs. Maybe she thought it was an overseas call, maybe her professor. She said she would love to come out to the Cayo, but she hadn't been feeling well. It was hard for her to talk freely in the middle of her landlady's living room. Before she hung up, she made me promise to invite her again.

"Please," she said. "I want to see where you live."

Miss Beard squinted out at the street and coughed softly.

"Sure," I said. "I promise."

So I bought a cup of ice cream from Miss Beard and wondered if I was pathetic, and I called Price's flat. Price had a telephone, of course. If it had been wartime, Price would have had stockings and chocolates and brandy. He was happy to come see me. He was fighting with Candace and needed to get out of the city for a couple of days.

"Candace wants to have a baby," he said.

"Whose baby?" I said. "Not your baby."

Miss Beard sat up in her chair. She looked straight at me. Her cigarette drooped at the corner of her mouth.

"Don't worry," I told Price. "We'll talk about it when you get here."

I hung up the phone.

"Have another ice cream," said Miss Beard.

"It's late," I said. "I have to go."

"Don't rush away," said Miss Beard.

I put some dollars on the counter. When I looked out the window, the street was dark. It felt like we were the only two people left in the whole town.

"Maybe Uncle Patel will come in," said Miss Beard. "He sometimes comes in late for a strawberry."

"Another time," I said, and I realized with a little dread in my heart there probably would be other evenings in Miss Beard's ice cream shop.

When Friday came, Price rode out on the late bus. The baker's boy met Price at the bus stop and walked back to New Hope with him, and then the boy posted himself on my steps for the rest of the evening. Albert made Price nervous, but everything made Price nervous. I didn't think we had to worry about Albert. I liked having him around. We spent the evening drinking rum and the orange powder. I gave Albert some orange drink without the rum, but he didn't care for it. In the morning, I woke up hot and thirsty and not at all well. Albert wasn't on the steps. My head hurt, and I couldn't get up or stay in bed either without feeling sick to my stomach. It was a familiar feeling. I kept thinking I'd turn around and see the ghost of Hobson out on the veranda. Price didn't know what a hangover felt like. He watched me curiously for the first hour we were up, then went out for a long run and came back much cheered up, a string bag over one shoulder, six bottles of beer in it. I had no idea where he might have bought the beer. I didn't ask. I was lying in the hammock. If I placed all of my pillows in just the right position in the hammock, it was possible not to feel completely lousy.

"I figured out what I'm going to do," said Price. "I'm going to tell her I already have children." He was rummaging around in the kitchen for an early lunch. "I'm going to tell her," he said, "they're back in the States."

"Who?"

"My children," he said. "I'm going to tell Candace about them. They're problem children." He opened one of the bottles of beer and put the others in the refrigerator. "There's something wrong with them. Something genetic. You think she'll believe me?"

When he handed me a beer, I couldn't drink it but I held it against my head. The cool bottle felt comforting.

"I think she probably will," I told Price.

I was watching Albert and three other boys cut the grass in front of the schoolyard with their machetes. They looked thirsty, and I thought I should take them some water. I was afraid if I stood up, the floor would tilt.

"Will what?" said Price.

"Believe you," I said.

"Who will?"

"Candace."

"What are we talking about?" said Price.

I handed him the beer I had been holding against my forehead, and he exchanged it for one from the refrigerator.

"We're talking about turning over a new leaf," I told him. "We're talking about drinking less and not smoking when we're drinking, and generally becoming sober upstanding individuals. We could be good."

"Oh that," said Price. He opened the not-so-cold beer and drank half of it down. The bottles were small.

"I was afraid you were being serious for a moment," he said.

I told all of this to Croker. We talked until I had to go to work. I'd lost track of the time. It's the sort of thing that happened to me, now that I worked while other people slept.

"I need to go to bed," said Croker. I knew he kept a little cot in the next room, and a hot plate. It suddenly occurred to me that he might live back there. He made his voice sound wretched, as if he was dying.

"That's not all of it," I said. "That's not the whole story."

"It's three o'clock in the morning," said Croker.

"Is it morning," I said, "or is it night?"

"Don't ask me that," said Croker. "I just want to be a lawyer now. I want to sue people and get them out of jail. Don't ask me to do more than that."

He went and lay down on his cot. I could see him through the doorway. He still had his shoes on.

"Croker," I said. Then I said it louder. "*Croker.*"

But he didn't answer. So I rode my bike to work and baked the morning bread.

Next day, I met Katherine in the park. I waited for her by the giant propeller that came off some old riverboat, on the bench where we always met. I told Katherine everything I'd said to Croker. It took me an hour and a half. I was getting faster. Sometimes I thought she was going to hug me, and sometimes I thought she was going to hit me. I just kept talking.

"It's a start," said Katherine. "I have to go now."

All of a sudden nobody had time for me.

"I've got to get home," said Katherine. "The midwife is coming over."

There was no point in arguing with her. That midwife had a place in Katherine's life, one I couldn't challenge. I'd tried to get Katherine to go to a doctor, a man who would wear one of those mirrors on his forehead and prescribe medicine in handwriting that only a trained pharmacist could read.

"The midwife again," I said.

"Don't push your luck," she said. "Don't tell me what I should do. One trip to the sperm bank doesn't give you the right to make suggestions."

She was determined to use a midwife and she wanted to deliver the baby in the house. I'd never met a midwife before Katherine's. This one was young, from Boston, and she spoke very precisely and sometimes wore a leather coat with the words *Bitch Mama* stitched on the back. She said she could only wear it around people she was comfortable with. Katherine said the midwife, the Bitch Mama, was a warm and loving person. She said the jacket was a joke.

"You better call me soon," said Katherine. "Don't wait too long or I might not answer."

"I'll miss you tonight," I said. "I'll miss you when I take my nap and I'll miss you in a few hours when I wake up and go to work."

"You know where I live," said Katherine.

"I could visit," I told her.

"No," she said. "There will be no visiting. If you come back, you come to stay."

We were walking down the path that runs next to the river. There's an iron railing there to keep little kids from falling in, and up ahead was a little place where people stopped and looked out over the water. A young black man watched the barges moving slowly up the river, a man with grass in his hair standing absolutely still, unnaturally still. I took hold of Katherine's arm to make her stop.

"What is it?" said Katherine. "You know that guy?"

"I don't know," I said.

The young man turned slowly to face us. Two little children ran up the path, their hands full of freshly cut grass. They threw what they held in their hands at him, their father I suppose, adding to the grass clippings they'd already thrown in his hair. He let out a shout but he wasn't angry, and he chased them back the way they came. Katherine laughed. I realized I'd been holding my breath. I would have sat down if there had been a bench to sit on. Katherine looked at me in that funny way pregnant women look at people.

"Stacen says I don't have much time left. She says I need to make up my mind about becoming a father."

"Stacen's pretty brilliant," said Katherine.

"I was afraid of that," I said. But I didn't get to say more because she got into her car and left. She said good-bye first. Sometimes she doesn't say good-bye. I knew it wouldn't do any good to call after her. I've tried that before. With Katherine, when your time's up, your time's up.

7

ome days passed. Some more days passed. I didn't keep track of the days like I used to before I changed my station in life. When I got to work mornings, there were great stacks of canned goods at the back door and more bags of doubtful yeast waiting to be stowed away in the freezer. The usual noises drifted down from the apartment upstairs, comforting noises as long as everyone up there stayed between the lines. Like my old friend Price would have said, every place had a thing and there was a thing in every place. Even the smells were the usual smells—bread and coffee mixed up with the odors from the pet store next door.

I would have liked to go into the pet store more often, but those guys next door were some more guys Stacen didn't get along with. She would have taken it as disloyalty if I went over and made friends. The only time she spoke to anyone next door was when their animals made a break for it and she found them first thing in the morning sliding across her dining room floor. I wasn't crazy about reptiles myself. An older guy and a younger guy ran the pet store together—I figured they were related somehow. The younger guy was in charge of the birds, and he looked a little like one of those birds when it would ruffle all its feathers so it could do that bird thing with its beak. The older guy looked more like a salamander, all red and splotchy in the face. The red face was partly my doing. He was more or less permanently angry with me since the night I let one of his snakes go out the back door of the café. I didn't try to stop it. It was a fat snake the size of a man's arm and making good time when it came out from under the stove and headed for daylight. I dropped the big frying pan on it. The frying pan hardly made a dent in that snake. My mistake was, as soon as it was daylight and the man opened up his store, I went over and told him about it.

Stacen went with me but she wouldn't go all the way into the pet store. She stood behind me at the alley door and yelled over my shoulder at the man with the red face. I shouldn't have mentioned the frying pan. He said it wasn't a poisonous snake. After he calmed down.

"Keep an eye out," he said. He seemed to think I should have caught it for him. "Maybe it will show up again," he said, hopeful.

"Best place it could show up," said Stacen, "is in the big wok over at Liu's."

That isn't all Stacen said. She wanted to call an exterminator. She told her pet store neighbor she'd find someone to fog the whole block with some kind of snake-killing all-powerful poison if another one of his clientele presented its snaky head in her kitchen. I thought the guy was going to have a stroke over that. He was going to call the police, start a lawsuit, start a lot of non-sense. I thought I might have to call Croker and get us some help. But these things blow over. They haven't had any escapes since then.

Another evening not long after that, during all this passing-by of evenings and days, a bunch of little kids came to the door of my apartment in costumes, so I knew it had to be Halloween. I was pretty sure. I gave each of them a dinner roll for a treat. They studied what I gave them suspiciously. When they left, they threw their rolls into the next yard for the Rottweiler. I didn't let it bother me. I carried on. I worked my shift, I talked to Katherine, I met her for tea, I bought her cheeseburgers. Her belly grew. I missed her, especially in the small hours of the morning, but I was working those hours and that's how I coped. I tried not to think. I watched my back.

And then out of the blue, Stacen told me she was going to shut down for two days because it was Thanksgiving. I knew Katherine would go have Thanksgiving with relatives. She has a boatload of cousins. I didn't care about Thanksgiving, having no cousins. My mother moved out to Kansas years ago to be with one of my brothers, the one who can read. I hadn't spent a holiday with family in a long time. I stayed home. I baked a couple of loaves of seed bread. It was something to do.

One cold morning in December, I rode the blue bicycle through the dark to the café. This morning I'm telling you about should have been a good morning. First, there were no snakes under the stove, and second, no ghosts at the window, and third, I pulled the perfect raisin bread out of the oven. Not a sweet raisin bread. Anybody can dump a box of sugar into a bowl. These were small brown almond-shaped loaves. Each slice tasted like autumn. We'd seen the last of autumn. The only way you could get that autumn feeling again was if you drove south, maybe to Florida, or ate fresh raisin bread, not too sweet. It was the middle of the morning and I was in the back washing dishes, glancing at my loaves every now and then to gloat over them, feeling comfortably tired out. That's when she walked in, the girl who, in a better world, would have been my classmate. Sara.

Sara stood a long time and very still at the counter. She studied the forty varieties of tea and coffee we have posted on the wall, most of which I think actually exist somewhere in the café. If we get busy and I can't find a particular tea, I just serve the customer peppermint. It's the rice-and-beans of the tea world. Stacen doesn't want me out in the dining room anyway. We have to be unusually slow before I go out there and help people with their orders. To me, most of our tea tastes like peppermint. Some of the coffee does. Sara wasn't after a special cup of tea. She ordered the last thing she read on the big chalkboard behind the counter. The way she looked around the room and tried to see farther back into the kitchen, I knew what she was up to: she was looking for me. I thought at first she must be wearing her hair up in a new way. Then Stacen put the girl's tea in front of her, and Sara took the teacup in her strong hands and went to sit at a table where she could watch the door to the kitchen, and I saw how that young girl had done the unthinkable. She had cut off her beautiful hair.

Twice, I had to pass in front of the kitchen door and I did it in a way that would make people believe I was the busiest man in town, no time to chat with old friends, that sort of thing. Sara was patient. She poured another cup of tea from the little pot Stacen had given her. She asked Stacen if she could use the restroom, which meant coming through the kitchen, and she walked through the door and stood for a moment at the prep table next to me. I was peeling garlic for the soup Stacen wanted to make the next day. I had a mound of peeled garlic cloves the size of Pennsylvania, but I pretended like I needed more. She waited until I stopped pretending.

"Sara," I said, a little surprise in my voice, as though I'd only that moment realized she was in the café.

"Mr. Johnson."

"Please," I said, "call me Tanner." I'd said that to her already more than once in Croker's office. This time we were in Stacen's kitchen and I was wearing an old T-shirt and a dirty apron. This time she listened to me.

"Okay," she said. "Tanner." And she looked at me in a way I've only been looked at a handful of times in my life. It was a look like when you've lost the most precious thing you ever owned, and you want somebody to say he's found it.

"I don't know what I'm going to do," said Sara. "I feel like Sara's disappeared."

She spooked me. I didn't like the way she called herself Sara. It was quiet out front. It gets that way between nine and ten most mornings. I was wishing we had a bigger crowd so I could act like I was too busy to talk to her, but there wasn't any crowd. Sara had pinned me to the wall with that look. I felt like one of those grease-spotted little notes Stacen is forever sticking up. *Tanner, wash the soup pot. . . . Tanner, peel these carrots. . . . Tanner, get your shit together. . . .* I sent Sara back out to her teacup while I straightened up the prep table. I didn't dawdle, but I didn't hurry. I took off my apron and entertained a last thought that I could duck out the door to the alley. It was the simple way Sara stepped around the counter and stood next to me that kept me from leaving, the tone in her voice that said, *I may be loony but I'm a grown-up, why aren't you?* I poured myself some coffee and carried it to her table.

"You've changed your appearance," I told her. I couldn't bring myself to say the word *hair*. She looked out the front window and I looked out, too. The sidewalk was a totally different sidewalk from the day before. It was the first time I'd noticed the Christmas decorations were up.

"Everything is changed," said Sara. "More than what shows."

The way she said it, she was resigned to it. She wasn't going to miss that hair. It was the same way my mother spoke when my father died and she took out his suit one last time, and she said, *There, I won't have to mess with that again.*

"Sara is losing it," she said. "I don't know who Sara is anymore. I can't find her."

"Hey," I said. "Hold on. Sara's right here." I squeezed her arm, as much to make me think she was real as to make her think so. I didn't know what she would say next. People like that can surprise you. They sometimes just start in quoting scripture, or singing. Or barking like a dog. Stacen passed our table with a bus tub full of dirty dishes. She was on her way back to the kitchen sink.

"I'm on my break," I said to Stacen. "Give me ten minutes." I didn't look up. I didn't give her the chance to scowl at me.

"All right, Tanner," said Stacen, sweet and reasonable. It made me nervous when she acted that way. I held my breath until she was back in the kitchen.

"You don't have to figure these things out alone," I said to Sara. "You can talk to your friends."

"I don't have a lot of friends," she said.

"No?" I thought hard about that one. "Well, there's Croker."

"Uncle Croker?" said Sara. She said his name slowly, like it wasn't part of her everyday vocabulary.

"He has all those degrees and certificates. I thought maybe he could help."

"I was hoping . . . you . . . would know something," she said. "You were there."

She had ordered an herbal tea, and she was one of those customers who likes to play with the tea ball. The smell of oranges and cinnamon got into the air. I thought she could be hungry, so I went back and cut her a piece of bread. She thanked me when I gave it to her. I didn't know what to say, what questions to ask. When she started crying, she kept it up for a while but quietly, wiping her eyes with the sleeve of her jacket. I got her a paper napkin, the large soft kind. I brought some more hot water for her tea.

"I don't want to go to court again," she said. "I don't want to see that woman. A month ago, they had it all set up. I was going to live with my grandmother, go to these meetings, see a counselor. See two counselors, the whole thing. Then they call me back to court. I'm having a lot of trouble. It's like the last time."

I didn't ask about the last time. She opened her tea ball and dumped the wet tea leaves into her napkin, as if she wanted to read them.

"Someone's following me." She spoke softly, a whisper.

"Who?" I said. "What does he look like?"

"I was at a meeting, and he followed me. Do you go to meetings?"

"I don't know about meetings," I said. "What kind of meetings? Never mind that. Who's following you?"

"He was gone when they got there." She wasn't pretending to drink that cup of tea anymore. She was just telling me the story. It was why she came.

"I called the police," she said.

I nodded to get her to go on. "You told the police about him?"

"I told everyone about him," she said.

I felt a little sick inside. I didn't know if we were supposed to tell anyone. Some things you keep to yourself. Sara picked at the crust of bread on her plate until I offered to get her another piece, but she wasn't hungry anymore. She let me bring her a new tea ball. I didn't ask what kind of tea this time. I thought she would like peppermint.

"Are you taking care of yourself?"

"I am," she said. "I'm doing everything they want me to. Mostly, if I stay away from people, I'm all right. I shouldn't be here this morning."

"I'm not people," I said.

"Probably not."

"What does he look like?" I said. "This black kid? How old is he exactly?"

"No," she said. She looked a little puzzled. "He's not a kid. He's not black. He's an old man and he has a paper bag, and I don't know what's in that bag, but it's for me. He could be Russian or something. He could be a Greek. He could be Irish. Whatever he has in that bag is for me."

"Wait a minute," I said. "He's not a kid? About this tall?" I raised my hand to the height of my shoulder. I looked at my hand and raised it a few inches higher.

"Of course I'm sure," she said. "What do you know about it?"

Her hands lay on the table. They looked so much like Ellie's hands, large and smooth and perfect hands that would give you strength if you held onto them, I reached over and picked one of them up and held it in my own hand. She let me, but it was a mistake and we both knew it. She was all out of strength.

Stacen caught my eye. She glared at me from the doorway to the kitchen as if I was a creep, some dirty old man. I'm not that old. I turned my chair so I wouldn't have to look at her.

"Listen," I said. "You don't have to worry. It was probably just a coincidence. A guy with a paper bag. Could have been anyone."

Sara wanted to believe me. I felt like a good person then. I'd found the right thing to say.

"I know one thing," she said. "I'm not going back to school."

"That's all right," I said. "What are you going to do? How will you take care of yourself?"

"I don't know," said Sara. "I thought, maybe, I could come to work here. I could work for you."

"For me?"

"I'm sorry," said Sara. "I've hardly asked about you. How's business? How long have you owned this place?"

"Oh my lord," said Stacen. Only it was like she was muttering to the wall, not to either of us. She must have overheard what Sara said. Stacen had carried the tub of dirty dishes to the back and she was dropping them into the sink one at a time. After she heard Sara say that, it was more like Stacen was throwing them into the sink from halfway across the room.

"Does he own this place? Oh my lord . . ." I could hear her talking to herself back there.

She chucked a couple of coffee mugs in with the rest. They made a sound like the bowling alley.

"Is he worth the grief?" she was saying, her voice barely more than a whisper. "Oh my lord . . ." Some of the dishes were breaking. She could have put a little more water in the sink.

"Is he an asshole?" she said. She threw a few bread pans into the sink, too. Just the small pans. "Oh my lord, yes," she said. "Yes indeedy . . ."

"I'm going to have to get back to work pretty soon," I told Sara.

"Is that your wife in the kitchen?"

"My God," said Stacen, her voice gone hoarse and raspy. I pretended I didn't hear her. Then I pretended she was addressing the sink or the refrigerator, or her fate, not me. Not Sara.

"It's too much," said Stacen.

"No," I said, trying to sound calm. "My wife works for the public school. She's a librarian."

"That's right," said Sara. "I knew that. She's doing okay? You're doing okay?" She let her eyes take in the rest of the café. "You're both doing okay?"

"She's great," I said. "We're great, Katherine and me. Really. Honest. Everything's so great." I clapped my hands together and tried to look upbeat.

"Oh, Mr. Johnson," said the girl. She sat up straight and took in the whole room, as if she was seeing the café for the first time. "I'm sorry," she said. "I didn't know. I didn't realize." Her eyes filled with tears.

"Really," I said, "you've got to call me Tanner."

"Tanner schmanner," said Stacen, throwing one of her cookbooks on top of the refrigerator. She wasn't exactly shouting but she wasn't using her inside voice either.

"Call me Tanner," she said. "Call me pain. Call me sorrow. Call me a dumb shit."

"What's wrong with that woman?" said Sara.

"It doesn't matter."

"I didn't know about you and your wife," said Sara. "I just didn't know."

"It's okay," I said. "Really I'm fine. There are lots of people worse off than I am. I'm just fine."

"Fine," said Stacen. I could hear her teeth grinding. "He's just fine. Until we kill him. And we're going to kill him."

But I meant what I said. Things were okay with me. I wasn't born yesterday. I hadn't just fallen off the turnip truck. I'd seen the way people's lives get screwed up.

It was nothing, what had happened to me.

I told Katherine about it when I called her that afternoon. I tried to get her to meet me downtown for a cup of coffee, but she didn't drink coffee now that she was pregnant. I told her she could drink decaf, and she said, what's the point? I told her she could watch me drink the coffee. She didn't want to do that either.

"Is there some connection?" she said.

"Between what? And the answer is yes, of course. Everything's connected. But what?"

"I'm talking about your friend," said Katherine. "Sara. And the baker's boy. Is there something I'm missing here?"

"No," I said. "There's no connection. None at all."

"You're a lousy liar, Tanner," said Katherine. "Tell me the rest. Let me be the judge."

Through my window, I could see the sky had gone gray, and I was tired, and I guess I must have been cold. I started shivering while I sat on my bed with the phone in my hand. I had to hug my elbows to my sides to make the shivering stop.

"*Had we but world enough and time,*" said Katherine.

"What's that?" I said. "That's familiar. Is that a song?"

"A poem," said Katherine. "It's a long-ass poem that basically says, get on with it."

I stalled. There wasn't going to be any point in stalling.

"*And at my back I always hear,*" said Katherine, "*time's winged chariot draw-ing near.*"

"I don't like that poem," I said. "It feels like pressure to me. It feels like harassment. Can a poem be harassment?"

"Tell me about the baker's boy," said Katherine. "Tell me about Albert or I'm going to hang up."

I didn't want her to hang up. So I told her.

I told her I didn't know what some of the Creole words meant, the ones Albert shouted down at me that night from his tree, and I didn't want to know. When the other boys brought the ladder out for Brother Constant, Albert gave up. He dropped to the ground where he stood very still and watched me drive off in the car. I knew he wouldn't cry out when he was punished. Brother Constant knew when to stop. Brother Constant was in the Salvation Army. I worried about it, though. I was afraid I would lose Albert. He could always ask to spend his mornings in the woodshop instead of com-ing to class, or he could go to the fields alongside the older boys.

I was wrong to worry. Monday morning, he was back in the school-room, in the last row where he took up his struggle with the times tables. In the afternoon, like always, he went to the kitchen. On baking days, he was the most reliable boy Brother Constant ever had. He was no trouble in the classroom either, even if he wasn't a fast learner. He couldn't read many words, but he did his best to imagine the scenes described in those books from Canada, the world of snow and bears and falling leaves. New Hope had nothing to do with snow or bears. It could be confusing for him and me both. I read myself to sleep every night from a bunch of cheap novels Hobson had left behind, the kind with a half-naked woman on the cover, where an occasional vampire shows up. I dreamed of Ellie. And every Wednesday and every Saturday Albert brought me a fresh loaf of bread.

Hobson sent me a carburetor kit from Chicago, a plastic bag full of little washers and rubber gaskets, and he wrote to tell me about a thin angry mechanic on the other side of the river in Spanish Lookout, where the Mennonites lived. *He can make water flow from a rock,* Hobson said in his letter. *He might be able to fix your piece of shit carburetor.*

So when I'd waited long enough, I asked Albert if he wanted to take a ride in the car. I told him I had to go see the Mennonites, although I knew it didn't much matter where we went. I let him choose a friend to come along. He picked the one they called Mickey Mouse, a skinny kid with big eyes and big ears. Albert got in the car next to me and Mouse sat next to the door where he could hang an arm out the window. As I drove through the gate and onto the main road, they tried to act cool, like boys with money in their pockets. A British jet, a Harrier, passed low over the road, and without even thinking about it I slowed down. Two years before, the Guatemalan generals had moved their troops to the border, and so the Harriers had come. They were still there, no plans to go home. The boys at New Hope loved to see a jet rise up above the school: it was magic, it was obeah. It made me wonder how often those pilots trained their sights on the classroom. I wondered if they ever pretended to shoot the Toyota, like some old horse. Albert must have read my mind because he looked at me and laughed. He wasn't worried about any pilot. He didn't care if he was dressed right or if a big cloud of black smoke came out of the tailpipe. Mouse didn't care either. It was enough for them to be in the car, to go somewhere. I laughed, too. I was glad Albert wasn't still angry at me. Sometimes you can't do anything, so you don't do anything but laugh.

To get to the Mennonite settlement, we crossed the river on the ferry, a creaky wooden raft attached to a droopy cable. I'd put off making the trip for weeks because of the ferry. You couldn't see the bottom of the river from that raft, even close up to the bank. You couldn't see the snakes. Some drivers got out of their cars to help the deaf man move the whole contraption from one side of the river to the other. He did it with a hand crank, like something you would see on an old ice cream maker. When I rode the ferry, I played it safe in the car until we got to the other side. Sometimes I stood near the edge in case the whole thing went down and I had to swim for it.

Those Mennonite farmers raised corn and wheat and dairy cattle, everything they needed. They were the plainest people I ever saw, especially the women in the shops. They spoke German to each other and English to me. If I brought the boys into the shops, the women didn't speak at all. They never spoke Creole, though they'd been in the country for twenty years. At the edge of the settlement, we found the garage we were looking for, and we drove into the yard, Albert, Mouse, and me. The boys made no move to get out of the car. Albert did his best to read some words hand-painted on a wooden sign: *Body Shop, Welding, Radiators.*

I got out so I could talk to the man who stepped out of his shop into the yard. I was pretty sure it was the mechanic Hobson meant me to talk to, the same one or his brother. He thought I was a nuisance until I said Hobson's name. From the front seat, the boys watched the mechanic glare at them through the windshield. He raised the hood and removed the air filter. It didn't take long before he pulled his head out from under the hood, as if he'd received a piece of bad news under there. I thought of Moses for a moment, when he came down from Mt. Sinai and saw himself surrounded by fools. The man thrust the bag of new parts, greasy now, into my hands. He growled at me in all the languages he knew.

"Wrong kit," he said. "No charge."

I had to prime the carburetor again to get the Toyota back on the road. The old Mennonite watched me the whole time.

I didn't feel good until we got off the ferry again on the other side of the river, and I wanted to feel good. The boys liked to drive fast and the road was empty. I cranked it up. The engine was loud. The windows were all down and the wind blasted through the car. I resented that mechanic.

"All those Mennonites can go to hell," I said under my breath each time I shifted gears. Only I wasn't saying it as softly as I thought. I realized that when I saw Albert grinning at me.

"All those Mennonites can go to hell," said Albert. I had to laugh.

Mouse put his head out the window. "All those Mennonites can go to hell," he yelled, as loud as he could.

"All Toyotas can go to hell," I said, shifting down to take a slight curve.

"All Toyotas can go to hell," said Albert.

"All Toyotas can go to hell," shouted Mouse.

"All Fairbankses can go to hell," said Albert.

"All Fairbankses can go to hell," shouted Mouse.

"All right," I said. "Take it easy." We would soon be in sight of the school. I could picture the long drive that led up to the cluster of buildings, the tall trees. It was like the road to a fancy estate. I told myself I would slow down when I reached the first of those trees. I had to yell at Mouse again. I wanted him to pull his head into the car. He grinned at me and shifted around, and his elbow hit the door handle. He opened the door an inch, and it was the wind, or the way he leaned on the door handle, or a thing as simple as my bad luck. Something made the rust that held everything together finally give way. I heard the moan of tired metal, and then the odd sound the door made as it broke away from its hinges and tumbled out onto the road.

Albert grabbed hold of Mouse, and I grabbed the arm nearest to me, Albert's arm, and somehow neither of them fell through the hole where the door should have been. I kept us out of the ditch, too, the best driving I'd ever done up until then, or after. I stopped the car and closed my eyes against what might have happened. When I opened them, I saw where the door had done its best to catch up to the car, sliding along the dirt road after us.

"A sled," whispered Albert. He looked over at Mouse. "It's a sled. It's winter fun," he said. The boys got out and ran after the door. Mouse couldn't believe the glass in the window wasn't broken. The mirror had come off, and he ran back down the road to retrieve it. The mirror wasn't broken either. Mouse was disappointed.

I looked down the road in the direction we had come. I knew I was going to have to get that door fixed. I thought about how the scene would play out, that mechanic again and recrossing the river on the ferry. In a car where I couldn't even shut the door.

"Don't go back there," said Albert.

"Why?" I said, although it took me a minute to get the word out. He wouldn't look me in the eye. I wondered if one of them could possibly have stolen something after all. I hadn't let them set foot out of the car.

"They don't like we," said Albert, finally. "They are not a part of we. Besides, we have one door on this Toyota. We don't need two." He grinned up at me, and I could have argued with him, but where to start? What part of what he said wasn't true?

We crept the rest of the way back to New Hope, turning down the long lane and slinking along to the office. Mouse kept jumping out of the car and running alongside, sprinting ahead and waiting for us with his hand out as if he were hailing the bus, a big goofy grin on his face. I made him get back in the car, and I drove a little faster to keep him there. The dust swirled into the car, settling on our skin.

"Look," said Albert. He held his arm up next to mine. I didn't see it at first and then I did. With all the dust, we were more or less the same shade of brown.

I parked in front of Fairbanks's office and the boys drew a crowd with their story. They said they had received a curse from the Mennonites, then they were sucked out of the car by a great wind, and when an enormous jet flew over and the door exploded, they were forced to roll off the road into the bush to escape being run over by me as I backed up, a crazy man, to retrieve the parts of the car that had followed them down the road like angry demons.

"Well, motherass," said Feliciano, his voice soft with wonder.

Fairbanks came out onto the veranda of his office to see what the noise was all about. When he saw the car door—Mouse had leaned it up against a fender of the Toyota—he shook his head, a distant look in his eyes. Clearly, everything Fairbanks suspected about me was true. He disappeared inside his office, but a moment later he came down the stairs to hand me a note. He told me to carry the note back to the Mennonites.

"I know this man who does the welding," he said. "He will give you a fair price." Fairbanks told five additional boys to go along with me to see that I got there safely.

"Perhaps you could do me one favor while you're out," said Fairbanks, as if it had only at that moment occurred to him. He nodded to another boy who was begging to go along. The boy ran around the car and pushed his way in. I distrusted Fairbanks in small things as much as in large things, but I wasn't in a position to say no.

"There's a new boy named Gillett who has neglected to come stay with us," said Fairbanks. He looked through a stack of papers on his clipboard until he came to the information he wanted. "Perhaps you could stop by his house and pick him up on the way back. His people will expect you."

While he talked, two more boys crowded into the car. There were eight of them now. Albert and Mouse were holding on tightly to their place in the front seat. One of the older boys pushed in beside Mouse. He made nine. I couldn't find any excuse to ask even one or two of them to stay with Fairbanks. I couldn't find my voice. I still felt guilty about the earlier time when I'd left Albert behind. And I'd never convinced any of them to think of their own safety. I imagined how hot it was getting inside the car, even with the door off. As I came down the steps and got in behind the wheel, the boys in the front seat grew quiet.

Mouse said the name: "Gillett." Someone in the back murmured the word again. "Gillett." I had to wonder how they knew where we were going before I did.

I didn't want to go back across the river. There was a letter from Ellie in my pocket. I had carried it around with me for three days, reading and rereading what she wrote. She was free for the weekend and she was coming to see me. The letter was as good as a promise. She thought she'd be able to talk Price into coming along. The bus from Belize City stopped at the New Hope road twice every afternoon, and I wanted to be there to meet them when Ellie and Price got off. I didn't want to be roaring down the road with a load of juvenile delinquents in the car. But the juvenile delinquents were already in the car, and Fairbanks was looking at me, waiting. I didn't have a choice. I turned the key and stepped on the gas, hoping for once I'd flood the hell out of that carburetor and not have to drive anywhere. The car started right up like it was in some Toyota showroom. It was nearly three o'clock, time for the early bus to arrive, so I drove out to the mouth of the road and idled there for ten minutes, waiting. The car looked like a nest filled with young birds, each of them poking his head out, each of them threatening to fly. When the bus appeared, they quieted down for a moment. Mouse was the one who told the others to sit still.

"Unu could jinx a bus," he said.

The bus grew large in my rearview mirror, then passed us in a hot eddy of dust. The driver didn't slow down. I thought I saw him laugh as he went by, and Mouse glared at the others as if they must have jinxed it for true, but there was no point in getting upset. I made the big boy move over so Mouse could perch by the open door again—he knew the drill by now—and I drove off in the same direction as before, but slower. The broken door rode in the back where two boys held it between them like some kind of gift. I tried to avoid the potholes that could send one of them or half a dozen of them flying out into the dirt.

When we drove back onto the ferry, the ferryman looked as though his inability to speak was a great burden to him, or maybe it was a great relief. He stared in amazement as all the boys climbed out of the car, one after another. He was counting them in his head, but he was counting them so loud in his head I could hear the numbers. The boys argued over who would turn the crank, and Simple fell into the river and had to be pulled out. He wasn't any the worse for it. As hot as the afternoon had turned, his thin shorts would be dry by the time we got back to school.

We found the Mennonite Fairbanks knew, a thickset man with scars up and down his arms from all the years of welding. He agreed to repair the door only if everyone but me stayed in the car.

"I know boys like these," he said. "These boys can steal." He snapped his fingers for emphasis.

I heard grumbling, but it was only because of the heat in the car. The boys weren't going to argue with him. They were all thieves. Two boys were crowded into the very back, Avila, a small Carib with red hair, and Benn. They passed the car door out over the backseat, and the younger one made a horrible smell fill the car. Benn slapped the Carib boy, and Albert warned Benn if he hit anyone again he would get hurt. It surprised me. Benn was bigger than Albert. He was tall and as strong as any of the men who worked at New Hope, but in the heat of the afternoon, none of that mattered to Albert. He had turned fearless. I made him sit next to me and told him to take it easy or I'd have to let Fairbanks know about it.

The work didn't take long. The car smelled worse after the door was replaced, shutting in the odor of welding with the odor of arms and legs and bodies. We left the shop to cross the ferry one more time, and this time all the boys fell in the river one after another. Several of them held onto the raft as it made its way across the water. When they piled into the car again, wet and steamy, and we turned back toward New Hope, I was already thinking about getting away from everyone so I could go for a walk where that same river ran along the edge of the farm, where it would be a little cooler as the sun went down. But not too near the river. Not *in* the damn river, for God's sake. I didn't let myself think about Ellie or Price or the late bus from the city because I knew in my heart my friends weren't going to be on any bus that afternoon. I was thinking instead about the book I could lose myself in, and a cold drink, when the boys began to stir.

"Gillett," they murmured, softly at first, then louder and all together, like kids will yell for ice cream. "Gillett. Gillett."

Mouse crowded up next to Albert. He made as though he would grab the steering wheel if I didn't stop. I let the car idle in the middle of the road until he put his hands in his lap again. They all grew quiet in a trembling sort of way. It was that delirious quiet I'd felt twice before at New Hope, once when a convincing preacher came and woke everyone up with his detailed description of hell, even woke Mr. Montrose up, and another time when a storm made the river rise above its banks and we woke in the morning to find two feet of water in the lower pasture and more on its way. I made the car die and when it wouldn't restart, I had to let all the boys out to push so we could get moving again.

I would have preferred to forget about whoever this Gillett character was. I could have explained my forgetting to Fairbanks, but I couldn't explain it to the boys in the car who were so eager to collect the new kid. I drove past the road that would have returned us to the school, and then I continued another five miles down the Western Highway. I kept going partly because I said I would, enough reason to do a thing in those days whether it was for good or not. I tried to drive with one hand and look at the directions Fairbanks had written down for me. The paper was sweaty and the ink had smeared.

"You won't need that," said Albert. His mood surprised me. Unlike the others, who were excited, he'd grown serious. We drove another ten minutes, and Albert showed me where to pull off the road. I didn't ask him how he knew where Gillett lived.

The house Albert pointed out to me sat on stilts like all the others. It had not been painted recently, if ever, and it seemed familiar to me. All the little wooden houses in Belize looked alike. Farther off the road, you could find roofs made of thatch, but this house had a gray tin roof like my own house. The front door stood open, and an old woman sat in a chair at the top of the stairs, her head wrapped in a bandana. Her black face shone, unsmiling. I recognized her, the woman I'd sat next to on the bus months before whose name I remembered, and I nodded to her and said it, Miss Penny. She wouldn't look at me. I told the boys to stay near the car. I would have made them stay inside it, but most of them were out already, walking around and grinning at each other. I didn't want them up near the house.

"Come ya," said the woman at the top of the stairs. She wasn't speaking to any of us. She was speaking to someone inside, the boy named Gillett I supposed. Perhaps all the people in the house were named Gillett. I guessed Miss Penny was the boy's grandmother, though she may have been older than that. This boy had to be the one she had tried to say good-bye to on that earlier day, when I rode the bus with Hobson. The boy named Junie.

He didn't come out when she called, and when she spoke to him again, this time less forcefully, the New Hope boys sensed she lacked the necessary resolve. They started up the stairs toward her front door. I ordered them back, realizing too late the position I was in. I had become an officer of the court, there to haul one of her children, her Junie, off to detention. It wasn't what I wanted to do. I saw no way out of the situation except to push straight ahead like the ferry and make it to the other side.

"He needs to come out now," I said to the woman.

I hoped I could keep the boys in line. If Gillett came downstairs quickly, we might be able to drive back to New Hope without losing any more parts off the car. Miss Penny had fixed her eyes on three scraggly banana trees at the edge of her yard. The grass had been cut there recently with a machete, and I wondered if her Junie had done it for her. I heard the sound of feet as they moved across the wooden floor, running through the house to the back where there would be another door. I must have given him away. It was hard not to give him away, though to tell the truth I wasn't against the idea of him running out the back door and into the bush where we wouldn't be able to find him. When the other boys sensed what was happening, three of them ran up the front stairs, brushing past the old woman. Simple and another boy ran around to the back where they expected Gillett to appear.

Gillett climbed out a window instead and up onto the tin roof. He had no place left to go once he was on the roof. I was afraid he would jump. The house sat so high off the ground, it would be like jumping from the third story of a building in the city. I'd seen boys at New Hope do crazy things and survive with scrapes and bruises. I didn't know about this jumping. I wasn't aware that I had climbed the front stairs myself, yet I found myself standing in the middle of Miss Penny's living room. The room was clean and spare. More boys followed me into the house. Albert tried to go out the window after Gillett. He fell back into the room when the frightened boy kicked him in the forehead. I couldn't see Gillett up on the roof. I only heard him up there, crying.

Once they were inside the house, the boys turned shy, unsure what to do next. Albert knelt on the floor and rubbed his head, and he looked at me as if he thought I could make sense of where we were and what we were doing.

The old woman watched me, too, waiting. But I couldn't make sense of it. Any one of the boys who had just climbed out of the car and run up the steps to this house might have tried on a different day to run away from the school. Several of them already had. Mouse had stayed out for eight months, working in the sugarcane, living with strangers, until the police brought him back. When they took Mouse from the cane field, the police beat him to make sure he wouldn't give them any trouble on the drive back to the Cayo, and the first thing he earned when he was turned over to Fairbanks was more of the same from Fairbanks's rope. Yet here were Mouse and Simple and the others, ready to do harm to Gillett if he didn't come along, hoping for the chance. I didn't understand it.

I put my head out the window and ducked when Gillett tried to kick me. It was the first time I got a look at him, how small he was. His face glistened and his hair, which was tangled, hadn't been cut in a long time. He would be the smallest boy we had at New Hope. I grabbed his leg and held it a moment until he could see who I was. When he saw me, a strange and skinny white man, his leg went slack. I let go and he backed slowly away from the edge of the roof.

"Come down off the roof," I told him. I hoped he wouldn't make more trouble. I climbed out next to him, afraid at any moment the roof would give way and we would fall through it to the rooms below. I couldn't tell how old Gillett was. He looked away from me, but it wasn't like he didn't want to look at me. It was more like he didn't want me to look at him.

"Them boys," he said. "I fraid for them." I was watching him closely, but only with one eye. With the other, I was being careful not to fall off the roof. There was something wrong with the boy's face. I couldn't tell what it was exactly. He didn't want to hold still. He was willing to jump, and would have, but Albert pulled himself out of another window and onto the roof. Simple pushed through the window behind me.

"Don't hurt him," I said. The roof creaked beneath their feet as the two older boys moved up next to him. Simple hit him once and Albert took offense at that. I thought Albert was going to shove Simple over the edge before I could get Gillett away from the two of them. I sent Albert and Simple down off the roof, one at a time. I told them to wait by the car. Gillett wasn't hurt, but he was sobbing, afraid. I told him I would get him a glass of water if he came down off the roof with me.

And he did finally. I passed the boy back through the window of the house into the front room where Albert held onto him, always Albert, until I could lower myself through the window, too. Gillett trembled, watching his grandmother put clothes into a bag. A man sat alone in one corner of the room. Perhaps he had been there all along. Hunched and motionless, he stayed in the shadow by the door offering no help and no resistance.

"*Da next bwai deh,*" the man said, "*da fi he own family.*" He repeated himself several times to nobody in particular. The Creole words were too hard for me. I heard them, but I couldn't tell myself what they meant.

"Good-bye, Junie," said the old woman. And then she said, "Take care of him." She said it to Albert, not to me.

I got the new boy in the car and had him sit next to me with Albert on the other side. Before I could get all the way into the car and shut the door, the boys had cuffed Gillett on the head half a dozen times. I had to threaten them to make them leave him alone.

"Unu listen to the man!" said Albert. And then to me he said, "Make we go." He didn't have to say it twice. I backed out onto the highway and drove fast back to the compound, only mildly trying to avoid the potholes. A cloud of dust behind us drifted off the road to the houses on either side.

I'd heard the boys sing on occasion, mostly the hymns the missionary groups taught them at Wednesday services. On the football field they might break into a few lines of a song from Radio Belize. Linda Ronstadt got a lot of air time that year, in English and in Spanish. The boys sang one of her songs in the car, then started in on an awful pop song titled "Let's Just Kiss and Say Goodbye." I was glad when they stopped that one. Mouse began a song I'd never heard before. The rest of them knew it, some better than others. It sounded to me like some college fraternity's song. Or as if the words, lost to my ears, should have been in German. It was the rhythm that registered with me, not the words. Their voices came in waves above the air rushing through the open windows, voices that grew deeper and gruffer than I expected. Fairbanks waited for us on his veranda, and the boys piled out of the car singing as loud as they could. They wanted to pull Gillett from the car. He was their trophy. I took him by the arm myself and walked him up the stairs where I gave him up to Fairbanks. Albert stood on Gillett's other side.

"Mr. Tanner, Mr. Tanner," said Fairbanks softly, a small smile at the corners of his eyes. Then he turned to the boy. He held Gillett's face up so he could look at it, and that was the first time I saw the damage there.

"What happened?" I said.

"It's an old injury," said Fairbanks. "Nothing our boys have done."

Fairbanks let go of the boy's face. He took Gillett's right hand and held it out. The hand was deformed as well.

"You should relax," Fairbanks said to the boy. "You'll be all right with us. You're here with your brother after all."

"His brother?" I said. I'm sure I hardly made my voice heard. "Who?"

I looked around. Nobody else was on the veranda except me and Fairbanks. And Albert, who looked at me as hard as I looked at him. Albert held the new boy by his good hand. I hadn't noticed that before.

And I hadn't noticed her, sitting just inside Fairbanks's office on a wooden chair. Ellie. She held a glass of water that trembled in her hands. It made me think of the glass of water I promised Gillett but never gave him. She said a soft word to me, some simple greeting. I couldn't hear her voice. Fairbanks hadn't stopped the boys from singing. There was no end to the number of verses to that song, each one as mysterious as the one before it.

"The door?" said Fairbanks. "You got it fixed?" He let his eyes pass over the boys crowding up the steps.

"Yes," I managed to say, "the door's okay now."

I must have introduced him to Ellie, though I didn't need to. She would have introduced herself already. Price had not come with her, or he was down the road somewhere buying beer, or he had stopped to talk to the girls who lived near the highway. I didn't ask. I didn't want to know right away. I led Ellie away from Fairbanks's office. I noticed how her blouse was sweaty, how it clung to her back where she had been sitting in the chair. I thought we might cool off by the river until Price returned. I hoped she wouldn't want to swim, because I wasn't going in that water. I hoped we wouldn't be able to hear the boys anymore, their singing.

8

I don't know why pregnant women make me think of cannibals. I asked Katherine to have Sunday breakfast with me, an early Christmas present. "I need real food," she said, "not just bread. I need protein." That's when I thought about cannibals. Tigresses. Lone she-wolves. I thought about sharks, and other things that live underwater. I offered to buy Katherine a cheeseburger.

"An omelet would make me happy," said Katherine. "I don't eat meat all the time. I'm still a vegetarian, practically."

She named a restaurant, a little place two blocks over from where I live, a counter with six stools and three tables. I knew the place. I was waiting for her when she got there, thinking about how much time I spent in cafés, wondering if I had some kind of problem, and there she was standing at my table. My heart paused. I gave myself a little whack on the chest to make sure it would start back up. Some women are beautiful when they're pregnant. They look as if they're on their way to the photographer, as if this is what they were born to do. Some other women look tired and a little angry. They've been asked to pack the car for the family vacation, and somewhere along in the eighth month, they find out there's no gas in the car and they have to push the damn Chevy all the way to Wyoming. Katherine was mostly beautiful, with an edge from all those hormones coursing through her body.

She had hardly settled into her chair before she said it: "Stacen tells me you have a girlfriend."

"You know better," I said.

"Sometimes I know better," she said. "Sometimes I wonder. Sometimes I think you're looking to replace me."

"It's not like that," I said. "It's not about replacing anyone."

"It's not?" said Katherine. "Then tell me something, Tanner, because I'd really like to know. What the hell is it about?"

I was glad the waitress came and hovered next to us, waiting for our order. That waitress was sort of pretty. She had hair a shade of blue I had only seen before on skateboards and a certain kind of church window. She was twenty years younger than Katherine and me, but she had her own problems. I wouldn't have to answer Katherine's questions with the waitress standing there.

"Isn't it time you told me?" said Katherine, the way a person might say *I hope the food is okay in this place. I hope there's pie for dessert.* "Isn't it time you told me what it's all about?"

"It's about breakfast," said the waitress. God bless her. "Hopefully."

I looked at the menu. I wanted it to be a bigger menu than it was. I was sorry it wasn't one of those menus with a story printed in the middle about the history of the town, or the establishment of the Tennessee Valley Authority, or something equally important. The 1923 World's Fair. The true meaning of Christmas. I wanted to tell Katherine what my life was all about. I'd have to tell her how for twenty years I've been followed around place to place, job to job, by an angry young man who may or may not be a real person. I'd have to let her know how I wake up nights and change my T-shirt because it's soaked through with sweat, how I used to get up from the bed even when she was right there next to me and walk through the house checking to see that every door was locked. I'd have to say, I'm all broken inside.

"You have eggs?" I asked the waitress.

"Jesus," said the waitress. "If you knew the size of my hangover, you would get serious here."

Katherine knew what she was going to order without even looking at the menu. I read the menu a second time. I looked for typos. I asked the waitress what kind of bread they used to make toast. She didn't know. I asked her where the eggs came from.

"They come from the chickens," said the waitress. "What I've been told."

I thanked the waitress for that bit of science. I ordered bacon and fried eggs.

"After all that," said the waitress. She poured me more coffee and steered her mean self away from our table.

"I hope you figure it out," said Katherine.

"I ordered, didn't I?" I said.

"Yes," said Katherine. "You ordered."

She got up to use the restroom. Pregnant women use the restroom a lot. Maybe cannibals do, too. It wouldn't surprise me. I sat for a good five minutes with nothing but my thoughts to keep me company. A long wait.

"Enough about me," I said when Katherine came back. "For now," I said. "Please. How are you feeling?"

"Abandoned," said Katherine. She saw how that hurt, even if I had it coming, and she would have taken it back. "Actually," she said, "can I be honest with you?"

"You haven't been honest up to now?"

"I have," she said. "I've been more than honest. This might make you give me another one of those pained looks."

"Sorry," I said.

And here's when I started having trouble listening. I was watching the little window in the back of the restaurant where the food always appears in that place. There was a new cook back there in the kitchen. I couldn't see his face. I could only see his arms in the window when he slid a couple of plates out to the waitress. The cook was too old to be called a kid, too young for a man. He had long thin arms, black arms covered with a light dusting of flour. How can I say this? I knew those arms. I closed my eyes and saw little bursts of red where those arms had been. I took a deep breath, and I told myself to take forty or fifty more deep breaths. It was our food he was pushing out the little window. The waitress brought those plates to our table, along with the check.

"Remember," she said when she placed the check next to my coffee cup. "I'm a working mother."

I looked at the food on my plate. "Is this what I ordered?"

"You don't remember either?" said the waitress. She picked up the check again to see if she had written anything down. It didn't matter what I'd ordered. I wasn't going to be able to eat that breakfast.

"I've been thinking," said Katherine, her eyes on her own plate. "I could do this by myself."

The waitress looked down at me. She was interested in what I would say to Katherine. I had to glare at the woman until she went away.

"Do what?" I said.

Katherine set her fork down. She closed her eyes and tilted her head to one side as if she was listening for something. Or she had a headache. "I'm not sure how your brain works anymore," she said. "We're going along having a regular conversation, talking about something important, and suddenly you're not here. Not even in the room."

"What did I do?"

"It's not what you did," she said. There were tears in her eyes but not the good kind of tears. She started to scoot her chair away from the table. The food hadn't had a chance to get cold yet.

"Wait," I said. "Give me another chance. I got distracted."

"You're killing me, Tanner," she said. "I know six-year-old kids in the special class at school who have better concentration than you do."

"Please," I said. I felt the waitress's eyes on the back of my head. I could tell the cook in the back was listening through his little window.

"Don't leave," I whispered. "Let's start over."

I forced myself not to look toward the back of the restaurant. I told myself to ignore the bad feeling I was getting. Maybe it was him back there, and if it was, that was bad news. On the other hand, if I didn't listen to Katherine, it was another kind of bad news.

"I want a cup of coffee," said Katherine.

"What about the baby?" I said. She glared at me, and I knew better than to say more.

"She wants coffee," I said to the waitress.

"Aren't you pregnant?"

"So what if I am?" said Katherine. "You never gave a pregnant woman a cup of coffee before?"

"Listen girl," said the waitress, "if you can eat the crummy sausage in this dive, the coffee won't hurt you."

"I heard that," said a voice from behind the little window. It could have been the owner's voice. It wasn't the cook's voice. The cook was going to have a boy's voice. The cook's voice would sound like cicadas and coconut milk and a bell ringing at the close of day. Like the Cayo.

"You didn't hear it from me," said the waitress.

"All right, all right," said Katherine. "Make it decaf."

The waitress left to get the coffee, and Katherine focused on me again. She studied me. She weighed how much I was worth. I could have been an old lamp at a yard sale.

"Go ahead and tell me," I said. "What you were going to say. Before I got distracted."

"Okay," said Katherine. "I will. It's like this. I've been thinking about doing it all on my own. The parenting thing. I've got a friend named Michael with two babies on her own, no father in sight."

"You know a man who can have babies?"

"Not a man," said Katherine. "Michael can be a woman's name."

"Yeah, but," I said.

"You sound like one of my little kids at school. Yeah, but."

"Sorry," I said.

The waitress brought the coffee. Neither one of us had touched our food.

"Eat up," said the waitress. "The cook has feelings."

"I'm trying," I said.

"Are you?" said Katherine. "Are you trying?"

I tasted my eggs. Maybe I was supposed to argue with her after what she said about going it alone. I'd been worrying about how much time I had before she started thinking about trading me in for some new guy. Now I could see she wanted to skip the guy part of it altogether. That was a step in a strange new direction. I was lost.

"Tell me about the young woman," said Katherine.

"What young woman? Sara?"

"I don't care about her," said Katherine. "I know about her already. Tell me about the other one. The one that matters."

"What one that matters?"

"Don't play games," said Katherine. "I want you to tell me about her. About Ellie."

I inhaled too fast and ended up with coffee in all the wrong places. I coughed and my eyes got bleary. Katherine kept her gaze on me. I tried setting my coffee cup down. I tried lining up the little packets of sugar, getting the pink ones on one side with the pinks, and the blue ones on the other side with the blues. They even had some white ones. I put those in the middle. With the other white ones.

"I'm still here," said Katherine.

"It doesn't seem right to tell you," I said. "It feels like I'm being unfaithful."

"To me? Or to her?"

"I don't know," I said. I thought about it for a moment while Katherine glared at me.

"When I think about her," I said, "I feel like I'm being unfaithful to you."

"That sounds better than 'I don't know.' Why haven't you told me about her before?"

"I must have told you something. How do you know her name if I didn't tell you?"

"So many secrets," said Katherine. "Why so many?"

"I don't know how they got to be secrets. I didn't mean for them to be secrets."

"Would I have liked her?" said Katherine.

It wasn't a fair question.

"You like everybody," I said. "You like Stacen and Liu and Croker. You like the Bobber, for God's sake."

"I like his wife," said Katherine.

"His wife's just like him. His kids are going to be like him. They're all Bobbers."

"I like the little one," said Katherine.

We were on dangerous ground. It wasn't a good idea to talk about kids.

"You like everybody's wife," I said. "You even like that midwife, the one with the leather jacket."

"It's true," said Katherine. "I like her a lot. You know why?"

I wished I hadn't mentioned the woman.

"I think I know why."

"She's going to be there," said Katherine. "At the house. When the baby comes."

Maybe I deserved that, but still I didn't deserve that.

"Tell me about Ellie," said Katherine, her voice soft and calm again. The waitress reappeared and frowned down at Katherine's plate.

"I can get you something else, if you want," said the waitress. Katherine exchanged one of those looks with the waitress that women are always exchanging with each other. The waitress seemed satisfied. She shuffled away to torment someone else.

"Surprise me," said Katherine. "Tell me the truth. Surprise yourself."

"How much do you have to know?"

"Look," said Katherine, "could we face the music here for a moment? Time's passing. I'm living in this house by myself, wondering how I'm going to pay the mortgage, who's going to mow the lawn, why I don't sell the place and move to Oregon. You're just a few winters short of fifty, Tanner. *Time's winged chariot,* remember? You don't have a lot of afternoons to mull things over."

We pretended it was my turn to let the words sink in. As if I wasn't thinking about this sort of thing at odd moments every day.

"What have you got to lose?" she said.

"I don't know," I said, watching my eggs. I thought I saw one of them move. "I should not have ordered eggs," I said. "I should eat something else for breakfast."

"Of course you should," said Katherine. "Talk to me."

"Did I tell you I'm thinking about getting a motorcycle? Not a real fast one. Just something to ride around on."

"You can get one," said Katherine. "Tell me about Ellie."

"I might have to move out of my apartment. Croker may have something in mind for that place. I can read the writing on the wall."

"You can move," said Katherine. "Right after you tell me about Ellie."

"I don't know how to begin."

"Take one of those deep breaths," she said. "The next word that comes out of your mouth should be *Ellie.*"

9

*E*llie. When I think of her, even now I can be overcome with shame. It's not for any of the obvious reasons. It's not about sex or meanness, or honesty, or the lack of any of those things. It's not about where we started or where we ended up. It's about one important difference, the one thing we did not share: Ellie was a real teacher and I wasn't, and I didn't know how to do the first thing about it. I didn't know how to ask for help. I had every intention of asking her. I wanted to get myself on the right track. Then Ellie and I would get together for an evening or a weekend, and I'd get lost looking at her hands, her smile, smelling her hair, touching her clothes.

That first weekend at New Hope, we slept in different rooms. Sunday morning, she woke up at dawn and dressed and was in the kitchen making breakfast for Price and me before I knew the sun had come up. It didn't upset me. I was happy she was there. I didn't expect more from her. We spent other weekends together, either at New Hope or at her place in the city, weekends with Price, and weekends without Price sprawled in the hammock or coming up the back steps with that grin on his face. In the city, too, Ellie and I stayed shy with each other for a long time. Sometimes in the evenings we held hands and walked in the street where we could listen to Radio Belize out of every open doorway, every shop window we passed. It was months before we slept next to each other, afternoon naps at first and then whole long nights. We weren't backward. We got around to it in time: we went to bed early and lay in each other's arms and did the small things lovers do, but not the one big thing. She let me know I shouldn't be in a hurry with her. It was her choice, but I was okay with it. I didn't have many girlfriends before Ellie.

We planned a long trip together, which asked for more trust than sleeping together. Price told us we were making a mistake. I didn't listen to him. Other cities, other countries, I wanted to share the world with Ellie. I wanted to share the people on the street who sell soft drinks, and the shoeshine boys so small, so young, they can barely lug around their kits, and all the strange buses holding peasants and peasant children and peasant goats. I wanted Ellie to sit next to me and doze off once in a while and wake up when I nudged her to show her the next amazing thing. I wanted to be in love with her. I welcomed it.

We were walking through the Belize City market, shopping for fruit and what vegetables we could find. Ellie wanted oranges so she could make juice, and Price was on a papaya kick. He ate it three times a day for a couple of months. He wanted to find a way to make a drink out of it. Papaya wine, he said. Papaya beer. Papaya margaritas. He and Candace were on the outs. He had told her about his children in the States but Candace didn't believe him. Ellie picked out a dozen oranges and tried her best to ignore Price. I tried to listen to him. I wanted to hear what his voice sounded like again, sober.

"The only way to travel," said Price, "is alone."

"What do you know about anything?" said Ellie.

"I know," said Price, wagging a cucumber in Ellie's direction. "I know some things."

"One dollar fifty," said the woman standing in front of Price. He had piled up tomatoes and carrots and a large mango, making a tower of sorts, and now the woman thought he ought to pay for all of it. He made a face at her, but then he pulled his money out of his pocket.

"I have been around," said Price.

"Why don't you come with us?" I asked him.

"No," said Ellie.

"Why not?" I said. "He could bring a friend. It'd be better with four of us." I was afraid I'd run out of things to talk about and Ellie would be bored with me.

"That's terrible," said Price. "That's the worst. Four happy travelers all off to discover the new world, and you're doomed."

We listened to him. Even the woman in the market listened to him.

"Sooner or later there's a pairing up, and usually it's your buddy who falls in love or some variation of love and leaves you to try to partner up with whoever's left over. That always turns out wrong because the girl you get is reluctant to spend that much time with you, and she complains and maybe gets sick with something that causes her friend to break away from your friend so she can spend several days nursing your friend's friend back to health."

"What?" I said.

"Or you discover there's a reason why your best friend fell for the other girl and not for the girl you're supposed to be hanging out with," said Price. "Your girl is opinionated as hell about some topic you hardly care about, the rights of the American Indian for instance, and everything she says makes you realize that in fact you *do* care about the rights of the American Indian, too, by God you have opinions, too, a whole lot more than you ever realized, and you also care about the degradation of the national parks and about the best way to teach young children to read and about whether *Time* magazine is a liberal or a conservative magazine. There's no end to the things you can argue about, and any one of those things will show you that you can't possibly fall in love with this woman." He shoved vegetables into one side of his backpack. He had papayas in the other side. They were ripe, and they were leaking juice through the zipper.

"What woman?" I said. "What falling in love?" I didn't think anybody could follow what he was saying.

"And she feels the same way?" said Ellie.

"What?" I said. I was reeling. "You're getting this?"

"Absolutely," said Price. "Eventually, the two women are huddled in some bus station and your buddy's sitting on a bench by himself and he's not speaking to you because it's your fault his new girlfriend isn't going to continue the trip with him, and now the two women are going to take a little time for themselves in Honduras, or travel up the Yucatán without him and more to the point, without you, and if you aren't careful, you find that the three of them are all flying back to Illinois together where your friend can start law school and a wedding is planned for the fall, where the girl you don't love is going to be the bridesmaid, and if you are in the area you could drop by, but you don't have to make a special trip for it, you don't have to interrupt your travels."

"Man," I said. "Could you repeat any of this if you had to?"

"Hell yes I could but I won't," said Price. He shouldered his backpack and held out his hand for his change. The market woman looked at him like he was a genius. "It all happens," said Price, "and then you're traveling alone again."

"What's so bad about that?" said Ellie. "I thought you liked traveling alone."

"Traveling alone isn't bad, except for the way you spend all your time trying to meet other people, especially the pretty girl who gets on the bus at the last minute, waving good-bye to her host family out the window, having a little trouble getting her bag in the overhead. You play it just right, not too eager to connect with her, but not holding back too long because there are always other guys on the bus who are traveling alone and they're better at this than you are, so you check your shirt, see if it's too smelly, then stand in the aisle and help pull her Goliath-size backpack through the window, the backpack she's never going to carry across even one plaza by herself, and you get it up on the rack while she says things in good Spanish to whatever person or persons are standing on the sidewalk—the fat woman and the man in the old hat—and you settle back in your seat, realizing at once you've made an error, you should have found a way to take the seat next to her . . ."

The woman in the market was holding her breath. She gave Price all his money back. She gave him a couple of extra dollars.

". . . the bus is filling up too fast, and you stand up again and glancing around you realize, with a great freefall in your gut, that all the people on the bus, all the Panamanians or all the Inca peasants or all the other students making their way toward the border, are watching you, all smiling to themselves, waiting to see if you're going to get away with it this time, if she's going to allow you to sit next to her, if she's going to turn red and stare out the window for the next eight days, if you're going to die of shame that you ever started the mile-long journey from your seat on the bus to hers. And of course, you stop in your tracks as though you only stood up to stretch, which you do then, before you sit back down and wait, and it isn't a long wait until someone a little hairier, someone with a paperback novel by a writer you have never heard of, someone who wears the shirt he bought last week in a market three districts farther south than you have been, gets on the bus and sits in the only vacant seat. The one next to her."

"Next to who?" I said.

The market woman made that sucking sound with her teeth and frowned at me.

"That's another thing," said Price. "You never listen."

"True that," said the woman, scowling at me.

"On second thought," I said, "don't come with us."

"Of course I'm coming," said Price.

"Like hell," said Ellie.

"I wouldn't miss it for the world," said Price.

"Go through, man," said the market woman, approvingly. "Go through."

But he didn't come with us. It was Ellie's idea not to tell him when we were leaving, the same way it was her idea to visit the ruins at Tikal. Herbert drove us down to catch the afternoon bus, smiling at us in the rearview mirror so often I thought he was going to wreck the truck.

"You can't get there in one day, you know," he said. "You must spend the night at my uncle's hotel. In San Ignacio." He winked at me. "It is a safe place to start your honeymoon," he whispered. I chased him around the truck two or three times until Ellie asked me what I was doing and insisted it was time to get on the bus.

It was almost dark when we got to San Ignacio, and in spite of my better judgment we went to Patel's hotel, a cinder-block building at the edge of town, as far away from Miss Beard's ice cream shop as we could be and still find ourselves in San Ignacio. I had never been this far west with Ellie, and I wanted to show her around. I wanted to walk her up and down both streets before dinner, but she chose to stay indoors that night, half afraid Price would find us out. When we were greeted at dinner by a short smiling man with a round belly, I let myself laugh. I knew who he was even before he brought us our menus.

"Herbert sent us," I said. Patel held the menus over his heart and smiled, first at Ellie and then at me.

"That Herbert," he said. "It's a wonder he didn't end up at your school for difficult boys."

Ellie was charmed. She made me feel charmed, too, as long as I didn't think about Herbert or how close we still were to New Hope. If there had been more time, Ellie would have spent some days of it in that dining room talking and laughing with Uncle Patel, but I felt the urge to keep moving. It didn't want to let me go. I promised to come and see him again when our trip was over and I was back with the boys at New Hope.

"Yes, come see me. Perhaps I can help you," said Patel. "In some small way."

The next morning, we took a taxi to the border. We showed our passports to the border guards and Ellie asked for directions to the bus station. We took the morning bus away from Melchor, and it had been raining all night, so the road was bad. I sat close to her the whole way, except when we had to get out and push the bus. It was a twenty-hour ride, and sometimes she rested her hand on my thigh, and sometimes I brushed my fingers along her forearm.

For six days, we shared strange and wonderful hotel rooms. We went to bed late and woke up early, and in between going to bed and waking up, she held me and rocked me, and she was willing to make me happy even if she wasn't willing, not yet willing, to let me be happy in the way that brings babies into the world. She had her lotions, and she let me touch her and smell her and kiss her. She wasn't teasing me. She hadn't been beaten by nuns or dragged through some awful childhood full of revivals and organ music, though she knew about those things, and life sometimes made her sad. She just didn't want me inside her yet, inside her heart or any other part of her because once she let me inside her, then she would love me whether she should love me or not. Loving a man was dangerous, and loving a boy was even more dangerous. She knew all that.

We played cards while we waited in little cafés for our meals of rice and eggs and tortillas. Her Spanish was better than mine, but she let me order the food and a soft drink for her, a beer for myself. We moved every day, long rides on buses that left at dawn and were crowded with people going to market or to the next town, wherever the small brown men in white shirts went, and the women in their layers of embroidery. In Flores, we spent the night in a room so narrow the door bumped against the bed, no radio and no television, just the two of us to talk to each other and touch each other, to undress in the dark and whisper yes and no and I'm afraid, and I don't want you to be afraid. And to make the bed damp, and in the morning to take a shower together and feel the soap on her body as I washed her long dark hair and dried her back. Those mornings I looked at the bed, I longed for it, but we had a ride to catch and that was the best thing, to keep moving.

From Flores, we drove out to the ruins in the back of a small truck with four other tourists, two who wouldn't meet our eyes. One of the friendly ones, a blonde Italian, gabbed nonstop with her companion and with Ellie.

"You're Italian?" said Ellie. "But your English is beautiful." Those four in the truck smiled at each other.

"Thank you," said the woman. "Your English is beautiful, too."

I felt bad for Ellie that morning. I would have picked a fight with somebody to defend her, but I didn't know who to fight. When the truck stopped, we climbed out of the back and we didn't talk to each other much for the rest of the morning. We spent that day like we spent the next one and the one after that, walking around the ruins, reading from our guidebook, climbing the giant steps the Mayans built around their temples. The Mayans walking along the road were short people, small as Japanese. I didn't understand why a short-legged people would build tall, steep stairways. I wanted to ask, but I was afraid somebody would take offense. Maybe the old Mayans hadn't realized they were short. Maybe the ones we passed along the road that morning thought *they* were tall. Who was I to bring it up? We had lunch in the shade, bottled water and some of Albert's bread from New Hope. The truck we'd arrived in came and went throughout the day, but we waited until the Italian woman and her friends were gone before we climbed back in and gave the driver our money. We waited too long, and because we were tired and hungry, the ride back was uncomfortable. Ellie's arms were burned by the sun and the wind.

We found a new place for dinner that evening. Inside a small dining room, the owner had collected an odd assortment of stuffed animals: small raccoon-looking things, and what might have been a young jaguar. There were a weasel and an owl. The animals were threadbare and looked as if they'd never been mounted properly. As a joke, the owner of the café had placed them all on a bandstand, had given each one an instrument to play. Anteater held a dusty clarinet. One of the raccoon things was suspended over a pair of bongos. There were music stands on the stage, some ancient brown music. The place had the look of a gag the owner had tired of a long time ago. The guitar that belonged to the largest animal, a yellow dog, had three strings missing.

Ellie didn't care about the band. That night, she wanted to tell me about herself, about all the life that happened to her before she found her way to Belize. She told me about her family, about her parents' divorce and her father's sadness, the little college she went to in Kansas, the plays she was in before she realized she wasn't any good at acting. I didn't believe that part.

"You were good," I said. "I know it. You have talent."

"You don't need talent," she said. "Just like, after a while, you don't need parents."

"Don't say that," I said.

She shrugged it off. "It's harder, though, to try out for parts after you know you don't have the talent. And then the shows. It's pretty miserable when you know you're going to be mediocre six nights out of the eight you have to perform."

I tried to imagine her on stage, but I couldn't imagine her pretending to be someone she wasn't. I couldn't imagine her doing anything other than sitting across that table and talking to me. I tried to think of some story I could tell her that would match what she told me. I found myself staring into the eyes of that guitar-playing yellow dog and thinking my life was tame. I told her about the time I drowned.

"We need to work on your self-esteem," she said.

"Why?"

"Self-esteem is good," she said. "Self-esteem is appealing."

The waitress took our plates away. We were among the last to leave the restaurant that night. We were four blocks from the room we had booked that morning, which was an okay room in the dark, but the room had no window and the ceiling was stained from a leaking roof, and Ellie didn't want to go back and look at any of that too soon.

"I wish we had our deck of cards," I said.

"I wish we were at Uncle Patel's," said Ellie, but she laughed to let me know she didn't mean it. I ordered a beer. Ellie said she would have one with me, which cheered me up. I thought she might make love to me if she had a beer or two. I didn't want her to get drunk though. I knew I didn't want that.

The waitress who brought the drinks set her tray down awkwardly and one of the bottles of beer spilled across our table. She tried to grab the bottle but it got away from her, rolling all the way across the room to the bandstand and dumping the last of what it held beneath the anteater's glassy eye. The waitress said a word in Spanish that was both soft and harsh, a word I thought might be useful if I could get her to say it for me again. I got up to find a towel and to help wipe the table. She began to cry.

"I'm sorry," I said, trying to give the bar towel up so she could finish cleaning the spill. "*Lo siento.*" I was surprised the words were there when I needed them. An angry man came out of the back room and glared across the table at the three of us. He looked as cross as any one of the animals in the orchestra, as if at any moment the big blood vessel in his forehead might burst.

"It was my fault," I said. The man kept his eye on me.

"My fault," I said again, patting myself on the chest. "*Mi falta, mi falta,*" I said.

The man narrowed his eyes, as though he was trying to see me better. He and the waitress exchanged a frown, and the man looked over at the anteater as if a dead anteater could speak Spanish better than me. The waitress managed a small smile and the man, who had to be the owner of the café, walked back to the storeroom scratching his head. Ellie finished cleaning our table. She wiped off the salt shaker and set it next to a little jar of hot peppers floating in vinegar.

"That was nice of you," said Ellie. "You didn't make any sense, but he got the idea."

"I didn't want her to get in trouble."

"You're a good guy."

I wanted to ask Ellie what she meant by that, by *good*. We hadn't used that word in a long time. I wanted to know if her ideas had changed. We sat down at our table again, Ellie beside me so we could touch each other while we talked, and so she wouldn't have to look right into the teeth of that musical genius of a dog.

"Who are you?" she said. "I want to know all about you. Tell me how to be good."

"I don't know how to be good," I said.

"You're good with the boys. At New Hope."

"I don't think so. It's not like that."

"Of course you are." She thought I was being modest. "You should try never to speak Spanish, but you're a good guy."

The waitress returned with more beer and a plate of small yellow cakes.

"We didn't order all this," I said, but the waitress left it and hurried away.

"She's giving it to us," said Ellie.

"I don't understand."

"You helped her out," said Ellie. "With her boss. She agrees with me. You're a good guy."

"You're wrong," I said. "You're exaggerating at least."

"Tell me a story," said Ellie. "Tell me right now. I need to know how to be good."

"I don't have any stories. Not about that."

"Everybody has a story," said Ellie. There was a new sound in her voice. She was frightened. She had told me too much about herself. I was slow to look at her. I knew, behind her eyes, all the wheels were spinning.

"Please," she said. "Please, please."

Which is why I started talking, and why everything I said was true. It wasn't any of it especially good, not as far as I could tell.

It happened the weekend after I moved out to New Hope, the weekend Hobson and I rode the bus into Belize City and part of the trip I sat next to Albert's grandmother, Miss Penny, but I didn't know who she was. Hobson had the last of his boxes with him on the bus. He was just days away from flying home, and he wanted to be done with New Hope. He didn't want to say good-bye to the staff and the boys and then have to come back for more of his stuff. The dogs and the motorcycle were gone. There was nothing holding him to the place.

Price had moved into a small flat with an extra room near the Fort George Hotel. He had a sofa and a mattress on the floor and he was generous. Anybody who needed a place to sleep could stay there, he didn't care who it might be, anybody in town from the districts. When Hobson and I got off the bus, we took a cab to Price's flat and Hobson found the key in a coffee jar under the steps. We threw open the windows to get rid of the smell. Someone had been sick there recently.

Hobson handed me a note he found in the refrigerator. It was from Price. The note said he would come by a little later.

"Only thing in the refrigerator," said Hobson, a little awed. "Leave him a note back. Have him meet us somewhere."

"Where?"

"The Bayview," said Hobson. He went into the bathroom and set his soap and shaving gear on the back of the toilet. "If he doesn't know where it is, he needs to find out."

I was thinking sooner or later I would have to disagree with Hobson about something. I didn't know what it would be. He knew me for a true follower. So I left a note for Price in the refrigerator and I followed Hobson to the Bayview, hoping the place would turn out to be a real restaurant. It was a bar next to the river on the usual stilts with a veranda that hung out over the water.

We climbed to the top of the stairs and slipped into a shadowy room.

"Two Heineken," said Hobson to a small man behind the bar.

"No Heineken," said the man.

"What?" said Hobson. He glared at the man, then looked quickly around the room to see if there were any Heineken bottles on any of the tables.

"Charger then."

"No Charger," said the man. "We got Belikin."

"Boy," said Hobson. "I hate Belikin."

The man shrugged.

"You got One Barrel rum?" asked Hobson, shutting his eyes tight against the coming disappointment.

"No must," said the man.

"Good," said Hobson. "Give us two rum and Coke."

"One Barrel?" said the man.

"No must," said Hobson.

I was thirsty from the ride on the bus, and I drank the rum and Coke too fast, and another, and then meant to order just a Coke while I waited for Price, but ended up drinking the Belikin beer Hobson ordered for me. I told Hobson I was going next door to get something to eat, and I stepped out into the street before I realized I didn't know where I was, where I would have to go to find food. Two small ragged boys ran up to me. They looked exactly like the boys I had left at New Hope earlier that afternoon.

"Shilling?" asked one of the boys. "Give me one shilling?" It was straight-up six o'clock and the sun was dropping into the river behind the bar. That sun and the boys and the smells of the river were all incredibly sad. I felt in my pocket for loose change, but before I could give it up, Hobson appeared in the doorway.

"More little shits," said Hobson. He spoke to the boys as if he recognized them. I suppose it was possible. "I know your tricks," he said.

The boys backed away, ready to run.

"It's all right," I said. "They're not picking my pocket."

"The hell they aren't," said Hobson. He wasn't drunk but he was on the way. He made as if to go after the boy closest to him, and both boys ran, disappearing into the gloom.

I could hear a radio playing in a nearby shop. There was only one station, and the houses were close together, all their windows open for the slightest breeze. Everyone in Belize City listened to a British radio play, *Dr. Garrison,* for ten minutes each evening. Standing on the street corner, I felt like I was eavesdropping, only it was more like I was expected to listen. It was the national pastime. The night's episode started with an urgent phone call, and Dr. Garrison had to leave his lovely wife at dinner in a terrible hurry.

"Stop listening to that drivel and come back inside," said Hobson.

There was a car crash and burning petrol. Dr. Garrison was unconscious. The flames were about to reach him in the car. I knew the flames were about to reach him because an old sheepherder who had come across the accident was saying just that.

Why, look out lad. Those flames are about to reach you. Let me see if I can get this door open. I don't know. With my bad arm, I might not be able to get to you in time. Before the flames reach you.

"Snap out of it," said Hobson. I was standing like a statue of a drunk on the sidewalk. I heard the sound of a car door open slowly, the straining grunt of the sheepherder.

"Goddamn it, Tanner," said Hobson.

His voice alone made me move. I climbed the stairs to the Bayview again and let Hobson move us out to the veranda where he ordered more beer.

"This beer is vile," he said, "but if you knock back a couple of rum and Cokes first, you can stand it."

"I thought we did that," I said. "We knocked them back. Don't you want to eat?"

Hobson stared at me blankly. "Eat?" he said. "There's an idea."

But he didn't get up from the table, and when Price came in an hour later, we were still trying to decide whether to go to the Chinese restaurant or to a greasy spoon called Mom's for burgers. I was worried about Dr. Garrison.

"Let's have one beer before we go," said Hobson. Price was game, only he told us he was taking some kind of medicine and wasn't allowed to drink for a couple of weeks. Hobson scowled at Price as if Price had just said the stupidest thing in the history of beer. Then they both looked at me, and I must have looked rough. Price wanted to call off the beer altogether. I told him it was okay. I let the man behind the bar bring me one more. I had no intention of drinking it.

"I have to take a leak," said Hobson. He got up from the table and headed for the door.

"They don't have a place in here?" said Price. The look Hobson gave him this time, you'd have thought Price had just said something bad about God. Hobson headed for the stairs to the street.

"He's tying one on," I said. "I've had too much myself. Dr. Garrison's in trouble."

"We'll get something to eat," said Price, eyeing me strangely. "You'll feel better." He picked up Hobson's lighter from the table and began playing with it, adjusting the flame as high as it would go.

"Don't," I said. "The petrol." But Price ignored me. Hobson had left a pack of cigarettes on the table, and Price helped himself to one. Angry voices came from inside the bar. A small boy ran out onto the veranda, followed by another and then by Hobson.

"I told you to piss off," said Hobson, trying to catch the nearest boy by the shoulder. They weren't afraid of him. They had seen large drunken men before and trusted that they could dart away safely into the night. The first boy did his best to dodge Hobson. The other slipped up to the table where Price and I sat.

"Shilling?" he said. "Quarter?"

Price laughed at this one's nerve and leaned back away from the table. The boy saw the lighter. It glinted on the oilcloth like a silver coin. With a quick motion the boy swept the cigarettes and the lighter into the front of his shirt and looked for a way around Hobson, who stood between the table and the only door.

"Wait," said Price. "What are you doing?"

"Bastard," roared Hobson. He grabbed the boy by the shirt, but the shirt was old and worn thin, and it ripped away from the boy's back. The torn shirt made Hobson more angry than before, and he lunged toward the boy with the lighter, hitting his shin against a chair. I was already on my feet. I don't know why I bothered to stand up, and I don't know why I would take Hobson's side. I was sick of Hobson and I was seriously looking forward to the day he got on a plane and flew back home. At first, I only meant to take a quick step in the direction of the nearest boy, to send him running out into the street.

"Big stinking white men," said the boy. "Unu smell like shit."

And I found I had the boy's head under my arm. I was squeezing for all I was worth. I felt Price try to pry my hands away from the boy, and then I felt stronger hands, Hobson's hands, break my grip easily. I laughed it off. As quickly as I'd gotten angry, I wasn't mad anymore. Hobson pulled the boy to the edge of the veranda, laughing, too, as he turned the boy upside down and held him out over the railing. A boy like that hardly weighed anything. Hobson was able to hold him by the ankles in midair, dangling him twenty feet over the river below. The boy swung his arms and tried to grab hold of the railing, but each time he did, Hobson gave him a jerk and the boy found himself dangling in space again.

"You want a shilling?" said Hobson. "I'll give you a shilling." He shook the boy until whatever small stuff the boy had in his pockets fell into the water. Price laughed and passed his hand over his mouth.

"Okay," said Price, "that's enough. You made your point."

But Hobson was gone. Somebody else was there in his place, or maybe this was the real Hobson, I don't know. All I know is I didn't do anything about it. I wasn't part of it anymore, just an observer. I didn't look around for the police or call for the owner of the bar to come out onto the veranda. I watched the other boy move in behind us and do a crazy thing. With the lighter he had stolen, he set fire to the thatch roof near Hobson's back. The dry thatch burned easily, and still Hobson kept shaking the boy he held by the ankles. Price beat at the flames with his shirt. The young boy who started the fire was frightened at what he had done, and he threw a glass of water on it. Only it wasn't water. It was the rum Hobson had ordered. The flash of flame drew Hobson's eyes back to the rest of us.

As he turned toward us, Hobson let go of the boy. I didn't hear a splash in the water below and I didn't hear the boy fall onto a passing boat, which would have made a different sound. I didn't hear anything at all. I didn't look over the side. The other boy ran out the door, and the owner of the bar hurried toward us with a bucket of water. The thatch was old and brittle, and half the roof of the veranda was in flames.

"Let's get out of here," said Hobson.

Smoke filled the room. Everybody else inside had already left except for two shadowy men behind the bar who were taking as many bottles into their arms as they could carry. The bartender tied a rope to his bucket to haul water up from the river, but the bucket wouldn't fill fast enough to keep up with the flames. The street below had been all but empty. Now it was crowded with people. I heard the sound of a bell approaching, some kind of alarm. A policeman cleared a path through the onlookers so that two young men could bring up a fire hose and aim it at the stairs. Thick brown smoke filled the doorway, spilling out into the night. The people in the buildings on either side of the bar came out into the street, their arms piled high with whatever they thought they wanted to save if the fire should spread. Price and Hobson and I helped pull the hoses into place. Price looked angry and Hobson looked angry, and I wondered if they were angry at each other or at me. There was no sign of the small boys.

We looked for something more we could do to help, but the fire was under control in a matter of minutes. The tavern was ruined. A shout went up from the crowd when what was left of the thatch over the veranda fell away from the rest of the building and dropped into the river. The men directing the water from the fire hoses were minor heroes. They had kept the fire from spreading.

"What happened to that kid?" asked Price.

I couldn't tell him. I didn't know.

"Doesn't matter," said Hobson. "You can't hurt the little pricks. I know that."

I had stopped feeling the drink, but now it all came back to me and I needed to sit down. A woman in the crowd, thinking I was overcome by smoke, handed me a cloth soaked in water. I heard the murmur of Creole voices. All I could gather was that they were talking about the three of us, three white boys. They thought we had done something worthy, saved a child from the fire.

"I'm leaving," said Hobson. He walked into the crowd as though he was following one of the fire hoses, as though he was problem-solving. I knew he wouldn't turn around and come back. Price pulled me to my feet and we moved off in the same direction, following Hobson.

What else could I have done? I couldn't answer that simple question at the Bayview. I couldn't answer it any better later as I told the story to Ellie over cake and beer in Flores. I didn't know about stories yet. I didn't know you got to change the ending if you wanted to. I couldn't look her in the eye when I was finished.

"I don't know what you were supposed to do either," said Ellie. She sat close enough to reach out and put her arm on my shoulder, and I thought, this was what it took, this was what would bring her to me. She wouldn't give herself to me for being good, but she would for a story like the one I'd just told. It was funny, but I didn't bring it up. I wanted her to love me that night.

We paid the bill and left something extra for the waitress, though not enough extra that she would hurry after us in the dark and return it. When we walked down the street toward the *pension,* Ellie put her arm around my waist. I stopped once to kiss her. She met my kiss with her soft open mouth.

"Let's go back to the room," she said in a murmur. "I'm cold."

We were on a little island. Looking over her shoulder, I saw the water in the distance and a long row of low stalls with flat roofs. I wondered if people lived in them, or if those were shops, the windows boarded up for the night. There was no life in this part of town after dark. I wondered if we were safe.

We passed in front of the row of stalls, an open doorway up ahead where we could hear voices inside laughing softly. Someone had left a small bundle on the sidewalk. As we got closer I could see it was a baby. It was wrapped in a blanket, so I couldn't see the baby's face. I was afraid of the voices coming from the dark. I tried to convince myself someone would come out and pick up the baby in just a moment. I told myself what looked like a puddle where the baby lay was really a trick my eyes were playing on me. I told myself it would be wrong to kneel down next to the baby, or to call softly into the doorway. I told myself, though I knew this was a lie, too, that Ellie didn't see the baby, or she saw it better than I did, saw the truth of the situation, that there was nothing to worry about.

She held onto my arm tightly.

"You are a good man," she whispered to me on the street, and again later in the room as she unbuttoned my shirt. "You are a good man." She waited for me to help her with her clothes.

When we lay down together, she stroked me in the dark, but when I closed my eyes, I saw Hobson standing on the veranda holding that boy over the railing by his ankles, and when I forced myself not to see that, I saw the baby in the blanket on the sidewalk. I couldn't have explained it to anyone, even to Price. Nothing wanted to work for me. She tried to please me but she couldn't. I tried to please her.

"Maybe it's the beer," she said. She kissed me on my forehead. "I'm sure it won't last. At least, you know I'm here with you."

She pulled the sheet up to ward off the chill of the night. A mosquito buzzed near my ear and I swatted at the dark and squeezed my hand shut and the mosquito was quiet.

In the morning, I woke and would have directed her hand down to where I lay full and hopeful again, but she was up already. She was dressed and smiling at me from the chair that sat near the small sink in the corner.

"Oh," she said, watching the sun come up through the open door, "how nice." I got up and dressed quickly, and washed my face in the sink. I dried myself with the ratty towel that had been on the bed when we arrived. I stood next to her in the doorway.

"How nice," she said again.

We bought sweet bread from a shop near the bus station and found places on the bus that would take us back to Melchor and the border. We would have had to sit separately, but a Guatemalan man, an Indian, smiled at me and stood to exchange seats. I sat down next to Ellie. Two rows behind us a man lit a cigarette, and I wondered if that was going to bother her. I could have said something to the man with the cigarette but I didn't want to move. I wanted to sit as still as possible and wait for the feeling that might come over me, whatever that feeling is that comes over a person on a bus early in the morning far away from home. It's not a bad way to feel, a little lonely. I wondered what Ellie could be thinking: the possibility of regret, now that she had given so much of herself to me and could see me again in the gray light of the morning. I was afraid of what she could see and what she could feel, and yet I knew if it was regret, there was nothing I could do to prevent it. So I waited for her regret, waited until I almost came to long for it, for the suspense to be over. She sat next to me and she was quiet. I wondered if she waited for the bad feeling, too. When we had been on the road an hour, when the bus driver had stopped for three drunken men and then refused to let them board the bus, and the bus had pulled away from them where they sat mean and sick by the side of the road, I realized the bad feeling had not come after all.

"How are you doing?" I asked, and she smiled and nodded.

"Are you hungry?" I said.

"No," she said. "I think I'm going to be happy."

10

I buried my head for days and did nothing but work for Stacen, ride the bike home, read a little, sleep when I could. It wasn't easy to sleep because I was thinking all the time. I saw my life more clearly than before, how I was different from other people. Katherine, for instance. Katherine who lived in the now. I lived in the now, too, but I also lived in the then. I was going back to Belize, I was going back every day, I had to. But I didn't stay there. I couldn't live in my imagination. I hung out there awhile and then I returned to the other part of my life, to Toddy's Café and Stacen and my room off Franklin Street.

At work, I tried to keep out of Stacen's way. I turned out some good bread, but most of it was going into the freezer. Nobody much walked through Stacen's front door the month of December other than a few college kids who asked for Coca-Cola and french fries and got miffed when they found out we didn't sell that sort of thing. I didn't call Katherine for five days after I told her about Ellie. It wasn't because I didn't want to talk to Katherine. I love talking to Katherine. If my ship goes down once and for all, I want Katherine in my lifeboat. If I'm stuck on a desert isle, I want Katherine. She's a great listener. Everybody says so. Katherine will listen to Republicans. She will listen to Baptists. She listens to other librarians.

The reason I didn't call Katherine didn't have anything to do with Ellie either. The way I felt about Ellie, that was all dead and gone for years. Katherine knew it, too. I was sure she knew it, but I was afraid to put her to the test. Because what if I called her and she wouldn't listen to me anymore? That would have been too much. It would have killed me. Instead, I just didn't call. Five days I stared at the phone and those red words on the wall, what I started to think was a message from God maybe, but I wouldn't read the last of it, the final word. If God had something to say to me, God could take a number.

But five days was a long time. You can clear your head in five days. You can get over yourself. I made the call. On the fifth day. Katherine had a lot to say about how long it took me to find the necessary gumption to make a simple phone call.

"The phone works both ways," I said. "You know my number."

"You're supposed to call me," said Katherine.

"Why?"

"That's the way it's done."

"Can't it change?" I told her. "Can't we change?"

"No," said Katherine. "Everything's change with you right now. I need something to stay the same."

So then we didn't talk for some more days, only now it was because she was sore at me, and every time I called she was busy. She was cooking. She was vacuuming. She was giving the cats a bath. We lost that week. It was no big deal. It was just time. It was just time's wounded chariot knocking at my door.

When business was bad, Stacen liked to brood. She'd pull a pencil out of her hair and start making lists on a napkin. Stacen loved lists. She read once in a magazine that you should write out your vision of yourself, where you want to be in five years, where you want to be in twenty. When she tried to take inventory—the flour, the cornmeal, the oil and sugar—she was reminded of the need to plan her life. Pretty soon she was scribbling away on a half dozen napkins, looking up now and then to scowl at the walls she needed to paint and the tables she should have thrown out, they're so wobbly. And then of course she looked at me and had to start a whole new list to number the ways I wasn't helping her get where she wanted to go, what a fool I was to leave my loving wife Katherine, heavy with child, just so I could come sit at one of her broken-down tables and hold the hand of a young girl who was not my daughter but could have been. The injustice of the world could push Stacen right to the edge.

I signed out early on a Saturday, business was so slow. I thought it might make Stacen happy if I got off the clock. I took a seat at a table near the window, the same table where I sat with Sara the week before. (I liked how Sara came to see me. When she left, I watched her walk away, and I realized how thin she was getting. I had a funny feeling about that, as if she were evaporating.) There hadn't been a customer in the café since ten o'clock, and the tension had built all morning in the kitchen. My table was close to the door, the safest place to be if Stacen came undone. I knew if I didn't get out of there soon, I would be on trial. Still, I couldn't move. I was out of energy, pasted to my chair.

Stacen came out of the kitchen to wipe down the already clean tables. She had the biggest knife she owned tucked under her arm, a knife that was supposed to be for cutting a cake but was so absurdly long nobody used it for cake. Mostly we used it to retrieve spoons and bottle caps from behind the espresso machine. That knife looked like a sword from the Civil War. A cake sword.

"Little enough to do," she said. She set her sword down on my table. "You might as well go home."

The words were a relief to me. I'd expected her to say something more direct, something like, who the hell were you sitting with here the other day?

She took one of those long Stacenish looks out the window. She could see things nobody else could see. She could see the back of Sara's head from the Saturday before as it floated down the sidewalk into the winter gloom. She could see Sara's thin shoulders.

"So," she said, her smile a little too sweet. She tucked her pencil back in her hair and felt around up there until she found another pencil, a sharper one. "You son of a bitch," she said quietly, pointing that pencil at my nose. "Who the hell were you sitting with here the other day? What little home-wrecking princess was that?"

I found I had the energy to stand up after all, and I did. I kept the table between us.

"It's not that way," I said to Stacen. "Sara's a friend. We had a class together." It wasn't exactly the truth. We never actually had the class. The truth can wear you out after a while. I thought we might give the truth a rest.

"Listen pal," said Stacen. And I started backing up. I did a lot of backing up around Stacen. A few minutes before, she had looked tired and as sweet as Stacen could look. Now her eyes were on fire. She took a step toward my side of the table.

"I've about reached my limit with you," she said. "You have a wife at home. She has a child growing inside her womb. This wife, this woman who I have known for years and who I seem to love far more than you do, she's being incredibly patient with you, waiting for you to get over this . . . this thing you're going through." She took another step toward me. I took a step away.

"Katherine let you quit your job," said Stacen. "She let you have your little panic attack. She let you move into that dive you live in now." Stacen took two steps in my direction. I took three steps away. It was like some kind of dance and we needed to learn it.

"She didn't even say much when I told her you've been sitting in my café with some teary-eyed . . . coed." Stacen pointed at me again and made me wish I was home in bed because she didn't point her finger and she didn't point her pencil this time. She pointed that sword at me, that cake harpoon.

"Damn you, Tanner."

"Take it easy," I said.

"Well, excuse me," said Stacen. "I meant to say goddamn you, Tanner."

Stacen didn't know what she was pointing at me. She didn't know she held a knife in her hand, I'm pretty sure.

"You better hear me out," she said.

"I'm listening," I told her.

"You see," said Stacen, "the thing is this—I am not Katherine."

"I know that," I said. "I can see that."

"I've got no reason to be nice to you," she said.

The door opened up behind me. I felt a gust of cold air come in and then I heard little feet, and Stacen's children were throwing themselves at her knees.

"Hey Stace," said Tony. "Hey Tanner."

Tony's a little on the heavy side, and having a wife in the bakery business hasn't been the best thing for him. There's more of him than there used to be. When he walks, you get the impression he's guiding his body in the general direction it needs to go. He guided it between the tables and headed for the cooling racks in the kitchen. Stacen had taken a batch of cinnamon rolls out of the oven. The smell of bread and sugar and cinnamon was thick in the air, like something you wouldn't mind swimming through.

Stacen put her free arm around one of her kids, the older one. Some of her anger seeped away.

"Tanner," she said, measuring my name out carefully. I thought she might put the knife down on the nearest table. I thought she might be worried about impaling a small child. "If you don't get yourself together pretty soon," she said, "I don't know what I'm going to do with you."

Tony reappeared from behind the counter, a hot roll in one hand, a cup of coffee in the other. "Is this one of those employer-employee things?" he said.

"I don't think so," I said.

"Yes," said Stacen.

"Yes, of course," I said. "It certainly is," I said. "I can see that now."

Her kids ran to the counter and pressed their faces up against the glass. It would have been another good time for me to leave, except Stacen had worked it so she was between me and the door. She stood there on purpose. It was touch and go—I might have a job another day, I might not. There was nothing new about that. The giant knife was the new thing. I closed my eyes and tried to make the words come to me, the words Stacen wanted to hear.

"Let me explain about Sara," I said.

"Shut up," said Stacen. "I don't want to hear about someone named Sara."

"Oh dang," said Tony. He was reading the newspaper at a table next to the espresso machine, his feet on a chair. Stacen hated it when he put his feet up. She glared at him, but he didn't notice. I would have noticed. When she glared at me that way, I could feel it.

"Did you have a good day?" asked Tony, his nose deep in his paper. "Did we make lots of money?"

I wished he hadn't said that. It was ill-advised. Tony had his attention devoted to some millionaire ballplayer in the sports section, but I could see the heat in Stacen's cheeks. Her eyes bore down on the top of her husband's head. She rested her hand on the table.

"Did you sell a lot of cookies?" said Tony.

"What's it look like to you, asshole?" said Stacen.

Tony is dull, but he's not that dull. Something in his wife's voice made him put the paper down and come over to my side of the table.

"When you look around the room, do you see a lot of customers?" said

Stacen. "Are they lined up at the cash register? Are they getting in their special orders for the holidays?"

"Honey," said Tony. He tried to backpedal, but that was the thing about Tony: he didn't know how to backpedal. He was a straight-ahead kind of guy. If he'd been a dinosaur, he would have put one foot in the tar pits and said, "What the hell," and tried to go on across to the other side.

"Things are going to get better," said Tony. "I'm sure of it. You're in a slump is all."

The front door opened again and I was glad for the distraction even though I couldn't believe my eyes. It was Croker, looking like he'd just escaped from somewhere. He had a white-haired lady with him, all pearls and cashmere. She looked addled to me. They both did. You could tell the way they stopped inside the door and stared that they hadn't been inside the café since Toddy's time. They were trying to remember what it used to look like. I didn't figure her memory could be too good, or why would she be out with Croker? The woman was better dressed than Croker, but older. Then I saw it, the resemblance. She had to be his mother. They had the same bushy eyebrows. If she'd had more of a mustache, she could have been his older brother.

Tony gave Stacen one of his wise looks, as if he thought these two were going to put Stacen's day back on the right track. I knew better. Croker was cheap, and his mother wouldn't have been able to buy all her fancy clothes if she was throwing her money away in restaurants. They would come in for a cup of tea and look at the cakes and the muffins and the little pictures of all the sandwiches Stacen knew how to prepare, and they would make the right noises, and on a good day they might order a bagel and split it.

"Sit anywhere," I said. "Someone will be right with you."

"Could I have a word with you?" said Croker.

I let him draw me aside. I didn't mind. I didn't think Stacen would threaten me in front of a customer.

"This is your mother?"

"Yes," said Croker. "How did you know that?"

"Lucky guess."

A shadow moved over the tables at the front of the café, someone passing by on the sidewalk. That shadow made me shiver. I didn't look to see who it was. Keep going, old shadow, I said to myself. We don't need you here today.

"We're looking for Sara," said Croker. For some reason he was speaking softly. He didn't want to bring his mother into the conversation.

"I haven't seen her," I said. I spoke softly, too. "It's been a few days."

"We were admiring your place," said Croker's mother. She doffed her hat. I'd never seen anyone really doff a hat before.

"We were what?" said Croker.

"We were admiring what this man has done with this old café," said the mother, raising her voice a notch, and pointing at me. "This place was a dump before he took it over."

At that, even Tony could see the fire in Stacen's eyes. If Stacen got any madder at me, she was going to do one of those spontaneous combustion things.

"Oh God, no," I said.

"Well, it's true," said Croker's mother.

"Stacen, honey," said Tony, "listen to me." His voice was meant to be soothing, directed only to Stacen. "They can't know this is your café unless you tell them it is."

"Was Sara okay when you saw her?" asked Croker.

"Why is everyone whispering?" said the old gal. "We're looking for my granddaughter," she said, this time to Stacen. "She said something about getting a job down here."

From the kitchen, I heard the unmistakable sound of a cake pan falling to the floor. One of Stacen's little girls began to cry, quietly at first, but it was going to get louder. It always got louder.

"Get the children out of the kitchen," said Stacen between her teeth. She was talking to her husband. Another pan fell, only this time it was as if a pan had been thrown down from a great height. It sounded like somebody making thunder at a student play over at the college. Both little girls were crying.

"Croker," said the older woman. I couldn't believe it. She called her own son by his last name. "Croker, what is that? What do I hear?" She had the look on her face old people get sometimes. She thought someone was trying to play a trick on her.

"Now, Mother," said Croker. She was carrying a lady's handkerchief. He watched her twist it into a fierce knot.

"Where's Sara?" said Croker's mother. "And why won't this woman wait on us? They could use a little help down here. If your friend's so smart, why can't he make her wait on us?"

Tony moved toward the kitchen, but he didn't take his eye off Stacen. He looked like a basketball player trying to cover two opponents at the same time. He tried to make it appear as if he wasn't in a hurry. Another crash, and both children came scooting into the dining room. The older daughter had to come around Tony, but the younger one shot right through his legs as if he wasn't even there. Tony could have been one of those bead curtains you don't see anymore. Both girls had flour in their hair, and the little one had blueberry stains on her chin and on her dress and a large muffin in her hand. The big one was trying to get it away from her. They made a parade, the littler kid chased by the big one, who was chased in turn by Tony. I would have chased someone, but Stacen had me trapped behind the table with a sword.

"I don't know," said Croker. His mother looked as if she was wired together with coat hangers and some of the coat hangers had got bent out of shape. Croker looked at me, and he looked at his old mother, and there was fear in his eyes. "We were hoping to talk with Sara. We were hoping for someplace quiet."

"You want it quiet?" said Stacen. "He wants it quiet?"

"I think . . . ," said Croker.

"Don't think," said Stacen. And I knew what was coming, but it was too late to do anything about it except to get a little closer to the wall and make myself small.

"Don't think. Don't offer advice. Don't sit down," said Stacen. "Don't even blink your eyes at me. Don't do it, don't do it, don't do it. Don't shit, don't fart, don't breathe. Just get the hell out of my bakery."

The old woman's head came up and her lips formed a small, straight line. She was Croker's mother, after all. I told my legs to have a little courage and make their move for the door, but my legs couldn't hear me. All they could hear was Stacen yelling *Don't, Don't, Don't.* Tony grabbed his older child by the shirt just at the moment the girl grabbed her little sister by the hair.

"My cake," cried the baby, watching her prize fall from her hands to the linoleum.

"It was mine first," said the older girl. She let go of her sister's hair and made a dive for the stuff on the floor.

"Who's she yelling at?" said the crone.

"You heard me," said Stacen to the only two customers she was going to see for the rest of the afternoon. "Go away from my café."

"*Your* café?" said the old one. She slapped at Croker's hands. He was trying to guide her to the door. "But *he* said . . ." The woman pointed at me.

"No I didn't," I said. "I said no such thing."

"I don't care what he said," said Stacen. "I don't care what he does. I don't care who he sleeps with. But as long as he's in this café," and she took a deep breath that made me want to sit down and put my head between my knees, *"He fucking works for me."*

The room went absolutely silent. Tony turned white as flour, and both of Stacen's little girls looked up at her in wonder.

"I never heard the like of it," said Mrs. Croker. "You told me there wouldn't be children underfoot. You told me we could talk to Sara." She was saying that to her son. "You know I don't like children underfoot."

I'd got my hand on the cake sword. I was hiding it behind my back, but it didn't make any difference. Stacen headed for the kitchen, where there were rolling pins and cleavers and worse. Tony and I had to work at it to get the two Crokers moving toward the door.

"Go on," said Tony, first to those two, who needed the encouragement, and then to me, who didn't. "You go home, too, Tanner. Give her room to breathe."

He pushed me out the door onto the sidewalk. I tried to give him the cake sword, but he looked at it as if it was a murder weapon. He didn't want his fingerprints on it. Croker's white-haired mother was moving down the pavement pretty well, considering her age. Croker was right behind her. He looked back one time as if maybe he wanted to apologize, and I waved the sword at him, and they disappeared around the corner.

"Go," said Tony. "I mean it. I have to see about the kids." He shut the door on me.

There I was, standing in the gutter with a lethal weapon and without my jacket, and it was getting cold, the middle of December. I knew better than to go back in the café for a thing like a jacket. What was pneumonia, after all, compared to the wrath of Stacen? I looked through the window and saw her at the counter. She was crying and shaking, and her kids were holding onto her knees. Tony was stroking her back. I wished him well because I think

Stacen is right most of the time. She has my number. The thing is, it's only part of my number. Though it could be most of my number. I looked at my watch and saw that it was four o'clock. I never stayed at Stacen's that late. It was the time of day I called Katherine and I had a feeling in my stomach that said I wasn't going to get to a phone in time, or I was going to call her and she wouldn't be home. I ran around to the back of the café, careful not to fall on Stacen's sword. I stashed that thing in the bushes. I grabbed my bicycle out of the alley, and as I rode to my apartment I tried not to think about Katherine being home or not being home, about Sara lost in the world, about Stacen's trembling shoulders. The afternoon was so cold my eyes teared up. I had to stop twice and wipe my face with the front of my shirt.

She answered the phone on the eighth ring.

"You're there," I said, making an effort to control my breathing. The apartment was as cold as the outdoors. I moved around the room as much as the cord on the phone would allow me to, putting on a sweater and my long coat, trying to stop shivering.

"What's wrong?" asked Katherine.

"Nothing."

"Tanner?"

"I'm cold is all."

I asked her to wait a minute while I got a blanket off the bed, and she didn't say anything more until I got settled in my chair. I tried not to let my teeth knock together.

"I've been talking to my cousin this afternoon," said Katherine.

"Which one?" She had twenty cousins. She had cousins all over the country.

"The one in Louisville. Married to the French teacher."

"The French teacher," I said.

"Yeah, well," said Katherine. "They've invited me to move up to Louisville, stay with them. I can stay as long as I want to. Have the baby in their home."

"You wouldn't do that."

"Tell me why I shouldn't," said Katherine. "Give me one lousy reason. No, don't give me a lousy reason. I'm tired of lousy. I'm tired to death."

"I don't want you to go," I said.

"I can't talk to you right now," said Katherine. "You're making me too angry."

"Tell me what I can do," I said. "Tell me how I can show you I want you to stay."

There was a long pause while she thought about it. There was static on the line, somebody else's far-off conversation, another state, another life.

"Katherine?" I said. "Are you there?"

"I'm here."

I tried to picture her. She was sitting in the chair I bought her just after we got married. It had one of those matching ottomans. I pictured her with her feet up. She has small feet for a tall woman, beautiful delicate feet.

"Talk to me, Tanner," she said. "Just talk to me."

11

*S*o I talked to her. I told her about Junie. Maybe I didn't tell her everything, but I told her the parts that mattered. I told her the boy's real name. I read it on his paperwork one evening in Fairbanks's office when nobody was looking. *Reuben Bonner Gillett, Jr., brother to Albert.* I told Katherine how, when the new boy walked upstairs to the office his first day at New Hope, he was so scared I thought he might fall over. He only managed to tell Fairbanks the one thing: "Please don't call me Reuben."

"Why not?" said Fairbanks.

"They call me Junie," said the boy.

He wanted nothing to do with his given name. But if he shared his father's name on some piece of paper in Fairbanks's office, it meant somebody loved him once, on the day he was born. Somebody wanted to honor the child and the father with the gift of a shared name. What happened to Reuben senior, I wanted to know. Where was the boy's mother? Where did a love like that come from, and where did it disappear to?

He didn't need to worry about his name at New Hope. We called him Junie from the day he arrived. We called other boys worse things. *Big Mouth . . . Nervous Boy . . . Squinty Eye.* One fuzzy-headed kid with a raspy voice was called *Power-to-Jesus.* His father was a failed preacher and a drunk. Another boy, Dale, was surprised with his pants down one evening at the edge of the bush where he was keeping himself company behind a tree. By morning, he was renamed *Treeboy.*

"Sake of, he could love that tree, boy," said Albert.

I told Katherine about the names, how sometimes a boy had to try on a few names before one fit. It happened that way with Feliciano, whose arm was broken when he was a baby. He never saw a doctor for it and his arm healed wrong. He walked around with his hand held away from his side, as if that hand was dirty and he was looking for someplace to wash it off. The other boys called him *Broke Arm,* but Brother Constant didn't like the name and tried to put a stop to it. He called Feliciano *Side Arm.*

"There's no broke to that arm at all," he said. "Just one lee turn to the side."

Brother Constant did all he could to make the rest of us say it, too, say *Side Arm* instead of *Broke Arm.* Some of the boys went along with Brother Constant until one evening, just as it was getting dark and time to go in, Feliciano got kicked hard on the soccer field. As he lay on the ground, weeping silently, nursing his privates, the boys gathered around him. *Broke Arm* became *Broke Dick.*

"Oh no," said Brother Constant. "No, no, no." He took a firm stand. "Not that. This boy's name is not *Broke Dick.*" He didn't want the name to take hold. That was a hard name to leave behind, *Broke Dick.* But we had a hot spell, and few of the boys had the energy to dodge Brother Constant for long. Ultimately, he chose a day and threatened to whip the next boy who used the word *broke* in any kind of sentence at all. By the evening bell, everyone at New Hope had seen the wisdom in giving the name up. They settled on a new name for Feliciano. *Side Dick.*

"That's better," said Brother Constant. "Give a boy some lee respect."

The day Junie arrived, Fairbanks chose not to beat the boy right away, whatever he was going to be called. He told Side Dick to show Junie around the school, and he let Albert go along with him. Fairbanks saw how it was. Albert didn't mean to let Junie out of his sight. The two older boys showed Junie the cows and the sheep, the chickens, and Albert's favorites, the rabbits. When they came back, Side Dick, that big talker, was silent, his face gray as ashes. The other boys laughed at him. They told Side Dick he was acting *serious*. It was a great failing on any boy's part to act serious.

"Unu could laugh," said Side Dick. "Unu could laugh now. But that lee boy up there in Mr. Fairbanks office, that Junie, that is no ordinary boy." And he went off to be by himself.

It was a mystery to me what Side Dick was going on about. Junie was just one boy in a sea of boys. He was not the youngest and not the oldest. He was small. He told us he was twelve years old, and it could have been true, but I've seen six-year-olds in Katherine's library who were taller and better coordinated than Junie. I didn't see what made him special. The boy didn't speak except to whisper, and still, everyone who came into a room where he was working or singing or fooling around with bottle caps soon came over to talk to him. He had the smile of a clown and the bright eyes of a boy who is either extra clever or already insane. He didn't look you in the eye. He looked at a place near your knees or in the dirt at your feet, and he held his body turned away as if he wanted to hide something he had stolen.

He was hiding his hand. When he was younger, when he and Albert still lived at home, there was some kind of accident and his hand was burned. It was the same situation with Side Dick and Bus'up, with half a dozen other boys who had strange lumps and scars. There was no doctor to look after Junie. Instead, he held the three smallest fingers on that hand tight against his palm, trying to hold off the pain of his burn. When the pain went away, his hand had a new shape. All he could use on that right hand was a thumb and one finger. The other fingers were glued to his palm. Another boy, someone like Albert, would have learned before long to do everything he had to do with the left hand, the good one, but Junie never learned. When he helped Albert in the kitchen, he passed out slices of bread with his bad hand until the boys objected, calling Junie names and throwing the bread back at him. Albert felt called upon to fight them all, one after another, and for a while he was punished after every meal. Fairbanks himself came to the kitchen and told Brother Constant to give Junie a different job, "One that will keep that bloody hand out of sight."

The hand was half of it. His face was wrong, too. When I went to collect him that afternoon at Miss Penny's, I thought the scar below his nose came from a harelip. I didn't look at it close up until later, when we were in the office and Fairbanks turned the boy's head to the light. Where a normal face would have two nostrils and a small piece of cartilage between them, some-thing I have learned to call a septum, Junie had only a single large hole the size of a nickel. I wanted to know about Junie's face, how it happened. Then again, I didn't want to know.

Fairbanks went to Jamaica for a three-week course of study, and when he came back, a different man returned to New Hope. Fairbanks had always been quiet. Now he spoke less than before. Most afternoons, he went into his office and closed the door and wouldn't answer a knock unless he knew it was one of the officers outside. When he came out of the office, Fairbanks took long walks around the grounds, mumbling to himself. He was wrestling with big ideas. I didn't know what to make of it. I stayed out of his way while he made his rounds and gave his blustery orders. *Boys, unu stand up straight. Boys, unu stop this foolishness. Boys, unu keep the noise down.*

"Boys, unu pick up this trash," he said one afternoon. He was walking past my house, trailed by two bored tough guys he had pulled out of the carpen-ter's shop. He left before they had a chance to obey him or disobey him. The two boys fell into arguing about which of them Fairbanks had been talking to. Soon enough they left, too, going off in different directions. When they were gone, I went down off my veranda and picked up the offending pieces of paper, half a dozen pages of arithmetic that had leaked out of the schoolroom.

"I see you're conscientious."

Fairbanks's voice startled me. He had nearly disappeared into the shade of a tree. It might have been the first time I ever looked right at him. He was handsome, I guess, a couple of inches shorter than me, six or eight years older. He didn't smile much, as if something in life hadn't gone right for him, something important. I tried to remember what I'd been told about him. He had traveled to the States a couple of times, to Philadelphia, where he stayed with his sister. He loved to play basketball. He had a ball under one arm now and he was looking for the school's air pump. It had been missing since he came back from Jamaica.

"I told those boys to police this area," said Fairbanks. "I didn't mean for their teacher to do it."

"Maybe it's my fault," I said. "Maybe I give them too much work."

"Maybe I should call them over and give them a good beating," said Fairbanks. The words were more bitter than anything he had said in weeks. I smoothed out the page of arithmetic problems I held in my hands. I hoped he wouldn't ask to see it. If he found a name on the paper, one more boy was in trouble.

"It's what the old Fairbanks would have done," I said. My voice wandered a little when I said it, but only a little. One of Ellie's words came to mind. I'd heard her use the word—audacity—plenty of times. Now I had it, too. I had audacity. I probably picked it up from Price.

"The old Fairbanks," said the headmaster. "The boys hated that old Fairbanks."

"He was a hard man to like," I said. My voice wouldn't behave. It didn't really tremble. It didn't break. More like it couldn't make up its mind.

"Maybe so," said Fairbanks. "Still, these boys need a firm hand."

"Boys need a lot of things," I said. I tried to say it gently. I didn't want to go any farther out on that limb. I'd used up all my audacity. "Sometimes they need a break." I looked off at the schoolroom in the distance, and at the sky beyond. The clouds had formed long gray beards of rain to the east of us.

"Rain di come," I said. It was a long speech for me in Creole.

"Right, right," said Fairbanks. He wasn't thinking about weather. "Rain di come," said Fairbanks. "Wind di blow."

The two boys who had disappeared returned, like magic. I didn't see them run across the grass. They simply took shape before my eyes, and a third boy with them, Junie. He stood in front of the other two. I had the impression he was leading them. He carried a small paper bag and searched the ground with the others, looking for the papers I had already picked up.

"Mr. Fairbanks, sir," said the largest boy, Benn. "We doesn't find any trash."

"This place here *clean*," said Junie.

Fairbanks looked at Junie, but even Fairbanks had to look away. He studied the others. He studied me.

"Look here," he said at last. "I don't want to see Mr. Tanner pick up after you again."

"No, sir," said Junie.

The rain began to fall as if someone had reached up and turned on the water. I knew the boys wanted to run for shelter. They stood very still, waiting to see what Fairbanks would do to them next. But he didn't do anything. He walked off toward his office. He wanted to stay out of that weather as much as they did. I took the stairs to my veranda and I watched from there. It was a look or a signal too small for me to read. I don't know any other way to say it: Junie dismissed those other boys. When the two of them had run off toward the dining hall, Junie stood alone in the yard, holding his hand up to the rain, holding his face up to it, as though the rain could wash away his wounds.

I tried to avoid Junie, but he drew me to him, the way he drew everyone to him. When they weren't fighting with each other, the boys stuck together, especially the young ones. They kept their secrets. Junie couldn't read, but the others tried to read to him. No, that isn't quite right. They read *for* him, as if they were trying to impress him. They surprised me, the things they did if they thought Junie was watching. Boomba loved to draw. It was a desire nobody could discourage, and if Junie was around to watch, Boomba filled page after page of notebook paper with drawings of fighter planes and Land Rovers, scowling the whole time as though he hated the power such a small boy could hold over him.

It was hard on Albert, having Junie at New Hope. Albert loved his brother, so he learned to be a fierce and dirty fighter who could hold his own with boys twice his size. Whatever it took to watch out for Junie. But it wasn't just Albert that kept the others from picking on Junie. Junie's wounds and his strange whispering voice frightened the others. He could act a little serious, too. Twice during his first week at New Hope, he called all the available boys together on the playground, once in the schoolroom during their recess. He asked them to pray with him. At first, the boys were willing to come to him. They believed in sin and shame. They knew they had displeased God, or displeased the people God liked most. That was why they were at New Hope. They were afraid to ignore Junie's call even when, after a few of his prayer meetings, they saw that once he got a crowd together he didn't know how to proceed. They stood around for a quarter of an hour, then sidled off from Junie with the same hangdog look they wore when they avoided the missionaries on Tuesday and Friday evenings.

I gave Junie a seat in the front row of the schoolroom where the smallest boys sat. I had to think the smallest were the youngest, but I couldn't be sure. More than one boy didn't know his own birthday. The lee boy named Darnell tried to convince me he had never been born at all. The older boys tried to explain the process to him.

"For you pa, he juke for you ma. He left one seed in there that grow huge like a watermelon. Then out you come, one bighead ugly baby."

"That never happen," Darnell kept saying. He thought the others were playing a trick on him. "I would know about that," he said.

I sat Junie down between Darnell and Boomba, but it was a mistake. Boomba was so small he felt like he had to talk tougher and act up more than all the rest put together to protect himself. He spent a morning drawing pictures for Junie. He had a fever for drawing pictures, showing Junie each one as soon as he made the last mark on the page. When he ran out of paper, Boomba jumped up from his desk crying, and he hit Junie on the ear with his fist. Junie knew less about fighting than he did about prayer meetings. He laughed when Boomba hit him, and then Junie threw his arms out like someone in deep water and made strange sounds in the back of his throat. Albert was late that morning coming from the kitchen. He appeared at the door of the classroom as if he had been summoned. He picked Boomba up and carried him outside and threw him into a prickly bush. Then Albert led Junie away by the hand. I let them go. We didn't see either brother again for the rest of the day.

I didn't think I could teach Junie much of anything. He smiled at me, whatever I told him, but the way he looked at a pencil, I wondered if he had ever seen one before. I knew I'd have to let him stay in the classroom as long as Fairbanks wanted me to, whether the boy learned to read or not. Junie wasn't much worse than the others. Darnell could still barely write his name, and Side Dick had made no progress with his reading. Side Dick tried to cover up the fact that he couldn't read by turning every lesson into a small exercise in pornography.

"She did what?" he would say, holding up one of the illustrations in the book, pretending he was indignant. "With that dog? Boy."

Before Fairbanks brought him to New Hope, Side Dick had lived in the marketplace, eating the fruit that was no longer fit to be sold. He bragged to the others about his life in the marketplace, but Junie wouldn't listen to him.

"No need for tell me about no marketplace," said Junie. "No need for tell me about no fruit. I know about boys like you."

"Boy, you no know me," said Side Dick. There was fear in his eyes. "You no know me at all."

A few days later, Fairbanks appeared at my door again. It was the close of day, and Darnell had just finished ringing the bell for the evening roll call.

"I'd take a cup of coffee," said Fairbanks. Clouds had formed once more, moving in from the east, heavy with water. It always rained when Fairbanks was around. I made two cups of Nescafé. There were cookies Ellie had brought out from Belize City and I shared them, but I thought hard about it first. We talked about basketball and cars. We talked about the boys.

"I don't want to beat them so much," said Fairbanks. He lowered his voice, afraid someone might hear him. "That Junie. I don't think I could beat him for true. Only, it's what they know."

"Yes," I said. "They know it."

Fairbanks gave me a weary look. I wondered if Hobson had been right about me. I seemed to be turning into some kind of liberal.

"Maybe the old Fairbanks learned something new in Jamaica," I said.

"I doubt it," said Fairbanks. "This Fairbanks is an old dog. You can't teach an old dog a damn thing."

I thought about that. I wondered if it was true.

"Did they beat you when you were a boy?" I asked.

"What?" said Fairbanks. "You can believe they did. Until I got bigger than my mother."

I started to ask about his father. I thought better of it.

"Oh, I know you Americans," said Fairbanks. "I know how you do it. Sometimes you just take away *privileges.* The credit card. The keys to the car." He laughed. It wasn't a mean laugh. "It's hard to take privileges from these New Hope boys. What have they got? What do we take from them?"

I laughed, too. But I was thinking about the bruises Fairbanks had left on Albert's legs after we ate the rabbit. And the way the boy named Gordon had been forced to kneel in the sun. I was thinking about my part in it. I got up from the chair I was sitting in and went to put more water on the stove. My hands wouldn't hold still. I held them out to the flame from the stove.

"Are you cold?" asked Fairbanks. He came to stand in the doorway to my kitchen.

"No," I said. "Well, maybe."

"I never feel cold in Belize," said Fairbanks. "Philadelphia. That was cold."

I hadn't been cold in a year. I wondered how I would recognize real cold if I felt it again. "What did you think of the winter?" I asked. "In Philadelphia. You liked the snow?"

"Snow," said Fairbanks. "Who could imagine such a thing as snow? Snow is bothersome. Snow is ridiculous. Why is there snow?" He watched me carefully as I waited for the water to boil. He could tell I was upset. Thinking about Junie was enough to upset anyone. Fairbanks didn't want to talk about the boy either. Together, we tried not to. We drank our coffee when it was ready. We talked about the seasons and about a girl he knew in San Ignacio, and about a Christmas party. When the second cup of coffee was gone, he stood up to leave.

"I have a friend coming this weekend," said Fairbanks. "He wants to see what we do with these boys. He was my English teacher once, a long time ago, at the Teachers College. He's a priest and an American, but he's been here a long time. Maybe we'll kill a sheep, have a barbecue. If we're going to take privileges away from these boys, we need to give them some privileges first."

He stopped at the screen door. He examined the screen, a place where it had been torn and someone, maybe it was Hobson, had mended it.

"I'll invite you up after dinner for a drink. We'll get our minds off things. This man, this priest, he loves to drink." Fairbanks couldn't bring himself to leave, quite. He had something to tell me.

"If you think too hard about all of this, you could go crazy. Look at me," he said, laughing. "Upset over a boy. It's too much."

I hadn't admitted to Ellie what a failure I was as a teacher. Ellie was my teacher. On the weekends, I shared her bed or she shared mine. Once in Miami, in an earlier lifetime, I'd longed to have her hands touch me, and now they traveled where they wanted to. Maybe it was trial and error, but I was learning to please her, too. When her time came, her small breasts grew tender and she asked me to be gentle. Sometimes when we were together, she cried without telling me why. I suspected it was something to do with her professor and the years she gave to him. I hoped it wasn't because of anything I did, or failed to do.

"No," she told me, holding me tight. "You're good. You're fine." And her mouth traveled down my neck so I wouldn't know if the wet places she left on me came from her lips or from her tears.

Ellie made a distinction between the loving we did and the loving we didn't do. I hardly thought about it. It was all wonderful to me. Lying with me in a dark room, she wanted me to tell her everything and anything. What I told her didn't always make sense to me, so I didn't see how it could make sense to her. I told her about the years I wasted in school, and she told me those years weren't a waste, not really, not yet. It was too soon to say a thing like that.

One night I was with Ellie, but I was thinking about Junie, picturing how he tried to hold a pencil in that wounded hand. "Tell me," she said. She traced her fingers over my lips to encourage me. I wasn't sure I knew how to tell her. It was the real stuff. Once I started, there would be no holding back. "Don't be afraid," she said. And she said my name. She said *Tanner,* over and over again. It felt as if nobody had ever said my name before.

So I told her about everyone at New Hope: Brother Constant and Señor Muerte and Fairbanks with his rope. We talked into the night. Mostly I talked and she listened. I told her about all the mornings I stood outside the schoolhouse door with a knot in my stomach, wanting to walk back to my house and pretend I was sick. I told her about the reading books from Canada and the books of arithmetic problems that were soiled and dog-eared and had so many pages missing I could seldom give three boys the same assignment. I talked about the vacancy in Junie's eyes. At one point I think I cried a little, but then I must have stopped. I didn't have a lot of experience crying. That was new to me, too.

"Do you have paints?" she asked. "For your classroom? Are there scissors and paper to make things with?"

I didn't have any of that. When she asked, it made me realize how grim it must have felt to Junie and the others, this going to school. My classroom was only a way to get out of working in the field.

"You could read to them," she said. "They would love to hear a story."

I got up from her bed and walked into the next room. She thought I was angry with her, but I wasn't. I hadn't figured that out for myself, the reading, though I spent as much of my own time as I could with a book, trying to shut out the truth of where I was with stories about other places, about somebody else's adventures.

• • •

Father Hugh arrived on the Saturday bus. Fairbanks asked me to meet him at the road and drive him back to school. I wanted Ellie to come out, too, even thought she might ride the bus with the priest. I wanted her to meet the new Fairbanks and his old teacher, Father Hugh, but she called at the last minute and said she wasn't feeling up to it. Maybe I described the event too well. The boys were excited about the barbecue. Fairbanks told Señor Muerte to kill a large sheep so there would be enough for everyone, and to make sure he buried the head and the offal before the priest arrived. And buried it deep.

"Those damn pigs," said Fairbanks. He was remembering the rabbit skins. "They get into everything. We should kill them."

"We could kill them," said Señor Muerte, his eyes glowing. He held out his sharp knife. "I can kill a pig."

Fairbanks's eyes grew wide. He looked at me, as if he wanted my support. "Just the sheep," he said. "We'll save the pigs. Another time."

In the kitchen, Brother Constant couldn't hide his great, toothless smile. He fussed around the stove and out in the yard behind the kitchen the whole morning, where he cut up the sheep and laid a fire in a barrel that had been sawed in half. When the coals were ready, he put the meat on to sizzle and smoke. I had never seen that much meat on one grill. Once I gave in to the fact that Ellie wasn't coming, I kept my eye on the barbecue, forgetting anything else. Fairbanks had invited his favorite girlfriend to the party, a small shy woman with beautiful brown eyes that could drift out of focus. I recognized the blouse she wore, pink against her dark skin. I had seen her in the blouse several times before. She watched from the edge of the ball field where Brother Constant had set up his grill, moving with a slow grace that might have hidden something else. She was sad, or she didn't feel well. She watched the meat on the grill with me. I wondered if she got enough to eat at home.

When the food was ready, the boys took their plates of meat and rice and flour tortillas, and they wandered off in twos and threes to sit on the grass with their backs to each other. They ate until their bellies were swollen, then sat and talked quietly. "Barbecue." I heard the word whispered here and there. The older boys slipped away to smoke, past Señor Muerte smiling and talking to himself, his hand on the knife in his scabbard.

After dinner, we went up the stairs to Fairbanks's house. Father Hugh sat down wearily in one of Fairbanks's chairs. I had talked to the priest a little during dinner. He was a small man with a big head and pale skin and arms that looked too short for the rest of his body. He had an East Coast accent, maybe from Boston. I couldn't be sure. The priest loved the bread Albert brought from the kitchen as much as I did. He had eaten most of a loaf at dinner and asked for more, but there wasn't any more.

"Forget the mutton," said the priest. "That bread is delicious." He watched as Fairbanks made the drinks, pouring from a half-gallon bottle of Scotch, a brand I'd never heard of before.

"Whoa, Matthew," said Father Hugh, taking a sip. "That's stout. Put a little water in the first round."

I hadn't heard Fairbanks's other name before. I said it softly to myself, Matthew, and wondered if I could get away with using it. I took a bottle of beer and settled into a chair near the door where I could look out and see the boys on the ball field. Junie sat alone off to one side. When the last bell of the evening rang, I watched the boys line up for inspection, Junie at the head of his line. The priest watched them, too. Each time Fairbanks brought him a fresh drink, he complained good-naturedly that it was too strong, but it didn't slow him down. Fairbanks kept up with him. He was bigger than the priest by a few pounds, and he was younger. He stayed sober longer than Father Hugh, who was slurring his words by ten o'clock and talking too loud.

"So," said Fairbanks's girlfriend. She sat like a prize next to Fairbanks. I had never been told her first name. I called her Miss Croft, the same as the boys did. "Tell me, Father Hugh. Was Matthew a good student?"

"Him?" said Father Hugh, swinging his big Irish head in her direction. "Oh, he was . . . a fine student. He could write an essay on just anything. You give him the topic, he wrote the damn essay."

Fairbanks smiled, but he didn't like the direction the discussion was headed. He wanted to talk about something other than his record at the Teachers College.

"Perhaps writing those essays was his best subject," said the priest. "Or math. *Maths,* you call it. Damn the British."

He stared at Miss Croft for a moment.

"Girls," he said, a note of disgust in his voice. "That was always Matthew's best subject."

Fairbanks smiled an embarrassed smile.

"Isn't that right, Matthew?" said Father Hugh.

I got up quietly and fetched myself another beer. I found myself enjoying my new friend's embarrassment.

"You say so," said Fairbanks.

"What was that girl's name?" said the priest.

"I don't remember," said Fairbanks. Miss Croft was watching him now. There was information she wanted, too. "I don't think my past is what we should be talking about here," said Fairbanks. "Hasn't anyone read a good book lately?" He looked at me hard.

"Well," I said. I knew I was grinning. I tried to stop. "I was reading, let me think . . ."

"Elisea?" said the priest. "Estanza?"

Fairbanks's face went darker, redder.

"Eustacia," said Miss Croft, so softly we could barely hear her.

"That's it," said Father Hugh. "Eustacia. Whatever happened to Eustacia?"

"She's fine," said Fairbanks. He turned to me. "What were you saying about that book?"

"And the child?" said Father Hugh. "A girl, I think."

"A boy," said Miss Croft.

"Was it a boy?" said Father Hugh. "Was the first one a boy?" He had that faraway look, like when you're trying to remember. "The other child," said the priest, "the one by the English woman, that was a boy, but I thought Eustacia's first child was a girl."

"The English woman?" said Miss Croft.

"I think I may start reading more myself," said Fairbanks. He was sitting up straight, on the edge of his chair. His eyes begged me to speak.

"Oh," I said.

"Yes," said Fairbanks. He was tipping right out of that chair.

"The Great Gatsby," I said.

Everyone in the room turned and looked at me, as if I had shifted to a different language, a strange one. Fairbanks nodded. He meant to encourage me.

"Now, there," I said, looking deep into the bottle I held in my hand, at the sweat that clung to the side as if there were secrets hidden beneath that sweat, secrets I had tucked away myself, "is a good book."

The room was quiet. The priest swirled the whiskey in his glass. A small bead of perspiration appeared on Miss Croft's lip. Fairbanks groaned, but he probably didn't realize it.

Side Dick appeared at the door with a question from Mr. Montrose, who was in charge of the boys for the evening. Fairbanks stood up and made a great to-do about responding to Montrose. "I better write this down," he said a little too loudly. "I need a pen." Father Hugh held one up, but Fairbanks pretended not to see it. He left the room and was gone for a long time, returning with pen and paper. He wrote a note in front of us with a great flourish and read it three or four times. He sent Side Dick after more ice.

"And maybe some more of that bread," he shouted after the boy.

"Sir, there is no more bread, sir," said Side Dick.

"But Father Hugh loves that bread," said Fairbanks.

"What bread?" said Father Hugh. He watched Side Dick go out the door. He kept his eyes on the empty doorway until the boy appeared again with the ice.

"Let me fix you a drink," said Fairbanks.

"Tell me about these boys," said the priest. "Are they good boys?"

"Now, that's hard to say," said Fairbanks. He was happy to have a new subject to talk about.

"They're not choirboys," I said. Fairbanks smiled and nodded at me. He looked grateful. "A choirboy wouldn't be living here," I said.

"Boy, that's true," said Fairbanks. "I mean, that's really very true." He turned to Miss Croft. "True that," he said, as if he was translating for her.

"Do you beat them?" said the priest. "Perhaps that's what they need."

Miss Croft had lost interest in the conversation. She was studying Fairbanks now, but it was a cold look she gave him, one that didn't begin or end with a smile.

"Why do you ask?" I said.

"Why?" said the priest. "I'd like to help, that's why."

"We could use more help," said Fairbanks.

"I volunteer," said Father Hugh. "I'll be the one to beat them. Well, just the big boys. They probably need it most."

"Probably," said Miss Croft. Her heart wasn't in it.

"We'd have to draw the line somewhere, wouldn't we? How could we do it? Do you measure them?" asked the priest. "I'd start by measuring them."

"The narrator of *The Great Gatsby* is this fellow named Nick Carroway," I said.

"Oh Nick Carroway, Dick Narroway, what difference does it make?" said Father Hugh. "Have you measured their cocks, Matthew?"

"I doubt that," said Miss Croft. "He's quite busy measuring his own."

"Man, oh man," I said, rising and stretching. "Tomorrow is another day."

"Mr. Tanner," she said, "I was wondering if you would see me home."

"You're not staying?" said Fairbanks. "Yes, you are. Both of you. You're staying."

I sat back down.

"I'm not staying," she said. "He can drive me home."

"I'll walk you home a little later if you don't want to stay," said Fairbanks. "You know that."

"Mr. Tanner can take me home. He can take me now in his Toyota. You stay here with your guest."

Father Hugh's glasses had slipped to the end of his nose and his mouth hung open. He had fallen asleep in his chair.

"I don't want to be alone in this house," said Fairbanks in a whisper. "Not with him."

"It's your party," said Miss Croft. "Perhaps you could get out your tape measure."

I wasn't sure if I ought to be the one to drive Miss Croft home. I didn't know where she lived. She always appeared at the school on foot. But when she started off walking into the dark alone, Fairbanks nodded to me. "Be a friend," he said. "Go after her. Take the car. Please."

So I did. It took twenty minutes to drive to her home. It would have been a good, long walk in the dark. It wasn't even a village she lived in, just three houses together on the road to Belmopan. In the car, she told me what she knew of Fairbanks's history, how he was a star at the Teachers College until he got one of the other students pregnant. The college had been upset with him. It wasn't unusual for young people to pair up, but the girl, Eustacia, had been one of their prizes, and Fairbanks himself had been a student they took some pride in. Father Hugh tried to get them to marry. Fairbanks had been reluctant, had refused.

"Now I know why," said Miss Croft. "He had another girl all the time. He didn't tell me about the English girl."

When we reached the house, she had me stop the car.

"Don't pull off the road," she said. She looked at me hard. I was scared for a moment she was going to try to kiss me.

"I only have one thing to say to you," she said. I couldn't look her in the eye. I looked down at her pink blouse. That was a mistake. I looked out the window. I looked at the steering wheel.

"Learn to be a man," she said softly. "There are many boys in this world already."

She got out and walked up the stairs to a small house with a thatch roof. She opened the door and let herself in without looking back at me.

The return drive was longer than the drive out. I made it take longer. I looked at my watch when I entered the grounds of the school again and saw it was after one. The lights were on in Fairbanks's house, and I could hear the priest had revived. He was reciting some kind of poetry.

"The grave's a fine and private place, but none I think do there embrace . . ."

I was surprised to hear a poem like that from a priest. I didn't want to go back over there. So I didn't. I climbed the steps to my front door and tripped over Albert and Junie. They had brought blankets from the dormitory and they were sleeping on my porch.

"Shouldn't you go to your bed?" I asked Albert.

"Please," he said. "This is better. A night like this. If you don't mind." Junie hadn't woken up. His legs moved in his sleep. "Please," said Albert again.

"All right then," I said.

He waited for me to go inside before he lay down again next to his brother.

Sunday afternoon, Fairbanks put Father Hugh on the bus to Belize City. He invited me to walk with the two of them out to the bus stop, but I told him I had work to do. I wasn't making it up. The old priest was a great motivation for me. He was exactly what I needed and he was everything I didn't want to be. He pushed me over the edge. I'd been making plans all Sunday morning, and I kept making plans until late in the night. I wanted to do better by the boys in my classroom.

The first thing Monday morning, I called them together. I wanted to make a deal with them.

"If you will all try," I said, and I had to stop. Side Dick was doing his dirty little rumba behind my back. I turned so I could face him and he cringed, but I didn't hit him. I made him sit down and listen.

"If you'll try to get along with each other during the week, try not to fight," and at this point in the conversation I had to calm Albert down. He glared at Boomba, who had made an evil remark to Junie.

"If you will try not to make me crazy during the week, on Friday I'll do something nice for you." I said it fast so I wouldn't be interrupted again.

They looked at me with doubt in their eyes. What had I ever done for them? What had anyone ever done? Junie smiled sweetly at me, and I wondered, not for the first time, if the boy knew anything at all, if he knew where he was, if he knew the difference between the heaven and the hell he loved to talk about.

"Maybe we could have one prayer meeting?" he said. The others turned away. I was afraid I was going to lose the moment.

"No meetings," I said. "No prayers."

"We could sing," said Junie. "Like church boys."

"Maybe," I said. "Sometimes. But for this Friday, I'll make you some popcorn and I'll find a story to read to you. We'll just kick back."

"Kick back?" said Boomba in wonder. It was a phrase the boys liked to use, but not one they'd ever heard from me. "Kick back for true?"

"For true," I said. I could figure it out. I could learn how to kick back.

The rest of the day, they worked at their desks. When Side Dick's pencil went dull, he didn't blame it on Boomba, and when Bus'up put his fists in front of him, expecting a fight from Power-to-Jesus, PTJ made himself walk away. Though he promised to take it up with Bus'up later that afternoon, outside.

"Kill you," said PTJ.

"Kill you," said Bus'up.

"Kill you good," said PTJ. Still, the next morning, they were both back in the classroom, neither of them dead.

All week I let as much go by as I possibly could. I stopped fights. I made people talk to each other.

"Talk, talk, talk," said PTJ. "With you, it's always talk. I get sick of this talk."

I reminded them about the popcorn.

"What is popcorn?" said Darnell. Junie wanted to know, too.

"Fools," said Side Dick. "Unu will find out."

Albert glared at Side Dick, but he let it go. We all chose to practice restraint. If it seemed like any boy was going to explode, I sent the whole group out to play ball. I found an easier reading book for Side Dick, and I let Boomba stay inside and draw on the board with three pieces of colored chalk that fell out of a shoe box. We got through the week, day by day.

Thursday afternoon, it rained hard. The boys took shelter where they could, under the eaves of the officers' houses, in the dining room with checkerboards they'd drawn up themselves. They had bottle caps for checkers. I was holed up in my bedroom, reading and drinking coffee, thinking about Ellie and the way her hands felt on the back of my neck, when Boomba and Side Dick and a third boy from the classroom, Peter Rabbit, came to see me. I'd been holding some money for the three of them. We had raised cucumbers together and sold them to the Mennonites, who complained we let the cucumbers grow too big before we harvested them, then paid us twice what they were worth. I was keeping a five-dollar bill for Boomba and another for Peter Rabbit. Side Dick had given me three dollars to hold for him.

"We're going to San Ignacio on Saturday," said Side Dick. "We want to buy some shirts."

I gave them the money. I couldn't think of any reason I shouldn't. I asked them about the classroom.

"Do you think it's an improvement?"

The boys looked at each other. They knew the answer I was hoping for.

"Oh, much better now," said Side Dick. His small round face lit up. When he was nervous, he hugged his bad arm with his good arm, and he sometimes talked so fast his mouth couldn't keep up. He ran over the words with new words before the first words were finished.

"Are you looking forward to the party tomorrow?"

"Oh yes," said Side Dick. The others nodded their heads. Boomba was the least willing to commit himself to a good time.

"Maybe I can buy some more colored chalk when I'm in the city," I told him, and I thought I saw a glimmer of interest.

"Oh yes," said Side Dick again.

"Oh yes," said Peter Rabbit, mimicking Side Dick. The others laughed at him, the same way I did.

The boys took their money and drifted away, and I went back to my hammock. I was reading too much in those months, sometimes a thin book in a day although it was hard to find anything good to read. I pulled out the book I was working on, another one of the trashy things Hobson had collected. It wasn't *The Great Gatsby,* but I was hoping it wouldn't be too bad, and I could pass it on to Fairbanks.

There was a knock at my door. On the other side of the screen stood Side Dick again, angry this time. He must have argued with the others. Maybe he'd asked for an equal share of the money and the other two had refused.

"I just want to tell you," he said, looking back over his shoulder as though the other boys were watching. He struggled to speak schoolroom English, not the mixture of Spanish and Creole that worked better for him.

"Them boys," he said, "they going sorry they chance me. Sake of, I know what they do."

"Slow down," I told him. I had heard so many small-time grievances at New Hope that little of what the boys said felt important anymore. I tried to make him think I cared about the story he was telling.

"I mi tell them," he said, "I going to tell you . . ."

"Tell me what?" I said. I knew I sounded sharp. I tried to smile. Side Dick's eyes narrowed and he looked away. He could sense I was impatient.

"I know what they mean by take seat," he said.

Take seat. It was a new expression for me.

"They never think I will tell anyone," he said. "I tell them I will tell you."

I had no idea what he was talking about. I didn't suppose I needed to know.

"And Boomba, and that Peter Rabbit," said Side Dick carefully, "they are the two worst."

"They're the worst?" I said. I smiled at his seriousness. "Worse than you?"

I meant it as a joke, but the look that came to Side Dick's face made me step back away from my door. It was as if I'd slapped him again. I reached out one hand to steady us both, but the boy pulled away. The dinner bell rang, and Side Dick moved off my porch to go to the dining hall.

"I'm sure it will all look better tomorrow," I said after him. The rain was pounding on my roof.

"Rain di come," I said. "Wind di blow."

The rain was beating on all the roofs of all the buildings.

In the early morning, the three boys stopped being angry with each other long enough to slip out the gate and make their way to the highway. They wore their best clothes and each of them had money to take the bus to Belize City. The bus driver knew he wasn't supposed to pick up poorly dressed boys on that stretch of the road. They must have combed out their hair and tucked their shirts in neatly. All of them had shoes, though Side Dick had to steal a pair from Bus'up, asleep in his bunk. I imagine them standing apart at the bus stop as if they didn't know each other, climbing on the bus separately so the driver wouldn't be suspicious. It was hours after the bus passed through before anyone told me those three were gone.

Usually when boys ran away, they went on foot, and it was true what Hobson told me: it was an easy thing to catch up with a boy on foot. Fairbanks had us all out looking. I drove down the road five miles in each direction. Fairbanks hadn't figured they would have bus fare.

"Is it true?" said Fairbanks. He came to find me, shortly after a lunch that was delayed by our search. Fairbanks had been to my house a few times since the afternoon we shared coffee, but it felt like the first time all over again. He stood on the porch and spoke through the screen door. I tried to invite him inside.

"You gave them money?" he said.

I admitted it. "It was money they earned," I said. "They told me they wanted to buy some shirts."

"What do they need with shirts?" asked Fairbanks, and I knew what he meant. He was asking the question I should have asked. "How many shirts can they wear at once?" said Fairbanks. "How many shirts does a New Hope boy need?"

Two days later, at his auntie's house in Belize City, Peter Rabbit was the first one caught. He came back to New Hope like a hero. Fairbanks beat him for running away, but Fairbanks liked Peter Rabbit so he didn't bear down. The other two didn't come back for the better part of a year. The boys whispered that Side Dick and Boomba had gone north to cut cane near the Mexican border. Side Dick was hardly old enough to do a day's work. He spoke Spanish, and that would have helped him find a place. Boomba was younger and smaller, and I didn't know how he could survive on his own.

"You don't know?" said Albert. I had the feeling he was laughing at me. It was the Friday after they left, and we had gone ahead with the popcorn and the story in the schoolroom, though the day was ruined, a lost day. I read them the first chapter of *101 Dalmatians,* stopping as often as I dared so I could explain the big words, until I lost interest and simply read the last few pages straight through. I passed out the popcorn after I packed away the pencils and anything else one boy could use to hurt another. I never realized all the ways they could hurt each other.

"What's he going to do?" I asked Albert. I tried to rephrase the question. "What could that lee bally do?" It made the boys laugh when I said a few words in Creole. This time, Albert didn't laugh.

"Take seat," said Albert, and several of the other boys looked his way, surprised to hear him say it. The smallest ones pretended they hadn't heard the words at all.

"What does that mean?" I asked.

Albert was embarrassed for me. "Mean?" he said. "You no know that?"

Junie hadn't been laughing with the rest. He pointed his ruined hand at his brother.

"You tell Mr. Tanner," said Junie, in his soft child's voice. "You tell him."

"Me?" said the baker's boy.

"Must," said Junie. "Tell him right now."

I was going to press Albert on it. He wanted to act silly, and I decided not to ask more questions until I could get him off to one side. I waited until it was nearly time to go to the dining hall. I let all the other boys go, but I made Albert stay behind. I let him think he was helping me clean up. When no one else was left in the room, I quit pretending.

"What does it mean?"

"You know what it means," said Albert. He made a big job of lining up all the desks in straight rows again, moving them slowly and deliberately into their accustomed places. "Don't make me say it," he said.

"He's selling himself, isn't he?"

Albert rubbed at a pencil mark that made a long slash across the desk in front of him. "You could say so. A part of himself."

"The big boys chance the little boys?" I had to know.

"They sometimes do," said Albert. He was fourteen, and although he wasn't the biggest boy at the school, what Hobson had said about him was true: he was not in the group of small boys anymore.

"They don't do it to me," said Albert. "I never let them. And they better not hurt my brother, that's all. I can't look after the rest."

After a month of good behavior at New Hope, Peter Rabbit was allowed to walk out every day to the public school where one of the teachers took an interest in him. Much later, when I was almost ready to leave Belize, Side Dick and Boomba returned to the place, separately. Side Dick's hair had grown to his shoulders. I had to cut it all off for him. It was the only way to get rid of the lice. I got him interested in reading again, though it took some time. Once in a while, he would simply put the book down and look out a window, or at me.

"This here book," he would say, "this is no story. Believe me, I could tell a better one. This is no story at all."

12

When you tell a story that counts, you take your life into your hands and turn it inside out so the secret part you always thought you could keep hidden is exposed. It's out there, in the light. Side Dick knew that. So did I.

"But I don't blame them for running away," said Katherine. "Those boys. How could they not run away?"

Katherine and I were on the phone again. We were always on the phone. My ear hurt from pressing the receiver up against it. I didn't have an answer to her question. I saw the truth of it a long time ago. With five dollars in my pocket and a head start? If I'd been a New Hope boy? I would have run away.

"That little Junie," said Katherine. "You didn't tell me how he got hurt."

"I won't be telling you." I'd told Katherine enough secrets for a while. I had the right to close up shop when I wanted to.

"Don't you know?" she said. "Of course you know."

I knew a few things. I knew I was tired and hungry, and I knew it was late enough I ought to choose sleep over food. It was bakers' hours. Nothing mattered more than sleep.

"You're not telling me everything," said Katherine. "You helped him. You did something for him."

"What could I do? He needed more help than I could give him. He needed counseling and physical therapy. He needed a good surgeon."

"A surgeon," said Katherine. "That's what he needed."

"There weren't any surgeons," I said. "Not in Belize."

"There had to be something you could do for a boy like that," she said. "There had to be some way."

It was funny to hear her. It was so funny I could have laughed out loud like an insane person. It wouldn't have taken much. Those were practically the same words I used to say to myself. There has to be something. A boy like that. There has to be some way, something I can do.

All my life, I'd read these heartwarming stories in the Sunday newspapers about the doctor who was treating the African baby with the miracle cure the African baby couldn't get in his village in Africa and how the doctor was doing this for the little African baby (only sometimes it was a Peruvian baby or a Tibetan baby) out of the goodness of his Baptist heart, or his Methodist heart or his Jewish heart. His Zoroastrian heart, it didn't matter. Those doctors always had kind hearts filled with some sort of religion, and kind hands, too, not like the doctors who used to stick their fingers up my scrotum every fall to see if it was okay for me to play more basketball. I needed one of those heartwarming doctors. I didn't know where to find one. In fact, they mostly live in the newspaper, but I wasn't smart enough to realize it. I wasn't going to give up until I explored all the possibilities. I had audacity. I had a bad case of idealism. I had poor judgment. I had Price Donelly whispering in my ear. Price led me astray.

Price could have led the Pope astray. One time we wrote a letter to President Carter. We hadn't been in Belize a month, but all Price had to do was to bring it up (*Just imagine Jimmy reading this while he's in the bathtub . . . Imagine him reading it out loud to Rosalyn . . .*) and two beers later I was trying to find someone who owned a typewriter, trying to find the White House zip code.

I had barely settled into my new job and I was looking for direction. Price thought the President of the United States could offer us direction.

"It's why we have presidents," he said. Price was fascinated by Jimmy Carter. He thought Jimmy Carter was a saint, a good president. He loved the president's smile.

"This is interesting," said Price. "George Washington Carver. Jimmy Carter. A lot of great men got involved with peanuts. Well, two men anyway."

He wanted to see if he could get Jimmy Carter to send a bag of seed peanuts to New Hope.

"Say this fast, three times," said Price. "Jimmy Carter's peanuts."

"Jimmy Carter's peanuts, Jimmy Carter's peanuts . . . Oh, stop," I said. I didn't want to grow peanuts. I didn't like peanuts. "I don't even know what part of a peanut you stick in the ground."

"The whole thing," he kept saying. "I'm pretty sure you plant the whole thing."

"It's ridiculous," I said.

"But wouldn't it make a great story," said Price. "In the newspapers. 'President Carter sends peanuts to Belize. Volunteers express profound gratitude.' That's you and me," said Price. "We're the volunteers."

"I know that," I said. "I haven't forgotten."

Price went ahead and wrote the letter, but he didn't sign it. That was my job. He took charge of mailing it to the White House. He couldn't trust me to mail a letter like that. It didn't matter who mailed it finally because nobody wrote back. We waited months, but not even a postcard. Price didn't understand. Some kind of response would have meant a lot to him.

"A postcard makes a difference," he said.

He knew what he was talking about. He told me this story. In high school, some of Price's friends drove out to Southern California. They made it to Disneyland, and Universal Studios, and they sent him a postcard from out there with a photograph of Lucille Ball on it. That picture meant something to Price. He showed me the picture. He let me hold it for a while.

"She wrote on the back what a great guy I was going to turn out to be," he told me, as though I couldn't read the words for myself. It was so late it was early, and we were at his place drinking beer and talking and thinking seriously about waiting to see if the sun would come up in the east, like it always had before. He had hammocks strung up in his front room.

"She said that about me—*great guy*—even though she never met me," said Price. "She didn't have a picture of me. She could tell about a person just from meeting his friends." Price looked at me then. He was wondering what Lucille Ball would have made of me.

"It's what I believed when I was younger," said Price. "I believed a lot of things when I was younger. She signed the card, *Lucy*. I'm sure that's her signature. I still believe that." He would get sad thinking about Lucille Ball. I knew how he felt. I was like that, too, wanting to believe.

When Price learned about Junie, he was quick to see the possibilities.

"This is perfect," he said. "This is what we're doing here. This is why we came."

"I don't want to save the world anymore," I told him.

"Forget that," said Price. We were at his flat, sitting at his kitchen table, waiting for Ellie to show up. "The world is too big," said Price. "We're talking about one good deed. One pure and perfect act. Decency and kindness. Did you bring anything to drink?"

We were going to cook some chicken, or we were going to try to talk Ellie into cooking some chicken. We were hoping Ellie would bring some chicken over so she could cook it. I didn't see how Price could care that much about Junie. He had just broken up with Candace for the third or fourth time, and all he wanted was a diversion, some project to take his mind off his loneliness. I expected him to forget all about Junie, maybe before the evening was over. I was wrong, though. He hung onto the idea of being good.

"I can't do it," said Price. "But you can."

"What do you mean, you can't do it?"

"Christ. Haven't you figured this out yet? You're the only chance we have. You're uncorrupted. Ellie and I are jaded."

"I don't think Ellie's jaded."

"You don't?" said Price. "Maybe we better not trouble ourselves with that."

"Maybe not."

"But you," said Price, "you have this incredible amazing unearned possibility to do a good thing. We have to work on this."

I was starting to wish I had something to drink myself. Price's left knee was hopping under the kitchen table. There was danger everywhere.

"Let's write the president," he said.

"We did that."

"Let's write him again."

I didn't want to tell Price, but I'd already thought about writing another letter to Jimmy Carter. The president had a lot of doctors, and he didn't get sick that often. One of those doctors might be available. I saw myself dropping the letter into the mailbox at the main post office in Belize City, and that letter growing little wings and flying all the way to Camp David the way you see it in a cartoon. I didn't receive even a form-letter reply the first time, or I might have gone through with it.

"I thought I'd talk to Fat Eric first," I told Price. Fat Eric Dickerson was our director. I don't know who started calling him that. It may have been Price. Eric was six feet tall and he weighed 140 pounds, although he ate constantly. He had a yellowish complexion and a big nose, and Price didn't like him much. The man had a mild case of dyslexia, and he sometimes referred to

Price as *Prince,* and once as *The Prince,* though it was hard to tell if Eric meant anything by it. I knew what Price was going to say. Fat Eric was a bad idea. I didn't even have a plan and Fat Eric wouldn't do anything without a plan.

"Good lord, yes," said Price. "Go see Eric." His knee was vibrating. My head was spinning. It wasn't what I thought he would say.

"You think I should?"

"He's a blockhead," said Price. "But that's where we have to start."

"Are we going to do this thing?"

"I'm with you all the way," said Price. "But no, you have to do it. It's your white whale, not mine. It's your road less traveled. It's your shot heard round the world. Your chance to have a cliché of your very own."

I was glad when Ellie showed up. We were pretty sure it was Ellie. Someone was knocking on the other side of the door and singing the "Member Me" song Candace had made up for us, what seemed like a long time ago.

"I don't want to tell her about this yet," I said to Price.

"I understand," he said thoughtfully. "That song. She's a very jaded girl."

"She is not."

He opened the door and she stood there with a papaya in one hand, a bottle of rum in the other. Her face was flushed. Her T-shirt hadn't been washed in a long time.

"What?" she said, looking from one of us to the other. "I like that song. What's wrong with that?"

"Oh, we have a secret," said Price. He took the bottle out of her hands and hugged it to his chest. "Now everyone has a little secret from everyone else."

Price wouldn't let me stay and have dinner with them. He sent me off to see Fat Eric, who was famished and who took me to the Chinese restaurant. Eric was always famished. Price used to say hunger was Eric's best attribute. I sat across from him at the table and for once I didn't play with the chopsticks or read the Chinese horoscopes on my place mat. I didn't even wait for the tea. I asked him point-blank to do something for Junie. He had been to New Hope. Eric knew which boy I was talking about.

"You're serious," he said. He was studying his menu, although I knew he had it memorized. "This is something you've thought about."

He shook his head at me sadly. It was a long head. Most of his weight was in his head.

"Do you know how many little deformed kids there are in the world?" said Fat Eric. "I mean, think about it. It's a large world." He waited a long time for me to answer. Maybe he thought I would come up with a number for him.

"A lot," I said.

"Very much so," said Eric. "Do you know how many little deformed kids there are in China alone?"

We were at the Chinese restaurant so I guess it made a kind of sense, what he said. He had ordered two dinners for himself and two dinners for me. The waitress wasn't surprised. She knew both of us, but she knew him best. Fat Eric could eat. I was hungry all the time, too, but nothing in that restaurant was going to fill me up. The waitress went away, and when she returned she brought platters of rice and noodles piled so high she was cheating gravity to get the food to our table.

"Eat," said Eric. "You look like a rail."

I tried to eat. I just didn't want what was in front of me. I would have settled for some of Albert's bread. I pushed the food around on my plate. I drank my tea. Eric cracked open a fortune cookie.

"Life's a bitch," he said.

"That's your fortune?"

Eric laughed. "I like you, Tanner," he said. "You're funny. You're really very funny."

I left the restaurant a little later on my own. Fat Eric offered to give me a ride but I needed to walk. I needed to listen to Dr. Garrison on the radio, the way his story would follow me through the street from open window to open window. I wondered why there wasn't a real Dr. Garrison I could turn to. I thought about a lot of stuff on the way back to Price's house, but I didn't come up with any answers.

"I don't think Eric's going to be much help," I told Price.

"Of course he's not going to be any help," said Price. He and Ellie claimed they had eaten dinner. I didn't see any signs of it. They were sitting in the same chairs across the table from each other as when I left them more than an hour earlier. The papaya was gone, and most of the rum.

"Listen to what I'm telling you," said Price. *"Think locally, act globally."*

"What does that mean?"

"I don't know," said Price. "I thought it might help. It's like a proverb. *When God opens a window, He closes a door somewhere else."*

"I'm not sure this is helping," said Ellie.

"Don't you know any rich people?" asked Price. *"Rich people are good to know."*

"That's a proverb?"

"Are you guys going to tell me what this is all about?" asked Ellie.

"Not yet," said Price. "We're not hatching those chickens before we count our eggs."

"I know one rich guy," I said. I must have sounded less than sure of myself. "In the Cayo."

"A Belizean rich guy?" said Price. "You're kidding."

"I could go see him."

"We don't know any rich guys in Belize," said Price.

"I think I do."

"You can't," he said. "Not really rich. It's against the rules."

I sort of bristled.

"Okay, okay," said Price. "What's his name?"

"I'm not telling."

"That's because you don't know him."

"He does, he does," said Ellie.

"Oh yeah?" He looked from one of us to the other. "Oh, I get it," he said. "I'm not supposed to know. Only Tanner can know a rich guy. Tanner's the good one."

"Be serious," said Ellie.

"I'm always serious. And remember this because this one is true: *Whatever doesn't make you stronger, will kill you.*"

"Oh God," said Ellie.

"What?" I said. "What is it?"

"Papaya," said Ellie. "More papaya." And she ran out of the room.

"I am serious," said Price, and he was sad for a moment, as if his heart was about to break.

I spent the rest of the weekend at Ellie's. We fought like children, then made up, then fought some more. I was distracted. I took the bus back to New Hope and fed the rabbits and taught the boys and tried to think. The rich man I knew was Uncle Patel, and Ellie wasn't sure she wanted me to go and see him. She wanted that night we spent in his hotel to be special, to be just about us, not about New Hope or Price or any of our schemes to do good. But when I talked about Junie's hand again, his face, she saw the way it had to be. I wondered how it was I hadn't thought of Patel before, how rich he might be. With his hotel in San Ignacio, he had the knack for making money. It's a mystery to me. I never learned how to do it. The man wasn't just rich, he was generous, too. I'd gone to see him again and again on behalf of the boys until he should have been tired of my begging. The month before, he'd given me two crates of soft drinks, and I'd asked him to foot the bill for our summer program. He was thinking about it. We didn't have a summer program, but Fairbanks said if we could get enough soft drinks I could go ahead and plan one. I didn't enjoy playing the beggar's role. This time I'd do it for Junie.

I drove into San Ignacio on a Thursday night, stopping at two of the small shops for groceries, at another place for a cold beer. I couldn't make myself go to see Patel right away. It felt like too much was riding on his response. I stopped in at Miss Beard's for ice cream. I had two. I had a soft drink. Pretty soon, I had a stomach ache.

"Go see him," she said, as if she could read my mind. "Uncle Patel is wanting to see you."

And he was sitting out back in a folding chair when I got there, a mosquito coil burning at his feet.

"Did you bring her?" said Patel. "Is Ellie with you?" He was disappointed I had come without her.

We talked, and he looked at me patiently. There was a long silence he was more comfortable with than I was.

"What is it, Tanner? What is making you so troubled?"

I told him about Junie. I told him why I was troubled. I told him Ellie was troubled as well. Pretty soon, Patel was troubled, too.

"Bring the boy so I can meet him," said Patel.

It wasn't like he could work miracles. We both knew it. He was no doctor. But I felt better, all the same. There was no good reason for him to want to see Junie in person if he wasn't willing to help. If Patel just wanted to put me off, he would do it more graciously than that. He was going to have a hard time saying no if he thought it would get back to Ellie.

"He's out in the car," I said. And he was, too. I'd lugged the boy around all night with me, filling him with ice cream and soda until he thought his life had somehow changed for the better.

Patel shrugged, as if to say out-in-the-car was no big deal to him. He let me lead him through the lobby of his hotel. I could have been another rich guy and he was seeing me off. He liked to stand in the street and wave and laugh and generally look contented. I knew that much about him. I didn't know much more. I tried to act nonchalant when I introduced him to Junie. If you have audacity, it's good to be nonchalant, too.

"This is the good man who helps out your school every now and then," I told the boy. Junie grinned. He held up his hand at just the right angle so that Patel could see the three hardened lumps, the fingers seared into the palm. The nails on that hand had grown long. They were black and they curved into the boy's palm like small cruel knives. I needed to cut them. I didn't have the courage to do it. Patel held onto his smile, but it went a little grim. He looked away from the hand. It didn't help. His eyes rested on Junie's face, on the place where a boy is supposed to have a piece of his nose. Patel swallowed hard. His eyes filled with tears before he went back into his office, waving me away as if I had disgusted him, frightened him.

"It's okay, Mr. Tanner," said Junie. "It's okay for go back now."

I didn't know anything else to do. We got in the car and I drove us back to New Hope.

I tried not to think about Junie for a while, and would have succeeded, but a few days later I got a note from Price.

Tanner, he wrote. *The British! Why didn't we think of them?* He wrote it with a pen on the back of his Lucille Ball photo and sent it to me. He wanted me to see how serious he was.

This is a colony for Christ sake, he wrote. *Rule Britannia. My Country 'Tis of Thee. Who do we know who's British?*

I put the card away, then fished it out of my drawer and read it again. The only British people I knew were the soldiers who lived down the road in their barracks, and I didn't really know them. They were mysterious to me, like the pilots who flew their jets over the school. They had a little store where you could buy liquor, if you liked to drink what British people drank. I hadn't stopped in there lately. The last time I'd knocked on their door, a sunburned redheaded soldier told me to bugger off, as if he was still mad about the War of 1812. I didn't let it bother me, though. We won that war.

I thought I'd try again. I had a good reason. I put Junie in the Toyota and drove out to the barracks. The soldier at the gate was the same one as before, or maybe he wasn't. All redheaded British people look alike. This one didn't remember me. He let us into a little room where he waited with us for the doctor.

"You got the clap?" he asked me.

"No," I said. He grew suspicious.

"What do you want with the doctor?"

"Actually," I said, "I'm not sure if I have the clap. It could be the clap."

Junie laughed at me.

"He's got the clap?" asked the soldier, looking Junie over. But the soldier didn't want an answer. There was a small desk in the room, and the soldier went over and sat down behind it. He was more comfortable with the desk between us.

The old doctor at the post was gone, and that afternoon we saw the new one. He had a large forehead and no chin and a look about him that said British people didn't need chins, not as long as they had a magnificent forehead like he had. I thought Junie might win that doctor over. But an army doctor? It's how those things go I guess. He had seen sights more horrendous than a small boy with a ruined hand and a deformed nose. Maybe. He tilted Junie's head back so he could see the injury clearly. Then he went to the sink and washed his hands. "How did all this happen?" he asked, his back still turned to us.

"We can't be sure," I said. I didn't want to put Junie on the spot. He was whispering to me. I hoped the doctor wouldn't notice.

"What did he say?" asked the doctor.

"For me ma," said Junie a bit louder.

"What about his mother?" asked the doctor.

There was a long silence. The room smelled like alcohol or formaldehyde, that medical smell. It had the heavy feeling of a room where the floor had been mopped and mopped and would never be clean.

"He said it was his mother," I told the doctor. I had no reason not to tell the truth. I didn't want the man to think New Hope had anything to do with the way Junie looked. The doctor turned pale in spite of himself. His big forehead did. I watched him, wondering if this piece of information would make him more sympathetic to Junie's condition or less.

"The shame," he said.

He didn't say it without compassion, but I knew the moment he said those two words we were wasting our time again. The doctor had already started thinking about the drink he was going to fix himself as soon as he got back to his room. Maybe he would drive into town later and sit in the dark tavern next to the bridge. He would write a letter home and play some cards with his friends and try to forget we ever came to see him.

"We've been told not to engage in any hearts-and-flowers kinds of things," he told me. I wasn't sure what that meant. I would have to ask Price. The doctor lit a cigarette and offered one to me. I didn't take it, but Junie reached up and took one from the pack and placed it behind his ear. I let him keep it for the moment. I tried to imagine him lighting it up, holding the cigarette between his two good fingers, letting the smoke come out of the hole in his face. I'd have to take the cigarette away from him before we got back to the school.

"We're all just trying to get home now," said the doctor. He meant the soldiers, who were looking forward to the day they could leave Belize for good. "Home's the best place for everybody," he said. He didn't say Junie and I should leave his office, but that seemed to be what he was getting at.

For two weeks I went about my job as best I could, and I didn't let myself think about Junie or his condition. There were other boys with problems. A boy named Charington had an abscess under his arm. Señor Muerte offered to lance it, and would have, but Charington fainted when the man took out his file and started sharpening his little machete. Fairbanks caught wind of what was going on and yelled at the good señor and sent him back to the sheep.

A boy named Pitts found a marijuana plant growing beside the road. He was beaten for finding it.

"I didn't smoke it," said Pitts, crying out between strokes of the rope.

"That's okay," said Fairbanks. "You should have left it there. You shouldn't even know what it is."

Simple, still confused, came down with hives. I watched him scratch himself one whole morning as he sat on a folding chair outside the schoolroom door. Eventually he fell asleep, still scratching. I thought maybe he was allergic to himself. Nobody else could stand to be around him. Another boy, Michael (but everyone called him Squinty Eye), needed glasses so bad the officers wouldn't let him work in the garden for fear he would chop somebody's foot off with a hoe. "No want no damn fool glasses," said Squinty Eye, and then he walked into a tree limb and knocked himself out. I thought I might have to take him to the hospital, but when he woke up, he said he could see a little better.

I avoided Junie. The more I avoided him, the more Albert brought his little brother around. "Help my lee brother," he said. Albert had Junie come by for my laundry. He had Junie deliver my bread. I told the baker's boy I was still trying. I told myself the suffering was too great and I was just one person. I wasn't that good.

On a Friday afternoon, Fat Eric came to New Hope in the Peace Corps pickup. It was a brand-new truck, shiny and blue, with the sticker still on the window. The boys crowded around, all of them wanting a look inside. One of them turned from the new truck and set his eyes on the familiar old Toyota, the paint peeling off of its hood.

"Cho," said the boy, and he spit on the grass. I didn't know what the word meant, and yet I had a pretty good idea exactly what it meant.

"Cho," I said, trying the word out. And when Eric got out of the new pickup, I said it again, "Cho," as though it was some sort of greeting.

Eric brought along a fellow named Dobbins who had made the trip down from Washington. I'd been working with the rabbits that afternoon, trying to straighten out the little book I kept my notes in. I kept a careful record of which of the does had been bred. They were all white rabbits, and I couldn't tell one from another, and neither could the boys. But I had a little tattoo kit and Albert and I printed blue numbers inside their long pink ears. We used numbers because if we gave them names, we would never eat them. In spite of my record-keeping, the wrong rabbits, the wrong females, were throwing litters. I thought it might be miraculous at first, biblical. It was less complicated than that: the boys were slipping in at night and putting the buck in with the females to watch them mate. My notes were going to be useless.

The man from Washington—Dobbins—walked between the rows of rabbit hutches. We'd recently built a dozen new ones, and Mr. Montrose had extended the thatch roof to cover them. "I used to raise rabbits," said Dobbins. "When I was a volunteer."

I looked at him, at his clean khaki pants that had been pressed before they were packed in his suitcase. It occurred to me to ask this Dobbins fellow if he could do anything for Junie. I didn't know if it was a good idea. I didn't have time to talk to Price about it first. Maybe Dobbins knew a doctor in Washington. It wouldn't have to be the president's doctor. Maybe Dobbins's own doctor would like to get his picture in the paper. I sent Albert to find his little brother while Dobbins admired our new rabbit pens. He said our thatch roof compared favorably with the thatch he had seen in Botswana and Fiji and Brazil. Dobbins knew a lot about thatch. He reached in to pet one or two of the rabbits, moving slowly so he wouldn't startle them. When he came to the end of the row of pens, he stooped down to look carefully into the last one. He was troubled by what he saw there.

"Something's wrong with this rabbit," he said. The authority in his voice caught my attention, and I dropped the water scoop back into the bucket. I crouched down beside him in front of that last rabbit. I didn't say anything at first. I didn't want him to get too worried about a rabbit. I was worried about a boy.

"This one has some kind of tumor," he said. "On the belly."

I wondered how I could have missed a thing like that. We'd never had one with a tumor.

"Better show me," I said. "Where?" A few of the rabbits had been acting listless, but I thought it was the heat. Or the late hours they were keeping.

"There," he said, pointing at the rabbit's belly where the skin was pink and bare. "Something's growing there," said Dobbins.

"You better take care of that one," said Fat Eric. "I wouldn't keep that one around. It could spread to the others."

"Cancer's not contagious," said Dobbins. "Not in people anyway."

"Still," said Fat Eric. "A tumor. You better get rid of that one. I wouldn't even eat the meat. Just take it out and bury it."

"He's probably right," said Dobbins. "It could go through the whole flock. Or herd. Or coven. Covey. Whatever the word is. It happens in cattle. Something like that happens all the time."

"It's not a tumor," I said. And then I wished I hadn't said anything. We weren't heading anywhere that was going to do us any good.

"You can see it right there," said Dobbins, pointing to where the rabbit's belly lay against the wire.

"What is it then?" asked Fat Eric. "No, don't tell me," he said, already disgusted. Eric could be squeamish. The last time he had come to visit, I'd made him shake hands with Junie. He moved away from the rest of us, out of earshot.

"I don't know," I said to Dobbins. I was hedging. "We're not sure what's up with that one."

"Sure we are sure," said Albert. He came up behind us so quietly I didn't notice he was there. "Least, I am," he said. I tried to hush him, but I wasn't going to get the chance. "That there for that bally there business, boy," he said. I knew neither of the other two men would understand him.

"Go feed your rabbits," I said to Albert.

"No, don't brush him off," said Dobbins. "You have to listen to children."

"Let him speak," said Fat Eric, who couldn't stay away. "Oh, forget it. My God, that's disgusting." He walked farther off yet, only to come halfway back again.

"What's wrong with your rabbit, son?" said Dobbins. He was speaking in a kind tone, the sort of tone he planned to use one day with his grand-children. Albert chuckled and pointed, first at the rabbit's belly, and then at the man himself. When Dobbins still looked puzzled, Albert spoke to him patiently.

"There is nothing wrong with the rabbit, sir. It is only his seed you are looking at. His sex organs. His balls. This is a man rabbit."

The rabbit passed water into the pile of manure under his cage.

"I wouldn't kill this one," said Albert. "He jukes real good. But if you want, I will kill one of the others for you. A lady one. I could cook her up nice for you," he said. "I know how."

"Not now," I said.

"They're good," said Albert. "Make you want to bite your finger."

Albert looked quietly from one of the men to the other. Junie came to stand next to his brother, and what had seemed to me like a weak idea, having Junie meet the man from Washington, now seemed like a truly stupid idea, a completely futile idea. Jimmy Carter's peanuts all over again. Albert tried to push his brother forward, but Junie held back.

"I could kill a young one for you," said Albert. "This is what we use." He held up a hammer as though he and Junie had been building something together. "Only if you're hungry."

Dobbins didn't want to look at that hammer. He looked at Junie, who smiled and held his face up at the worst possible angle, so the man could get the whole effect.

"Jesus," said Dobbins.

Fat Eric kept his eye on the rabbits. "They're pretty good?" he said. "To eat?"

"Rabbit meat," said Albert. "It tastes like chicken. A little like iguana. That tastes like chicken, too, except the eggs. I don't like the eggs of iguana too much. If you like them, I could get you some."

"What kind of eggs is he talking about?" asked Dobbins. He wasn't going to get an answer from me. Dobbins didn't look like he felt good. Fat Eric looked hungry. I told Albert he was wanted at the office.

"How do you know?" said Albert. Nobody had brought us a message. Nobody was waving to us from across the way.

"I just know."

"You never let me kill anything," said Albert.

"For me ma," said Junie. He was talking to Dobbins. "She cut me. This face here."

The man looked desperate now. He wanted more than anything to get away from the rabbits, from the smell of urine and manure, from the boy.

"How about that one?" asked Fat Eric, pointing to the buck. "You probably have to get rid of her anyway, what with the tumor." Fat Eric hadn't heard a thing Albert said. He was a marvel that way. Dobbins saw his chance and headed toward the pickup. I hadn't seen anyone move that fast in a hot climate. Eric must have left the keys in the ignition, for Dobbins soon had the engine running and the air conditioner on.

"Those are testiculars," said Albert.

"What?" said Fat Eric. Then, with a start, the man caught on. "I'll be damned," he said. "Of course they are. And there's his little thing. Would you look at that?"

So we all crowded up and took a good look together, pretending we hadn't seen one before. Eric moved off toward the pickup, shaking his head. He reached down without thinking to adjust himself as he went. Albert filled the dipper with water and handed it to his brother. He asked Junie to give the buck something to drink.

"Too bad," said Albert, once Junie had walked off a ways. "You tell my brother's story, you end up making one whole lot of happy people sad."

Junie and Albert took up one of their games, throwing cups of water at each other. I was too tired to scold them. I followed the men to their truck because I felt like I was supposed to. Dobbins moved over so Eric could get behind the wheel, but Dobbins wouldn't look at me. I had shamed him. I had not meant to. I wracked my brain for some polite word I could offer up. I couldn't think of what to say to a man who could confuse a penis with a tumor.

"Herbert said for me to tell you something," said Eric.

"How is Herbert?"

"He's fine. He's Herbert. He says for you to call Uncle Patel. Patel wants to see the little boy again. He thinks he might be able to help."

• • •

So, watching them drive away, I was hopeful once more. I had no reason to be hopeful. I knew I shouldn't be. But I felt good enough to let Albert kill three rabbits and take them to the kitchen for the boys' dinner. Before Albert carried them off, I let Junie pray over them. I didn't see what it could hurt. He tried to resurrect the first one. When that didn't work, he lined them all up on the bench and sprinkled water on them.

"Bless you," he said. "And you, and you," he said. "Bless all of unu. Amen."

"Enough," I said. "Take them to the kitchen."

"All right, all right," said Junie, as Albert gathered them up and headed for the gate. "Amen now and amen forever," said Junie. "Over and out," he said. "Amen." He ran after his brother to the kitchen, his lips still moving in some kind of prayer.

13

I started thinking about the big picture, and this is another thing you should never do, think about all the wrong decisions you've made in your life. It worried me. Leaving The Bobber looked like another wrong decision. I hated to admit it, but my future with Stacen appeared shaky. After the day Croker and his old mother came into the café, the trouble they made, the way Stacen got angry about her business and her life and about me most of all, I needed to stay away for a few days. On the wall of my apartment I could read a truth. The words were all there now: *People Are No Damn Good.* But I was holding out for the possibility that it wasn't the only truth.

People weren't any good.

Then again, sometimes they were.

For example, I was a good employee for Stacen. I worked at it. She, on the other hand, hardly tried to be good. She never had to try. At her worst moments, there was an unmistakable decent thing about Stacen. I could see the decency even when she had a knife in her hand. Most people couldn't see that. There was a problem with that kind of decency, though. It wasn't working for me anymore. I was losing interest in it.

I couldn't get over how she'd threatened me. If that was what came from being good, then I was tired of all this goodness. I'd done my last favor for Stacen: when I left her knife in the weeds back by the trash cans, I was looking out for her. I didn't want her to get in trouble. One less weapon in the café. But with Stacen, there were no guarantees. She could find the knife again or another one just as awful if she needed to find one. I was worried about her. Being good was hard work. Maybe she was losing her touch.

Stacen was all right, but Katherine was the best person I'd ever met. She was calm and understanding, and she tried not to judge other people. Sometimes I hated her for it.

I called the café and asked for some time off.

"Okay," said Stacen. "Two days. That's it. Then you get yourself back here. You watch your step."

I didn't know what to make of that. One minute the woman was angry with me out of all proportion to anything I'd ever done, and the next she was telling me I better not stay away three days in a row. This much I knew to be true: the people like Stacen, the pretty good ones, were harder to understand than bad people.

I met all kinds of people in Belize. Good people, bad people. I met some confused people. People could be good to you on Monday and cut your heart out on the weekend. Ellie was always decent, almost always. I remember riding a bus through the countryside with her on our way to a Garifuna festival in Dangriga, when I didn't know yet if she had to work at being good or if she came by it naturally. Four young men sat in the back of the bus, Americans, in that way that reminded me of high school, how we used to ride a bus to a ball game. The tallest guys, the ones with the longest legs, liked to sit in the very back seat, hoping they would attract women somehow, maybe by the size of their shoes, I don't know. It never worked for guys in high school, and it wasn't going to work on a bus to Dangriga. Then I noticed Ellie was paying a lot of attention to these guys who were talking about a brothel they had been to the night before. I didn't know anything about brothels. I couldn't make up a story about a brothel. The thing about those places, though, was you couldn't very well visit them and do good at the same time. Even if you were just there to listen to the music. It wouldn't be easy.

I didn't think at first I had much in common with those guys on the bus, but there was something familiar about them. The crummy clothes that didn't fit right, the haircuts they'd given each other. Pretty soon they started talking about their director, who they made out to be some sort of tragic figure on horseback, and I held out that maybe they were bad missionaries or college boys on a summer-abroad program who had gotten lost from the rest of their group. I couldn't hold off the truth forever. They were Peace Corps, same as me. They lived in Guatemala City and they were on vacation, also same as me. Ellie thought they were hilarious.

It made me think she wasn't especially good after all, no more than the rest of us. She did her work as a teacher of teachers, which was good work. I had my delinquents. Price had his girls school. Fat Eric said we were all there to do the Lord's work, even Fat Eric himself in his new pickup truck. Price didn't buy the part about the Lord. Price might do a little good, but it didn't mean he was picking up religion. He knew the difference if Eric didn't. Price set up a science lab at his school for girls, a good thing. But he liked to work at his own pace, a Price thing. He didn't mind when his supplies got stolen off the dock one morning, and he was left to wander around Belize City for four weeks drinking and gambling until another shipment arrived.

There was a brothel in Belize City, too, but I don't think Price went to it. He would have told me. According to Price, there was a secret to being good and being happy at the same time. The key was to be good enough that you did your job, you didn't mess up anyone's life, but not to get all Jesusy about it. Price would give away his lunch if someone else was hungry. He'd pick a drunk up out of the street, but he wouldn't do it religiously. He bought the orange drink for Candace's kid. Maybe that was good and maybe it wasn't. Candace was crazy about Price, all her talk about babies. I guess Price did the right thing when he broke it off with her. He didn't get her pregnant, which would have led to all sorts of not-good things. He didn't get a baby started and duck out, like some people.

Myself, I used to try harder. One week, when I was trying to do a little extra, I volunteered to go with the New Hope boys to a Christmas party at a local mission. I didn't ask what mission. All those mission people blended together. This group had a nurse, and I had been to their place once before when one of Mr. Montrose's girlfriends' mother's baby brother needed medicine for a fever. (I took the little brother there in the Toyota. I took the mother, too, and Montrose himself, and another man I didn't know. It was pretty damn good of me.)

This other day, this day I'm talking about, a day in December, I returned to the same mission with a car full of boys. Small boys, and it was a short drive, so I must have had twelve of them in the Toyota, as many as would fit. It was almost Christmas, but it was a Saturday. I figured I was safe from any kind of religious excess. The boys liked Christmas, and it was supposed to be some sort of party. What was I thinking? We got to the mission a few minutes before the service began.

I tried to do the right thing. When I saw it was church, I didn't start coughing and head for the door. I sat with my boys on folding chairs in the newly finished meeting room. I bowed my head when it was time to bow my head. I sang the hymns. I know a lot of hymns because I was raised to be good and that was part of it. The boys knew the hymns, too. I suppose it surprised the missionaries. Those boys had not been raised to be good, but they liked to sing, and when they weren't singing the rousing Nazi fraternity song they sang on the day we picked up Junie, they sang hymns.

"This world is not my home . . ."

When the New Hope boys sang that song, they didn't sound desperate, not like our hosts at the mission did. The boys had energy. They sang in earnest and nodded their heads. They danced a little in their folding chairs. They felt the spirit. The woman playing the piano scowled at all of us and played a little more heavily, a little slower, to rein us in. A couple of the boys couldn't sing at all, but they made as much noise as the rest. I have noticed this fact about boys: they don't have much notion of whether they are musically gifted or tone deaf, not for a long time. I wasn't going to be the one to tell them. Amazing sounds came out of our group. I was sorry to see the woman at the piano close up her instrument and go sit with the others.

We received the sermon from a tall thin man with white hair who spoke with a stunned look on his face, as if he'd been taken up in the middle of a backyard cookout in Indiana or Idaho somewhere and transported to Belize, to this mission in the jungle where they made a preacher out of him. Or maybe he had dysentery. It's what dysentery looked like, too. His wife sat close to the front on the right side of those assembled to help him through the sermon. He talked about how the world was six thousand years old, how the end times were coming. If he lost his place, she spoke up, not correcting him exactly, but reminding him what came next.

"Some of you boys," he said, "you may not have to die at all." He checked with his wife to make sure it was okay to talk about dying. She nodded. It was barely perceptible, a secret nod. "I'll probably die," he said. It made me think he might be sick after all. He had a frightened look in his eye that reminded me of a neighbor who fell out of a tree when we were kids. She was my age, nine years old. When she woke up, she didn't know how to do things anymore, like tie her shoes or write her name. I tried to help her out by drilling her on her times tables. You do what you can.

"So," said the man, daring to take his eyes off his wife for a minute. Maybe this part of the sermon was the part he was most familiar with. "The time is near," he said. "Jesus will come back and this world will come to an end." The scared look went away from his eyes. He liked to go over this part. "In fact," he said, "some people think these events may already have begun." He raised his hands as if he held a small ball in each hand to signify the two halves of his point. One ball was Jesus coming again, and the other ball was the end of the world. He weighed them and found they weighed about the same.

"Maybe," he said, "the world has already ended . . . ," he looked in the general direction of his wife, ". . . but Jesus hasn't arrived yet." I thought about it. The man's wife closed her eyes, but she let him go on.

"Maybe," he said, "there will be no tomorrow. Maybe . . . there wasn't even any today."

"Earl," said the woman.

"Maybe," he said. He had that look on his face like my neighbor had until she figured out she could walk again, what her feet were for. "May be . . . ," he said, and now it was two words. Then he didn't say any more. I thought his wife would have to cut him off, but he just stopped.

"Earl," she said, "let's have a song."

So we had another one, a last hymn, and the boys sang with honest sorrow in their voices. I wished it all could be true what they sang, that they could just pray and Jesus would change their lives completely and forever. I wasn't wishing it half as hard as they were. Two or three of the roughest of them closed their eyes tight as they prayed. I didn't want to know what they were praying for. I closed my eyes and prayed this wouldn't be how I spent my last afternoon on earth.

We sat down outdoors at a collection of tables, some round, some square, a couple of them leaning to the right or the left. All of the boys were seated off to one side it's true, but as far as I could tell, we were served the same food as everyone else. The food was fine, if you liked vegetables. I liked vegetables. The boys didn't know what to make of potato salad or coleslaw. They would have preferred a nice piece of chicken, but these missionaries were not meat eaters. I thought about that, whether meat on the table was a good thing. I thought about the rabbits we raised back at the school, and I realized it was best not to mention the way we cooked them up, or the way Albert hit them behind the head with his hammer. The more I looked at those plates of sliced tomatoes and little red radishes, the more I wanted a small steak, or a hamburger. Sardines in oil.

"One thing I don't understand," said Darnell, who found very little he could eat at the mission, but who didn't eat much on the best of days. He was thin as air. "Why do all these people come to Belize? They don't have sinners in America?"

I tried to tell him how the mission folks were doing their best to do good, how they were trying to help.

"You're glad they're here, aren't you?" I said. "You're glad they came to do a little good."

"I wish they knew about rice," said Darnell.

"Good is okay," said Junie. He'd sat with his disfigured hand in his lap the whole day. He became self-conscious about his hand when there were church people around. "It's not the good good people that matter so much. It's the bad good people."

"If you're good," said Darnell, "you can't be bad. At the same time."

"Don't know about that," said Junie. He was staring at his lap, one hand cupped in the other. Nobody felt it was safe to argue with him.

"What are you thinking about?" said the wife of the man who had been preaching. She said it kindly. She hadn't sat with us during dinner, but she had come out several times to where we ate under the trees. She had offered us different dishes made of canned green beans and sweet potatoes. When she stood at our table, she listened to the boys with respect, like the good woman she was. "Who do you know like that?" she said. "Who can be good and bad at the same time?"

"For me ma," said Junie, and he smiled at her sweetly and showed her the missing part of his nose. She didn't want to turn away. She couldn't help herself. She hadn't seen anything like it before.

"That's not what I think it is," she whispered to me later, when the boys were filing back inside for more singing. She gently touched her own nose. "They don't have that disease in Belize," she said.

I thought I knew what she was talking about, and I wondered what would be the good thing to do. Should I let her think she had been in the presence of something that horrible? Should I tell her how Junie's face had been disfigured? There wasn't a good choice. Junie looked at me from his chair and he smiled, and I decided if you have to choose between good and true, sometimes you choose true. I told her what Junie had told me, about his mother.

"The woman put a hot coal in his hand," I said.

"Why?" she said.

"He took money from her purse without asking."

"Dear God," said our hostess. She was already very pale, and she lost what little color she had as she thought about Junie's hand. Her chin trembled.

"His mother cut his face, too," I said.

"Not his face," she said, her voice barely a whisper. "Why would she do that?"

"She wanted him to stop singing."

We were near the door when I told her. The mission group owned a half dozen cars and trucks, and they were parked in a neat row outside on the grass. The preacher's wife brushed past me to get outside. She stumbled over to one of the cars, a green Chevrolet covered with a fine layer of dust. I suppose it had been her car once. I gave her a few minutes before I slipped out after her to see if she was okay, but she got inside the car and rolled the window up and she stayed there until I went away. She wanted to be a good woman. It just wasn't easy. She didn't come back into the building for the singing. She wasn't there with the others to say good-bye when we packed up and shook hands with everyone and drove home.

Some days I wanted to think that good and bad didn't exist, that people just *were,* like the clouds and trees. Like the Belize River that flowed past the school. It was not a good river or a bad river, any more than it was a large or a fast river. It was an unexceptional river in every way, though beautiful to watch, especially in the evening. The water was a murky green, and once in a while we saw a snake swim down with the current, looking back at us. There were fish in the river. The Mennonites knew how to catch them in traps they baited with bloody hunks of liver. The boys swam near the bank on hot afternoons. I watched them swim, but I didn't care to go in. They swam naked, and so did Price when he came out to visit, unless Ellie came with him. Then everyone found a pair of shorts or swam in his underwear. Some of the boys were old enough to know what it was the buck rabbit did to the doe rabbits, what the ram wanted with the ewes. There was a house out by the road with two wild daughters. Sometimes those girls walked up to the gate to hang around, hoping a boy could slip away from his work in the field. I didn't want to know more than that. But Peter Rabbit and Side Dick and Boomba ran away, and some of the boys were going off with those girls, and some of the others were going off with each other. The smaller boys were at the mercy of at least some of the older ones. I told Ellie how things were. She made me see I had to try to find out more about it if I wanted to do good.

"They need someone to talk to," she said.

I didn't think I was the someone they needed. Most of my bright ideas had gone nowhere. Like the first Christmas, when I tried to start a choir. I had all the boys in one room, and I knew how they loved to sing, some with not-so-bad voices. We sang the songs I hoped most of them would know the words to. I didn't dare stand in front of them and raise my arms the way I had seen directors do in church choirs and high-school choirs. I sat at a table in front, and the boys sat stiffly in their desks, their desks in straight rows. We sang "Silent Night" and a couple of songs about Santa Claus. They were missing some of the words, but they sang with enthusiasm.

Oh, you better watch out
You better watch out
You better watch out
You better watch out
Santa Claus is coming to town . . .

Some of them loved that song. Some of them laughed. I didn't know if they were laughing at my voice, wavery in the still, warm night, or if they were laughing at each other. They were more wavery than I was.

"What else would you like to sing?" I asked.

"Ask Treeboy to sing," said Benn. Benn was the biggest boy at New Hope after Simple, and he was a bully. "Treeboy could sing, for true," said Benn.

The one they called Treeboy turned red. He looked like he might like to sing if given the chance.

"Why should I?" said Treeboy. I knew the boys had long-standing feuds. I tried to imagine the one between Benn and Treeboy.

"What should I ask him to sing?" I said.

Treeboy blushed a deeper shade than his usual red. He was a Carib from Dangriga, where Ellie and I had gone to the festival.

"Have him sing 'Hand Box,'" said Benn, looking down at the desk in front of him.

"'Hand Box'?" I said. Several of the other boys looked as though they wanted to laugh. They weren't sure if it was okay to laugh. Treeboy shook his head silently back and forth.

"I don't know that song," I said. There was more laughter.

Mouse, who was one of those boys who could sit quietly for days at a time and then explode in a fit of explaining, shouted to me from the back row. "It's one song about masturbation."

And Benn and Treeboy were fighting in the middle of the schoolroom, Benn laughing so hard he could barely defend himself against the smaller boy. Fairbanks must have been standing outside, listening to our caroling. When he stepped through the door, the boys stopped fighting. Treeboy ran out of the room, his face bloodied.

"Mr. Tanner, Mr. Tanner," said Fairbanks. "We can't have this fighting." He took Benn with him to the office, dismissing the other boys to wash up for bed. I walked the grounds, looking for Treeboy, but I didn't find him. Later that night, after most of the boys were in bed, I heard Benn crying as Fairbanks whipped him. And the next morning, I heard Treeboy crying.

I knew better than to go off half-cocked with some new proposal to Fairbanks. Even after Side Dick and the others ran away, I dragged my feet. One afternoon, I went down to the river to talk to Mr. Montrose. I wanted to get him to build a small wooden chest for Ellie. The boys were swimming, and Montrose was keeping an eye on the younger ones like Junie who hadn't shown him they were safe in the river. Most of the boys had grown wary of Junie. They couldn't decide whether he was a saint or a lunatic. He was standing alone on the bank of the river when Darnell ran up and pushed him off into the deep water. Junie went in with his hands at his side looking straight ahead, a great smile on his face. Albert had to dive deep and bring him up off the bottom. He had gone down like a stone, and when Albert brought him to the surface, Junie was still smiling. Albert dragged him ashore and pushed him up on the riverbank. The smaller boy's eyes were wide open. He made a quiet, high-pitched noise. It was terror or it was joy, I couldn't tell. I was afraid of what Albert would do to Darnell, once Albert caught his breath. Montrose grabbed Darnell roughly by his wrist.

"He wanted me to do it," said Darnell, struggling to say the words so Montrose and I would both understand.

"You could have drowned him," said Montrose. He slapped the boy hard on his bare bottom.

"He wanted me to drown him," said Darnell. "He wanted me to. He asked me."

Montrose looked at me and he looked at Junie again. The boy was still smiling, staring out across the river as though he could see a vision on the other bank. Someone rang the dinner bell, and the boys pulled themselves out of the water and grabbed their clothes, running half-naked back through the pasture toward their dinner. Montrose threw his arms to his side and looked up at the sky as if there might be an answer to all of his questions there. He followed the boys up toward the dining hall. I wanted to be alone, and I grew irritated at two older boys who tried to hang back from the rest. I cursed myself, not for the first time, for being afraid to swim in the river. The boys were still wet. They looked cool. I was hot and tired.

"Go on," I said to these last two. "Go play ball until your tea."

"Yes, Mr. Tanner," one of them said. It was Caesar, a boy who dressed better than the others. He went out to work four days a week at the feed mill. "Could I ask you one question first?"

"What is it?" I said to Caesar. His friend held back, but he was listening.

"You know a lot about medicine, no true?"

Caesar was wrong, but I didn't know how to tell him he was wrong. Some of the boys had ulcers on their legs that wouldn't heal. Simple had an especially painful-looking one, and I had cleaned it and wrapped it for him, but I didn't know anything about medicine. I wasn't going to lie.

"What's the problem?" I said.

"I have one sore," said Caesar.

"Where?" I said. Then I took a step back. The boy was holding out his penis as if it was a little animal he had found on the riverbank.

"This is my cock," said Caesar.

"Yes, I can see," I said. "I know what it is."

I waited, looking from one boy to the other, wondering if they were making fun of me again. Neither one of them laughed. I let myself look at Caesar's brown uncircumcised equipment. I wondered if he expected me to touch it. At the tip, near the place where the foreskin closed into a hood, was a sore like a blister.

"Did something bite you?"

"What?" said Caesar. He stared at what he held in his hand. The thing might have grown there overnight.

"Mr. Tanner asked if she bit you," said his friend, a boy everyone called Corky. Maybe it was his real name.

"No," said Caesar. "I don't think so. Maybe she did. I guess she could have."

"That's not what I meant," I said. I wondered who she was. The girls from the house out by the road. "I thought maybe that was a bug bite," I said.

"No man," said Corky. "Is it, Caesar?"

"I guess I know if something bites my own cock," said Caesar. He thought we were making fun of him.

"Don't get mad," I said. "Nobody's chancing you."

I convinced Caesar I'd seen all I needed to see. Corky wanted to show me his, too. "So you could compare," he said.

I told him it wasn't necessary.

"How long has the sore been there?"

"Two weeks now," said Corky.

"Let me talk," growled Caesar. "This belongs to me."

"He's worried," said Corky. "Sake of, that sore won't go away."

"They can give you a shot for that," I said. I remembered the word Beliz-eans used. "An injection."

"Injection?" said Caesar. "I hate one injection." He swallowed hard.

"Injection don't hurt, boy," said Corky. "It probably hurted more to juke that girl than an injection going to hurt."

"Boy," said Caesar.

"This is important," I said. "You don't want to let this go. You could go blind. Or crazy." The words sounded lame, like threats.

"Could it fall off?" said Corky.

"I don't know about that," I said. Then I noticed how relieved Caesar looked. That wasn't good.

"Maybe it could fall off," I said.

"Boy," said Corky. "I told you."

First chance I had, I drove Caesar to the army doctor, who started him on a series of injections. I'd considered taking him to the mission where I'd taken Montrose's people, but decided not to. I didn't know if the missionar-ies would have as much experience with syphilis as the British Army would have. I'm not saying they would or they wouldn't. I didn't know.

"What did the doctor say?" I asked when Caesar got back into the car.

"It won't fall off," said Caesar.

"Well," I said. "That's something."

"Still, I hate these injections," said Caesar. "That needle. I going to give up juking, boy. The time being."

After that, I thought I should watch the others while they swam, for anything like what happened to Caesar. It wasn't easy. I didn't want to stare. Once or twice I thought I saw a certain look on the part of some older boy, Benn in particular, as he watched the shiny brown bottoms of the younger ones. I saw Caesar and Corky swimming with the others, and later standing side by side and pissing into the bushes.

"It never did fall off," said Corky. He sounded disappointed.

Fairbanks and I were walking back from the basketball court. The boys had gone ahead to their supper. I tried to make my case. The old Fairbanks was gone and the new Fairbanks was my friend, and that gave me the nerve. I told him he ought to provide the boys with a simple lecture or two, so the boys could understand their bodies, so they'd have a chance to get along with girls when they got old enough to leave the place, if it was girls they wanted to get along with. I was careful not to give away the names of the boys who already knew too much.

"Of course they need that sort of thing," said Fairbanks. Relief washed over me. For once, he and I were going to agree.

"When can you start?" he asked. "Tonight?"

I felt like I'd fallen into a big hole, or been pushed. The trapdoor had closed above me. I wanted to argue, I meant to argue, but Fairbanks stopped me before I had a chance.

"Who else is going to talk to them?" he asked. We had stopped in the shade of a tall tree. He passed the basketball from one hand to the other.

"Sure, all the officers know how to juke," he said. "You think I'm bad. That damn cook has kids all over this district. The boys need to know more than how to get a girl pregnant. It's either you or me to tell them." He held the ball still.

"It can't be me," he said. "They need someone who isn't going to punish them for sneaking out at night, for whatever else they've done. If I catch them, you know I have to punish them."

Fairbanks listened a moment, weighing the sounds that came from the dining hall. "I have to punish them," he said. He had overcome the worst of his qualms about the rope. He used it regularly again. The boys were grateful when he didn't put salt on it.

When I look back on that time, I think, that wasn't me. It was someone else who met with the boys that evening after dinner. They crowded into the schoolroom and sat in the same straight rows as when they came for Christmas carols, and a young man stood in front of them, a man who looked a lot like me and whose voice sounded like mine, but who certainly wasn't me. This man was going to try to talk to them about the body's great mysteries, about love and desire. It couldn't have been me.

I supposed the first thing to do was to find out how much they knew already. It was about what I expected. The older boys knew the mechanical part of it. The younger ones suspected what the older ones knew. They learned some of it from watching the rabbits and the cattle and the sheep. The rest they learned the old-fashioned way, from the big talk of boys older than they were. For two hours that night, and for two more nights that followed, I tried to answer their questions about their bodies, and about girls' bodies (where their ignorance was only a little more scary than my own), and about disease. I tried not to say words like *juke.* I tried not to make it sound like sex ranked right up there with cigarettes and barbecue. I didn't use big words either. We were getting along okay, better than okay, until the third night when Brother Constant came to the schoolroom and stood just outside the door.

"Why are you talking to these boys about juking?" asked Brother Constant. "What makes you some big expert about sex? Are you a doctor? Are you a preacher?"

The boys froze. They sat in their chairs without saying a word, waiting for me to answer him. I saw the fear on their faces, that I was going to let them down.

"You know I'm not a doctor," I said. "I just try to listen. They have questions. I don't always have the whole answer." I could have told him I was trying to be good. He might have understood that.

"Maybe it isn't God's will that they have all these answers," said the cook.

"I don't know about God's will," I said. "I don't think it can be God's will for a boy to have syphilis."

"Depends on the boy," said Brother Constant.

"Look," I said, "You can help me. You can tell the boys what you know, too."

Brother Constant looked suspicious.

"If we don't tell them," I said, "who will?"

"I'm not sure they need to know," he said.

"That Peter Rabbit could know some things," said a voice from the back of the room. It was Albert, the baker's boy. He sat at a desk in the very back, his elbows on his knees. He looked at the floor. Nobody would know it was his voice if he didn't say anything more. Peter Rabbit looked up quickly. The boy glanced around to see if anyone would laugh at him. Nobody did. Then Albert spoke up again.

"Side Dick could know some things, too," said Albert. He met Brother Constant's eyes. "Boomba, he probably knows a lot of things by now."

Albert's words made Brother Constant stop there in the doorway and hold himself very still. He might have been saying a prayer.

"You could help," I said. "It would be good if we did this together."

Brother Constant looked out at the room full of boys, not letting his eyes rest on any one of them too long. One or two of them looked back at him. Most did not.

"Not tonight," he said. "I have to watch the office. Maybe next time."

He slipped away from the door. When he left, the room seemed unnaturally quiet to me, nothing to hear but the cicadas. I struggled with my thoughts. I looked at the chalkboard, at the poor drawing I had made of a female body. I saw how much I didn't know, made worse by the fact that I couldn't draw a decent naked woman. I was embarrassed that Brother Constant had seen my drawing. He'd been standing outside in the dark, like Fairbanks, listening.

"We going on with our meeting, Mr. Tanner?" asked Treeboy.

I looked at the chalk dust on my hands. I looked at the boys the way Brother Constant had looked at them, not at each face, but at the lot of them, as a group. For once, they weren't laughing at me. I saw sorrow in their eyes. Caesar and Corky sat together in the last row. Albert stood up slowly, ready to leave, a tired look on his face. Whatever I did now would not surprise any of them.

"We'll have our meeting," I said.

"All right," said Treeboy. "You heard him. Sex meeting tonight, boys."

A shout went around the room, a cheer. I was sure Brother Constant could hear it back in the office. I hoped he understood.

"Next question," said Albert. "And boy, speak up. Mr. Tanner doesn't have all night here."

I kept them later than I had planned. I didn't think I would have them again. A little after ten, they hurried over to stand in their lines in front of the office so that Brother Constant could count them off and send them to bed. One boy lagged behind in the dark. It was Treeboy.

"You sure about everything you mi tell we?" he asked.

I took a deep breath. "What are you thinking about?"

"About hand box," said Treeboy. He said the words so softly I had to strain to hear him. "About masturbation. Some people say it's wrong. Some people say you have one sickness if you do that."

The dew had already fallen. I walked with him through the wet grass wondering what I was supposed to tell him. I didn't want to sound like I was dismissing a question, not a question as important as that one.

"A lot of things I don't know," I said. "Brother Constant is right about that. But I'm pretty sure about this one thing. I don't think you have a sickness."

"It's just nature, right?" said Treeboy.

"Don't worry about it," I said. "Don't hurt yourself. Don't hurt someone else. That's what I want you to remember."

I left him and went down to the river to be alone. The mosquitoes were fierce, and I couldn't stay long. I scooped some water up and wet my face, washing some of the sweat away. I was afraid of the animals that came down to the river to drink in the dark. I wondered if Ellie would think I had done any good.

A few days later, I was called to the phone. It was Patel, from San Ignacio.

"The Lions," he said, all excited. As if I should understand about lions. I didn't know about any lions in Belize.

"The Lions Club," he said. "I'm a Lion. Aren't you?" It took me a few minutes before I caught on. The lions were for Junie. Patel thought he had figured out a way to help Junie.

"Come and see me," he said. "Next Saturday night at the hotel. We're having the Lions Club meeting."

Junie or no Junie, what Patel was asking was the last thing I wanted to do. I had plans. After the Saturday at the mission, I'd had my fill of do-gooders. I wanted to go into the city and drink beer with Price and Ellie and eat a big meal. Then I wanted to go back to Ellie's place and lie in bed all night and talk, and make love without making love. What we did, what we didn't do. Ellie's hands were what I wanted. I was afraid to ask for more, but after my Saturday with the vegetable people and after my fainthearted attempt to teach the boys about their bodies, I wanted to go see Ellie, have too much to drink, and get carried away, or almost carried away. I wanted meat and drink and love.

Instead, Saturday night, there I was at Mr. Patel's hotel, at the Greater San Ignacio Lions Club meeting. I had never been to a Lions Club meeting. My father and mother didn't join clubs. I had no experience of it. Fairbanks went with me to the hotel, but he was no Lion. It was strange seeing him in this light, laughing at the Lions' jokes and singing the Lions' songs. I didn't trust Fairbanks. He was having a good time. We brought Junie with us and sat him down at a table in the bar with a soda. We left the door open so I could keep an eye on him. Fairbanks worried about Junie and kept slipping out to see how he was doing, but I didn't worry. I knew how Junie dealt with stress. He floated away from the rest of us and went someplace in his head where we couldn't follow. I asked him once what he thought about when he was in one of his smiling trances.

"I'm having one meeting," he said. "With Jesus."

Fairbanks and I were meeting with the Lions Club in the public room of Patel's hotel, and Junie was meeting with Jesus in the bar. I kept trying to figure how the evening was going to work to Junie's advantage. Patel hadn't said a word to me about the boy. Fairbanks, once he was sure Junie had slipped off into suspended animation, got into the swing of Lionism, but I couldn't. I felt too cranky about not being with Ellie.

The whole evening was a test. I can see that now. Patel wanted a better look at Junie and a better look at me before he introduced us to a visiting Lion from Guatemala City, a plastic surgeon it turned out, who was educated in Mexico City and after that in Iowa. Patel and I went into the bar and broke Junie out of his dream. Fairbanks had bought the boy five soft drinks by then, and Junie had to go relieve himself before the doctor could examine him. When he did get a good look, the doctor's sad brown eyes filled with tears. Patel spoke Spanish and so did Fairbanks, which was a surprise to me. The two of them talked shop with the Guatemalan surgeon. I sat next to Junie feeling stupid, wondering if that was maybe what it felt like if you were good. I was a little tense about it. I don't know why. I didn't have enough practice with that sort of feeling.

"So, it's settled," said Patel suddenly in English. I was glad to hear it.

"This is wonderful," said Fairbanks.

Then the doctor turned and spoke to me. He sounded like a Midwesterner who was trying to sound like a Mexican. "We will look for you sometime next month. When the transport can be arranged."

"You mean the boy," I said. "You'll look for the boy."

"The boy can't go to Guatemala City alone," said Patel.

"You'll take him," said Fairbanks, who had already told Junie about his coming trip. "It will do you both good."

Junie said he wanted to pray about it, and I wondered if just this once, prayer would be appropriate. But Fairbanks said it was late and we had to get back to New Hope. He said we could pray all we wanted to in the car.

From that night, I was no longer in control. A plan fell quickly into place. Fairbanks talked to some of Brother Constant's relatives who did business on the Guatemalan side of the border, and Patel pulled strings through his Lions Club, and someone, I never knew who, managed to get us two seats on a Guatemalan army plane that would fly to the big city. I took the boy to a shop in Belize City two days before we were to leave so I could buy him clothes. Fairbanks slipped me money, and so did Brother Constant. I bought Junie four pairs of underwear. The boy was amused.

"Why four?" he said. "I only wear one at a time. Two at most."

I told him the others were spares, like the extra tire for the Toyota. He laughed again, and I pushed him into a cab and we rode out to Ellie's house. I didn't know how long I would be gone. I had to see her.

She met us at the door. She had waited all day. Ellie fixed Junie something to eat and sat him down on a chair in her living room, then pulled me into the kitchen where she threw her arms around me and kissed me. She had been eating mangoes. Her lips were red and swollen from it.

"I'm proud of you," she said.

I thought it over. Maybe this was what it felt like to be good. I was surprised at her warmth but not too surprised. I had figured there would be some sort of reward in it for me. "I want to make love to you," Ellie whispered.

"Right here?" I said. "Behind this door?"

She made a soft humming noise and she kissed me again, but she didn't mean that exactly.

"Can't you send him off somewhere?" she said.

"I wish I could. I have to keep him close by. We have to catch the bus in an hour."

"I'm going to miss you," she said, and she kissed me so hard she made my lip taste of blood. Then she did for me what she had done before, this time in her kitchen. I had to keep an ear open for the boy in the next room, in case he stirred. When she finished with me, and I leaned against the kitchen wall unable to open my eyes or to move any of my limbs, she leaned next to me and whispered in my ear.

"When you come back," she said. "We'll be together. Completely and always. When you come back."

I had that to look forward to, and it was a lot to look forward to. I gathered up Junie's new clothes and I got him onto the bus. On the ride to New Hope, we sat in our separate dreams. He thought of his version of paradise, and I thought of mine.

14

I took my days off and stayed away from the café. It was best that way. I slept through a night and a day, and woke up at midnight to red words glowing in the dark.

People Are No Damn Good.

It made me sick at heart, and I blamed Croker. I called him to tell him where he could jump off. I planned it out, how I was going to yell at him, *You're the one, Croker. You're the one who's no good. You're the worst of all.* I woke him up to tell him that, but when I heard his voice on the telephone, I lost my train of thought.

"It's you, isn't it, Tanner," he said, resignation in his voice. "My mother says I shouldn't talk to you anymore."

I wanted to tell him about his mother.

"She says you have bad energy," he said. "She says you exaggerate."

I wanted to tell him about bad energy.

"What about the words, Croker? The writing on the wall?"

"What words?" said Croker. "Look, it's late. Get some rest. Call me next week."

He hung up on me, and he unplugged his phone so I couldn't call him back. I got back into bed and slept until noon. By then, it was Saturday. I must have been tired. But I promised Stacen I wouldn't miss more than two days of work, and I meant to keep my promise. It's a small thing after all, getting to work when you're supposed to. I've kept bigger promises than the one I made to her. I wasn't going to let her down.

A steady rain fell Saturday night, and then the stuff coming down couldn't decide if it wanted to be snow or ice. December was late enough for snow, but this part of Tennessee, tucked up against the border with Kentucky the way it is, could stumble into every kind of storm. I read and listened to the radio as long as there was music to listen to. If the news came on, I turned the volume down. I lost track of whether the sun outside my window was coming up or going down. I watched for a while, trying to figure it out, then fell asleep again at the table and woke up to find the apartment had gone dark and cold. It was gray outside. My watch said it was half past four in the afternoon. Somewhere nearby, a tree limb had collected more ice than it could hold, and when the limb fell, it took down the first power line.

The thought of being cooped up in a cold apartment for another day gave me the urge to go out and buy a television set, the biggest, fanciest set they had at one of those stores with thirty or forty TVs turned on all at the same time. I'd have to ask for one that ran on a battery, the sort of thing you might take camping. Then I remembered I didn't have any money in the bank. There have been plenty of times in my life when I had money in the bank, including when I lived with Katherine. My finances were in a definite reversal. If they ever brought back the debtors' prison, I'd turn myself in.

I had to get out of the apartment. I used every drop of warm water in the pipes to take a shower. I brushed my teeth twice, afraid to look in the mirror because of the seedy guy who kept looking back at me. The weather wasn't any good for a bicycle. I thought about getting in my truck and driving to the mall on the other side of town to see what was playing at the movies, but I hadn't started my truck in a month and I didn't have confidence in the battery. And it had at least one flat tire. The idea of a shopping mall at the beginning of Christmas gave me claustrophobia anyway, or agoraphobia, whichever phobia it was that filled a person with fear in a shopping mall. I had both phobias. I thought about walking to the grocery store by the river and reading the magazines on the rack. The last time I'd gone into that store, I had to quit shopping early because of the music on the intercom, the kind of old love songs where the singer comes out years later with a different version of an earlier tune only the different version is slower and has more violins in the background than the original. That music made me cry on the frozen vegetables, little frozen tears that some other shopper took home and stored in her deep freeze. I didn't buy half the things I set out to buy.

When I walked to the door and stood on the front stairs, I realized I didn't have anywhere to go. It made me stop on the top step, a man frozen by his indecision as much as by the weather outside. I don't know how long I might have stood there if the phone hadn't started ringing. I hurried back inside hoping it might be Katherine.

It was Croker.

"I'm trying to get the rent together," I told him. "I've been off work a few days."

"It isn't the rent," said Croker.

"I apologize about your mother."

"It isn't about my mother."

We were quiet a moment.

"You're going to tell me what it's about?"

"It's Sara," said Croker. "I got a phone call from her. She's upset. Then her phone went dead."

"It's the weather," I told him. I knew that was too easy. "Where'd she call from?"

"I'm not sure," said Croker. "She said she was going out for a walk."

"In this? Is she nuts?"

"She mentioned the café. She said she wanted to say good-bye to you. You going away?"

"I'm not at the café. She wants to say good-bye to me, she's gone to the wrong place."

"She said something about the park by the river. She said . . ."

And then my line went dead, too.

I wished I hadn't picked up the phone, or better yet, that Croker had never called. I could have crawled back in bed and pulled the covers up over my head. Now I couldn't do that.

I grabbed a green slicker from a hook by the door, a raincoat I still have from those days in Belize. I started down the steps thinking I'd figure out where I was going when I was halfway there. I needed to move. I didn't intend to go anyplace in particular. I didn't intend anything at all. It was habit that led me downtown to The Unreformed Temple of Caffeine. It was late, but it was still Sunday afternoon (I was almost sure of that), and I didn't even know if Stacen would have the place open. For a month or so when she first took over, she tried opening up Sundays for the after-church crowd. It didn't work. The after-church crowd is peaceful and quiet. They get on Stacen's nerves. She tried hard, though. She tried anything she could think of to draw customers. Summer evenings, she invited young people to come play their guitars, but the café is small, and there isn't one good corner where a guitar player could sit and not get bumped into by the paying customers. When there were any of those in the place. It wasn't summer anymore. There wouldn't be any guitars. It was coldhearted December, ice in the street, and hardly a soul downtown. By the time I got to the café, I could do the little thing where you run a few steps and slide along on the frozen sidewalk. I hadn't played around like that in years. I saw two drivers barely avoid smashing into each other at an intersection, the only two drivers on the street. That made me laugh, to tell the truth, but I didn't laugh out loud because I didn't need one of those drivers to get out and punch my nose, which was cold from being outside so long. And because, just as they nearly collided, I looked across the street and saw a young man loitering beneath an awning. I couldn't see him close up. What I noticed was he didn't have any winter clothes on. He was thin and black, familiar to me as my own shadow.

The wind was at my back. When I thought about turning around and going home, I let the wind talk me out of it. I picked up my pace, and the guy across the street started walking along parallel with me, him on his side of the street, me on my side. I could have walked in the middle of the street, the whole town was so quiet. I stayed on the sidewalk, uneasy at the way the streetlights switched on one by one as we passed, as if some hidden presence watched our progress across town and turned the lights on each time we walked through an intersection. As I neared Franklin Street, I saw Stacen's café lights were on. I stood back from the window in the shadows so I wouldn't be too noticeable. I didn't want to go in. I tried to imagine where the guy across the street was hiding. I couldn't hear his footsteps. I heard singing, faint singing, some sort of gospel singing. *This world is not my home.* My feet were wet and cold. I hadn't had a cup of coffee in two days.

Stacen looked up from her work and focused her eyes directly through the window onto me, and I couldn't leave. It would have seemed like I was sneaking away. When she turned the outdoor lights on, it reminded me of the morning in September when the boy showed up and asked me for money. I was the one this time startled out of the shadows by the light, like a raccoon, or a small bird, no place to hide.

"Nice evening for a walk," said Stacen.

"It's not that bad," I said.

"What are you doing out here?" said Stacen.

I mumbled a poor answer: I was after the exercise. I was looking for a friend. I was trying to kill myself the slow way, frostbite, an inch at a time.

A long black car slid sideways through the intersection, clipping a taillight against the don't-walk sign. The driver straightened the car out and kept going, a boat crossing a perfectly smooth and wintry lake.

"I didn't know you had any friends," she said. She watched me the way she would watch a new dishwasher, some high-school part-timer fumbling with the cups and saucers. "You better come inside," she said. "Warm up a little. But don't stay long. Tony's coming to pick me up. I want to go home."

I followed her into the café and took my slicker off, dropping it by the door. I was frozen to the bone. Stacen poured me a coffee and I loaded it up with cream and sugar so I could get a little nutrition. I wondered why she was open at all. The welcome sign wasn't turned around in the window. The oven was on low. I think she was afraid if the power went out, she wouldn't get the gas lit again, but she didn't have to worry. That oven was so old there wasn't an electrical part on it anywhere. I saw a yellow legal pad on Stacen's table, a long list of figures. She was doing some serious thinking.

"Is it bad?" I asked. I tried to keep my hands from shaking by holding tightly to my coffee cup.

"It's kind of bad," said Stacen. "It's not so bad we have to close up tomorrow. We can hang on. We can lose a little more money every month, do without the extras at home. You know, the luxury items. Shoes. Milk." She drew a straight line across the page, carefully, as if it mattered how straight she drew the line. "I can work longer hours and have the girls hang out in the back of the place with me instead of those two mornings a week at day care. I'm not going broke in a hurry. I'm going broke slowly."

I was worried about her. It was way too calm for Stacen.

"I try and try to think of something different," she said. "Something to grab people's attention."

She didn't ask if I was hungry. She opened a bag of day-old muffins and set them in front of me.

"You need a plate?" she said. "You want me to get you some butter?"

"I'll do it," I said, but I didn't get up. I took the wrapper off a muffin and turned it around and around in my hands. I didn't want her to know how hungry I was. Every bite I took, I felt a little more human. I could hear the radio in the kitchen. The announcer cautioned listeners about the roads. Three or four snowflakes fell outside, not enough to give anyone hope. It wasn't going to snow. It was all ice now, and already more of it than I'd ever seen. I heard a siren in the distance. The sound cut off abruptly with a strange gurgle, as if the driver had left the road and gone into the river.

"Feels like winter out there."

"It's been winter all day," said Stacen. "Didn't you know?"

"I was napping."

She was quiet for a moment. She had her own thoughts.

"Why don't you go ahead?" I said. "I can lock up for you."

"I have to wait for Tony. He's got the girls. We're going home." It was the second time she said the word *home*, like it should mean something to me. I let it pass. "Katherine's coming, too," said Stacen. I felt my heart speed up. I wanted to see Katherine. For three days, every time I woke up, she was on my mind. Katherine, and the baby. The baby and Katherine. But I didn't want her to see me. I looked too rough.

"I'll just finish my coffee," I said. "You want me to sweep up?"

"Don't bother," said Stacen. "Sit still."

So I did. We sat at the table in the corner, and she didn't go back to work on her accounts. Maybe she was done before I came in, or maybe she lost heart. We didn't talk about it. I ate three of Stacen's muffins, but then the sound of my own chewing made me too self-conscious to eat another.

"Maybe you could raise your prices."

"Maybe I should give the food away," said Stacen.

A car came slowly down the road. In its headlights, I saw how the trees across the street, the trees old man Liu had years ago planted in front of his restaurant, were glazed with ice. A branch had broken on one of Liu's trees. Another was bent over, its top nearly touching the sidewalk. The car slowed as it approached the café, then slid sideways and came to rest across the street against a pickup truck.

"What a dumb ass," I said.

Stacen pushed herself up from the table and headed for the door.

"Turn some more lights on," she called to me. "That's no dumb ass. That's my husband."

She was moving too fast when she took the steps to the sidewalk, and her feet came out from under her. She went down, falling against her arm on the bottom step. I got the other lights on like she told me to, and then I ran to help her. As soon as I went out the door, I slipped on the top step, too, but I managed to grab hold of the doorknob. I went down on one leg. Stacen lay on her side on the icy sidewalk below me, holding tightly to her arm. Across the street I saw Tony get out of his car and try to plant his feet on the ground. He was letting go of the car door just to see if he could when he looked across the street and saw Stacen on the sidewalk. He gave a little swoon when he saw her. I thought he was going to fall down, too.

Stacen moaned where she lay sprawled on the bottom step. She was in a bad way, and I could see Tony wasn't going to be a lot of help. He was a history guy. He wasn't any good at current events, like his wife falling down the stairs. I looked everywhere, and there was not another soul on the street. The pet store owners were never in on a Sunday. A light was on in the back of Liu's, but he might as well have been on a boat to Shanghai for all the good he was going to do Stacen. She didn't even like Chinese food. I was the only one who could do anybody any good. I hate it when that happens. Stacen looked at me with the pain showing in her eyes. A little cut on her forehead was bleeding down the side of her face. I heard the girls inside the car ask their father what was the matter, why was he standing on the street like a lamppost.

The weight of all that need was hard to bear. I stepped back inside the café and I thought maybe I should call the police about Sara, or a tow truck for Tony's car, or a doctor for Stacen. What I really wanted to do was head straight for the back door and start walking and never turn around, not go back to my room for anything, just walk and walk, and do that little run-and-slide thing, and walk until I couldn't walk any farther and then put out my thumb and see how that worked, how far away from Stacen and Tony and Katherine and Croker and this whole disappointed town I could get. I went as far as the kitchen door. I tried the knob. It wasn't locked. I could have done it. I could have been gone.

I heard one of Stacen's girls cry out in the cold—it must have been the little one because she could cry the loudest—and I found myself looking around the kitchen for something I could put on the icy ground to make the walking easier, so I could get out there and see if she was all right. A little girl, after all. A child. I needed to find something to add grit to the street. There was salt, but there wasn't enough salt to get me all the way out to the car. There wasn't any sand, which would have worked better, but why would there be sand in a restaurant? I could imagine Stacen asking that question. I once had an old farm couple help me get my car out of a snowbank by bringing me ashes from their wood stove, but Stacen didn't have a wood stove. All I could find was a fifty-pound bag of whole-wheat flour, full of the little brown stuff that makes it bake up nice. I didn't know if it would work. I thought it was a dumb idea, but I found the biggest scoop Stacen owned and I filled it with flour and went outside and started sprinkling it everywhere.

"What the hell are you doing?" asked Stacen. She didn't say it in a mean way. She was sitting up. She hadn't tried to get to her feet yet. Her face was bruised, but she didn't know it. It could have looked to her as if I'd lost my mind.

"It works," I said. "Look."

I tried to give her a hand up. She waved me off.

"Come on," I said.

"Leave me alone," said Stacen. "I'll let you know when I want your help."

The way she held her arm, I knew she was feeling pretty bad. What she felt was worse than pain. It was deeper than any broken arm. I knelt beside her.

"It's okay," I told her. "You're going to be okay."

"No I'm not," said Stacen. "I'm not okay. I'm so far in debt I'm terrified. I'm tired as the Christmas goose. And I've broken my arm."

"You have insurance," I told her.

"You don't know shit," she said.

"You have me."

"Oh my God," said Stacen.

Tony watched us from the street. He must have had on the world's worst shoes to go along with his world's worst jacket and his world's worst haircut. He fell down in the world's most pathetic heap. One of his girls put her head out of the open door of the car. I called to her to stay where she was. For the only time in her life, she listened to me.

"Come on, Stacen. I need you to get up."

"It doesn't matter," said Stacen. "I'm not getting up. People are going to have to stop needing so much from me."

"I wouldn't know about that," I said.

"Sure you would," said Stacen. "You know all about it. I don't want to take care of people anymore. I don't want to look after Tony or Katherine, or your sorry ass. I want to quit like you quit. You're on your own now. That's how I want to be. On my own."

"Only one of us can quit," I told her. "One at a time."

"It's my turn."

"Too late," I said. "You missed your turn."

I grabbed her under the arms and lifted her to her feet. The move hurt her. I could tell by the way the blood drained from her face as I held her up. I thought she might faint. "Come on," I said, and I wished like hell there was a railing on those café steps. Somehow I got her inside, and I sat her down in a chair.

"I'll be all right," she said. "Jerk." She said it all through clenched teeth. "Go get my girls," she said.

I got a big bowl of flour this time and made my way down the stairs. Tony watched in amazement as I advanced slowly across the street tossing handfuls of whole wheat in front of me. First I got him to his feet and leaned him up against the good fender of his car. Then I got the girls out of the backseat. I didn't dare pick either of them up. I led them cautious as cats across the street and inside and sat them down next to their mother. I took more flour outside so I could work on Tony, and together we could take a look at his car.

"I think I can drive it," he said. He had a puffy bruise on the side of his face. He wasn't standing up straight. It didn't look to me as if he could drive anything.

"I don't think so," I told him. "We're going to push it out of the street and we're going back inside to see about Stacen."

He wanted to argue, and would have, but he was having trouble with the words. That little accident knocked the wind out of him. I got him to sit inside his car and had him turn the engine on just to give him something to do. Then I sprinkled the last of the flour in my bowl all around the wheels of his car. We got the car away from where it pressed up against that pickup, the wheels spinning and smoking. I cursed Tony and I cursed his car and he cursed me, and the little girls looked on in wonder from the front door of the café, all that terrific language. The big one was memorizing every word. We parked the car as close to the curb as we could get it.

Once inside, we found Stacen's girls leaning against their mother, wiping their eyes on her dress as if they'd been to see a sad movie. The way they stared at Tony and at me, you might have thought they didn't know us. Stacen had managed to clean the blood from her face. There were those little Catholic candles on each of the tables, and Tony lit them all, thinking we might lose electricity. The candles didn't give off much light. They made the girls feel better.

"You all right?" said Tony. He knelt next to Stacen. "Is it your elbow?"

"My arm," she said. "It's completely broken, I'm pretty sure."

"You think?" said Tony. "You're going to be fine, hon." He gave the wrong hand a squeeze.

"Do that again," said Stacen, "and I will kick you so hard you will pee sitting down for the rest of your life."

Tony stepped back from Stacen's table. He needed to think about it.

"I can splint it," I said.

They both looked at me as if I'd spoken a foreign language.

"The arm," I said. "I know how."

They looked at me again. This time they thought I was crazy.

"I learned about splints in the Peace Corps," I said.

"Right," said Tony. "Well," he said. Then he said, "Gee."

"Oh shut up," said Stacen.

"I'll drive you somewhere," said Tony. "To the hospital."

"Not on your life," said Stacen. "You, me, these kids, all camping out in the emergency room. It's too much."

"We can leave them here," he said. "They can stay with Tanner."

Both girls turned their heads slowly toward me. They began to cry harder than before.

"I guess not," said Tony.

I went to the kitchen and brought back two long wooden spoons, a dish towel, and a roll of masking tape. I had Stacen come over to the counter where there was more light, so I could get a closer look at her arm. She must have been in a lot of pain because she did what I asked without arguing. I was sure she was right about the arm. It was broken, but it wasn't like half of it was shooting off at some crazy angle.

"I won't try to set it," I said. "We're not desperate. Just let me splint it so you won't bump it on anything."

I wrapped the dishtowel around her arm then placed the wooden spoons on either side. I used the whole roll of tape to make it as snug as I dared. I taped it so she couldn't move her wrist or her elbow. It didn't look like much, but I thought the pressure might help ease the pain, and when I was finished, Stacen had a look on her face I hadn't seen before. It was gratitude or something that would pass for gratitude.

"I lied," I said. "I never learned this in the Peace Corps. I never did a splint in my life."

"I know," said Stacen. "It doesn't matter. You would have learned it wrong."

"It's cold in here," said Tony.

The girls carried on with their weeping as if they were on stage. Tiny supporting actresses.

"It'll be all right," I said. "You had a little bad luck is all. Everything's going to be fine."

There was a knock at the side door, and the girls wailed louder for their new audience. I stepped over to the window where I could see who it was, thinking Katherine, but it was the people who lived above the café, the young man and his redhaired girlfriend. They didn't appear to be fighting. They were fully clothed. I opened the door a crack.

"Your lights are on," said the man. "We saw the candles. Are you open?"

"Well, no," I said. "I don't know. I don't think so. What do you need?"

"It's cold upstairs," he said. "We've been gone all day. I'd give anything for a hot drink."

They knew how to warm each other up without hot drinks. I would have turned them away. Stacen wouldn't let me.

"Tell them to come inside," she said.

I went to lock the door behind them and saw a car inching slowly down the street, as if the driver was sneaking up on someone. The driver moved as cautiously as a driver could, but the car swung around in front of the café much the same way that Tony's car had swung around in front of the café: the street had become a river with a small whirlpool right in the middle. The driver hit Tony's car where we had pushed it up against the curb, caving a front fender in, killing the engine. Stacen closed her eyes, though her lips kept moving. I thought she might be counting to ten, or counting to a hundred.

"I'll get the flour," said Tony. "You start the coffee."

I was glad I didn't have to go outside again. I put coffee in a filter and loaded up the machine, and I didn't look out the window to see who it was this time. I opened up the last bag of day-old scones and muffins before Stacen had a chance to tell me to do it. I felt a gentle humming up and down my spine. I felt a buzz in my heart. My brain was calling out to the night, let it be her, let it be her. Tony returned a moment later, a beautiful woman clinging to his side, her face pale as the gray night. She walked like a duck and her coat wouldn't button over her belly, and I thought I would weep with the little girls at the joy of being in the same room with her. She didn't see me at first.

She wouldn't let go of Tony's arm even inside the café until he passed her to Stacen. The way he had wrenched his back, I knew she was hurting him.

"I was trying to get to the café," she said. "I stopped by Tanner's place . . ." And then she saw me. I think she was happy to see me. She buried her face in the collar of Stacen's coat. She had been crying out in the car. She was leaning up against Stacen's bad arm, but Stacen didn't say anything about it.

"It's going to be okay," said Stacen. "Tanner," she said. "Get over here. Sit by your wife and keep her from having her baby in this dirty dining room."

"Oh," said Katherine, as I sat next to her. "Oh, oh." She struggled with something she felt she had to say. We waited for her to compose herself. We had nowhere to go. Stacen gave her a one-armed hug. Tony hugged her and Stacen's kids jumped up from the table and ran to hug her, too. Everyone was careful not to look at me, and Katherine looked down at her belly. I had to get into the kitchen and be by myself for a few minutes because I was so much in love with her and had been longing for her all that day and all that week and the week before, and yet nothing had changed, I was still confused and scared, the same man I had always been. It would take more than ice on the trees, more than a night on the town, to see where I fit into Katherine's world.

When I could make myself do it, I came back into the dining room from the kitchen. Stacen handed me a bottle of round white pills and I took the cap off it for her. I gave her four. "Anybody else need a little painkiller?" she asked, a surprising kindness in her voice. The redheaded woman from upstairs held out her hand, sheepishly I thought. There must have been a question in my eyes. There was a look of pleading in hers. I gave the redhead two tablets.

"You need anything?" I asked Katherine.

"I'm okay," she said. She didn't look like she was okay. "Nothing in that bottle's going to do anything for me."

She buried her face in her own collar this time. I put my arm around her. She let me.

"What is that?" asked Stacen. "My God."

She was looking at something, someone, through the window. I held my breath. I was prepared for the worst. I stood up, ready to defend my wife and my child if it was time for that. When Stacen pointed, we all saw the apparition, a double apparition, though it wasn't the apparition I was expecting. It was Croker shuffling up the sidewalk with Sara at his side. She slipped and he grabbed onto a light pole so he wouldn't slip, too, looking around dazed at what he saw, ice everywhere, nothing but ice. Stacen looked at Katherine, a question in that look, and Katherine nodded her head yes.

"Get them in here," said Stacen. Tony moved to the door again. The tall boy from upstairs went with him.

"Are there any more refugees at the door?" said Stacen, kindly I thought, when you consider she was sitting there with a broken arm, too tired or too broke to get up and take herself to the emergency room. She was addressing all of us and none of us. She was showing an amazing amount of control. Stacen was not ordinarily a calm woman. She was not happy with her life so far.

"If there are," she said, "tell them to come in."

From across the way, like some kind of Chinese ghost, Mr. Liu came gliding silently over the frozen street, slipping and sliding on a pair of old house shoes, beautiful to watch. He looked like a figure skater at first, an Olympic speed skater warming up before the big race, until he tried to negotiate the curb and stumbled a little. He caught himself. His knee never touched the ground.

I opened the front door and asked him to come inside. He wanted me to come out where he was instead, where he could have a private word with me. I compromised and stood in the doorway.

"I saw what you did with the flour," said Liu. "We don't have flour. We're all out."

"What does he want?" asked Stacen, looking at me.

"Whole wheat, or white?" I said.

The man smiled and nodded his head. "Whatever you have."

I passed his request on to Stacen in a whisper, as though we two were keeping the worst of the news from the others.

"Hold just a little back," she said to me. "You may want to do some baking."

15

*L*iu took his bowl back to his own kitchen across the street, tossing the flour in front of him, moving as carefully as if he was crossing the thin ice of a Chinese pond. I didn't count on seeing him again. But twenty minutes later, after I brought Katherine a mug of hot water and a tea ball and put a tray of frozen croissants in the oven, the old man came back, followed by his wife. Each of them carried a plate, hers piled high with fried dumplings and his with egg rolls.

"Nobody is come to our place for dinner tonight," said Liu. "So we decide to deliver." Liu was small, even for a Chinese person. He didn't weigh a hundred pounds. His wife was smaller than he was. She looked frail, as if that one plate of food was all she could carry, and she looked half frozen. It was because of her, said Liu, they came back across the street.

"She gets lonely tonight," he said. "She gets lonely all the time. I don't know why. I'm here."

Mrs. Liu ignored the old guy and passed around the platter of dumplings. I offered to bring her tea, but she said she hated tea. I poured her a cup of coffee. She dumped four spoonfuls of sugar into it.

"I like a little coffee," she said. "From time to time."

Stacen announced hot scones would be coming out of the oven soon. Stacen announced it twice, and the second time I realized she meant for me to get in the kitchen and start baking scones.

"You have more flour?" asked Liu.

"Ask Mr. Pillsbury," said Stacen, and she lifted her chin at me as if I'd squandered all her precious flour instead of using it to rescue her.

"We have a whole bag we haven't touched," I said.

"So, go touch it," said Stacen.

"Shouldn't we get you to a doctor?" I said.

"Soon enough," said Stacen. "It's like Toddy used to say. You can't break what's already broken."

"I heard him say that once," said Croker. "In court."

"It doesn't hurt?" I said. "Your arm?"

"It's supposed to hurt." Stacen was talking to me slowly, the way you would explain something to a child. "I would just like to sit here awhile," she said. "I want to enjoy seeing my café full of people. It does me good."

"I can bake," said Liu.

"You don't know how to bake," said his wife.

"Tanner can bake," said Stacen. "It calms him down."

So I went into the kitchen and mixed the flour and leavening and slapped some dough together. I listened for Katherine's voice, and even when I couldn't hear her voice, I could feel she was out there. I peeked through the door once and saw her talking to Sara and Croker, as if they were old friends. Katherine was so much taller than Sara, the girl could have been one of Katherine's library kids. It wasn't easy for me to leave Katherine out front, but if she had tried to slip out of the café and go home, I would have known about it.

"This is how we have a party," said Liu, "in China."

We had finished the egg rolls and a tray of croissants. The boy from upstairs started a plate around to take up a collection for the food, but Stacen wouldn't accept it. She couldn't get any of us to take the money back either. The plate full of dollar bills sat on the counter, and every time the little girls got loose and ran around the room, some of the dollars fell onto the floor.

Sara went over and picked them up and tried to stack everything back on the plate. The Lius were beyond weariness. His accent had grown thicker than before. His skin, and hers, looked like paper that had been oiled so you could see through it. They were having the time of their lives.

"What part of China are you from?" asked Croker.

"Me?" said Liu. "I'm not from China. I'm from Kansas. I'm from Kansas part of China. That's the middlewest of the far east."

"Stop telling lies," said his wife.

Liu laughed, his small chest rising and falling. It made me think he hadn't laughed in a long time. The part of a person that laughs can get rusty. It was hard not to laugh with him. I wondered why he thought he had to hide in the back of his restaurant when he could have been out front with his customers having a ball.

"He had cancer," Mrs. Liu whispered to me. "He had it pretty bad. Them doctors got it. He's not strong like he used to be."

"This is what we do," said Liu, "in China." He had taken a position near the front door, the redheaded woman on his right and Sara on his left. "We sit in a circle," he said, "like this."

"Old rooster," said his wife.

I saw we had formed a circle of sorts, with only the tall boy sitting out of alignment. When he realized he was out of place, he moved his chair against the wall next to Mrs. Liu.

"We all take a turn," said Liu. "Provide some fun for the others. No radio, no TV. Everybody join in. Like communism."

"Not in this life," I said. I didn't mean for anyone to hear me, but it didn't matter if anyone heard me or not. There wasn't going to be any amateur hour for me. The radio was on low so we could hear what the weather was doing. Stacen reached over and turned it off. She did it mostly because I didn't want her to.

"Just us," said Liu. "We are our own entertainment."

"What do you do to the guy who refuses to take a turn?" asked Stacen. She nodded toward me like I would be the one person who would ruin Liu's fun. She probably thought Liu knew some ancient methods of torture. Stacen watched too many bad movies.

"I don't know," said Liu. He was stumped. "It never happened. Everybody has one thing they can do."

Looking around the room, I wasn't so sure. I figured we were a tougher crowd than he thought. I felt safe. We weren't the kind of people who worked at some summer camp for difficult children. We weren't fools.

"You came to the wrong party," I told him. I didn't say it to be mean. I just didn't see why I should let a man get his hopes up.

"I love it," said Tony. "I absolutely love it."

I gave Tony a look. I gave him several looks. I wanted my look to say, *Don't suck up to this guy or someday the commies will get you, just like they got him.* My look didn't faze Tony.

"I'll start," said Tony.

Of course he would start. Somebody had to start. Why not the big homely man who read history books for fun? All the same, I knew Liu's plan was doomed. It wouldn't get past the wishful thinking stage. If it was strip poker, we'd never get our hats off.

"Good," cried Liu, and Mrs. Liu clapped her hands.

"What will you do?" she asked. "I think you will sing?"

"How did you guess?" said Tony.

This was more than I was prepared to do, listen to Tony sing. He didn't know how to sing. He wasn't musical in any way, although whatever he did, it would be loud. He had one of those voices you could hear from a mile away, underwater. Even as he spoke, his girls were shoving their fingers in their ears.

"What's your name?" asked Mrs. Liu.

"Anthony," said Tony. As if he had more than one name. When he sang, he was Anthony. When he ran around bashing his car into other people's cars, he was plain old Tony.

"We always must introduce you," said Mrs. Liu. She turned and spoke to the rest of the room in Chinese, just a few words. She could have been saying, *Shoot the ugly dog of imperialism.* Or, *Remember those opium wars.* Croker smiled at her as if she'd nominated Tony for a Nobel Prize, as if he understood every word she said.

The room got quiet so Tony could make a fool of himself. The older girl curled up next to Stacen, and the little one came over and crawled up in my lap. I did not invite her. I was going to tell her to move along, keep looking until she found a better lap, but Stacen was watching me, and even with a broken arm Stacen could scare the hell out of me. I sat very straight in one of Stacen's wooden chairs. It's how I would sit if I were waiting for a miracle or a vision. Right away that little snaggletooth girl in my lap fell asleep. I felt like I was holding a sack of rocks.

Tony stood up and took a deep breath. I didn't think the room could get any quieter. Then it did. There weren't any cars in the street, no television noises from upstairs, no noises of any kind. It surprised the hell out of me when he started singing "Danny Boy." The man started out as if he knew what he was doing, but I've heard that song plenty of times. I've even tried to sing it myself when nobody else was around, when I was out fishing all alone and pretty sure nobody was around the next bend in the river. I knew there was this place near the end of the song where you have to hit a couple of notes that are way up in the rafters—*'Tis I'll be h-e-r-e* . . . and that word *here* shoots off into outer space. Tony was not going to be able to pull it off. It would be the end of show-and-tell at Toddy's Café.

He sang away. I didn't interfere. He came to that high part and he almost got it. I mean, he pretty much got it. You could say he got it completely if you wanted to be charitable. Nobody noticed the high note was ragged around the edges. Maybe it wasn't ragged. I can't say, anymore. The little redhead from upstairs had been bringing out a fresh pitcher of cream. She stopped next to the counter with her mouth open, and Katherine gave off this glow, and Stacen looked like she might cry or be Irish herself or some other nationality equally foolish.

"Wonderful, wonderful," said Mrs. Liu. People were clapping. Don't ask me why.

"That's a Chinese song," said Liu.

"Be quiet," said his wife. "You think any song about going home, it's some kind of Chinese song."

"I heard that one in China more than once," said Liu. "Long time ago."

Mrs. Liu called on Tony for another song, an encore, and this time he did a small piece of opera he said was by Puccini. Who knows? Maybe it was. I never met Puccini. When Tony was through, Liu tried to speak up. He was going to claim Puccini for the Chinese, too, but his wife caught his eye and he kept quiet. Tony sat down, all that applause hanging in the air. We clapped for a long time because the clapping gave us time to think. I wasn't the only person who was nervous. None of us wanted to see this crazy Chinese entertainment go any further, none of us except for a couple of crazy Chinese who should have been back across the street tucked in next to the stove with a quilt around their feet.

"I'll go next," said Liu. "I have very little talent. It's best for me not to wait too long."

"Oh you," said his wife.

"I will do a whistle song," he said. I didn't know what he meant. I had never been to a Chinese party. I hadn't planned on attending this one.

Old Liu puckered up his lips and started to blow. Until that night, I never heard anyone whistle an entire song, just a few bars of something from the radio, maybe the intro to a TV show. Liu whistled all the way through "The Yellow Rose of Texas." I didn't realize it before, but that song is about Chinese people. Without stopping, he whistled a John Denver song. I wondered why Chinese people like John Denver. He ended with "Rocky Top."

"Good lord," said Stacen. I thought she must have moved her arm too suddenly, but then I could see she liked the whistling. The timer went off in the kitchen. I passed the little girl I was holding over to Sara, who looked happy to have her, and I went to the kitchen for the scones and butter. In the bad light I burned my hand and swore and Stacen followed me in to tell me to watch my language.

Katherine came through the kitchen on her way to the restroom. She was in there awhile with the water running. I waited outside the door for her. When my wife came out, the look she gave me, I could tell she'd been hoping I'd be waiting for her.

"Hold me," she said. I did exactly as I was told. I put my arms around her, and I felt as if I was falling through piles of clean laundry, as if I had discovered a hidden valley in the high mountains. As if I'd driven home safe on a cold and snowy night.

"I wanted to be with you," she said. "That's all."

"You're not going to have the baby anytime soon, are you? You're not planning that for tonight?"

"It only happens that way in the stories people tell at baby showers," said Katherine. "It's early for that. But here," she said, and she put my hand on her belly. I felt the movement, like snakes in a bag, like a garden hose let loose in a swimming pool. I'd felt it before somewhere, I don't know where, but not like this. It was scary and it was magic. In Stacen's darkened kitchen, that baby was trying to talk to me.

"What part is that?" I said.

"It's a knee," said Katherine. "I think."

It was a knee or a foot, or maybe it was a head. It didn't matter. It was a baby part. It belonged to me a little bit. I felt myself falling again, and I grabbed onto the sink and tried to steady myself. I was out of control.

"Let's just pretend," she said. "For tonight, pretend we're together, like we used to be."

I agreed to that. I would have agreed to a lot of things at that moment if Katherine had wanted to take advantage of me. We went back into the dining room. Nobody paid attention to the fact that we sat down together, except Stacen, who smiled at Katherine and glowered at me. Mrs. Liu was doing magic tricks. They were jokes, really, not tricks. One involved making a set of chopsticks disappear. Her husband watched her closely.

"I been seeing her do that for thirty-one years," he said. "I still don't know how she does it." He acted as if it disturbed him.

"Of course you don't," said Mrs. Liu. "It's Chinese magic." She sat down, and everybody clapped some more, maybe because of the way she sat in a chair. Maybe because when she smiled, we had to see how beautiful she was. Tony hugged Mrs. Liu and she hugged him back and grinned at her husband, and everybody got into the hugging for a few minutes. They finished with that and they started looking my way. As if they wanted something from me.

"What?" I said.

"You," said Mrs. Liu, still beaming from her recent triumph. "It's your turn."

"Me?" I said. "No way."

"Why not?" said Mrs. Liu. "What are you afraid of?"

Stacen leaned forward in her chair. "Tanner," she said, and from the tone of her voice, the pain relievers were wearing off. "Is there anything you're not afraid of?"

I didn't like that. I wanted to tell her, sure, there were things I wasn't afraid of, but then she probably would have told me I had to list them. Nobody can list the things he's not afraid of. So I did what anyone would have done in my place. I stalled.

"Those guys haven't taken a turn yet," I said.

I pointed at the young couple who lived upstairs. They hadn't sung or whistled or stood on their heads. Neither had Katherine. Katherine was off the hook. This crowd wasn't about to abuse a pregnant woman.

"Tanner will take a turn," said Stacen. "But first," she drew her broken arm slowly across the table to her side, "I want to sing." She caught me off guard. I hadn't even considered Stacen, what with her injury and her sour disposition.

"I'm sorry," I said. "It's funny, but I thought just now I heard you say you wanted to sing."

"Be quiet, Mr. Tanner," said Mrs. Liu. "Don't be a stick up the mud." She caught me off guard, too. Nobody had called me Mr. Tanner in years. I didn't want to be a stick up anybody's mud. I just didn't know if I wanted to hear Stacen sing. Tony was sufficient for one night. I would have gone back to the kitchen and mopped the floor or changed a lightbulb, but Stacen wouldn't let me get up from my table. She told me if I left the room, I was fired all over again.

"What about the rest of the scones?" I said.

"I'll get them," said Tony. He jumped out of his chair and disappeared into the kitchen.

"Now, Miss Stacen," said Mrs. Liu. "You forget about that poor arm and sing for us. It will make you feel better."

Stacen swallowed another handful of ibuprofen and washed it down with coffee. She started a Christmas song, you know the one, about snow coming down, and *in the meadow we can build a snowman,* and that sort of thing. Her little girls watched her. They could have been looking at Santa himself. Maybe they hadn't heard their mother sing in a long time. Everybody loved it, old Liu and his wife most of all. They clapped. They wanted to make Stacen the queen of China.

"Now that," said Liu, "is a Chinese song. I heard that one plenty of times before."

"All right," said Stacen. Her song and her broken arm and the fresh round of painkillers had put a happy glow on her face. She looked my way as if to say, take that, Tanner Johnson, and you better be ready, because your time is running out.

I was granted a reprieve by the young couple who lived upstairs. They said it was their turn next. They hadn't been together long enough to know many songs they both could sing. They sang a few words of a couple of songs, but most of their music didn't have a lot of words. When they tried to whistle, they were booed until they had to stop.

"Give us a dancing," said Liu.

They looked at each other and smiled, and Stacen turned the radio back on, but soft. We had to stop being rowdy to hear the music, some kind of waltz. It was clear to me neither half of that twosome ever took a dance lesson, but we pushed the tables from the middle of the room, and they gave it a go. The boy towered over his ladylove. She studied his chest. He didn't step on her feet for a long time. The waltz gave me a minute or two more to think, to wrack my tired mind for one song I knew all the words to. I didn't want to look foolish. I tried to recall if I'd ever been able to whistle. I was having trouble swallowing, when I looked at all the people in the room and realized there was something that would work, something I knew how to do. It was watching the dancers, especially the young woman, the way her face turned red, that made me think of it.

"Now you," said Stacen, and by *you* she meant *me*. "No more excuses. It's a party and you're not going to ruin it. You do something, Tanner. Everybody can do something."

"Of course he can," said Mrs. Liu.

I didn't argue. I took a deep breath and I tried to clear my head. I was going to tell a joke. About fishing tackle. It was a pretty funny joke I heard once at The Bobber, about this catfish who was an atheist, and a Baptist preacher who couldn't swim, and a Jewish rabbi.

"Wait," said Katherine. "I'd like to go next."

I don't know if she was trying to save me or what. It was sweet of her, though.

"Bravo," said Tony. "I've heard her sing before."

"You have?" I said.

"I'm not going to sing," said Katherine.

"When have you heard her sing?"

"I'm going to recite a poem," she said. "It's by Andrew Marvell. It's called 'To His Coy Mistress.'"

"Wait a minute," I said. "I've read that poem."

"You shut up, Tanner," said Stacen. "I mean it."

Katherine stood from her table. She looked up at the ceiling once, then closed her eyes.

Had we but world enough and time,
This coyness lady were no crime . . .

She said the poem start to finish. Everyone loved it. They clapped a long time afterwards, but before they clapped, Tony murmured the last lines with her, giving them a flourish. It seemed everybody knew the damn poem.

Let us roll all our strength and all
Our sweetness up into one ball,
And tear our pleasures with rough strife
Thorough the iron gates of life;

Thus, though we cannot make our sun
Stand still, yet we will make him run.

There I was. Me and time's wasted chariot, both of us laid low by a beautiful woman on a cold night. Everyone looked my way, but there was nothing left of me, no more surprises. So when there was a new movement at the door, a little surge of that fresh, cold air, I was happy for the way everyone looked at the door instead of at me. I was so happy I looked at the door, too, a big stupid smile on my face as if someone had just arrived with pie. Only it wasn't pie. I knew it wasn't pie, I knew it could never be pie, I knew there was no pie left in the whole world. The door opened a few inches and it closed, all of its own accord. Everyone else acted as if it was nothing or it was the wind. Only I knew.

"All right, Tanner," said Stacen, "it's time to sing."

"Oh God, no," said Katherine, and the two of them laughed, like what a funny joke. Pretty soon they had everybody else laughing with them, everybody except me.

"I can sing a little."

"I'm sorry," said Katherine. "Honey, you go ahead and sing if that's what you want to do."

"I'm not going to sing," I said. My feelings were hurt. Maybe I don't know Puccini, but I can still sing.

"Another dancing?" said Liu.

"I don't dance in public, I don't sing in public, and I don't know any jokes fit for the public," I said.

"Maybe we could burn you at the stake," said Stacen.

"No," said Katherine. "That could be fun for you. I wouldn't enjoy it."

"Me either," said Sara. The girl hadn't spoken much that evening. She looked at Katherine to see if was okay to say even that little bit. Katherine smiled at her.

"If he can't sing . . . ," said Tony.

"I know what he can do," said Katherine. And everyone turned to look at her. I looked at her, too. I figured she owed me some kind of escape from my situation. "It's the best thing he does," said Katherine. Some of the others stared at her swollen belly, laughing, thinking, *Oh no, we're not going to have any of that at this party.* I watched the door out of the corner of my eye. Whatever I did, it wouldn't matter because *he* was out there waiting to stop me in the middle of it. *He* was going to stop me for a liar and a fraud.

"Tell us a story," said Katherine.

Sara smiled and Liu clapped his hands, and Mrs. Liu gave a little girl's jump of delight. I saw Tony nod his head once just for show. Goddamn Tony, anyway.

"I wouldn't know how to begin," I said, trying to get Liu to bail me out. This was his party. Maybe he could do some card tricks. Shadow puppets. Play the spoons.

"Tell us about the boy," said Katherine, "about Junie."

"It's not important," I said.

"It is important," said Katherine. "I want to know the rest."

"Junie it is," said Tony, sitting down next to his daughters.

"Junie," said Liu.

"Junie," said Stacen. In my mind I heard an echo: *Gillett, Gillett, Gillett.*

Katherine poured a cup of coffee and handed it to me. "We want to hear about Junie," she said.

"Precisely," said Mrs. Liu. "And that's that."

So I told them. Ice falling in the street, the lights flickering, I told them about Junie and about the baker's boy, and about Ellie and Price and me and Fairbanks and Patel. I didn't tell it all in order. I left out parts I shouldn't have left out. I didn't say half of it right. I just told them. It took a long time, they listened to every word, nobody else came into the café. Nobody left.

16

We arrived at New Hope shortly before dinner. Junie and I had only planned this much, to take the evening meal and then to ride in a taxi to the border. We would walk across the bridge to Melchor de Mencos and meet with our Lions Club friends. They would help us find the small airport on the outskirts of town where we would get on a plane for Guatemala City. I went to my house to clean up for the trip. We left the little suitcase with Junie's new clothes in it on the veranda outside the office. We set it right there in the open so we wouldn't have to look for it when it was time to go.

I regret many things from that time of my life, from all the other times, too, but nothing so much as the way I left that suitcase on the veranda. I should have told Albert to watch over it, or I should have taken it with me to my house, kept it by my side long enough to wash my face and pack a few of my own shirts, a clean pair of pants. When I came back, Junie was crying and Albert was beside himself. He was walking around in little circles, stopping now and then to reach out to Junie or to stare at the boys playing ball on the field below. The suitcase was gone. One of those boys had stolen it.

Then, of all the words I could have said, I said the wrong words. I only meant to make that other boy, whoever he was, give the suitcase back. I didn't mean to say anything that would hurt Junie. I didn't intend to put pressure on Albert. I stood on the veranda and I looked out at the boys who were coming in from their game, slowly forming into their lines for roll call, but I looked without seeing. I spoke without thinking.

"That suitcase had better show up," I said, "and I mean now. Immediately." And I didn't just say it. I pronounced it, the way Hobson might have. The way Fairbanks talked to the boys.

"If it doesn't show up, if it doesn't reappear right here where I'm standing, Junie and I won't be able to go. We'll have to cancel our trip."

Fairbanks came out of his office to stand next to us on the veranda. He stared at the place where the suitcase should have been, as if there might be a clue there to tell us who had stolen it. He brought his rope out with him. I'd thought of that rope as something that belonged to the old Fairbanks, but now I could see how much it belonged to the new Fairbanks, too. All the boys looked at me. They tried not to look at Junie, who was so disappointed by the loss of his suitcase, those four pairs of clean white underwear and the red sweater. Junie's lips were moving, but I couldn't hear any words. The boys looked at Fairbanks, too, at the rope he was swinging against his pant leg. Fairbanks wasn't the one who frightened them the most. I don't mean to say it was me. I didn't frighten them at all. The most frightening person on the veranda was the baker's boy. Whoever had stolen Junie's suitcase couldn't give it back now. The thief faced a beating by Fairbanks. Looking up at Albert, the tears on his face, the thief knew he had a worse beating coming from Junie's brother.

Albert looked from one boy to another, trying to read guilt in a boy's laugh, in another boy's trembling lip. Fairbanks shouted at them to line up, and they moved grudgingly into their ranks. They had learned a long time ago they could find safety in order. But before they could get themselves properly arranged, Albert ran down the stairs and flew straight at the boy who headed up the first line. It was Benn he picked out. Everyone knew Benn was a thief, in that place of thieves. Albert bloodied Benn's nose and knocked him off his feet. He was on top of Benn, choking him, before anyone knew what he was doing. Four boys grabbed at Albert and tried to pull him off, and Fairbanks came up behind him with the rope, lashing Albert hard across the back. It didn't have the effect Fairbanks hoped it would. Albert was so wound up he reached out blindly and grabbed for the rope, and caught it, and pulled on it hard enough that Fairbanks stumbled and fell. Albert found himself standing over Fairbanks. When Fairbanks reached out to grab the boy's leg, Albert kicked the man in the side, made him curl up on the ground, and then it was madness, a free-for-all, some boys trying to stop Albert before he did things he would never be forgiven for, and others just trying to hit someone, anyone, to even the score. I don't know how I moved off the veranda and entered into the middle of it, the whole ugly, horrible moment. I went to rescue Fairbanks or to protect Junie or to calm Albert. All I know is I ended up with Fairbanks's rope in my hand. There were boys on the ground and boys trying to get out of the way. A brown foot delivered a message to me, a hard kick so near my groin I doubled over and tasted something bitter and hateful. I turned around and lashed out with the rope more than once, paying no heed to any boy's cry of pain. They scattered. I made them scatter, the way the wind blows leaves across the ground in a dry yard, each of them running in a different direction except Albert, the baker's boy. He lay on the ground with his knees drawn up, staring at me. It was only then I realized I had directed most of my blows onto him. The bloody rope. The sound of tears.

When everyone stood still, the noise from the nearby bush, the insect sounds and the bird sounds, filled the air louder than ever, out of proportion to the time of day. The boys looked at me. The bigger boys placed themselves in front of the smaller ones, their arms spread from their sides as though to protect the lee boys from me. Fairbanks approached me slowly, a smile on his face that wasn't a smile at all. He held his hand out for the rope. I gave it to him quickly. I didn't want to touch it anymore. I wished I hadn't touched it. I could see by the looks on the boys' faces it was too late for a wish like that. That afternoon, I lost everything I'd worked for, every inch I had traveled up the long lane to New Hope. A year and a half, and I was a stranger again.

Albert got to his feet and looked at me, then past me to the place where Junie had been standing.

"Where's my brother?" He asked the question in Creole, but I no longer have the heart to try to say the words that way. Then he asked it slowly in English, looking at me, letting me know he held me responsible.

"Where is my brother?"

All the boys glanced around, as if they were looking for a coin someone had dropped in the dirt. Fairbanks and I looked, too, but Junie was gone.

We searched for him right away. It wasn't like before with Peter Rabbit and Boomba when we let them get a head start. We looked everywhere. I called Junie's name again and again until I realized nobody else was calling his name. The others went about looking for him quietly, grimly. Two boys went on foot to the mouth of the road. Others ran to all the old hiding places: the hen-house, the laundry, the storage shed where we kept feed for the chickens and the rabbits. I looked under my house and in my kitchen, and I unlocked the schoolroom, but nobody was there. We searched until it was too dark to search anymore. In the confusion of Junie's disappearance, we forgot to keep an eye on Albert. The baker's boy must have known how much trouble he was in. He had dared to strike Fairbanks. He couldn't expect anyone to forget that.

"Tell him to report to my office," said Fairbanks.

"Right, right," said Brother Constant. "Tell who?"

"That baker's boy."

So we looked for Albert, too. We called his name. But nobody could find the baker's boy.

• • •

I took the Toyota and drove along the highway, first to the east, as far as the house where Junie had lived with his grandmother, Miss Penny, before he came to New Hope. When I drove up to that house, it was dark, and the place looked abandoned. I made myself climb the steps and peer in the window, startling a large orange cat that had been asleep by the door. The house was empty. Part of the tin roof was missing, as though someone had stolen it. I wondered if Albert and Junie had told me something sad about Miss Penny and I hadn't understood, or simply hadn't listened.

On a hunch, I drove in the opposite direction toward San Ignacio. I crossed the bridge and kept going, drawn on in the direction of the border. A group of Indians passed me, walking into town. I tried to ask them if they had seen either of the boys, but they pretended not to understand me, or they didn't understand me for true. It didn't matter. The sun had set and I worried the Toyota would break down and leave me stranded in the dark. I saw a figure up ahead. I slowed to an idle, half expecting him to run, but he stood without moving in the glare of my headlights, waiting to see what I would do. It wasn't Junie. It was Albert. His face was dusty and swollen.

I pulled the car off the road, dimming the lights. I got out and stood next to the car, one hand on the door.

"No luck?" I said. Albert didn't respond. He looked past me into the car, afraid I had brought the others with me.

"Maybe we should go back," I said. I nodded in the direction of New Hope. I never expected Albert to get in the car. I never expected him to forgive me. I never expected to see him again by day or by night. I closed my eyes for a moment so he could slip away into the dark beyond the edge of the road. It seemed to me like the decent thing to do.

I went back to the school exhausted, numb from disappointment, but I didn't sleep that night. The boys didn't settle down either. Several of them came to my house in the dark and threw rocks against the walls or up onto my roof. I was afraid they would break a window or put a hole in the roof, so I turned on all the lights, hoping it would scare them back to bed. I sat up the rest of the night.

In the morning, I drove the roads again, this time all the way to the border, right up to the little building where the border guards examined passports. It was foolish to depend that much on the Toyota, but I drove anyway, unable to think of anything else I could do. Shortly before noon, I thought I'd drive to Miss Penny's house again. Then I changed my mind and took the road that led toward the Mennonite settlement. I waited at the ferry, unsure whether to cross over. When the ferryman was ready to go, I let him go on without me. That's when I saw him, Junie, standing at the edge of the river. He stood utterly still, a look on his face I have only seen one other time, on the face of a very old woman who was dying after a long and painful illness. Junie may have stood there all night. He was there and he wasn't there. He was gone to the place where none of us could follow. He was having a meeting with Jesus. When I called to him, he heard me on some level, though he didn't turn to face me. He stepped into the river, and with each call of his name he moved in a little deeper until only his head was above the water, his arms out to his sides, and he was adrift, floating away down the river, his face just above the surface or not above the surface at all. In his short time at New Hope, he hadn't learned to swim.

I willed myself to go after him into the river. I took steps in that direction. A small solid object fell into the water three feet from the bank, from a tree that hung over the water's edge. It could have been a lizard. It could have been a dead branch falling after months of lying up there on top of another dead branch. It could have been anything. I couldn't see the bottom of the river. I didn't know what might be in the water, big or small. If I needed help, there was nobody there to save me.

I must have kept on calling out Junie's name. I moved ahead slowly, as slowly as Junie had moved, until I was in the water up to my knees and three big boys came running down the road from New Hope. From a different direction, though I couldn't have said where, Albert appeared. He had changed his mind in the night about crossing over to Guatemala. He had come back for his brother. His hair was uncombed, his shirt dirty. He'd spent most of the night walking. If he'd rested at all, he must have crouched beside the road with no blanket, nothing to eat or drink. I pointed to the place where Junie entered the water, and Albert and two of the others dove in after him. The current moved through that stretch of the river steadily. The boys tried to gauge how far downstream a small boy would travel, how fast. They dove and called and climbed out to look in the weeds for what felt like an hour but was surely less than that. In time, they gave up.

"Give us a ride back," said the boy who had been diving the longest, the deepest. It was Benn. The words caught in his throat. Those three got in the car and looked out at Albert, expecting him to follow.

"Come with us, Albert," I said. One of the boys eased the door open on his side of the car, not Benn this time, one of the others. I thought he might rush the baker's boy, try to force him to go back with us. And I knew it would be like the night before. Albert stepped down the bank of the river and slipped into the water again. He let the current carry him away, watching us at first to see if we would follow. Fifty yards downriver, he turned and looked in the direction he was moving, away from New Hope, toward Belize City. In this way, Albert, too, disappeared before my eyes.

When I finished telling Junie's story, the mood had changed in Toddy's Café. It was what the baker's boy used to say: "You tell my brother's story, you end up making one whole lot of happy people sad."

The night didn't feel like a party anymore. It just felt late, and my chair felt hard, and the room was colder than before. Stacen stared at the floor. Tony looked stunned. You might have thought someone had come up behind him and knocked him down, and for no good reason. Liu sat straight-backed at his table. His wife tried a smile but she couldn't pull it off. As far as she was concerned, an icy night and a couple of car accidents out in the street and a room full of bone-weary people, that was nothing. Let Tanner Johnson run his mouth and the real worries showed up.

I saw the sadness in Katherine's eyes.

"I wanted him to make it," said Katherine. "He deserved to make it."

"It's too bad you can't sing," said Tony.

"God, Tony," said Stacen. "You are such an idiot." She squeezed her eyes shut rather than look at her husband. It was the same way she refused to look at the slugs that turned up on the doormat in the summer, the ones her girls loved to pour salt on. I did not expect any support from Stacen. It was decent of her to stick up for me. I wondered if she meant it.

"Well," said Tony, "anyway." He looked around at the rest of the people who had taken shelter at Toddy's. "What are we going to do next?"

The others weren't talking. Mrs. Liu made herself small in her chair, like a child. She pulled her knees up to her chest and held on tight, as if she was pressing against a great sadness. I didn't know her sorrows. She didn't want any of us to know. The upstairs couple huddled together in their corner. Sara stared out the window. I was sure the only thing she could see out that window was the sky, and the sky was completely dark.

"Come on," said Tony, "it was only a story. It's not like any of that really happened."

Sometimes silence can weigh a place down, like a heavy coat or a backpack full of books you'd rather not read. I don't know how long we would have sat there without moving if it hadn't been for Sara.

"If everybody has had a turn," she said, "what I'm wondering is . . . ," and she looked at me and then looked away, and it seemed like she couldn't make herself look seriously at anybody. So she looked at her shoes. "I never got my chance."

"Your chance at what?" said Tony.

"I want to sing," said Sara. Liu looked up from his table. His face had lost what little color it had left. The old man grinned at the girl. He was game.

"She doesn't have to take a turn," said Liu. "This girl is cold and tired. It's only if she wants to."

"I want to," said Sara. Liu made a gracious bow in her direction.

"If you will sing," said Liu, "then afterward we can all go across the street. I will cook some pork, some chicken. I'll cook some rice. For everybody. We don't need flour for what I'm going to cook."

"You're worn out," said his wife.

"Old woman," said Liu, raising his voice a little. He said a few words to her in Chinese, but he kept most of it in English for the benefit of the rest of us. "I told you before," he said. "I been telling you for years. I never get worn out. And this girl wants to sing." Liu pointed his finger at Sara, like it proved his point.

I wondered what she would sing. Her short dark hair framed her face in the night. I guessed she would do a song from her generation, one I didn't know. The radio was full of those songs. I didn't try to keep up. Sara cleared her throat and she pulled her hair back and let it go into the air, as if she was checking to see which way the wind was blowing. I couldn't tell if she wanted us to stop looking at her, or if she wanted to make sure we were giving her our full attention. I tried to make myself small.

"I'll sing the rain song," she said softly. She looked at all of us again. She wanted to see if anybody had a better idea. "It helps little kids go to sleep," she said.

I couldn't remember the last time I'd heard that song. In all the recent afternoons I'd sat in my apartment with the radio on, I hadn't heard it even once. I didn't know what to expect from the girl's voice, either. I wondered if she would have a beautiful voice, if she was someone who had put in her time in a church choir. I wondered if she would have one of those whiskey and cigarette voices. Women will fool you.

Stacen's girls were fighting against sleep. They ran their engines hard all day until they dropped and slept deep and still, sometimes in the car, sometimes in the back of the café or draped across a table where they had just finished eating muffins. They had no schedule. Even for them, the hour was late. The clock was in the kitchen, and I wasn't going to go back and look at it, but I knew it had to be after midnight.

Sara took a sip from her cup of tea and set it carefully on the table in front of her. Looking at a spot on the wall a few feet above the little girls' heads, she opened her mouth and began to sing. I was right about her voice. It sounded scratchy at first as if she hadn't used it recently or she had used it too much, but it was a moving voice, innocent and weary at the same time.

Rain, rain, she sang, *Go away. Come again some other day.*

There weren't many words to the song. She sang it the way Peter, Paul and Mary used to sing it on a long-ago record album, so there was a part where she sang the counting words: *five, ten, fifteen, twenty. . . .* She told us about the old man who bumped his head, and then she sang *rain, rain, go away* again, and the rest of us sang the song with her, but quietly. It was her turn, after all. We didn't horn in on that. We sang it four or five times. I know it makes a better story if I say the little girls fell asleep, but the longer we sang the more they perked up, and by the time we were through they were climbing all over their mother, and Mrs. Liu had raised her head and even the sleepy Katherine looked as though she was good for another go-round.

"I never heard you sing before," said Croker to Sara. He said it the way a father would say it. I understood completely, how we love someone through and through and for years, and don't know all the sides of that person. Katherine, for instance. Would I ever know her? Or Stacen, who had one girl hanging around her neck and the other one sitting in her lap. Stacen smiled at all of us with a dazed look that said she might never sleep again. When the girl hanging from Stacen's neck, the little one, let go and fell to the floor, it gave us all a start.

"Oh," said Katherine.

The little girl cried a bit, but she looked okay.

"Oh," said Katherine again.

"It's nothing," said Stacen. "She's just tired."

"Oh, no," said Katherine.

"What is it?" said Mrs. Liu. "Are you all right?"

And then it was happening, the thing that only happens in the stories you read in Dear Abby. There we were, taking shelter from a storm late at night, almost every car disabled, and out of nowhere a small puddle appeared beneath Katherine's chair. We looked at each other, Katherine and I. Tony's eyes lit up. Somewhere in one of those history books he must have learned how it goes with a birth. "Ah," he said, pointing his finger at the wet floor. "Amniotic fluid." Then he passed out onto the table in front of him.

"Katherine," I said. I said it twice as loud as I needed to, but I didn't care. I went to her side and she let me put my arms around her.

"Is that your water?" asked Mrs. Liu. I thought somebody might want to help with Tony, but Mrs. Liu was unable to take her eyes off the puddle underneath Katherine's chair.

"I'm so sorry," I said. I don't know where those words came from. I buried my face in her coat. I didn't want to say anything more, which was good because I didn't know what I was going to say, and my voice wouldn't work, and there was the sound of the ocean roaring in my ears. Rain, rain, go away.

So much water I was drowning. I was falling apart. Nobody acted surprised. After all that had happened that night, why would the fact that I was having a nervous breakdown be a surprise to anyone?

"I'll come home," I said, or I tried to say it. I croaked it out. I kept my eyes buried. It surprised me, what I'd just said. I was determined to shut up. I mean, all this talk was far too personal to be said in a public situation. I was not going to say another word.

"I was a fool," I said.

Who knew what I was going to say next? I'd lost control of my mouth.

"I *am* a fool," I said.

Katherine had her arms around me and she was crying, too.

"Yes, you are," said Katherine, but she didn't say it in a mean way. "It's okay, Tanner," she said.

"How fast are the contractions coming?" asked the redheaded woman. "Do you want to lie down? Do you want to walk around? Do you have names picked out? Should we call a doctor?"

"Your water is awfully brown," said Mrs. Liu.

"My water?" said Katherine. She laughed and spread her legs and looked down at the floor. I had never been around a woman giving birth before, but I thought the laughing was unusual.

"That's not my water," said Katherine. She grabbed me by the lapel and held on tight. "I spilled my tea," she said. She kept hold of me when she said it, as if she was afraid I would jump up and run away.

"Your tea?" I said.

"I'm sorry," said Katherine.

I saw the empty cup on its side under her chair, and the tea bag in the middle of Katherine's brown puddle.

"Ginger Peach," said Katherine.

"Everybody can relax," said Liu. "Nothing to worry about. Just your strange typical couple has a life-changing experience here. Strong tea does that. It's a false alarm."

A great rain of feelings fell on my head, gently at first: relief that I had told Katherine I was coming home, fear that maybe I hadn't meant it, more relief, disappointment, too, that the baby wasn't coming. Liu brought Katherine a towel and he patted me on the shoulder. I wanted to hug Liu. I wanted to tell him where to go. I didn't know what I wanted to do.

"Now then," said Katherine, "here's something to watch." And the puddle under her chair, as if by magic, doubled in size. Water dripped down between the chair rungs, first a trickle and then a real torrent. If before, she had spilled her tea, now she was spilling the whole teapot. It didn't look as brown as before.

"Katherine?" said Stacen.

"Oh my heavens sakes," said Mrs. Liu.

"This time, we can get excited," said Katherine. She settled slowly back into her chair. "There goes my water now."

"No," said Tony, still a little groggy from the last time.

"Oh yes," said Katherine, and Stacen let out a whoop, and her kids shouted, and Tony's head hit the table. If I'd been that baby, I'd have wondered what I was getting myself into.

I was on uneven ground. They got Tony to lie down on a sleeping bag before he fainted again. I felt like I might have to lie down myself. Mrs. Liu laughed and clapped her hands and shouted at the others. Sara and Croker were laughing with her as though they had been waiting for someone to tell them to laugh. Katherine held on to me as if I were a fugitive from justice and she was bringing me in for the reward. After a moment, she gave me a little break. She made it possible for me to stop hugging her if I wanted to stop. I think she wanted to see what I would do. Mr. Liu was talking softly to Mrs. Liu, trying to rein her in, and the young woman from upstairs was clinging to her boyfriend over by the window. Stacen sat down next to Tony. She was talking to her daughters, explaining the puddle on the floor. That was about them all loving each other, too. Everyone had it figured out, everyone with the exception of me. It occurred to me that Katherine was the real storyteller, only she was telling the story of her life and mine, and the story of the baby she carried. She was doing it without worrying over it the way I worried over it. She was a natural.

"Come home with me now," said Katherine.

"I can't deliver a baby," said Liu, getting up slowly. "I better go cook."

"You can't cook, you old fool," said his wife. But it wasn't like she thought she could stop him. "It's too late for cooking," she said. "Besides, it's too slick for all these people to cross the street in the middle of the night. And this woman is having a baby."

"You can't have the baby in a café," I said to Katherine. "There's ice in the street. Another storm is coming. We have all these people to feed."

She looked at me sadly. "There will always be people to feed," said Katherine. "There will be other storms."

I looked around the room. People were trying to do what was right, trying not to stare at us. Tony leaned up against the wall and closed his eyes, and the redheaded woman placed her hand on her heart as though she had just been visited by an awful thought. I knew better than to look at Stacen. I didn't want to make any decisions based on whether or not Stacen was going to kill me if I chose wrong.

A low rumble came from outside. A large truck moved down the street, the salt truck. It passed in front of the café making a lot of slow noise, spreading salt and sand behind it. It would be safe to drive on that street again, at least for half an hour or so, until fresh ice covered up the sand. It was too cold for the salt to do much good. It might be days before the road looked better than it looked at the moment.

"First babies take a long time," said Stacen. "Meanwhile, people need to eat." She looked at Liu. "You can cook right here. I'll help." Then Stacen looked at Katherine, as if she wanted to help Katherine make up her mind.

"I want to stay, too," said Katherine. "I want to stay a little longer in this room."

I thought about insisting she go home. The woman was having a baby, for Christ sake, and the whole sweet lot of us were acting like crazy people. Katherine gave me a teary smile. I didn't want to disappoint her. I didn't want to look like a worrier.

"Okay," I said. "We'll stay as long as you want. But when you're ready to go, I'm going with you."

It must have been what she wanted to hear. She smiled her old smile, the one that made her face go soft. I hadn't seen that smile in a long time.

"At least for tonight," I said.

She frowned then, as though she was having another contraction. I knew that wasn't it. It was me, still causing her pain.

"See," said Liu, looking at his wife with that mixture of true love and annoyance that people who stay married a long time like to show each other. "Anything is possible. Like I always say."

Liu and Tony went slipping and sliding across the street to bring back Liu's wok and some seasonings and rice. The old man and Stacen set to work in the kitchen as if they had grown up cooking together. Sara offered to time Katherine's contractions.

"I just want to be helpful," she said.

"You are," said Katherine, and she smiled at Sara and squeezed her hand. The contractions hadn't started yet, not in earnest. Sara looked across the room where Croker had nodded off in a chair. When she went over to see about him, Katherine and I were left alone for a moment.

"Did you ever see him again?" asked Katherine. She couldn't let the other story go. She was thinking about Junie. "Did they find him?"

I felt tired, as if I'd been talking for days and days.

"They found his body a week later," I said, "a mile or two downriver. The Mennonites came to tell us. I was packing my things. My time was over at New Hope. Fat Eric had a plane ticket for me. I was on my way home."

"What about Albert?"

"I'd rather not tell you any more about Albert."

"You have to," said Katherine. "You're this close. You have to tell me the rest."

For a moment, I thought about running again. The back door, and the night beyond. But only for a moment. In my heart, I knew she was right.

"I will tell you about Albert, and about Price, and Ellie," I said to Katherine. "And then that story will be done. I won't have any more of it to tell."

17

I spent my last days in Belize City in a constant ugly mood. I didn't understand what happened at New Hope. I didn't understand what was happening with Ellie, either. We were standing on opposite sides of a river, and we didn't know which one of us was supposed to cross over so we could be together again. Her love was slipping away. I knew it had everything to do with my drinking, with my late nights with Price, my sorrow. But if I didn't go to some club and put my coins in the jukebox, if I refused to sit around in the evening at Price's flat listening to his crummy, worn-out tapes, all I could think about was the baker's boy and his lee brother Junie. I'd see the distant look on Fairbanks's face, the look I saw when I packed my boxes into the back of a pickup so Herbert could carry me away from New Hope. I wasn't sure if there was anything left for me in Belize. But there was always Price and there was always another glass of rum, one more bottle of beer.

In that city, on every other block, tired men and women sold liquor and beer out of small shops that didn't sell much of anything else. Price wanted to try all of it. He had a drink in every dive that crossed his path. We drank One Barrel rum, we drank Three Barrel rum, we drank rum from Mexico and Trinidad. We drank on the street corner. We rode bicycles out to a small village on the highway to Orange Walk where a crippled man sold Nescafé and kidney beans and drink in a badly lit shop just off the road. We bought the drink. Later, a little boy led us farther back off the road to a small gray man with red eyes and a worried face who worked a still. The man sold us a rum that didn't come with a label, in a short green bottle stoppered with a cork. Price called it village rum. The old man called it white oil.

Price took a Friday off from his girls school, and we drank away a whole weekend with friends he had made, two coolie boys who had moved to the city from Punta Gorda. Sunday afternoon, we were drinking the village product. It was enough to make even Price slow down.

"This one is not so good," said Price's new friend, the boy who talked the most. "They didn't wash out the bottle. You can taste it." He was a thin boy with an odd triangular face. His first name was James. We had just determined his father's first name was James, too. The boy was young, but he already had a son, himself. His son's name was James.

"Taste what?" said Price.

"Some bally used this bottle one time already," said James. His mouth frowned even when the rest of his face showed no emotion. "I hate that taste."

"What taste?" said Price.

"Kerosene."

James took another drink from the bottle and wiped his mouth on his sleeve. He handed the bottle to Price, who looked at it for what seemed to me like a long time.

"Oh," said Price. And then he said, "Well, well." And after that he followed me outside, and we stood next to each other by the water tank and were sick together.

Late most nights when I had my fill, I tried to get back to Ellie, but I spent the early part of every evening with Price. We drank with his Belizean friends. When his Belizean friends weren't around, we drank without them. "Two or more, gathered in my name," said Price. He had started talking that way. He liked to pour out a little rum onto the ground, the way he saw those coolie boys do. They said it was for the ancestors.

On the Fourth of July, we went to a party hosted by a woman who worked for the consulate. We watched Arnie Svenson drink thirty-one beers that night, Charger beers, which meant they were the small bottles. Arnie weighed 280 pounds. According to Price, beer didn't count. "With beer, you're just replacing fluids," said Price. "A kind of recycling." He wrote the number *31* on a little piece of paper and put it in his wallet anyway, as if it was important.

I didn't enjoy it the way Price did. I could never drink enough to lose track of every foolish word I said, though I tried. What I liked most of all was to have a couple of drinks, then go listen to the radio or sit with the little tinny tape player Price took around to parties. I wanted to crawl right up into the speaker with the music. I sang with Price if he knew the words. If he didn't know the words, we sang anyway, tearing up those lyrics. One evening when we were still halfway sane, a woman named Carly saw a small shadow move behind her door. She ran into her bedroom and brought out a hammer and she used it to smash a cockroach. Price took the hammer from her, cleaned the roach parts off of it, and spent the rest of the evening singing to it, as if the hammer were a microphone. When he went home that night, Price had the hammer sticking out of his back pocket.

I could have charted our months in Belize by what Price drank. And the way he felt about roaches. On the afternoon we first arrived, we sat in the airport lounge waiting for Fat Eric to pick us up. Price asked for a rum and Coke like everyone else, everyone who wasn't a Mormon or already in AA. He asked for a slice of lime in his drink. The man serving us laughed out loud.

"If you got the money," said the man, "I got the lime."

He didn't have any limes. It was just a joke. But Price didn't mind.

Those early days, he could lose interest in what was in his glass. If he saw a cockroach crawl across the floor of someone's flat, he set his drink down long enough to open the door and shoo the roach outside, staying as far away as possible as if it might turn on him and attack. He could forget all about his drink that way. He was unfocused. If he had two cigarettes in an evening, he said he was trying to learn how to smoke, and if he had three cigarettes, he told us he was trying to quit. I wrote a letter home about Price, the same way I wrote about the trees and the flowers and the fruit I bought in the market-place. I took pictures of each of my new friends next to the schools where they taught. I took as many pictures of Price as I did of Ellie.

By our first Christmas in Belize, Price was drinking rum with every kind of soft drink, even the grape kind. Anytime we saw a cockroach he threw a shoe at it, and if he missed, he grabbed the shoe and kept after the roach until he was sure it was dead. He could do it without setting down his drink. I would have written about that in a letter, too, but I'd stopped writing letters to people I didn't love. I was tired of describing scenes that didn't mean anything to them. I sent an occasional postcard home, but I found it hard to understand my old friends. They had new jobs and they worried a lot about their cars. Price and I talked about going home as if we actually looked forward to it, and Ellie had to tell us it was too soon to think about leaving Belize. Price had quit smoking by then, twice. After three drinks, he wanted to talk about Candace, and after a couple more he talked about a girl he loved more than Candace, but the next day when I tried to get him to talk about the girl he loved so much, he insisted I was making it up.

On his school vacation, he left town without saying where he was going. He said he had to get away from Ellie, away from me. Traveling by himself, he drank a beer with every meal, just one, but even at breakfast, and he ate food he knew he shouldn't eat and only got sick once, and that time he blamed it on the water. He mailed us a postcard from Honduras. It was the only mail I received that month. I read Price's postcard to Ellie more than once, until I realized it embarrassed her. He'd met some girls who worked for CARE in Tegucigalpa, and he had too much to drink and went home with one of them. He ended up at a strangely familiar house with a toilet that ran all night and cockroaches in the kitchen. In the morning the girl put on a bathrobe and made him breakfast. She pretended she did that sort of thing all the time back in Iowa or Colorado. He pretended to believe her.

When our first year was complete, we had a little conference to mark the halfway point. By then Price had stopped wearing socks and only wore underwear on special occasions. The first day of the conference, he led us to the bar once the afternoon meeting ended. The second day, he started out alone at the bar, skipping the afternoon meeting. The last day, I could hardly find a seat in the bar because they were all there by eleven o'clock, even Fat Eric, and there was no more Charger. Everyone drank rum, and since it was morning, we drank it with milk, hoping the milk was safe. We listened to Price talk about ways to kill cockroaches, some of which involved torture. He said *fuck* a lot, especially when it wasn't appropriate. He seemed never to have learned when a word like that was appropriate.

That second Christmas, Price traveled again without me or Ellie, though before he left he made a promise to me he wouldn't get drunk two nights in a row. He kept that promise. He said it wasn't so hard. He found a couple of paperbacks at Ellie's house and he took them along on his trip so he could read in the evenings instead of drink. One of the books, a murder mystery, had the last page missing. Price was angry about it. In Nicaragua one night, he took a stab at writing his own ending, and the writing was so bad he had to get drunk since the hotel had good beer and he hadn't been drunk the night before. At the bar he talked to a beautiful woman from Los Angeles who was traveling with her girlfriend and who smelled good, he claimed, from five feet away. In the middle of a conversation about Afghans, or Airedales, he couldn't be sure because he got those two breeds of dogs confused, a cockroach hurried across the bar, and without thinking, Price smashed it with his palm and rubbed his hand on his pant leg. The girl excused herself and he never saw her again that night or ever, though he thought he would remember her as long as he lived, her beautiful posture and her scent and the way she never stopped smiling as she headed for the door.

We made a calendar so we could mark off the days until we would go home. We knew it was a foolish thing to do, like counting the days until we were dead. Life was meant to be lived, every day a celebration, and still we counted them down. Price kept the calendar pinned up beside his kitchen table. He tried to find his way back to Candace, but she was counting the days, too, until Price would go home and she could be decent again. He thought about asking Candace if she wanted to get married. He drank rum with the powdered orange mix. A cockroach ended up in one of those drinks. He'd set the drink on the floor for just a moment while he went to find a pencil. When he came back, there the thing was, floating with the ice cubes. He fished it out, and wrote letters that night to people he had been neglecting. He read parts of the letters to me, but they all turned out badly and he didn't put any of those letters in the mail. He went ahead and finished the drink. He didn't think I would notice.

Then we were done. Our time was up. We took down the calendar and burned it in the yard in a serious ritual, and we packed our bags to go home. There were two parties for Price in the city, one of which was so boring he drank rum straight up and left early with a headache. I helped him mail a couple of boxes home. In two years, he hadn't managed to accumulate much. He hardly had any clothes left, and he started an argument with me over a pair of blue boxer shorts. As quickly as he started, he dropped it and fixed us both a drink. He went to the barber to get a shave, as though a shave would make a difference, but he couldn't go through with it. I met him on the way back from the barbershop and I took him to dinner. A young boy came into the restaurant where we were having rice and beans. The boy placed a packet of marijuana on the table and Price panicked, thinking he was being set up, suddenly terrified he would have to spend the rest of his life in a Belizean prison. The boy ran outside when Price shouted at him, but he waited for us on the street, like a threat. We could see him through the window. We slipped out the alley door, back to Price's empty flat where the cockroach he had been keeping in a mason jar was trying to climb up the side of the jar to freedom. The roach had gone without food or water for two weeks, and still the thing mocked us. That roach meant to outlast us. Price poured two fingers of rum into the jar and let the cockroach drink himself to death.

I had taken care of my affairs. I could fly home any day I wanted to. I was putting it off, dancing around the subject with Ellie, around other subjects, too, hanging around the city until finally Fat Eric lost patience with me. He told me I had a week left, and then he would see that my visa was canceled. I was going to be illegal if I stayed any longer. That must have been what the party was all about, a going-away party at a house on the edge of the city. We only sometimes had a reason for a party. Dicky Roy had a party when his father came to visit. It was strange to think Dicky Roy had a father. Arnie Svenson had a party when he learned he was accepted into law school. Carly and Harris had a party when they got engaged.

We drank, we danced, we sang to the hammer. Afterwards, we caught a ride home in the back of Carly's pickup. Carly, with her blond hair and her bad eyes, was the girl who planned to get married, the one who knew what love was all about. She had been drinking, too, but there wasn't any traffic, and it was her pickup, sort of. It was a consulate pickup, to tell the truth, but it wasn't anybody else's pickup, and Carly was the one with a driver's license, so she drove. Everybody else was drunker than Carly. I was, and Ellie was.

Price was sad that night because I was going home, and he would be leaving, himself, before long. And because there was some big story he said he needed to tell me. I was sad, too. I had failed to accomplish the one task I thought would make my life mean something again in a small way. I'd failed to find Albert.

I had an address where some of Albert's people lived. I went to the house repeatedly, but by the third visit, they knew the story about Junie. Miss Penny rode the bus in from the Cayo to tell everyone what had happened to her grandson. After that, her people turned their backs on me. I walked all over town hoping I might run into Albert, and twice in the marketplace I thought I caught a glimpse of him, once on a fishing dory as it moved away from the dock. I called to the boat, but it kept on going. I just wanted to talk to Albert, to tell him I was sorry. It was selfish. I had nothing left to give him.

The night I went to that last party, I'd had the feeling all day the baker's boy was watching me. I walked through the streets on my way to the party house, whirling around every so often to catch a glimpse of Albert in the shadows. I knew he was there. I didn't know why he was following me. At the party, I drank Charger and played the fool and stood with my arms around Ellie. She hadn't given herself to me after all, and I wasn't sure if it was because she had changed her mind, or if I just needed to ask again. I couldn't make myself ask again. When the noise and the music got to be too much, I went out on the porch where I waited for Albert to come up the stairs and sit beside me, the way he used to at New Hope. Once, I saw a movement in the alley, and I thought it might be him. And then Ellie came outside and leaned up against me. She said she'd decided not to leave for a while.

"You aren't ready to leave this party?" I said. Although I knew what she meant.

"I'm not ready to leave Belize," she said. "I know you have to go, Tanner."

I had suggested we go home together. I wanted that, to go home together. We could go see her parents first, then go see mine.

"I'm going to stay here, work a while longer," she said. "At least until Christmas. It's the right thing to do. A good thing." She smiled at me weakly.

I didn't know the good thing to do anymore.

Some of the night passed. Ellie went inside. More of the night passed, and Price stood on the porch next to me. The cicadas were raising hell, and the smell of Belize was all around us, cigarette smoke and salt in the air, and an open sewer a few blocks over. I stared hard at a clump of bushes across the alley, trying to make one of the smaller bushes turn into the baker's boy.

"You know, when we first got here?" said Price. "Two years ago? In May?"

The bushes were moving so much I couldn't look right at them, or my head was moving. I tried to focus on the porch rail in front of me, but it seemed we weren't on the porch anymore. We were standing next to Carly's truck while Carly looked through her pockets for her keys. Some more of the night must have passed.

"Tell me about May," I told Price. "I forget how we got here. Did we come on a boat? On a bus? Did we fall from the sky?"

"I'm serious," said Price. I wanted to tell him I was serious, too, but I didn't think I could make him understand. It wasn't good to be so serious.

"It was before I knew you well," said Price.

"Shut up," said Ellie. At least it was Ellie's voice. In the dark, I couldn't see her.

"I can't shut up," said Price.

"I have achieved drunkenness," I said.

"You already said that," said Ellie. "Stop saying that. It's stupid."

We no longer stood beside Carly's pickup. We sat in the back of the truck and Carly, sweet nearsighted Carly, was driving the truck very care-fully, not speeding or making the tires squeal, concentrating on her driving the way only a drunk person can concentrate.

"Stop the truck," I said, not because of what Ellie said, and not because I was going to be sick, which is what everyone thought, but because I saw *him* then at last, Albert, that baker's boy, outside a small shop where they sold groceries and cheap underwear. It was dark on the street. Nobody else saw him. Nobody else was looking for him like I was.

"Don't stop the truck," said Ellie. She pounded once on the cab and pulled me down next to her, our backs against the rear window. If you slapped the top of the truck once, it meant go on. If you hit it several times, the driver knew you wanted to stop. Everybody knew that drill.

"There's this thing I want to tell you," said Price.

"Shut up, Price," said Ellie. "I mean it."

Price moved away from her and took a seat a little higher than us, up on the side of the truck. He wanted to put some distance between himself and Ellie.

"I have to tell him," said Price.

"You don't have to say another word," said Ellie.

"You tell him then," said Price.

That's when I must have started pounding on the cab. The truck slowed to a stop and Ellie, who was now in tears, shouted to Carly that she should ignore me, that she should keep going.

"Just drive," said Ellie. "Please."

"No," I said. "We have to stop." I could make out Albert's shape in the faint light of the moon. He was following us from block to block, a thin black shadow moving like birds move over the river just after sunset. He must have been running from the dark side of one building to the dark side of the next. Or it was obeah. He was fooling around with the spirit world. I thought Albert might be waving at me. I thought he was calling me over.

"I slept with her," said Price. He was crying like Ellie was crying, only Price could cry quieter. "It only happened one time," he said. "We were drunk."

"Slept with who?" I said. I was on the lookout for Albert. I wanted to get down out of the truck, but Carly was driving on again, sweet Carly. Price wasn't talking about Carly.

"What is he talking about?" I said, and when I looked at Ellie, she sat with her knees drawn up close, hugging herself, breathing like a swimmer who has just pulled herself from the water.

"I don't know if you'll want to be friends anymore," said Price. He stood up in the back of Carly's truck. He was unsteady on his feet, a man crossing a river on a log.

"Sit down," I said.

"It's okay," said Price.

"No," said Ellie through her tears. "Tanner's right. Sit down here with us."

And she would be glad for the rest of her life she said that, I'm sure of it, because as Carly drove around the next corner, and she was driving slow really, really she was, Price tumbled over the side of the truck. I reached for him. I was on my knees and I saw him land, his head hitting the pavement. He fell over and he arched his back once, and then he didn't move, even when we pounded on the roof of the truck like thunder and got Carly to stop.

"Make up your mind," said Carly. But we were already running back to where Price lay in the street. I tried to pick him up. You're not supposed to do that, but it wouldn't have made any difference. Great ropes of blood came from his mouth. I knew he was dead before I could lift him from the ground, before we could drive to the hospital racing through the streets faster than any of us had ever driven the streets of Belize City.

There were tears. Carly screamed it was all our fault, and Ellie slapped Carly, and Carly would have run out into the traffic in front of the hospital, but there wasn't any traffic in the middle of the night. I held Carly and held her, and she fought against me, and I thought she would slap me, too, but the nurses took her from me and walked her to the end of the corridor, and then Candace was there. I don't know how she found out. Candace looked stunned. She didn't remember our names. Fat Eric was there. We were all telling him, *Look, you have to understand, it wasn't Carly's fault. He was drunk. Price was drunk. He wouldn't sit in the truck like he was supposed to. Ellie asked him to sit down just before he fell out. It was his fault. It was our fault. We shouldn't have been drinking. We were drunk. We were all so drunk.*

Fuck, I said. *Oh fuck, fuck, fuck. Oh Price. Oh fuck.*

I went back to Price's flat in a taxi. Ellie didn't go with me, which was okay. I went to bed and woke once near dawn because I thought I felt a bug, a cockroach, crawl across my face. I sat up in the hammock, relieved that I was just hung over, that it hadn't really happened, that none of it had happened, that Price was asleep in the other hammock. I started to look in the other hammock, but I didn't look because it would be dawn soon, and there would be time then to look for Price. I lay back down. It didn't matter. I couldn't get any more sleep that night. I was afraid I never would sleep right again.

When the sun made it light outside, I had to leave the flat. I didn't want to be sick indoors, and I knew I was going to be sick, at least for the rest of that day. I went back to the street where Price died. This is the strange part because I remembered the other thing had happened, too. It was the same street where I saw the baker's boy, where I saw Albert. When I got to the place, there was still blood on the street. A group of young men were hanging out on the corner, talking about the wonder of it all, how two such things could happen on the same night. I asked them what they meant by that, by two, and they told me: *the one thing, and one other thing.*

And I asked first what the one thing was, and they told me what I already knew, that the Peace Corp volunteer died in the night, right where I was standing, after he fell out of a truck.

That bally was drunk and standing in the truck. Boy.

And like a fool, I asked what the other thing was, and they told that, too. How a young troublemaker broke into the back of that shop, *the one right across the street there,* a Belize boy. How he climbed the tall fence and broke in through that door, and when he came out of the shop, the night man saw him on top of the fence, and how the night man will be okay because he called to the boy first, and the boy wouldn't come down, *he just froze up there,* then made as if he would go over the other side, so the night man shot him, and the boy died in the night, in the dark. Only, when the night man got to him he found the boy must have been crazy because of what the boy stole from the place.

I asked what he had taken, and they told me. He had the following items tucked into his shirt: *flour, yeast, oil and salt.*

I asked why that was, why that and not something else, and they said they didn't know exactly. *But he could find water anywhere.*

They looked at me. They were measuring me. *You know that yourself, man. You know that for true.*

I didn't spend another night in Belize. Fat Eric put me on the plane to Miami with a connecting flight to Atlanta. I arrived at my parents' house the next evening, after an all-night wait at the bus station and a five-hour ride on the bus. The weeks that followed, my family asked me to tell them stories, but I didn't have any stories to tell. None they would believe. I didn't want to be a teacher anymore. I took a couple of classes and then I stopped. I did my time with the want ads. I bounced from job to job, from state to state. Sometimes you don't know what you would rather do, so you keep on doing the same thing, or something different. If you don't understand how that can be, you're very young or very lucky. I didn't want to live in the world anymore, much less change it. I just wanted to do my job and pay most of my bills and get by. I did it just that way for a long time, until I moved back to Tennessee and went to work selling fishing tackle, and Katherine came to that party at the Bobbers' one night, and my life got complicated all over again.

I never saw Ellie after that, and I never saw Fat Eric again, or Carly or Arnie, or Brother Constant, or Mr. Montrose or Fairbanks, or Boomba or Side Dick. I never saw Belize again. I never took another drink of rum.

18

*I*t was cold in Stacen's kitchen, even with the oven going and Liu's wok smoking away on top of the stove. I was glad for the cold. It meant I could sit close to Katherine, and I could put my arms around her and rest my head on her shoulder and smell the good smell of her hair. I could have spent the rest of the night there with her, listening to the clatter of Liu's knife, watching the candlelight on the walls. But Katherine couldn't get comfortable. I tried placing my hands on her belly to see if I could make the baby calm down. It didn't work. Katherine had been having mild contractions all day, though she hadn't said anything about it, not to any of us. After she spilled her water on Stacen's floor, the stronger contractions began.

"We have plenty of time," she said. She was just talking. She didn't know how much time she had. She was afraid I was going to drive her to the hospital and drop her off and drive away again, drive and drive and keep on driving. Katherine wanted me to stay with her. It must have been one a.m. It didn't matter what time it was.

Myself, I wasn't worried. I had read all about it in a book about babies. Early contractions can last a long time. I told myself that again as she tried to find a more comfortable chair—early contractions can last a long time—and I said it once more when she went to the restroom, where she stayed a lot longer than I would have liked—early contractions can last quite a long time—and I told it to myself again when Katherine asked me to go find Mrs. Liu and borrow her cell phone.

"I don't know how to use one," I said, as if my being a fool could keep the baby from coming. "Anyway, early contractions can last an awfully long time."

"Stacen," called Katherine. Then she called louder: "Stacen."

"*Stacen*," I shouted.

"What?" Stacen shouted back. She stood in the doorway to the dining room, her arm wrapped in my splint, one size fits all, her hair and the shadows of her hair going in every direction. "Don't tell me you spilled your tea again," she said. Stacen took a good look at Katherine, and I think she bumped her arm at the same time because what Stacen did next I would have to call a full-scale swoon. She leaned against the wall and called for Tony.

"Oh, right," I said. "Tony."

"First babies don't come fast," said Stacen. Katherine was panting and Stacen was panting. I was trying not to pant. "We have time," said Stacen.

"Call the midwife," said Katherine.

"Yes," I said, "somebody call the midwife."

I thought about Katherine's midwife, about that leather jacket and *Bitch Mama,* and the way when I first met her, she shook my hand as if she was cleaning up after the dog. I was going to be a major disappointment to her. When the midwife came, it would be like having another Stacen in the room.

"Let's stay calm," I said. "We really need the midwife? You're sure?" I didn't know if I could take two Stacens.

Katherine held her breath through a sharp contraction. I knew she wasn't supposed to do that. She was on her feet, leaning against the wall as if she needed to keep that wall from falling down. She tried to close her eyes against the pain, but only one eyelid agreed to stay shut. She bit down on her lip.

Then she stopped biting on her lip long enough to say a certain twelve-letter word in my direction.

"Lord, yes," I said. "We need the midwife."

"How early are you?" asked Mrs. Liu.

"A couple of weeks," said Katherine. "Three at most."

"You'll be fine," said Mrs. Liu. "My grandmother had eight children. In ten years. In the rice field." She smiled at Katherine, and I thought Katherine was going to swear some more.

"We have to get Katherine to the hospital," said Stacen.

"She wanted to have the baby at home," I said.

"She isn't at home, is she?" said Stacen. "I'd love for her to have the baby right here, but you may have noticed it's dark and it's dirty, and it smells like the pet store, and if the lights go out it'll be cold as an Eskimo's pecker in this café."

"All right," I said. "All right, all right, all right."

"It's okay, honey," said Mrs. Liu. "You're a man. We don't expect much from you at a time like this. I don't anyway." She smiled sweetly, and she took the phone from me and dialed the number Katherine recited to her, the midwife's number.

It took four tries before we got through. The midwife was stuck on the other side of the Kentucky border, helping a farmwoman give birth to twins. I tried not to be the one to talk to the midwife, but that wasn't how it turned out. Mrs. Liu was the kind of woman who would dial a phone number and then at the last minute stick the phone in your ribs and walk away.

"I'll never make it down there," said the midwife. "I'm too far away."

"What about the backup midwife?" I asked.

"She's in a ditch between there and Nashville."

I reported it to the rest of the room.

"Give me the phone," said Stacen. I would have given the phone to her gladly, but she took it from me before I had the chance.

"What about the backup to the backup?" asked Stacen.

Stacen didn't look as if she liked what the midwife told her.

"What did she say?" I asked.

"She said you're the backup to the backup," said Stacen.

"Get Katherine a chair," said Croker. Katherine was making slow circles of the room, stepping around people and chairs and tables. I'd taken over her job of holding up the wall.

"Get a chair for Tanner, too," said Croker.

"Everybody stay calm," I said. "The only really wrong thing we can do right now would be to lose our heads." It was what the midwife had said to me a moment earlier, before Stacen grabbed the phone. I didn't believe it. There were some more things we could do wrong. There had to be.

"I suppose you know how to deliver a baby," said Stacen. "I suppose you learned that in the Peace Corps."

I started to say no. It was ridiculous. We weren't allowed to have babies in the Peace Corps. Where would we have put them? But the way Stacen glared at me, I could see *no* would be the wrong answer. And Katherine had a certain hopeful expression on her face. Her tired, tired face.

"Sure," I said. "We learned that stuff. Mouth to mouth. Heart attacks. Babies. It's amazing what we learned. We covered a lot."

"Good," said Stacen.

"Can't you take her home then?" said Mrs. Liu. "Nothing feels better to a woman than her own home."

"No," said Katherine. She sounded a little hoarse. Her words were a whisper to me. "The plan has changed. Let's go to the hospital."

"The plan has changed," I said. "We've got a whole new plan here. We're going to follow the plan." Everybody kept staring at me. I was feeling an old familiar anxiety, but I couldn't put my finger on it. Something like stage fright. I was about to give a speech, and I didn't know what I was supposed to say. I didn't have anything written down for my speech, not a blessed word. I don't know how long the others would have kept looking at me, all those horrible expectations, but Katherine let out a low moan and they decided to stare at her again, or to look away, or just to close their eyes and hope for the best.

We got Katherine, my wife, up on her feet and walked her to the door. Tony went out ahead of us to start up his car, so that once we got out to it, the backseat of that car would be warm. We stood for a moment on the threshold of the café, and we heard the salt truck pass on a main road a few blocks over. It was a welcome sound, though I couldn't tell how far away it was or which way it was going. Liu and the boy from upstairs went ahead of us to push Tony's car away from the curb. They stepped out slowly, cautiously. The surface of the road was already icing over again. Stacen came next, with me, to guide Katherine across the street. Everyone smiled brave smiles. We made our way to the car, all of us taking little steps and holding our breath against Katherine taking a fall.

Tony opened the car door and swung his legs to the road.

"I don't feel so good," he said. He didn't look so good either.

"I'll drive," said Croker. "Tanner, you get in the back with Katherine."

"You want me to come?" asked Stacen.

I would have said yes.

"Stay with your children," said Katherine. She was leaning up against the car, gathering her strength to pull herself into the backseat. "Tanner will be with me. Tanner has done this sort of thing before." I felt my face flush, and Croker said some words under his breath that sounded doubtful.

"It's going to be all right," said Katherine. "I'm so glad Tanner's here."

Stacen and I got Katherine into the car. She could ride comfortably as long as she knelt on the backseat with her legs slightly apart. She could rest her head on the front seat.

"You're timing those contractions?" asked Stacen.

"No," I said.

Stacen placed her hand on my shoulder and leaned her head softly up against mine. I changed my mind.

"Yes," I said. "With the next one. I'm timing them."

The tall boy brought down a pile of towels from upstairs and he put a sleeping bag in the car next to Katherine. His girlfriend stood with Sara, their arms around each other, both of them trying not to shiver. Sara wanted to come with us, but Katherine didn't want anybody else. She only wanted me.

"Just Tanner," said Katherine. "He's my doctor."

"Come back inside with me," said Stacen, leaning on Sara just enough to make the girl feel important. "I'll teach you how to steam milk."

"Really?" said Sara. She smiled and stood up straight, her eyes filled with tears. "Good luck then," said Sara. They were all saying it. "Good luck, Katherine, you're going to be fine, what a story this is going to make, you'll tell your baby about it someday." I was vaguely aware they were waving to us and saying encouraging words, and then I got in the car and Tony shut the door, and I couldn't hear them anymore.

"Sara will be all right," said Croker, looking out at the café. "This is a good place. She'll be okay here."

"How can you be so sure of me?" I whispered to Katherine. "What kind of doctor am I? I'm nobody's doctor." The rain and ice were falling again. Inside the car, moisture lay thick on the windshield. Croker got the defroster going, and the wipers.

"It's time," said Katherine.

He eased the clutch out slowly, trying to get some forward momentum. He had to work for every little bit of traction. Liu skated along with us the way you would skate alongside a train, if you were in a movie and there was a train in the movie and you weren't too old or too crippled to skate after a train. It was exactly like that. Then we were moving too fast for him to keep up, and Liu was waving to us.

"Everybody takes a turn," he said. His words felt like they were caught in my ears. I didn't know what they meant.

"Don't look back," said Katherine. "Don't stop."

"I won't stop," said Croker. He shifted into second gear, and the tires slipped on the icy street, and then they caught and we were fishtailing on our way. "I won't stop for anything," he said.

He was good to his word for fifteen blocks, maybe twenty, until we got past the bank parking lot and the German delicatessen and the Presbyterian church, past the place where volunteers serve free food to homeless people at noon, past the front gate to the college, and then left onto College Avenue, not a main thoroughfare and it still hadn't been sanded, and we were almost there, almost to the road that runs five miles south to the fairgrounds and north the other way to pass right in front of the hospital, where we were headed. We were that close when I saw someone crossing the street, someone whose thin black arms weren't dressed for this weather. Someone who shouldn't have been there. I thought Croker was going to hit him. He turned the steering wheel at the last minute and lost control, and we slid sideways up and over a low curb into a parking lot. No harm done. Croker tried to keep us moving in a more or less forward direction, but he couldn't find the traction on that frozen asphalt, and we made a great slow 360 degree turn in the empty parking lot, then a smaller one, and another smaller one after that, and another, until we came to a stop, the tires of Tony's car whining against the ice. Croker tried to get us going again. All he managed to do was to turn the ice dark beneath the tires.

"Not so good," he said.

He looked back at Katherine's pale face. I caught a glimpse of Croker in the rearview mirror, and he didn't look so good himself. He opened the car door slowly. He had to talk himself into it. I was sweating like a man who had been standing in front of a hot oven for hours and hours. I couldn't stand it. I had to get out of the car, too, and I threw the rear door open. The cool air felt good to me. I looked around for Croker.

"Where did he go?" said Katherine. "Where are you going? Don't leave me."

But I wasn't worried about Croker. Croker could run away. I didn't care. I was looking for someone else.

"He's here," I said.

"Who's here?" said Katherine.

"He's always here. Every time something bad happens, he's here."

I stepped out of the car and looked around, first to the right, then to the left. I wasn't sure I knew exactly where we were. We weren't far from the hospital. We might as well have been twenty miles away.

"Tanner," said Katherine. She was reaching out to me. "Don't leave me here."

"Hush," I told her. "Sit still. I'll only be a moment."

I shut the car door. We were alone then, just him and me, though I couldn't see him. I knew he was there.

"What do you want?" I shouted into the night. "Isn't it enough? Haven't I paid enough?"

The wind had stopped, but there were no cars in the street, and the town was as quiet as it was dark. A young man stepped out of the darkness. He looked cold, dressed the way he was, his dark arms bare. He could have been drunk or high. He had cloth wrapped around his shoes. It helped him walk on the ice.

"I'm not here to do you no harm," he said. "I never did you no harm."

Something in his hands reflected the light from the car. It was a long knife. It looked like Stacen's knife from the alley. It could have been the same. He must have found it back there next to the garbage cans.

"What's the matter with you?" he said. He saw me looking at the knife, and he held it away from his side awkwardly. He looked past me, through the window, to where Katherine knelt in the car.

"Take care of your woman," he said. "You don't need to fear me. You don't never need to fear someone like me."

I heard Katherine call to me, and I opened the car door an inch or two so she would know I was there. I tried not to take my eyes off him, but as I got back in the car, I looked down at Katherine's legs, pale in the car light, and when I looked up, he was gone. I didn't see which way he headed. I only knew Katherine needed me. The engine was still running, so we had the heater to keep us warm. I couldn't hear anything else over the noise of the car engine. All my senses were shut down except for one, and with that sense I felt the baby trying to come into the world. It was a feeling of terror. There was no stopping Katherine's labor. There was no stopping a baby like that, one who had his mind made up.

Katherine was panting for real. I'd gone to two childbirth classes with her before I moved out of the house, but the sounds she was making were nothing like the practice sounds she used to make for me. The seat between us was wet, and everything that was wet felt cold.

"Give me your hand," said Katherine. I gave her my hand and squeezed hers. It was supposed to be an encouraging squeeze. Her other hand gripped the upholstery, as if she planned to tear big chunks of it away from the front seat.

"No," said Katherine, "not like that. Here," she said. She took my hand and pulled me closer. "Feel," she said.

She had on a long loose dress, and she had taken off her underwear. She guided my hand up between her legs. Her thighs were heavier than before and slick with the water from her womb.

"Feel," she said again. "Reach inside me. You can feel the baby's head."

I'd put my fingers inside her before, a hundred times, a thousand times. Maybe not a thousand times. But a lot of times. And now in the backseat of that car, I was timid.

"You be ready," she said. "I need you, Tanner. We're going to have this baby."

I did as I was told.

I held her hand and told her I loved her.

I cupped the baby's head, which felt like an enormous wrinkled piece of fruit Katherine was somehow, impossibly, squeezing out between her legs.

I promised I would be home from that moment on.

I promised her the moon and the stars, and fresh bread every week, and a story every night when we went to bed.

I promised I would return to my classes at the college.

"You don't have to go that far," she said. She pushed the words out between short quick breaths.

I promised to tell only good stories where people loved each other and didn't hurt each other and forgave each other for everything.

"Just help me," she said. "Catch the baby."

I put my hands between her legs again, and she groaned in a different way from all the sounds she had made throughout the evening. It was a groan like no woman ever made since the history of women. And it was exactly like the groan her mother must have made on her night, and her mother's mother before that. I felt a new gush of water and blood, and I knew I had to turn the baby's head a little until that part, the head, came out. I couldn't make myself do it. I was unprepared for it. I never studied how to do that in the

Peace Corps or anywhere else. Then Katherine looked at me, and it was as if she could see me and see through me to the other side as well. She knew the birthing part was going to come out okay. I found the strength. I turned that baby's head just right. Katherine rested a moment before she pushed again. When the whole baby came out, it was too slippery for me to catch, but I held on anyway, and I played out that umbilical cord like an anchor line. I got Katherine to sit back in her seat. It was too cold to spend a lot of time wiping the baby down, so I just wrapped him in one of the tall boy's towels. Katherine and I fumbled together at her buttons until I could put the baby next to her breast. I said a prayer. I had not prayed all evening, and even then I could not have said who I was praying to or what language I was praying in. I prayed the car would keep running and the heater would keep us warm until help came.

I said to Katherine, "Did you notice?"

"Did I notice what?"

"It's a boy," I said.

"Of course it's a boy," she said. "I told you it was a boy."

That's when somebody came to the window and looked in. I don't know who it was. It was a shadow in the night.

"I'm frightened," I told her.

"Don't be," said Katherine. "It could be somebody here to help us."

"You don't know who it is," I said.

"Maybe I do," said Katherine. "Maybe I know more than you think I do."

"It's always this way," I said. "Ever since Belize, every bad thing that happens, he's here."

"Maybe not," said Katherine. But she was tired. She didn't know what she was saying. How could she? "Maybe you've been wrong all along," she said. "Maybe he's been here looking out for you."

So I thought about that, and I thought about it some more. I felt him move away, whoever he was. He moved slowly, like he would have liked to stay a while longer, but he had other places he had to be, other windows to look in.

"We can have a girl next time," said Katherine.

"We're going to do this again?" I said.

"I'd like to. Next time, in the summer."

I promised her we would do just that, and she grew quiet. I told her stories until the windows fogged up with our talking. She heaved-ho again and delivered the afterbirth. I wrapped it in a towel, and she said she felt a little better for that. I told her more stories, until the car ran out of gas. The night was quieter then. I didn't want it to be quiet. I cursed Tony or Stacen or whoever it was who was supposed to keep a gas tank full on a night like this. I cursed their whole family. Katherine told me to hush.

"They've been good to us," she said.

She cried a bit. She was shaking. We kept the heater running even with the engine out of commission, until the lights on the dashboard dimmed and the battery failed. It didn't take long. I had been shivering from the cold that filled that car. Now I began to shiver twice as hard. Where we were wet from the birth, my hands and legs, nearly everywhere for Katherine, we grew numb with the chill. I helped her get the baby as close to her breast as she could, skin on skin. I piled on every towel and blanket we had, the tall boy's sleeping bag. I wrapped my coat around the mound that enfolded the baby and willed myself to stop shaking so Katherine wouldn't know how tired I was.

I had no way to follow the time. The windows had a thin layer of ice on the outside and more gathering on the inside. We could no longer see through the glass, and I was afraid someone would come for us and I wouldn't be able to tell they were there, afraid they would keep on going because I hadn't called out to them. I told Katherine I had made up my mind, I had to go for help, but Katherine begged me to stay with her. She had run out of steam, out of bravery. I watched her teeth chatter, her lips turn blue. I was afraid to look at my son, afraid I would be looking at him and he would stop breathing. Katherine could not stop her gentle weeping. I tried to think up lies to make her feel better.

"This is nothing," I told her. "People do this all the time."

"What people?" said Katherine.

"People like Indians," I said. "People in Antarctica."

"That's the South Pole," said Katherine. "Nobody has a baby at the South Pole."

"They do sometimes," I told her. "I read about it in *National Geographic.* There's a movie about it."

"What if nobody comes?" said Katherine. "What if it's Junie all over again?" It was a sign of her weakening. "It's going to be Junie and Albert, only worse. We can't stop it, any of it."

"No," I said.

"What?" said Katherine.

"No." I held her and that baby closer. In the dark car, I searched out her face, her eyes.

"Say it again," she said.

"No," I said.

"No," she said, and she didn't say it with as much conviction as I did, but then we said it once together, and another time, and the more we said it, we got better at it.

"No," I said.

"Keep saying it," said Katherine.

So we did.

We said no while that baby took milk from his mother's breast. We said no while our clothes turned stiff against our legs. We said no and the rain fell, and the rain turned to ice.

We said no until the fire truck arrived. The men and women on the truck brought blankets, but I already had my wife wrapped up in a sleeping bag. My son was bundled up next to her, his skin against hers.

"Come with us," said a man in a long black coat. An ambulance had pulled up behind the fire truck. Croker stepped out of the ambulance and fell down.

"No," I said.

"Yes," said Katherine.

"I mean, yes," I said. "Sure," I said. "Of course. Lead the way."

We got my whole family into the back of the ambulance. It was dawn, and the faint light was frozen, and tree limbs were breaking all over town, and I had to piss like a racehorse, but I was happy because that was my family in the ambulance. That was my wife and my child. That was my racehorse. That was my Croker. Those were my ambulance guys. Nobody was ever happier than I was that morning. Nobody ever will be.

We took my wife and my new son to the hospital and I left them there. Katherine sent me home to rest. I told Katherine I would be back soon. She smiled at me.

"I know you will," she said.

A police officer gave me a ride home. Not to the apartment on Franklin, but to my real home. He showed me into the dark house with his flashlight. There were warm blankets on the bed and the sheets smelled of my wife. I took my wet clothes off and washed and dried myself as best I could, and I went to bed, eventually to sleep an hour or two, but not before I had a chance to think about a lot of things.

What I have learned is this, and maybe you will learn it, too, but maybe not: joy is not the thing that takes away sorrow. Joy follows sorrow, and sorrow follows joy, as I will one day follow my young son through our house from room to room, from sunshine to shadow. Sorrow may come again to me. My house may be filled with it tomorrow, this house I plan to share with Katherine, with children. I can't stop sorrow, any more than I can stop the night or keep the morning from following one day to the next. I mourn those young boys and the men who are lost to me. And the young girls, and the women. I have to pay sorrow's due. I remember Junie and Albert, and Price. Ellie. I give them their memory.

But for now, for as long as I can, I plan to live in a house of warm sheets and laughter and too many books and not enough spoons. I will live in a house of joy. There. I have told the story straight, and all the way through. I have not strayed from the simple truth, not once.

I think it will do.

BARRY KITTERMAN has lived and taught in Belize, China, Taiwan, Ohio, and Indiana. The fiction editor of *Zone 3 Magazine*, he has had stories published in many literary venues, including *The Long Story, Cutbank, California Quarterly,* and *Carolina Quarterly.* He currently teaches at Austin Peay State University in Clarksville, Tennessee, where he lives with his wife Jill and their children Ted and Hannah.